Living Stones

52 Love Letters

DIMITRIA CHRISTAKIS

Living Stones

Copyright © 2021 by *DIMITRIA CHRISTAKIS*

Any similarity to real persons, living or dead, is coincidental and not intended by the author.

Unless otherwise indicated, Scripture quotations are taken from the New American Standard Bible (NASB) from Bible Gateway.

Connecting the Dots... An Unanticipated Journey of Finding Faith is available as another work written by this author.

ISBN
978-1-954932-55-5 (Paperback)
978-1-954932-54-8 (eBook)

This book is dedicated with love to every
person addressed here *and* to the next
fifty-two …......

"Teacher, *which is the great commandment* in the
Law?" And He said to him, "'YOU SHALL
LOVE THE LORD YOUR GOD WITHALL
YOUR HEART, WITH ALL YOUR SOUL,
WITH ALL YOUR MIND." This is the great
and foremost commandment. The second
is like it, 'YOU SHALL LOVE YOUR
NEIGHBOR AS YOURSELF.'
— Matthew 22:36–39, emphasis mine

And coming to Him as to a living stone which
has been rejected by men, but is choice and
precious in the sight of God, *you also, as living
stones*, are being built up as a spiritual house for
a holy priesthood, to offer up spiritual sacrifices
acceptable to God through Jesus Christ.
— 1 Peter 2:4–5, emphasis mine

Contents

Preface

"Make my joy complete by being of the same
mind, maintaining the same love, united in
spirit, intent on one purpose. Do nothing from
selfishness or empty conceit, but with humility
of mind *regard one another as more important than
yourselves*...
— from Philippians 2:2–3, emphasis mine

"And let us consider how we may *spur one
another on toward love and good deeds*, not giving up
meeting together, as some
are in the habit of doing, but *encouragin one
another*
— and all the more as you see the Da
approaching.
— Hebrews 10:24–25, emphasis mine

You may wonder why I would start with the biblical quotes above. You may also ask why I wrote another book when my last one, *Connecting the Dots...*, proved a massy memoir on top of being a personal testimony. I'll tell you why: while the prior publishing process was underway, my mind and heart were still reeling and churning to say more; only this time, it wasn't my yarn I wanted to spin. Also, at this time, I was searching for a way to continue serving Him. Completing that book did not give me the satisfaction of feeling *done* in what He would yet have me *do*. Not knowing what the next form of giving would look like, I considered sundry ways to serve Him and even briefly contemplated visiting souls in prisons; I ended up getting involved in a local feeding program for the homeless. That was and is fine, but I felt that the action did not quench me, or, more accurately, did not seem to have His stamp of approval or calling placed on my life. Therefore, I just kept talking to Him, and what the Holy Ghost prompted me to do was *more of the same*, only this time from a different angle: I should look *out* instead of *in*, yet still *for* and *with* Him. What kept welling up within me was that I wanted to showcase His love through showing appreciation for dear ones He had placed in my life.

I felt compelled to share my heart and tell them *why* they mattered to me. Sometimes talk is cheap; therefore, I intended to take my time and linger in love over each one. I searched to see if this impulse was biblical as well as logical, and, as you can read from my proofs above, it is! I wanted to cherish others and rally them with my words; to do so would necessitate self-sacrifice and obedience. *Thy* will be done, not Dimi's! It makes sense that He'd have me proceed from the revelation of the new creature *I* had become in Him by loving on *others* in a way both completely natural *and* enjoyable for me: through writing. At the moment, it may not make sense why I would feel motivated to share all this with *you*, my gentle reader. I ask that you continue to the next section in this Pay-It-Forward lesson and learn how I came to proceed. In the end, I will back full circle to loving my Lord who loved me first. Oh, what that you might do much the same! This is how my humble knee bows...

Prologue

"My message and preaching were not in persuasive words, but in a demonstration of the Spirit and of power so that your faith would rest... on the power of God... *We speak God's wisdom* in a mystery, the wisdom which none of the rulers of this age has understood. Just as it is written, *"THINGS WHICH EYE HAS NOT SEEN EAR HAS NOT HEARD, which HAVE NOT ENTERED THE HEART OF MAN, ALL THAT GOD HAS PREPARED FOR THOSE WHO LOVE HIM."*
—from 1 Corinthians 2:4–5, and 7–9

"Coming to Him as to a living stone which has been rejected by men, but is *choice and precious in the sight of God, <u>you also, as living stones,</u> are being built up as a spiritual house for a holy priesthood, to offer up spiritual sacrifices acceptable to God through Jesus Christ."*
—from 1 Peter 2:4–5, emphasis mine

Let me start off by thanking you for reading this introductory section. Though the Preface and Prologue are not technically a part of my collected letters, they do provide critical explanatory background information that will boost your understanding. I consider it crucial to share the impetus that gave rise to what you are reading as much as to the content itself. As the passage above from Corinthians informs, you have not *yet* read anything like you are going to, nor might you realize that, as Peter says, you, too, are or could be a "living stone." We are *all* called to serve Him by loving others. No, I did not anticipate having the desire to write another book — *this* book. This confirms to me that I am no longer my own anymore; when He beckons, I move, and priorities shift. There is not a doubt in my mind that God prepared and jumpstarted the longing in me to write others and share my love. You will witness what I have to say to these beneficiaries of a double-stacked love, both human and divine.

Did you notice that the sub-title is "52 Love Letters"? Did that seem odd to you? I can assure you it is not a list of paramours! Allow me to explain. As a high school teacher, I am asked to write letters of recommendation all the time, and in my thirty-year career, I'm sure I've written *hundreds* of them. When I finish one and take it to the guidance counselors or mail it off myself, I have the sweet sense that not only do I *know* I've made them *look* good by focusing on the best that's in them, I actually feel like I've written a love letter. In fact, I have! Not only this, but because I share a copy of what I've written with the students who make the request, they who silently gulp in my plaudits of praise as their eyes snap across the page, they often tell their *other* teachers about my "bragging" on them. Perhaps they hope that other teachers will do likewise and pat them on the back, too. Teachers have asked me how I do it because it *can* be hard to put pen to paper and write these, one after another after another. If I know the student well enough to vouch for his or her character, my response to being asked to write a letter of rec. is always *yes*. I can cast that honest vote of confidence, and then I find myself desiring to share the good that's in them *with* them. If I don't look for the best, the letter will come off sounding stiff or stilted, an obviously contrived effort that bears no certificate of authenticity, no seal of *truth*. Secondly, to those teachers who seek advice as to how to craft such letters, I respond that they must be as detailed and specific as possible, giving real examples from both *in* class and *out* where these students shine spectacularly. I would have you know that I applied this same mindset and method here and now to the loved ones of my *own* choosing. There are no recommendations, just my attestations. Of course, not one of them was expecting to get a letter from me, *especially* one of this nature, but, beyond a shadow of a doubt, I know that they, like we *all*, could use a heaping spoonful of praise.

This leads me to my next point. We all have unique gifts and talents through which we are good at *expressing* love; not only that, we each have ways we particularly like to *receive* love. I reviewed the main types of "love languages" which Gary Chapman coined. They include words of affirmation, acts of service, spending quality time, giving gifts, and physical touch, the last of which I believe is fundamental. It seems to me that it is also an act of service to gift people with words of affirmation that touch the heart and feed the spirit, so I figure, I'm hitting three of his five suggested ways to give when I write. It might even lead to a hug! *Your* way of showing love is going to look different than mine, and that's as it should be! Still, I would contend that in this dog-eat-dog world which is regularly tampered with by the Enemy, we all would be better off if we got a dose of His love, so I decided to use my words to show folks love. How could I not? Every morning when I read His Word, I read God's love letter to me — to us!

Love is love. No other reason makes sense for me to have undertaken such a work of faith. We all want to know *we matter*, and we also crave to know *why* we matter. No one wants to feel unseen. I will not go into gifts of the Spirit here because I have already discussed this before. Anyway, you can read it for yourself in 1 Corinthians 12 and also in Romans 12:6–8. Please do. That said, I need to reveal my gifts with you; it'll be just one more reason to justify how and why this book of love came to be. The bottom line is that God fashioned me an encourager as well as a teacher; the one often goes hand in hand with the other. I witnessed optimism in my father's nature; building people up came naturally for him. There are many different types of gifts; mine just tend to pile up in a couple of baskets; I am no Jack-of-all-trades. There are many things I fumble and stumble at, but finding the right thing at the right time to say to reflect the gold I see in *you* is not one of them. A strain of the wordsmith lives in my quiet mother, too. Writing to someone is an incredibly powerful and intimate act, both for the writer while she is in the process of pondering over her loved ones *and* for the recipient. Doing such means you are going to get inside the r soul, both for visitation *and* gifting; this is a task that carries a heavy responsibility. Hearts are entrusted in your hands; therefore, sensiti ity and honor are due. Writing is also potent because of its potential to leave a lasting mark, so, for the record, let me say that I hope never to "kill anyone softly with *my* song."

Instead, I would rather heed the advice of Billy Joel, who says, "You've got to tell her about it before it gets too late... Let her know how much she means." More often than not, we do not tell folks how we feel because, except for the regular annual celebratory events, there isn't the occasion to do. Maybe it's more accurate to say that we don't *seek* the opportunity to do so. Communicating love comes more naturally when we are falling into it and are basking in the splendid glow of it. The opportunity presented itself to me *here* because it occurred to me — and with quite a sense of urgency — that *I do not want to wait for my loved ones (or me) to be dead and gone so that I miss my chance to tell them what they mean to me.* We ought not to wait when we are left standing around someone's deathbed to say to him or her in their final moments just how much we love them. I don't want to be that one either! On the other hand, my love letters will not have that sense of insistence or finality; in fact, I hope each letter comes across as a sort of affectionate commercial break with God as my sponsor. Eleven years ago, I had to write my father's obituary. Even though I articulated his accolades, accomplishments, and essential life markers, I felt constrained, and, as a result, I never felt like I got to the core of all my heart wanted to say about him. Plus, sometimes you just have *no words*. Thus, for this book, I decided that I was going to take that time right here and now to express my love; it's the least I could do! I spend enough time on things-n-stuff, activities, busyness, and work; oughtn't I spend *more* on *people*, on my loved ones? You bet! You, too, have many.

Next, I anticipate you asking me why you would want to read about people you don't even know. Good question. As one who has taught thousands of students, I have come to notice that, year after year, certain types come and go. Yes, of course, individual names, identities, and personalities differ, but there is a foundational imprint or stamp on each that I come to recognize. I'll bet if you think about it and without too much effort, you can come up with some parallels or underlying commonalities among the people in *your* life, too. As one who teaches language and literature, I am familiar with and now choose to review some archetypes commonly found in real life as well as fiction; I'll bet you know them. I'll list a few here to jog your memory. There's the battle- ready *warrior*, the *child* whose hope springs eternal, the *orphan* who seeks a sense of belonging, the *artist* who is driven to create, the *explorer* or dreamer who seeks new vistas, the caregiver or *healer* who wants to make it all better, the *sage* person whose wisdom makes him/her a mentor to many, the *joker* or fool who delights us with unexpected revelry, the *ruler* who is a natural-born leader, the *rebel* whose free spirit is double-edged, and finally, the *lover* who is ready to sacrifice all for a passion, ideal, or person. Yes, there are others and combinations thereof, but you get the idea. In so doing, I hope to provide you with a bridge or conduit that can connect my world to yours.

Although technically, you have not met these ones here I have showered with love, I'll bet you can come up with many who fit a near description of such sorts in your own life. No, you will not find me labeling or reducing my chosen ones by type; I merely list these classifications here to help you recognize *your* people while I am in the thick of reminiscing my peeps. There are many other related considerations and identifiers I'll be using which you might recognize more readily than the archetypes above. By the end of this book, my addressees will no longer be no strangers to you, and you will inadvertently discover much about your author, too. This was not part of the plan. I also pray that amidst these pages, you will have an encounter with our maker *and* our Savior. Please know I do *not* intend for my readership to be limited to one stratum of society. *Living Stones* is for non-Christians and Christians, men as well as women, family members along with co-workers, adults as well as children, and *any* friend. This book is for *you*!

You may be curious as to whether I have given my letters to their recipients, and the answer is *yes*; therefore, before this book was ever officially published, it has already been released. In planning on making this collection of letters available for public consumption, I have been extremely selective in what I have chosen to reveal as regards intimate or delicate details that I know. I am careful and tread lightly to make no wrong turn and inadvertently injure one with some revelation. Anyway, this book as about basking in love; this is not a tell-all book! In fact, nothing could be further from the truth. We are far too complex for that. I also need to ask you to please be patient when you come across things you might not understand because you lack the inside knowledge to get it. Just let that pass on by and seek the universal in what is personal. My pastor says nothing becomes dynamic unless it is specific, so I *have* to be detailed for it to come to life, even if you don't know all the pieces. Might these ones to whom I wrote feel I was being disingenuous by their coming to realize I had forethought and intention to share these letters at some later date? Maybe, but I'm telling you unless you undertake a hefty endeavor of love like this one, where purpose and vision materialize only through prayer, planning, and *His* timing, you'll just have to take my word —

and His — that *love is meant to be shared.* Anyway, naught will come to the good, let alone to fruition unless He wills it. This labor of love was not natural, but it has been incredibly rewarding and often profoundly moving. Many moons before this *book* came to be, they each read their *letter* in the privacy of their own rooms. In the end, each letter is still theirs alone. Nothing changes that.

I hope you will benefit by bearing second-hand witness to my love and get a little of it on your sleeves, too. There is no time like the present, but for things to work out well, you can't force your hand or the matter if it is not ready. For me, this means being patient and persistent and sensitive to God's timing, but, I tell you, my being middle-aged gives me a sense of imperative that you don't have when you are younger, when the world is your oyster, and you feel you have all the time in the world. It is not lost on me that with every passing year, the living-to-dead ratio will reverse and with increasing momentum. There will come a time for me when there will be more dead than alive. This is hardly novel, but I will speak more on this matter later. If you are a Christian, you may refute and tell me here that since I am a "whosoever" who *does* believe, I "will not perish but have eternal life" (John 3:16); therefore, what's the big deal? You are correct, but right now, I'm speaking of my *mortal* life, this beautiful, confounding, and messy life in the flesh. I will be vulnerable and admit I sure hope I am a *long* way off from my last lap, but the truth of the matter is, when it is all said and done, we do not know if we have one year or one day left. We just don't know.

We *are* told that "the days of our life [are] *soon gone, and we fly away.* Teach us to number our days that we may present to You a heart of wisdom" (from Psalm 90:10–12, emphasis mine). Don't *you* want to be wiser, *too*? It is definitely a blessing that we can't see one second ahead into the future, yet knowing that there *is* an expiration date and that we don't know how long our shelf life is, I am driven to make my moments count. For me, this includes thanking God for putting particular people in my path whom I've come to love deeply, and, as a by-product, getting a taste of *His* love in the giving and taking of it. Like you, I want to live my life fully, yes, drink it down to that good-to-the-last drop. For *this* endeavor, I imagined that if I had a time limit of *one year*, whom all would I want to express my gratitude and love towards? How would I go about doing it? This dream gave birth to the vision of fifty-two letters I would write because I thought, surely to goodness, I could commit to writing a letter a week for a year. I prayed I would do Him proud *and* bring Him glory in the process.

And yes, there was a process, a method to the madness, as they say. Let me tell you about it now. First of all, I set myself a couple of conditions: the first is that my recipients must all be *living*; you will find no obituaries here or notes to the dearly departed. This is no *Spoon River Anthology* chronicling dead residents through pithy epitaphs. Secondly, they have to be persons who have had a significant impact on my life in some capacity; it matters not how long or little I've known them. Next, I set about making a roll of persons to whom I wanted and felt I *needed* to write, and it is a different list than one would make for sending Christmas cards. The catalogue I came up with is hardly exhaustive! Heavens! My love is certainly not limited to the fifty-two people here, so please know this isn't a list with a purposeful cut-off. There are *many* more souls I cherish *deeply*! I humbly request you neither be disappointed nor dismayed at whom I've chosen here today. It also occurred to me that had I undertaken this endeavor ten years ago, I would have included some over others not yet known to me then. Should I have waited to do this ten years from today, I might have missed out on writing some who might no longer be with me. Of course, there would be new ones I would want to add. These are stone-cold facts that set my heart on fire, and I have a sense of urgency to grab the bull by the horns and share the marks many have made on my life. I thank God for them all. You will notice that I organized my ones by fitting them into themes I established for each month. Some are ones you'd anticipate; others will be new for you. It made it easier for me to collect my thoughts this way, and I hope it will make more sense to you to look at twelve months' worth of letters rather than fifty-two random pick-me-up cards in this deck. That said, you will also notice something unconventional in my calendar: it commences when I actually started my journey, that is, mid-September, and not January. Please recall that this idea came to me shortly after *Connecting the Dots...* was released. As it turned out, when I turned the corner and came back around to the last three weeks that *following* September, I experienced an unanticipated joy in finding myself addressing one person I had not planned on.

How could this be? I allowed myself a little wiggle room by purposefully *not* picking every person from the start because it occurred to me that there would likely be one or two more persons that would come to my mind *as* I was writing. That's just what happened, and it was good. You'll see. When I got down to the brass tacks of writing, I would first jot down a skeletal list of memories and good traits I wanted to be sure I included. I then committed to writing a little every day; I rested only on the Sabbath. Stitching the moments and memories together while singing praises had me weaving a beautiful tapestry I did not see coming. So incredible is each person! I did not force myself to a fixed timetable. In fact, you will notice a progression in the length of the letters from when I first started. This project was a process of discovery for me, and, as time went by, I found myself having more to say. The length of these letters ranges from less than one page to seven pages, but the span does not reflect any differentiating degree of love. Looking back now, I am not surprised that the further I went, and the more involved I got, the longer my letters became as more was being culled from me. I managed to keep up the pace and match the message with its correct date until summer when I took nearly three months off. The recipients of letters from *after* summer break would have been bewildered by the months-off date, but

I let it fly anyway. All in all, it took about a year and a half to write one year's worth of weekly letters.

After my introductory description of each person which precedes the actual letter, you'll also find a few questions for *you* to ponder. That way, I hope you will find yourself more involved, engaged, and invested. The questions I offer you on the front end will till your mind for considering those in your own life while you are reading about mine. I am sure you will be able to glean prayers implied within my questions to you which I hope will have us *both* seeking ways to fortify and galvanize our love into the lives of others. I concentrated on revealing the *best* in my persons. Once I got started, I found myself surprised at how much I remembered and had to say. There is a wellspring of love inside each of us if we should tap into it; love has no end. You don't have to have a title or be famous to rock someone's world and change someone's life. Remember that. While I was writing, I felt like I was living a double life in being both author *and* His amanuensis. I both do and do not entirely understand how these epistles seemed to write themselves of themselves. Every now and then, you'll see I got creative and switched things up a bit. Rather than write the person directly, I might have written to *another* person in his or her life as if I were writing *about* the addressee. You'll also notice I included select quotes, lyrics, and/or Scripture before I launched into the letter. Doing so helped put me in the frame of mind and prepare myself for them as if I were standing in a mental narthex before the sanctuary of their soul. I also hoped it would draw in my chosen one with something familiar to him or her. You might be inclined to skip over them, but please do not. They will shed insight into the person, and I explain why I chose the quote within the letter.

Other than fixing a typo here, swapping out a word there, or compressing some quotes, I have not changed the contents of these letters. Finally, I can hardly wait to tell you about the two final finishing touches I added after I had completing each letter:

I made the decision to sign each letter in *purple* ink because I am the daughter of King Jesus. His royalty deserves and receives a stroke of purple! Anyway, He was with me the whole time. It may be just little-old-me to them, but I wanted to remind myself that *I am special to Him*. The second custom I established was a holy one: after I folded and slipped the letter into its envelope and before I sealed it, *I prayed over the letter.* I prayed to Jesus to bless the person I'd just written to, prayed that blessings and His abundant love and glorious grace would fill their life! After my prayer, I opened my eyes and felt *such* an incredible hope and joy for the person! How could I lose? How could they not gain? Won't you join me now and walk with me as we witness these precious lives?

September

Those Nearest & Farthest

Like many of you, when I was a child, I associated September with the time of year when school started back up. It seemed we played our hardest on Labor Day, giving our all and coming indoors only after we had squeezed every drop we could get out of the day. There was a good chance that we would come in with rings around our sweaty necks, knees green from grass stains, and our throats a little hoarse from yelling. Our days of freedom and frolic could not have been more different than the days that followed when duties were imposed on us, all "for our own good." We got down to the business of learning, and before we knew it, we were absorbed because brains and passions were captivated. Freedom for my spirit and discipline for my mind were drawn on the blueprint of my youth. Mind and body, emotion and spirit all teeter-tottered to stay balanced within me. Sometimes things get off-center and can't be righted because they become part of some new system or better way. There are people I know who are vital to me, and I cannot imagine my life without them any more than I can see myself without a limb. We have much in common, be it something ordinary like a similar life experience, or it could be that we share a mutual interest, hobby, vocation, or same bloodline. Sometimes a slight shift occurs that can bring about an unexpected turn or departure. The result is that despite the outward or ostensible connection being unbroken, the other person and you can feel a million miles apart. What may have seemed like no big deal can turn into a full-blown divide or gulf. The difference may have come about swiftly, or it may have taken a decade or two for the crack to split wide open. Regardless, some people who are as familiar as your own hand can concurrently feel alien to you. Ones we have long loved can seem as if they are living on another planet for how their values, beliefs, and life choices have shifted. Yours may have altered from theirs, and they may have been the ones who remained the same. It also might be that the person is simply in another place in life than you. Nonetheless, these ones remain precious; you love them. It can also turn out to be that the person becomes more to you than you ever imagined. As with the full expanse of the days of my youth, these people here run the gamut. One lives right around the bend; the other resides across the ocean. Both are woven into my emotional landscape, and my life would not be the same without them. In just under a year from now when I finish up September's weekly entries, the similarities and contrasts of ones I share with you will be of a different nature.

1. Stephen

Meet my brother, Stephen. Although the letter that follows is technically the shortest, let me assure you that when I started this, he was the *first* person that popped into my mind as one to whom I wanted to write. Stephen and I share the same blood, a similar enthusiasm for our heritage and Mediterranean food, and a mutual love of nature and travel. His being seven and a half years my junior, there still remains in me a knee-jerk reaction to play the part of his oldest sister. Still, he is every bit a man, weighted down with responsibilities that are equally matched by his many capabilities. Even though he seeks and achieves material success, fatherhood is his most sacred charge; the means and manna he gains go towards his family and their fun. My brother is deeply devoted to his family. Yet, like many adults, he has experienced the fractures of a broken marriage that add complexities he grapples with in his life today. No big sister cannot make it all better. I hope he attains not only the professional acknowledgment and other successes he seeks, but even more importantly, I hope the Holy Spirit will draw him to desire a spiritual center of gravity with Jesus smack dab in the middle. I pray he has a real encounter with Him that will overwhelm him with love and move him from the inside out. In the meanwhile, I'll love on my brother where he is from where I stand with all I've got.

Who is your brother or a man that is as close to you as if he were your brother? What is your favorite memory of him? What makes him so unique to you that it would seem as if it needs no mentioning, but that he would surely appreciate hearing knowing the good you see in him? Do you need to receive forgiveness from this man? Do you need to extend it? Close your eyes to any seeming

*flaws in him, just as you would have him overlook yours.
If he is your actual brother, how has he come to mean
more to you now than one connected by genetics or shared
history? When was the last time you looked him in the
eye or touched him on the hand and told him you loved
him, that you couldn't imagine life without him? What
do you need to say to him today?*

Let's meet Stephen now.

"Joy is not getting what you want. It's
appreciating what you have."
— From Mark Batterson's *If* (2016)

September 23, 2018

Dear Stephen,

I saw this quote, and it made me think of you because I believe that *appreciation* is a value you are intrinsically attracted to and aspire to show. I like this, too, but I freely admit, I don't come close to demonstrating it as often as I'd like. Therefore, I thought I'd implement it today by regarding not a "what," but a *whom* I am grateful for — you! When I look back on my childhood, I will always remember the day you were brought home from the hospital. It was like a holiday! Oh, what joy we had blowing up balloons and decorating the entry hall as we were awaiting your arrival. Like a halo of our family, we all fanned all around mom while she was holding you in her lap in that plush rocking chair. We beheld you in silence and wonder; it seemed like we were witnessing our own Madonna image. We held your little fingers; you stole our hearts. Regardless of how imperfectly I did so, caring for you when I was a girl through my teenage years was both a pleasure and a privilege for me. I know I was not always kind in my care of you. Though much of your youth is *not* a part of my recollection of you, this is not essential. Certain intrinsic qualities of yours remain and have expanded to make you the man you are today. Oh, what a full and rich life you have built for yourself! You love your family, and you sacrifice time and resources to make memories with and give the good life to your loved ones. Your wonderment of Nature; your passion for delectable food *and* feeding your babes; your ambitions and aspirations at work; and your patience, steadfastness, and resolve to stay the course for those people and ideals you cherish are all hallmarks of your character. There are many more good things to say about you, and I hope to have a lifetime to enjoy them and see more come to fruition. Know that I always want to be in your life. In short, I just wanted to hit pause and, for no particular reason, tell you that I am proud of you and that I am glad you who you are. Know that...

I love you always,

D.C.

2. Erike

Meet my nephew, Erik. Unlike my brother's sons and daughters who live just a couple of hours away from me, my sister's children have spent the bulk of their lives over a thousand miles from where I live. This is not a criticism; it is a reality of contemporary American culture for grown family members to reside in different pockets of the country. I think that more is lost than gained from splintering far off from one another. Erik is a very bright young man who has a delightful sense of humor and a passion for history. He cares deeply for the disaffected and those who have lost fundamental rights to those with or in power. Perhaps because he has experienced frustrations for feeling powerlessness himself that the topic of independence is near, dear, and yet elusive to him. His sense of sight is profoundly impaired. Indeed, it might be easier if he were outright blind, but since he is not, most can't see that he can't see. Therefore, he lives in a limbo-like state of looking the part of one with no disability but unable to act it through without great stress and strain. I feel immensely for Erik. He resides in a world skewed and bent towards isolation. It is so much easier that way. When you meet him, he is courteous, respectful, and even deferential, but I am sure that the struggle has been and continues to be real to keep his spirits up. It isn't easy to have family and friends that are further than can be measured in miles or geographical location. Therefore, even though there will be no reply, I will reach out and write him. What that I could also show Erik love through time and touch.

Do you know someone who has a disability or an impairment that makes life more challenging for him or her? Do they have the right resources available to help them? Do they have a support system or network of people who can empathize? Can you put them in touch with those who are like they are and with whom they can share a bond that you are incapable of providing? Does this person know you care about and love him or her? What life choices has he or she made that you admire? What do you both have in common that you enjoy and could spend time together doing without even saying a word? Do you have a relative whom you know and love but lives states away or countries apart? How will you reach out to that person and let him or her feel that you are grateful she or he is in the world and in your life?

Let's meet Erik now.

"Am Ende wird alles gut sein. Und wenn es nicht gut ist, ist es nicht das Ende." "Everything is going to be fine in the end. If it's not fine, it's not the end."
— Oscar Wilde, translated into German

September 29, 2018

Dear Erik,

I think it has been well over a year since I last wrote to you, maybe longer, and I apologize. I know only scant details from whenever I ask your mother how you're doing. She tells me that you have your own apartment and that you are teaching in some capacity, and I hope this brings you contentment. I should also like to add that your mom did *not* ask me to write to you; in fact, she does not even know I'm doing this. I'm not sure if you knew it, but I took a quarter of German at the university, and the above quote is what I remember from that course that *did* please me.

I recall back in 1987 when I took a train to Germany from Russia to come to visit your mother; I had just completed a full semester of study in Moscow. I hadn't seen my sister in well over a year! She was so proud to show you to me, and as she held you in her arms, we both took delight in you when you reached with all your might for a lamp that was turned on. You just kept saying, "*Light! Light!*" I believe you *still* crave the light, whether it is seeking knowledge or a suffusing glow of sustaining love. To be honest, there are few people in this world with whom your mother can giggle, take delight in, or share the same sense of humor that she has with *you*. That's the truth! Later, as a little boy in your bedroom, you would draw soldiers at battle for hours on end. Oh, what *was* their cause? Was it *your* war cry? And as a boy, that you held a funeral for one of the Guinea pigs speaks of your innate reverence for life and your capacity to love; these qualities do not depart even if they aren't apparent. When you were a teenager, at the lake one summer, I remember how much I was in awe of you when you showed me how you had to give yourself a shot daily. In a sense, you were already a soldier then. I am pretty confident this isn't in your current mindset now, but it's still in me to want to share with you, that is, this courage of yours.

To be frank, I'm not exactly sure why you are still living in D. Do you love it there or prefer it to the States? I'm just curious is all. I wanted to let you know that no matter where you are, you have someone — many

— who love you *very* much. I am one! I have always admired your go-to reflex to be respectful, kind, and considerate, no matter who the person is you're around or what the occasion. Other than specific historical- political figures, I really don't know for what your heart beats or what moves you. I remember when I sent you a Soviet poster when you were in high school, I wondered what it was about these socialist movements that captivated you so. Was it the revolutionaries' willingness to live for something greater than themselves?

I think that perhaps, deep inside you, *you* thirst for righteousness, freedom, and empowerment, and I want you to know how awesome I think that is. So often in life, the ways of the world subsume or squelch our purest tendencies, and it's easy to fall into the trap of cynicism and fatalistic thoughts. I have done so in the past myself, but no longer; I now have both hope and faith. Ah, do *you?* John Donne was right: *no man is an island*; we are connected by tectonic plates. I know that your grandparents are not too far from you, and I wonder what kind of relationship you have with them. I wonder how they show you love. I ponder over the longings of your heart. If I could reach out, I would surely give you a big hug right now; I know that's no panacea, but it is my sentiment. I also love looking back on our trip to Greece in 2011. I was so proud of you when we went on that hike that ended up in a mountainous ravine as we trekked our way back to the village. I know every day presents its unique trials to you the likes of us will never understand. For this and more, even if you get weary or frustrated, I admire your tenacity. I also think about the basics of your daily living, but even more than that, I hope you come to know the essential in life, that is, realizing that you are *loved* and that *you matter*. This vital fact is worth the fight for all of your life.

Sorry for the lack of organization in these my scattered thoughts to you; I'm just letting them flow is all. In short, I wanted to send a shout- out to you to tell you that *I think about you*, and I'm *always* hoping for greatness for you, Erik — not only today or tomorrow, but forever.

I remain...

D.C.

October

Pastor Appreciation Month

For October, I will focus on celebrating Pastor Appreciation Month. You may find it ironic that I have not included our senior pastor among this group of people; instead, I have chosen to highlight other pastors and another who supports him. These are the ones whom he tasks a host of roles and responsibilities; there are many necessary for shepherding a community. Don't worry; I will address this man elsewhere; honestly, he defies classification. Before I became a Christian, I was unaware of any such designation for October, but now I see why. A pastor is on-call *all* the time, and he chooses to bear the burden, responsibility, *and* privilege of representing Jesus at all times. That means a life of servitude. Pastors are never not to be available, and people both in and out of church come to rely on these men of God for material and spiritual aid. They also get scrutinized like few others. No, of course, they are not perfect. More than most, these men must try to abide by the calling placed on their lives. They take the high road and walk that straight and narrow path, but they can't leave others in the dust. We trust that they dwell in the Word and get sustenance from it when we tax them with our many wants and needs. They become physicians for our souls. Pastors do their best to love and live by the standards Jesus modeled with authenticity, compassion, zeal, and ease. A pastor ought to be capable of inspiring or spurring us to live more like Jesus. It means doing the hard but right thing, even or especially when the world says we are out of touch or missing out. This job necessitates good stewardship as well as being a visionary for the church — and I don't mean just the physical building. A pastor must have sound leadership and exist in a permanent state of being in-tune with the Holy Spirit. That means he must spend much time in prayer; in fact, it should be an automatic reflex for him to talk and listen to God. A pastor also knows when and how to really rest. Restoration is needed; in fact, it's biblical. Just as there are Monday-morning quarterbacks, there are even more who think they have a right to insert criticism, to pull rank or weight, or to steer the pastor into following some plan that may have little or no bearing of God's stamp of approval. Such judgment can wear on a pastor: after all, he must be sensitive, flexible, and aware of the pulse of his people. At the same time, he cannot become distracted to the point where he pays more attention to man than Maker. For all the pressures a pastor feels, I've also recently learned that this is a profession which has a low survival rate, so how can I not acknowledge the pastors I've come to know and to whom I am personally grateful? Yes! Love on your pastors!

3. Melanie

Meet Melanie, our pastor's wife. Right off the bat, there was no question that I should start with her. Jesus speaks to and through her husband, our pastor, to further His kingdom in our neck of the woods. Yet it is Melanie who makes it possible for Pastor Mark to have the freedom of mind and time to devote himself to God's calling on his life. Unsurprisingly, although he places a premium on words, she prefers not to be in the limelight and would rather not speak in public. I will confide that even though we are church family, I neither know her well, nor would she call me a close friend. However, as our senior pastor's wife and the mother of Mark's children, I view her as unique because she loves the man who is our pastor. It is she who sees his frailties, knows his vulnerabilities, and spends a lifetime in the shadows protecting, guarding, and bolstering him as he pastors his flock. She may be invisible to some, but she clearly has his ear and will help discern friend from foe. It cannot be easy to be a pastor's wife, for not only does she hear his dreams, know his thoughts, and see all the good he does, but she hurts as he keeps battle scars hidden or when there is little support or even scorn and silence. She also witnesses adulation from enamored ones who will be here today, but likely gone tomorrow and therefore miss out on Him. More often than not, her husband's time and energies are divested in the community so much so that when he comes home, he is drained and finds it hard to be the man of her hour on his own home front. His children may land on the last nerve since his patience has long since been spent. At times, she may miss her best friend, but she still waits until it is *their* precious time. Therefore, I consider Melanie an unsung hero and one to whom I owe my thanks. It is long overdue; she, too, is on double duty. Her support, love, reliability, and soft strength make it possible for him to do what he does. Though our pastor bears his soul and prays to God, he shares his heart and life with *her*.

*Do you know the wife of a pastor? Have you considered
what she endures in supporting her husband? Can you
see that she could use encouragement and praise, too?
Consider those who ground your leaders and make it
possible for them to do the job you've come to rely on.
Who are the less obvious ones in your life that you may
have taken for granted and those to whom you need to
drop a coin of heartfelt thanks? Tell or show her today!*

Let's meet Melanie now.

"An excellent wife, who can find?
For her worth is far above jewels.
The heart of her husband trusts in her,
And he will have no lack of gain.
She does him good and not evil
All the days of her life."
— From Proverbs 31:10–12

October 2, 2018

Dear Melanie,

The day I began writing you was the triplet's birthday, and I thought it would be the perfect day to start my unexpected letter to you. In less than a week, it will be October, which is Pastor Appreciation Month. I'm well aware that Mark receives adoration and attention because he is in the limelight. This is to be expected because he is our church's pastor, a natural leader, and an impassioned exhorter. But I wanted to take the time and celebrate *you* and who you are. I will start with the obvious: I know that you are Mark's wife and a mother of five, and by now, I'm sure you are used to his being on-call 24-7; you well know how people need him, cling to him, question him, and can take much of his time and energy, even if he gives of himself freely. Although I am his friend, I have been such a one, too; therefore, I wanted to take a moment and say *I appreciate* you for your patience with me. Even if you are used to it, it can be trying to share your husband, our preacher; he has a position that has no set hours. You understand and have Mark like no other person, and what you share with him goes way beyond description, comparison, or title. That's exactly as it should be.

Today I wanted to hit pause and say *thank you* for the time that *you* give that makes it possible for him to fly like a butterfly and lead like a Moses. Many people may not realize or think about the concessions, conciliations, and extra work *you* have to make and do in order to give Mark the freedom to do his job at our church, that is, to counsel, to plan, to dream, yes, to play, and to grow God's Kingdom in his unique fashion. It's not that you would have it any other way or that you are seeking acknowledgment; you are a strong, practical, allegiant, and wise person, it seems to me. As a mother of five, I also want to say that I have tremendous admiration and respect for you, all the more so because you have three boys the same age, and this can sometimes put at least a triple burden on you. Mark says if you want to know how he is as a parent, look at his children, and I would say that that is exponentially the case for you! They are level-headed, clear-hearted, and full of life!

Although I don't really know you all that well and probably haven't spoken more than several hundred words to you, I want you to know that *I see you* and notice what is dear to you, and I am moved. I will always remember our being together on our church's Footsteps of Paul Tour in Rome and Greece. From your posts on FB, I can tell you treasure a gorgeous sunset on an East Tennessee lake and childhood's most sacred and simple moments, including an innocent babe asleep in your back seat, your boys out on the ball field, or the many zany and humorous expressions of your youngest! You are present and accounted for in all of life's messy moments, be it baking hundreds of cupcakes because one son wanted to give one to everyone in his class or another son who needed you by his side in the hospital, be it for diabetes or a broken bone. Your daughter is your princess, and one day, she will watch over you two, too. I'm glad you have your inner circle of girlfriends who are close to you. Still, as one on the outside looking in, I want you to know that for this Pastor's Appreciation Month, I believe you are not only the wind beneath our pastor's wings; you are the earth beneath his feet. For this and *so* much more, I thank *you*, Melanie! Please know, I remain...

Your sister in Christ,

D.C.

4. Todd

Meet Todd. He is one of the pastors at our church; what he consistently brings to the table is mercy. He happens to be closer to my age than the other two pastors. He can also boast of a full career spent teaching and coaching in a public high school; therefore, he has had to straddle two worlds for a long time. That he has been both a teacher and pastor means that he serves in the public eye and is under its constant scrutiny. That is no big deal for Todd. He is an open book, and his character is sterling. He is aware of the impact he makes on those around him, and he takes his responsibilities seriously. His manner is gentle and his humor fitting. This is a man who believes in miracles, and he has witnessed some. I find it adorable that he always has his notes on standby should he be asked to teach or preach. What I appreciate most about Todd is his steadfastness and willingness to be there for you — *especially* when you are hurting, injured, or infirm. He is also present and accounted for if you have someone close to you suffering or even dying, and you need ease for all your worry. He is that pastor who will visit you in the hospital and be the first to come beside you and put his arm around you when you get on your knees to pray. He always leads his prayers by calling out to our "Father God," and you will see him shine and come to life most when he is serving on the mission field in Nicaragua.

What pastor or person do you know who is there when the chips are down or when you feel down-and-out or blue? Whom do you turn to when you need comfort, confidentiality, or a perhaps a rick of firewood? What man has broad shoulders for you to lean on or cry to when you are down on your luck? What man would hold your hand when you are too sick to hold up your head should you feel the need to pray? Is there a person — a man like Todd, whom you can count on when a crisis arises? To whom you would reach out for support because you well know he or she would come to your rescue or to be by your side? Whom do you see Jesus working through in order to bless those who mourn?

Let's go meet Todd.

"Then Joseph threw his arms around his brother Benjamin and wept, and Benjamin embraced him, weeping. And he kissed all his brothers and wept over them. Afterward his brothers talked with him."
—Genesis 45:14 (NIV)

October 14, 2018

Hello, Todd!

With this being Pastor Appreciation Month, how could I look over the past five years or so and not remark with gratitude all that I've learned from *you*? Numerous times you have told us that you love the Book of Genesis, and of all the passages you've shared and explained, it is the time in Joseph's life quoted above I recall most fondly. You made me feel like I was right there; such a joyful moment this was for him! This also captures the love I think you have for our church family! Plus, when you teach the Bible, it's like you rediscover these beloved men all anew! Of all the leaders in our church, I believe you are the one who best exemplifies humility. You wear a lot of hats, and you are ever-ready to do so for our sake. You are clearly the go-to person who makes sure that nothing falls through the gaps, that everything runs smoothly, and that all gets off the ground without a hitch. Not only that, but you are the quiet, steady type, and you remind me that it is the tortoise that wins the race. You are a sensitive man who is the epitome of patience, righteousness, and faithfulness, and you expect goodness.

How else would Mark have come to our church, had it not been for you? I know you've been a pastor at your own church elsewhere, but I look up to you for your loyalty and service here and now. I remember once when you were showing us slides from your serving on a mission trip in Nicaragua, you were beaming. You explained that a part of you really comes to life there in doing simple, honest work for a grateful people. This told me more about you than many other things combined. I didn't know you all that well before you took on a greater responsibility at the L.C. campus. I genuinely believe you were its saving grace there, and I will always cherish our Wednesday night meetings even though there were only just a few of us present. Your kindness to Bonnie is also a quality of yours for which I'm appreciative, not that it doesn't come naturally anyway. I will never forget that it was you who were the first to greet Bonnie at the hospital that early morning on the day of her surgery. I believe you are a tender-hearted man, and though you drive a big truck and know all about farming like the back of your hand, it is your giving spirit that is evident in all you do and for which I have come to know and love you. I am confident that all the students you've taught and coached would attest to this.

You are a fellow teacher, and, day in and day out, you spent a career in front of a sea of students; this speaks of perseverance and steadfastness, too. I can just hear you say, "Can I get an amen?" to that! Speaking of which, when you pray, I feel His Holy Spirit in you; so reliable, sweetly sincere, and connected you are. And I know when someone is sick, you are one of the first to pray over that person. Much in our lives seems to flow at such a hurried pace; therefore, I wanted to slow down a moment and tell you that I love you, my brother, and that I think you are a great man for living out the "second greatest commandment," as you once put it.

Yours in Christ,
D.C.

5. Thomas

Meet Thomas. At the outset of this book, Thomas was still one of the pastors on staff at our church. This man was an integral part of the leadership there, and his unofficial role was that he was the one who made things happen and brought Pastor Mark's projects to fruition, be it installing a new sound system or ordering group tickets for a mission trip abroad. He is gifted not only in administration and in the execution of plans, but he is steadfast, dependable, and rock-steady. This man switched out of the engineering program in college because God had a calling on his life. Being more of an introvert, if it were up to him, I'm not sure if he would have sought the spotlight or faced a congregation in the pulpit. That was on God. Studying compelling arguments presented by the logical Apostle Paul as well as finding innocuous ways to show people how Jesus moves in powerful and practical ways were more to his liking. Over time and with experience and help, he grew as an orator and came out of his shell. He traveled to Europe and broadened his horizons. Then he underwent another powerful shift in his life's direction. Thomas decided to put his time and talents to reach those abroad who did not know Jesus, so he moved his family and now lives in another country. There he is a teacher, preacher, and leader to other pastors. I believe this second ninety-degree turn in his life had to do with the fine-tuning of his innate gifts in a place God had in store for him elsewhere. Therefore, I am grateful for the interlude of time I got to spend with him face-to-face. Who knows what's next?

Whom do you know that has made a radical change or shift in their lives? Whom do you admire for his courage because he followed bold dreams, even if at the outset, it didn't make sense to you or others? Though this person

*may be distant, how can you speak into his or her life
today so that he or she knows that you still care? What
challenges do or did you face when they left? Assuming
you don't see this person very often, what do you find
inspirational about his remaining true to himself because
it reflects what Christ would have him be and do? Can
you can tell that this person's life impacts and touches
many for the better?*

Let's go meet Thomas now.

"Therefore, *we do not lose heart*, but though
our outer man is decaying, yet *our inner man is
being renewed day by day*. For momentary, light
affliction is producing for us an eternal weight
of glory far beyond
all comparison, while we look not at the things
which are seen, but at the things which are
not seen; for the things which are seen are
temporal, but *the things which are not seen are
eternal*."
—2 Corinthians 4:16–18, emphasis mine

October 16, 2018

Dear Thomas,

I've been thinking about you a lot lately, and I'm not going
to be conservative with my affection for you, my Christian
brother, and not tell you that I miss you. I do. When I read
Paul's excerpt above, it puts me in the frame of mind back
when we four were in Corinth three years ago reading this very
passage engraved in a marble pedestal. Mountains enfolded us;
the sea was calling in the distance; and columns, temples, and

ruins abound in the immediate vicinity. Our imaginations filled in the gaps and brought to life what Paul meant when he spoke of the sacrifices he was making for Christ. It is likely that what brought physical discomfiture or despair delivered delight to his soul. I see much of Paul in *you*: there is the lawyer's love of logic and what some might call a fierce mercy that dwells within your breast. You eschew modernity and its flagrant and unapologetic moral compromises, hyperbolic and unchecked greed, and, above all, man's intentional blindness to suffering and blithe ignorance. I have never told you this before, but in a lot of ways, you remind me of a Russian monk. I am not referring to Drago in *Rocky IV*; I'm talking about the fact that you possess a form of asceticism, purity, and intentionality which reflects Christ's unconventional and astonishing love. Few people are willing to go all out like you are. You don't need to don a clerical robe for me to know what's inside of you. No, it doesn't mean that you can't live in the real world and be a vibrant partaker of life's splendors. Despite the worldliness and flesh about that can bring you agony, you find strength in the seeming contradictions Christ promotes: you, *too*, have made yourself weak so that much may be made of Him. You have literally repositioned yourself so that those who don't know Him can be saved, and you pour yourself out as a drink offering so those who have little can drink Him in with liberality. It may be wrong to say so, but for your desire *and* ability to make such sacrifices, I am jealous of you. You may not be aware of it, but you have helped me, too.

When you came on the Vision Quest trip to Greece I planned in 2015, I really didn't know you all that well. I just knew you were Mark's right-hand man at church, a guy who helped make many of his plans come true and in a timely fashion, including the monumental makeover of our church's interior which you both orchestrated and worked on. When we were in Greece, I got a chance to observe you closely as you took in with wonder all you had previously imagined Paul did. I was grateful that you read Scripture to us at apt spots all along the way on this tour. One year later, through your extensive preparatory research, you filled in the gaps with even more teaching, some of which our local guides hadn't known. By fusing your mission-mindedness with a local evangelical church's philanthropic activity there, you made this trip like no other. I have learned much from you here at home. For example, I hope you know that when I included your explanation of the interlocking box analogy in my *Connecting the Dots...*, it was a sign of respect. You clarified how God sees only our imputed righteousness. I value your theological prowess and attempts to make Jesus and Paul more accessible and understandable.

Although you wore a lot of hats at our church, the Lord was working behind the scenes in your own life and preparing you to launch out, boots on the ground, to serve a needful people in Nicaragua. How were you going to say, "No," to where He was directing your steps? I hope that you are learning a lot down there right now, and I mean more than just the language. I know that you have a special appreciation for the simple things in life which is reflected in the lifestyle of these people. May I also say that over the five years of watching you as a preacher, I believe that you have grown more passionate, clear, and in tune with us so as to better expand our understanding of Jesus. I like that you want to show as well as tell us, and I will never forget your presentation of the seven stations of the cross and having us partake of the Seder meal; you made it a rich sensory experience for us. You really did Jesus proud in showing us all of that. It was that night I witnessed that there was a unique fire in you which was going to take you elsewhere, yes, even before it was formally announced. You also visited Israel on your own then. Wow! I don't know what's in store for either one of us, but here it is Pastor Appreciation Month, and I certainly didn't want to let this year go by without telling you how dear you are to me *and* that I'm proud to call you both friend and brother. In short, all I want to say is, may God continue to bless you and your family for His glory!

I look forward to seeing you again the next time you visit. We can hang out together and enjoy a big fat Greek salad (or pastry) as we catch up *and* look ahead, in over our heads for Him!

I love you, man.

D.C.

6. Timothy

Meet Timothy. He is the other pastor at our church who is the youth pastor, but he is also the one whom our senior pastor is pouring into to grow him as a preacher, teacher, and especially as a leader. These two men have spent countless hours together, and they have shared life, shot hoops, cut up, and related their innermost thoughts on faith and other matters to one another. They have a pact of confidence that is solid; their affection for one another is hearty and genuine. I mention these things about Timothy because you might not know that this man, who is under thirty and a good decade younger than our senior pastor, has a wisdom beyond his years. Timothy's competitive spirit helps keeps our pastor on his toes and looking ahead as well as around him, and, as a result, both of these men continue to bring their A-game to us. Even if Mark and Timothy look nothing alike, they are both dreamers with the same vision and have ready hearts for Christ and man. Timothy is in the first stages of starting his family, but he has a way about him that I am sure will keep him ever-approachable to our youth and young adults as he matures.

Who is a leader of youth that you know? Is she a coach? Is he your church's youth pastor? What makes it so easy and natural for teenagers to want to hang around, laugh with, or be able to confide in him? How does he keep life fresh and fun such that kids don't even realize that they are being shaped and stretched and challenged? Whom do you know that is like a pure-minded Pied Piper and leads youngsters through his infectious joy, an all-in commitment, and sincere happiness that lifts kids' spirits up and points them to His path of righteousness? Whom do you know who meets and loves kids right where they

*are and fills them with confidence such that they can
better become who they are meant to be?*

Let's go read more about Timothy.

"Hear, O Israel! The Lord is our God, the Lord
is one! You shall love the Lord your God with
all your heart and with all your soul and with
all your might.
These words, which I am commanding you
today, shall be on your heart. *You shall teach them
diligently to your sons* and shall talk of them when
you sit in your house and when you walk…"
—Deuteronomy 6:4–7, emphasis mine

October 21, 2018

Dear Timothy,

Perhaps when you first came to our church, you felt like you had "become a foreigner in a foreign land" (Exodus 2:22), and compared to Mark, initially you may have felt like you were "slow of speech and slow of tongue" (Exodus 4:10), but look at you now! You have become his right-hand man, have brought countless youth to Christ. You preach movingly and with both a vulnerability and strength such that we all love you! You are a living beacon of Moses' command quoted above! As this is Pastor Appreciation Month, I thought it was only fitting to write you a note of thanks and to let you know how grateful I am for you. Maybe it is your height, perhaps it is your potential, but I can imagine you like Moses in long, flowing robes with a staff, wearing sandals, and with a face bold and shining from having been in His presence. Your eyes are large and luminous and convey goodness and mercy that words cannot capture, but which are apparent in just a glance. Like you, I understand what it is to desire to draw the best out of youth and to try to bring them closer to Christ such that, hopefully, they will cultivate their lives in Him. This comes so naturally to you! There is a compassion, commitment, and optimism in you that children of *all* ages can sense. That is why they are drawn to you like bees to honey! I have seen how students open up to you, how little kids climb all over you, and how you, too, can hardly wait to get to them to share Christ through word, play, or deed. I am certain He is well-pleased in you!

I can relate to your passion for youth; their desire for honesty, authenticity, and trustworthiness above all things is evident, and you deliver the Truth they seek. That you are willing and able to let people see *your* weaknesses bespeaks a humility which is incredibly attractive because it is rarely found. I am sure you do much behind the scenes with and for our senior pastor that we congregants are unaware of, so calmly do you bear your weight. We all know that Mark is your mentor and is one molding you, and you are obviously a quick study because you are growing by leaps and bounds. We can also see that you have his full confidence, and none takes this for granted because, truth be told, personal trust is not easy to give or to come by in a man of his position and experience, so that says a lot about you. Loyalty is such a precious commodity, and it is evident that you both respect and protect one other.

Speaking of "senior," your working with Mark helps keep *him* young at heart. That you are ready to be both real and relevant, as well as to keep on the sunny side of life, serves you well in maintaining a groove of deep joy, yes, even when the weight of the world falls upon your shoulders. That you can cut up and joke as quickly as you can choke up and mourn reveals a keen sensitivity you possess. I also think that your competitive streak serves you well in challenging yourself *and* others; there's nothing more important than staying on-point for Him, right?! Next, how could I forget our trip to Greece together with Thomas in 2016? I was only beginning to know you then, but on that trip, I saw a young man who drank in the import of all he saw in this ancient world and one who was awestruck and in wonderment by standing on Mars Hill or at Acro- Corinth. You are fully one who is ready to go, go, go for Christ, yet your pace is steady and sure. For all these reasons and more, I admire you and wanted to tell you that I can see that Christ lives in you abundantly. When you preach to us, it is clear that you want to give Him away with all you've got; you hope for us to be emboldened by Him. That last month you chose to talk about God's commandment for us to love all people was quite relevant because you are such a one. What a bright future you have! Anyway, Timothy, I'm proud to call you my brother, and I am happy to take this moment to encourage you and thank you for all you do for us.

Grace be to *you*!

D. C.

November

Thankful For, To, and That

As we exit October and move into November, yet another school shooting has taken place, this time in Charlotte; one child perished. Soon after and on the heels of this tragedy, eleven people were massacred in a synagogue in Pittsburgh. With every passing year since I have become a Christian, regardless of the mayhem and murders I see around me, I am still filled with an underlying joy and hope I never knew possible. You may say, "Oh, you are out of touch." I call it perspective. Either way, the world is indeed fractured in ways we haven't borne witness to before. Prior to my coming to faith, I might have looked to this or that political pulse, economic plight, or sociological phenomenon as the reason for the madness. Now I understand that once we tilted off our axis in the Garden, it comes as no surprise that we have been spinning off-kilter and into chaos ever since, regardless of astonishing advancements and creative acts from that time hence. Does this mean that there is no hope or that we cannot take delight in our beautiful and incredible planet?! No! We *ought* to do that and more, not the least of which is to be good stewards of our planet and lovers of our fellow man, starting with our neighbor. Thanksgiving is my absolute favorite holiday. It is uniquely American and hearkens back on a time, even if in our collective memory, when people of differing backgrounds and ethnicities came together to share the bounty of the land through a common feast. To this day, we may have no other expectation than the hoped-for joy we will have just to *be* together. There also may be geographical or emotional hurdles to overcome in getting or staying there, but since the time and place are provided, we will also have a venue or opportunity to try and make things right, if not better, with our loved ones. How exactly can we do this? What does restoration, reconciliation, and improvement look like? You have to let go of the past to let them into your present. One way to facilitate this is to tell each of your family members how grateful you are for them and how thankful you are that they are in your life. And who better for *me* to start with and to show my appreciation for than by thanking my mother?

7. Mom

Meet my mom. A mother ought to need no introduction, but each mother is different in her own right. My mother is not and never has been like other moms I saw out there in my world. Maybe that's why for me, she fits better in this month's category. She was not one to get up and make us breakfast, gloat over us, or up and snatch us close for a hug us for no apparent reason; in fact, she didn't hide her mild disdain for those mothers whose singular topic of conversation was on the latest goings-on of their children. Ho-hum. How droll. And yet... she invested her time and shared her mind with me; I knew her for better and for worse for all that she confided in me. I know now what I couldn't understand then, that this shy woman did not receive caresses from her own mother, and her father was a disciplinarian who inspired fear and dread. She was filled with trepidation for want of adoration. Thus, this little girl became a woman who didn't know how to show affection.

That said, she had and still has a passion for doing all she can to support and uplift her community; it's as if her home fires extend to a bigger nest that she sees needs tending, sprucing, or restoring. As a youngster, I did not appreciate this, and I felt myself longing for her beyond words I knew to say. She was the opposite of my father, and as a chip off his old block, sometimes I felt our differences brought my mother and me to unintended odds. On the other hand, there is no other person in the world with whom I can get tickled at over an absurdity here or a spoonerism made there; oh, how we can giggle or burst in delight in simultaneous union! Today we live five hundred miles and three states apart, and it takes great effort and planning to meet. Still, when we do get together, even though it's only a couple of times a year, in no time at all, we get in our groove and discuss the latest in the news or what's going on in each other's spheres. We can stretch breakfast out into lunch. As she crests into her golden years, I find myself incredibly grateful and full of love for her. You'll also see that I long to share my faith with her.

In what ways is your mom unique? Can you think of memories that you share only with her? What particular values did she instill in you that remain with you today? Which have not? Have you ever considered the impact your mother's parents had on her formation as a girl that you can observe in her as an adult? What can you put behind you that may have hurt or bewildered you as a youngster that bears no practical relevance to your life today as an adult? What do you need to let go of to be able to hold her? What do you cherish and admire about her as a person that you see in no other person, let alone, mother? How will you show her your respect and gratitude today?

Read on to meet my mom.

"Dear common flower, *thou art more dear to me*
Than all the prouder summer-blooms may be.
Though most hearts never understand To take
it at God's value, but pass by
The offered wealth with unrewarded eye…
My childhood's earliest thoughts are linked with thee;
And I, secure in childish piety,
Listened as if I heard an angel sing
With news from heaven, which he could bring
Fresh every day to my untainted ears When birds and
flowers and I were happy peers.
How like a prodigal doth nature seem, When
thou, for all thy gold, so common art!

Thou teachest me to deem
More sacredly of every human heart..."
—From "To the Dandelion" (1848), by James
Russell Lowell, emphasis mine

November 4, 2018

Dear Mom,

How many scores of letters and notes have I written to you throughout my life? Goodness only knows! There are many more in my mind which I've never penned, and others never sent, but this particular one I write with great gratitude and with no conventional or annual prompting. The excerpt of the poem above I choose as if I were now handing you a freshly-plucked dandelion in spring. Ah, the intensity of the rich but "harmless gold"! I remember your once telling me that any mother would welcome a bouquet of common dandelions given in innocent love over a spray of a dozen proud roses. We are those few who understand "the offered wealth most hearts never understand," aren't we? It is *you* who first taught me to value "the sacredness of every human heart." How so? By your life of service to your community, regardless of where you live. Admittedly, it can be hard for a child to feel like she must share her mother, but I stand in awe of how you divest your time and energies. It all boils down to a life of giving to others, trying to uplift those who are disenfranchised, and adding beauty to places so in need. Perhaps this action on your part also keeps some malaise at bay, where quiet pangs of missing us need dampening or a busy mind craves direction. However, a life of contributing takes on a momentum of its own, and yours surely has. There is no historical marker that could ever capture all that *you* have done for your community. We, your children and beneficiaries of a perspicacious and logical mind, also appreciate the absurd and sublime and cherish home and hearth. Some might find it ironic that you have come full circle and moved back to Indiana; I myself think that, as her native daughter, you are one of her national treasures.

When I look back over the course of my life, although it is dad whose energy I have inherited, it is your attention to detail and sensitivity to life's often overlooked moments that I favor from you. You appreciate amazing artistic creations of man, like the rough-hewn Chippewa canoe and Frank Lloyd Wright's *Fallingwater.* You are moved by Debussy's *Clair de Lune.* Music produces within you an irrepressible desire to dance, as I've seen when "Boogie Nights" or "Kansas City" strikes up on the radio. You are a rich and complex woman who values the essential and the rare, the simple and sophisticated, the local and global, and both nature and art (as the former possess the latter). You respect the sanctity of a child's mind and spirit, and you pledge allegiance to conservationism. With all due respect, I half-jokingly tell others that I never know where to throw away my rubbish, as little is actually "trash" to you. Who else but you would cry, "Hurrah," for a frog caught and presented to you as if it were an emerald, would save scads of carpet samples for the possibility of one day stitching a new and more impressive one, or would promote art and music over sports and fashion? When I was a young girl, you spent much time nurturing my interests and talents, be it listening to me practice the violin or, later, reading my essays when I was in high school. Through it all, you lived out Mr. Rogers' credo. Everything you did echoed his words; it was if *you* were the one singing, and I believed you when I heard him say, *"I like you as you are; I wouldn't want to change you."* I am all the stronger for it, and I humbly thank you.

When I ponder about the formation of *you,* I am filled with gratitude to our Supreme Creator for making someone as unique as you, you who have always had a quiet thirst for freedom. In fact, you are still a rebel, only one with a cause. As was told on the Sermon on the Mount, I think your heart, too, "hungers and thirst for righteousness." Whether you volunteered with the

League of Women Voters, helped resurrect iconic buildings in a condition of sad neglect, worked to restore a sacred document belonging to a Native American tribe, or plucked your young daughter from a chapel service that left her feeling ostracized, any way you slice it, you honor the sanctity of the child, the defenseless, or the innocent. Even as an octogenarian, you are still concerned for me regarding matters of faith. Though it may bewilder you, the irony can't be lost on you that I am now a Christian. I'm reasonably sure that the very word instantaneously evokes images of fire and brimstone, or worse, self- righteous, stiff-necked, and sanctimonious church-goers.

Yes, Jesus had to deal with such types, too. They murdered him. When I read Jesus' words in the Gospel of Matthew, "I did not come to bring peace, but a sword... For I came to set a daughter against her mother" (10:34–35), I shudder. Can it still be so? Is *this* what's happening? Oh, but this *can't* be the end of our story, and it is not! Instead, I prefer to think that this pen may be mightier than any sword with the help of His Spirit to help us both and me here now. I am also told, "If possible, so far as it depends on you, *be at peace with all men*" (Romans 12:18). Let me switch places with you for a moment, go back in time, and tell you that I wish I may, I wish I might have been among the congregation when you were that grade-school girl who read the sacred passage from the second chapter in Gospel of Luke recounting the nativity of Christ. I'm sure you would have loved to have had parents out there who could have caught your eager glance, so hopeful for affirmation. I would have cupped your face in my hands, smiled and kissed you, and told you how proud I was of you, and, yes, also for all those verses you'd memorized and received stars. Instead, such was met with lukewarm reception as for an idle accomplishment, one to put behind you once you were no longer a youngster; so many more fascinating and important things were there to discover. With no one to encourage you or to help you grow your faith, it is no wonder that your sense of wonder in your faith desiccated. Nonetheless, what was done can't be undone, and I take comfort in the fact that your salvation can't be put asunder. All that notwithstanding, I am also incredibly grateful for Aunt Carrie, your own sort of saving grace. Of all people who have passed, it is she whose memory moves you to tears at the thought of her bravery and independence in laying stake to her right to determine just how she chose to live *and* die. Though I am glad for the affection and affirmation you got from Aunt Carrie, she, too, was hurt by a young Catholic man who spurned her and broke her heart, and for that, the Church paid the price for the grief a very imperfect boy inflicted on her. It's easier that way and less personal; one bows to the god of Reason when the messy affair of life's private casualties can't be explained or vindicated. More often than not, we neither forgive nor forget, and such a state leaves our hearts to rancor or sour.

Love abounds in me for you, mom, and even if you are out of the habit of looking beyond the surface of past pains and prejudice in order to accede and look back squarely into the face of the man who is *also* our messiah, He still knows you and loves you. Thankfully, our Heavenly Father is nothing like your (or anyone's) dad, believe you me. Your dad's stoicism and withholding affection hurt the girl and damaged the adult; it became easier to join the superior cynics than to reckon with *no* cause for his harshness and neglect. You need not recoil at the name of "Jesus" for the atrocities *the Church* has committed; there are many more of His martyrs that have kept the faith *and* contributed to do the good than the other way around. It's just that bad news travels faster and farther. Oh, but goodness still glimmers. Was not your grandmother a beacon of kindness for you? My hunch is that your own father saw an angel dwelling within the mother she was.

Good works may be great, but without faith, we really won't get far for lack of fuel. And like the little seeds we plant in fertile soil in some Styrofoam cup at church, though they appear inert, these seeds will surely sprout. What that I could water the dormant seed of your distant youth! Say the word, and I'll rush back your Bible to you, presented to *you* by Central Christian Church, Sunday, Sept. 28, 1947, so you can re-read all about the Good News for yourself. His Word has not changed its message or lost its veracity or potency. In fact, "the word of God is living and active and sharper than any two-edged sword, and piercing as far as the division of soul and spirit, ... and able to judge the thoughts and intentions of the heart" (from Hebrews 4:12). Mom, the whole of this book is greater than the sum of its parts (or genres)! Its promises are "sweet to the soul and healing to the bones" (Proverbs 16:24).

I know you are a sensitive and introverted person, and it's easier to tuck in your head like the box turtle does than to feel what may seem like a glaring light to you. I don't intend my focus to be thus. In fact, in my mind, I am holding a single candle, a faint but glowing one, that I give to you now. Let me hold your hand and your heart and reassure you that *I love you*, mom. I hope you can forgive *me* for any disappointments I may have caused *you*, and I pray you are liberal and open-minded enough to look past man's many imperfections and to check back in with the man who gave us His all. I offer you here what we all long to get: nothing else but "the greatest of these": *love* (1 Cor. 13:13).

Know I'll always be. . .

Your *D. C.*

8. Ronnie

Meet Ronnie. I met him when we were both in junior high school, back when his being two years older than I felt like he was twenty years my senior. He had it all: charisma, intelligence, charm, looks, athleticism, and vast musical talent. There seemed to be nothing he couldn't do, and he never met a stranger. From the moment we got introduced, we hit it off because we could see in the other a twin facing us. It was immediate and complete and lasting. In fact, I could spot him a mile away; he always and instantly brought a smile to my face. Though we traveled in different circles at school and then diverged later in adulthood, to come upon each other even once a decade felt like we were back on home base. He made his mark in music and became a jazz and blues singer, playing the circuit in a band in the capital of country music, no less. Once he came to my work as a motivational speaker for the freshmen class, and fourteen years later, when I came to have faith in Jesus Christ, he was one of the very first ones I could hardly wait to tell the good news. It felt like he bound through the phone for the warm joy I detected in his voice. What a cheerleader he was and has been to me! A year or so following this, I can't tell you how many times I called about this or that biblical question. Living life to its fullest (and having bad genes) can sometimes lead to unintended consequences, so when I came to learn through FB by the literal hundreds of posts attached to the news of Ronnie's having had a massive stroke, I fell to my knees and wept and prayed. No longer able to walk or to use his left arm, bedridden but not broken, he still possesses hope, a steady faith, and a readiness to love. I can't imagine my life halted with such force; therefore, Ronnie inspires me daily with his persistent optimism, and I am full to the brim of gratitude for this man.

*Is there someone in your life who has suffered great
tragedy or is now afflicted or permanently disabled?
When was the last time you spoke to or saw him or her?
How has he impacted your life? How has she changed
your measure of success? What might you share of your
faith with him or her? How can you concretely show
God's love and your gratitude for his or her being a part
of your life? Won't you tell him now?*

Please read on to meet Ronnie.

"To see the heaven in your eyes is not so far
'Cause I'm not afraid to try and go it
To know the love and the beauty never known
before I'll leave it up to you
to show it
And golden lad, golden lad
I'd like to go there…"
— Adapted from Stevie Wonder's "Golden
Lady" (1974)

November 11, 2018

Dear Ronnie,

You are one of my few true-blue friends who not only goes back over four decades in my life, but you are undoubtedly also one of God's anointed. I am grateful for your friendship, and now, more than ever, I am *so* thankful that you're still here. Stevie said, "lady,"; I write, "lad." Your voice is powerful, and His presence in you is discernable. I'm thinking about just where you are right now in life, *mi amigo*, and from an earthly perspective, it may seem perplexing, but when it's all said and done, whether we have one day or a decade, it all boils down to *what we do for Him* in the life we are given by Him. When I consider this, then you have seemingly lived *several* lifetimes! Not only this, you still have much more life remaining *and* a new body yet to come!

When I first met you or, rather, heard you in junior high, it was your laughter resounding down the hallway that prompted me to quicken my step to spy who this person was walking so confidently and with such joy. I felt your energy, and, much to my delight, there *was* a next time: I saw you was when you popped in to visit our teacher downstairs in the science wing. Eyes met, contact was made, and a friendship was struck. I was thrilled and even a little electrified because I did not know that it would be in the stars for me to see your handsome face and full smile that matched the laughter I had heard! Your charisma and magnetic energy were arresting then, and I can only imagine the spell that you cast upon the many thousands who heard you sing over the course of your career. Oh, to have witnessed your dazzling and soulful self sing! When I saw you with some regularity at school, you seemed more "grown-up" to me then. From the perspective of a teen in junior high or high school looking at one a year or two older, this stance is the norm. Still, I felt a sure connectionwith you, and I knew that it would not be broken even after we took off in our own life directions.

You and I have a similar spirit that matches in our souls, but it would take me half a lifetime to know that it was the gift borne from Christ's passion, which was yet to be born in me and that already resided in you. I had yet to gain His Spirit. You are a full-spirited man who enjoys and appreciates the fact that God thought to make women; there is also something in you that is drawn to the pure and righteous. In middle- age years, we may call it "conservativism," but all it boils down to being centered in Christ's holiness. Your close relationship with your three beautiful daughters, your life centered around music, and your natural evangelism all testify to your generosity. I know passion is sometimes borne in pain, and among other life circumstances of yours, may I also take this moment to humbly pay my respects to your brother, too. Though you are now living close to where we grew up, distant from your career and Music City, who knows what future purposes God will call you to over the rest of your life? When you came to visit where I teach as a motivational speaker to our freshmen class — which now seems eons ago

— I was *so* proud of you. In fact, you brought a blush to my cheek and a gladness for the students because of the fantastic job you did encouraging the students through entertaining them, all with a motivating message on the side. Afterward, when you dropped by to visit me and we actually got to chatting about what we believed in, I'm sure I have told you that when you announced, *"God penetrated the cosmos through the gift of His Son,"* then and there, even though I would not claim Him for myself for some years to come, your words got permanently etched in my brain.

Catching up with you and recollecting stories about folks whom we know from those early years in the seventies never tires me because it's nice to have a few familiar things to ground you in life. In the past five years, I find myself drawn to you again, only this time, for fellowship, and like a child seeks answers to riddles, I divined to know what God intended for me. You are one who not only drew me closer to Him, but I felt myself drawn to you, a mature believer, and I asked you questions that had been vexing me in my fledgling faith. Knowing my core as well as you do, you instinctively knew what to say and how to answer. You patiently answered this or that question in love, grace, and with not a hint of condemnation or condescension. And that was over the phone, not face-to-face, with a stretch of years since we'd seen each other! Just recently, in the two or three times I have gotten to visit you in the past six months, I have been moved because, first of all, I am impressed with the progress that you have made in your physical rehabilitation, *and*, to be honest, I am *still* awestruck by your vitality, resilience, depth, and zest.

You and I are also ones similar in that we are strongest when we get still and quiet — not that we can be contained, praise be to Him! I don't pretend to know what you have recently gone through or fathom how, in private moments, Satan might still try to mess with your mojo. Still, I *can* say that you continue to inspire me. That I get to call you my brother in Christ alongside your being my lifelong friend is an identity I cherish. With Thanksgiving coming up in a couple of weeks, I had you on my mind to tell you in this way that *you* are *golden* to me!

Your sister in Christ and friend for life!

D.C.

9. Rick

Meet Rick. Here's a guy I've known for over twenty years and in a singular capacity: we both are "gym rats" who have gone to the same gym at around the same time for many years. Rick is one of those men who has a salesman's personality, except you wouldn't know that it's actually Jesus Christ he represents. For years, he would engage me in light conversation, seemingly going nowhere except for his wanting to chit-chat with a person there for the same reason as he. We were regulars. I knew he was a Christian because I regularly observed him rattling off Scripture, talking about his men's small group for Bible study, or conversing about matters of faith just as naturally as if he were talking about who won the game or describing the weather. I watched him but remained at arm's length; two or three times he invited me to church. We got a kick out of each other, and the extrovert and optimist in us ricocheted off the other. Mainly we checked in about each other's day, all the more so had it been particularly high or low. Without fail, he always shared some Scripture with me. At the time, I didn't get it; I just knew it was normal for him to spout off a verse or two when we met. Other than that, this was the extent of our contact. When I came to faith, he, too, was one I looked forward to telling. He hugged me right then and there. We were brother and sister! From there, our friendship shot off like a rocket, and he became a spiritual mentor to me. He took the time for me when I had questions. Sometimes we might lean against a fitness machine for fifteen minutes at a stretch for how in-depth was our discussion. Whether I was going through a typical day or one fraught with trials, I always could count on his humor and banter which brought me back to civility and sense. He is that constant Christian companion outside the church we each attend, out there in the so-called real world, right where and when we need a brother or a sister.

*Not including work, home, or church, who is a person
in your life that you see regularly? What is the basis of
your friendship, and how might you foster an even better
bond? What have you learned from him or her that has
brought clarity, wisdom, and insight into your life? What
have you shared that has been instructive to him or her?
What might your prayer be for them? Have you ever
served with them in some capacity? Have you told them
that you are grateful for them?*

Read on to really meet Rick.

"Your words were found and I ate them,
And *Your words became for me a joy and the delight of
my heart; For I have been called by Your name,*
O Lord God of hosts."
— Jeremiah 15:16, emphasis mine

November 18, 2018

Dear Rick,

Long ago, some twenty years before we became friends, I used to catch a glimpse of you arriving at the gym at the same time as I did, and I would ask myself, "Who is that handsome guy rolling up in a shiny black Porsche, dressed in suit and suspenders, carrying an old leather gym bag, and obviously looking forward to a good work out? You had an air of confidence and success about you, but there's no way I could have known then that it had nothing to do with your outer trappings. I believe I've told you before that I thought you looked like a white version of Lionel Richie, being both winsome and personable. How could I *not* have noticed your warmth and friendliness around so many people? I came to understand that you have the heart of an evangelist; whether you are on the treadmill or walking around the track with another, deep in conversation, like some modern-day apostle, I have observed you witnessing to people through the power of everyday conversation. Out of the corner of my eye, I could see you speak to friends, acquaintances, and the stranger with equal ease, and it became apparent you had much on your mind to share, and it emboldened you. I did not know what "it" was, but more often than not, I'd see a smile on your face, a desire to share a joke or laugh, and an easy comradery soon established. I, too, became such a one.

I think what you do is hit upon some essential positive truth about the person, take note, and, through the help of the Holy Spirit, see where that takes you as you witness about Him. I can hear you now laughing, saying, "Well, I don't know about all that!" You are quick to self-efface and note the best in others, and this is the basis from which you launch a conversation about life, Jesus, or Scripture. I don't remember the moment when you introduced yourself to me, but it was well before I became a Christian. I knew *you* were one, and it became apparent when I'd relate some happening of the day or a lecture of mine to you that, more often than not, you would gently steer the conversation toward its Biblical application or Christian principle. Your comments never turned into a diatribe; you did not overwhelm me. If I shared with you points about the Puritan period or some dealing with a troubled student, you were particularly attentive and encouraging, and I think that's when you hit upon your stock phrase when we'd part and go about our day. I can't see you without hearing you call out, "*Strong* Dimi," when we meet and "*Persevere!*" when we part. I chose the quote at the top of your letter because I think it captures you, you who *so* love His precious Word and because you speak of His foreknowledge of us. Until you, I'd never met an actual person whose normal conversation was peppered with memorized Scripture, and you weren't being a fake or show-off either. What a pillar you are!

I was amazed that you could so readily find words of wisdom applicable to everyday life without trying to do any of the changing yourself. My strides or falls are on me! I had never met one, who — no matter what the latest shocker, trouble or woe that had arisen in politics, economics, or society — found all unsurprising and inevitable. No bad in this world surprised you. Our system is tainted, and we are spoiled *and* rotten. With a smile on your face, you broadcast a future replete with better times of a radically different nature, and I was all ears and all in. Your jocularity and familiarity infused with His tonality were the footers of your *modus operandi* of communication. You do not wield His Word as your personal weapon. His words are edifying, encouraging, or convicting enough, and you know they need no help, just a voice. Indeed, all I sensed was that you and I had similar energy even if at the time, we had little in common. Regardless of the topic, you always found some parallel in the Bible with Godly advice embedded; to hear you talk about Biblical figures felt as if you were talking about your own relatives! And how many times did you invite me to church? It's too many to count, yet you didn't hold it against me when at the time, I didn't respond, commit, or accede. Like water rushing over a rock, through the years, you were unknowingly massaging my heart and helping to ready me for new possibilities.

You were the first person I'd ever met that not only wasn't afraid to die; indeed, you told me you looked forward to it because it would bring you in His presence. You informed me that even though "this world was perishing," someday, "we'd get a new body." Later on, in casual conversation, it was you who first carefully explained to me the upcoming New Heaven and the New Earth and how all of creation would be made anew and *spectacularly* beautiful. For me, it was like listening to the sneak preview of the most incredible movie for its seeming so amazing, even surreal, yet for you, it was the plain and glorious fact. Could it really be? Fast-forward to my ostensibly getting saved in 2004, when I acquiesced that I was indeed part of "the *world*" that Christ "so loved." I was anxious to tell you I had gotten baptized as if I'd gotten a badge of membership. You went from your normal mirthful self to solemn *and* celebratory in that split second. Based upon your reaction and a quick hug, I felt the weight of the immensity of my decision, and I was moved. Fast forward another nine years to when I'd gotten invited to a church, befriended a pastor, and became receptive to the Holy Spirit's whispers to really believe that Christ came for and loved me *personally*, and our frie dship took off like it was on steroids! I want to thank you for the many conversations around this or that exercise machine since then.

You may ask yourself, why would I focus on the time before I became a Christian? There are others like me out there who don't know Christ, so I want to encourage you to use your gift of gab *and* evangelism that He has prepared in you because *it works*: slow and steady, happy and friendly, courageous and encouraging, compassionate and principled you are. Your offer neither too little nor too much, make gentle reproofs, and shine a shaft of His light where it might not otherwise have been. Since I have come to know Christ and have been trying to catch up and grow, I particularly look forward to seeing you at the gym. It's as if I were in a sea of foreigners trying to spy out my fellow countryman, we who do not live by the ways of the world. No matter what is going on in my life or in the times in which we live, I can count on you to bring a smile to my face, to make me laugh, or to see the light. I like that you enjoy being playful with me and joking around. Why? We know the Good News of what is yet to be! Should the need arise and in the blink of an eye, we dive into the richness of His Word.

Let me tell you, my friend, you are my "mighty Rick"; you are *my* hero. I also appreciate the songs in your soul that you have shared with me! You've got a band playing in your heart yet! When I have been at my wit's end and troubles abound, you remind me that, after all, today *is* just another day, that there really is nothing to fret over, that *He's got this*, and I know you are right. You have shared some of your dark days, too, with me. His mercy has helped you in the sleepless watches of the night when you have faced torments of your own. When you felt unworthy, you, too, have had to cling to His promises and take comfort by reminding yourself that you are one of His beloved. Through your actions, you have shown me that your faith is alive: you've taught Sunday school, held men's weekly Bible study groups for *years*, and have ministered to countless individuals like me and a man formerly Jewish, who is now enthralled by His Word that you now read and study with him weekly. Like Bonnie, you are a prayer warrior, and the troubles of many touch you. This letter of mine may be unexpected, but consider the truth that He will come "like a thief in the night" (1 Thess. 5:2). Therefore, while we are on this side of paradise, I wanted to pause my busy day and mind and place this letter of sincere gratitude to you as if it were an offertory in His plate.

God bless *you*, Rick!

D.C.

10. Gwen

Meet Gwen. She is my sister and the one closer to my age than my other two siblings. As sisters who both possess spirit and spunk, each in her own measure, we got in many a catfight when we were young. She'd tease, I'd hit, she'd tattle, and I'd get in trouble. My parents would extract an insincere apology from me. Rinse and repeat. Our roads diverged more dramatically when we got into middle school, the period when kids grapple with shifting alliances and experiment with new identities and categories of friends. Although we lived under the same roof, by the time we were in high school, it seemed as if we inhabited different planets. We co-existed as lionesses in our private zoo. When we got to college, circumstances were such that we ended up sharing an apartment for a couple of quarters; suddenly and somehow, we were young women united as "survivors" of our parents' divorce, and this put us back on the same side. We *still* combusted, but now it was from spontaneous amusement or a mutual delight. In our adult years, we have lived at least two states apart, and due to differences in life experiences and choices, we have had a more significant emotional barrier than distance could measure. But you can't keep good women down; Gwen and I have overcome past frictions; communication is always the key. Though in different capacities, we also share common ground in being long-term educators and mentors. You never know what's going to happen or come up around the bend in life, so I'll skip to the next and more critical track for you: I'm pleased to report that that she and I are back in each other's lives. In fact, we are in a better way than I can recall having been in for a long while. She is still many miles away, but I don't have the slightest hesitation that when she crosses my mind, I am quick to pick up the phone to check in on her. I am thankful for the goodness in our relationship today.

Who is someone in your life with whom you've had a vitriolic or a trying relationship? Have you rectified the matter? Did you forgive and forget and move on to greener pastures? Have you at least learned how to agree to disagree? Have you quit giving her the cold shoulder or him the silent treatment? Have you pledged not to stir the pot any longer? Are you still holding on to a resentment from childhood that has no place or value now? Do you hope to be taken for who you are today rather than someone you were in the past? Ought you not offer that same grace to another? Won't you try to today?

Read on to learn more about Gwen.

"Well, we all have a face
That we hide away
forever
And we take them out
and show ourselves
When everyone has gone
Some are satin some are
steel
Some are silk and some
are leather
They're the faces of the
stranger
But we love to try them
on."
—From "The Stranger"

"I said I love you and
that's forever And this I
promise from the heart I
could not love you any
better
I love you just the way
you are."
—from "Just the Way You
Are"
—Both songs from Billy
Joel's
The Stranger, 1977

November 25, 2018

Dear Gwen,

As I write you now, it's as easy as talking aloud because I've known you for so long; as I've mentioned before, I share more childhood memories with you than with any other person on the planet. Maybe this is stating the obvious, but it is a fact I do not take for granted. Youth is the period when our brains are the most supple, and I drink up these memories of you now like there is no tomorrow. In primary years, our cycle typically revolved around teasing, hitting, and playing hide-and- seek with our feelings of love and mutual distrust. The game would repeat itself until sometime in middle school, when we each dabbled in different social spheres that occupied too much of our energies and corroded our sensibilities. Yet, such put us back on even ground. Your nightmares from childhood finally receded into the recesses of your mind, and new hopes transformed your dreams to days ahead of your own. In college, when you moved to where I attended school, we got to share an apartment together for about a year. Though I might not have said it, I was so happy to have that settled feeling you get when your family is with you. That you had nothing printed on your first quarter's schedule other than something to the effect of "See Head of Department," printed multiple times, as if the brains of the university had gone mad for a moment, made me feel extra protective of you. I recall your coming home on snowy winter evenings after school or from work at Wendy's. At times, I might have gotten you a Rooster sandwich to greet you; we didn't have to talk to understand one another. You might have taken comfort in eating a snack from our childhood days: graham cracker sandwiches with chocolate icing in between. Sharing a cup of cheer, we might have dared to talk about taboo topics that remained unspoken and unsolved mysteries in our family. You and I understand each other's gestures, interpret one another's facial expressions, and translate utterances in mere nanoseconds because we speak the same non-verbal language. Add to that, too many memories to count, moments of comfortable silence, raucous laughter, tears trapped, or a lump in our throats, and you've got an inkling of what it's like for us to be together. We also knew when to leave a tender moment alone; after all, smoke might get in our eyes. Nothing is off- limits because we were each other's home base without our ever needing to go back home. Decades between then and now have been punctuated by pain and promise, and we have gone from hiding to healing our hearts. I treasure my closeness with you; it is inviolable.

Oh, you are my loyal and brave one! The likes of your capacity for devotion, allegiance, and fidelity are not to be found in many, and your gift of organization and prioritization reflect the premium you place on peace and order because it brings tranquility. Even now, when life seems to have spit out various cryptic or indecipherable messages, I want to assure you that *you are loved* beyond measure. I love you! There is more goodness in store for you in days ahead than any malaise that lingers from the past. A mother's love comes through and provides and sustains, but even *that* has been provisioned by the love of your heavenly Father, one that no dad can ever give fully either. He finds ways to murmur continually to you, "*Do not be afraid. I am here to help you*" (Is. 41:13). I know that you have dealt with life's pains in your own fashion and at your own pace, and I'm so glad you've gotten the support you need. Still, I *also* want you to know that though you and I have reconnected yet remain geographically apart, *you are nevermore alone*. Even if getting grounded came about through a breaking down of your fragile fortress, I'm relieved you reached out and found a steadfast foundation you've been searching for, be it 1111 P. St., a hug from mom, or affirmations from friends both old and new; indeed, they have all been provided *for* you! Can you tell? You have *much* more than a past, and as life moves onward and forward, I am filled with joy that you and I have *decades* of closeness between us left! When I saw you back at grandma's funeral and I felt how natural it was for us to just sit back on mom's patio, catch up, laugh easily, and reminisce, it brought me such relief and gladness! In fact, in a way, it felt like no one else was there; time had been zip-compressed. I was anxious that dad's latter decisions would mar your view of me, but it did not. I love talking to you about mom and about what makes her tick; it's our oblique way of dealing with the tangential, though still-connected threads you and I possess. I well know that you and I each and both have a complex relationship with her. Life may not look like what you thought it ought to, and it may have involved experiences and forces that you could not have foreseen, but we *all* have scars. It's just that some aren't so apparent or as noticeable; pain is subjective, unique, and intimate unto oneself, known fully and completely *only* by the Omniscient one, that is, God. Know that Jesus "*cares for you*" (1 Peter 5:7). In fact, He compels me to tell you all about the good things that are and the ones yet to come! It is for this reason that I choose to write and tell you right off the bat that I am *so* grateful that you are my sister, thankful that you were born, and I believe *the best is yet to come for you*! I can tell from when I saw you last Thanksgiving and this past summer at the lake that you just keep on getting stronger. Your life will continue to blossom and get richer. I'm glad you have a place that you can call home, even if it is not where you expected. I am proud of you for taking care of yourself through the nurturing of *all* things, be it cultivating plants, being on-call as a humble "sherpa," helping students of all ages, and pursuing relationships that may have fallen by the wayside. I love how you express yourself through other creative endeavors, be it writing poetry, stretching body and soul in yoga, or putting out tender feelers for making new friends right where you are. These are all ways for you to establish harmony and a beautiful Fengshui for life!

Spending time with you last Thanksgiving was moving for me, and even though by some people's estimations, this time may have looked dim, I consider it a *turning* point. Your holding on to me showed me you were clinging to life. When we look deep within and find life wanting, do know that the very fact you exist means there's something *far* more significant in store for you than that which our parents could have conceived of in the conception of you. You have been known and were intended to be — the whole of your existence — since before your birth! I have read that it is hard for people who have issues with their fathers to really fathom the love of a Heavenly Father, but that is just the case, and my prayer for you is to experience it. It doesn't matter about mom, S., dad, or *anybody* else; beyond them, you are very much loved and purposed to be in this life! I, for one, also embrace you for the fact that I *get* to be your sister *and* friend for life! When I hear about your giving or doing for folks, I am encouraged; *to give is to receive*, and, regardless of the job, such will bring *you* joy and meaning in life.

As far as I'm concerned, the whole month of November is a month for thanksgiving, a time to be still and bask in gratitude, so I just wanted to say *I am grateful that you are my sister.* I am relieved you are in a safe place, and that you are restored enough to take baby steps forward, proving the story of the little engine that could translates to your becoming the resilient woman that *can* and *does*. Here's to your future full of bright hope and silent nights of heavenly peace.

I love you

D.C.

December

Great Givers

onsidering December is the month when we celebrate Jesus' birth and participate in the giving and receiving of presents to (hopefully) bring to mind *the* greatest gift of all time, it should be no stretch for you to figure out why I dubbed this month as I did. If you celebrate Christmas merely to get presents, no matter what you get, you've missed the point. If I am describing you, I hope you ask someone who knows and that he or she will take the time to tell you all about the huge deal that happened 2,020 years ago. Something you may not have considered are those ones in your life who have made it a part of their lifestyle to be in the *habit* of giving the *rest* of the year. They find a way to be generous on a regular basis by offering themselves through the gifting of their talents, time, or resources. There is a selflessness, a focus on the *other* guy (even if he or she is a stranger), and an instinct to respond to needs swiftly. I believe this is a learned behavior, so I pray that there are many teachers out there. Perhaps givers instinctively know that it just as easily could be they who are in a dark pit of need; after all, life can change on a dime. When I watch these ones dispense or provide, they do not heed the warning, "Look before you leap"; they are all in before they know it, and we are all the better for it. I'm not implying that they are careless or mindless with their generosity. Some givers have to be prudent because they realize they might find themselves spent or give out if they don't pace themselves. Yet they *also* know, Jesus' provisions never fail; they are in surplus supply. Loaves will be leftover! When we give what's needed with no questions asked, we give *Jesus* away! We must meet people right where they are, not where we think they ought to be, and this means looking to those with outstretched arms and hungry or hurting hearts. The gift may come in the form of food, a helping hand, or a cheerful smile. It could be a ton more. When it's all said and done, I think that maybe we should invert our way of thinking. Instead of mulling over what we would like to fill our bucket list with, such as things to do or places to see before we die, we should focus on *emptying* our bucket when and where we can. That's my personal takeaway. It matters not the size of your bucket, either. Remember the poor widow who gave two small copper coins: Jesus was impressed with the all she gave. You may be a mover and a shaker, or you might be the one who is in abject need who becomes the impetus or catalyst for generating the flow of others' resources. Either way, God will use anyone and in any way He can to provide. To *Him* be the glory! I think He smiles when He catches a glimpse of the Ebenezers out there who discover that by giving, they don't *have* to be a scrooge or grinch. We gain by letting go.

*Who are the givers in your life? In what way can and
will you give of yourself today?*

11. Mark

I recently confided to Mark about this book and told him that because I had written him so many texts and letters before, for this entry, I wanted to mix things up and write from a different angle. What I didn't say was that, in writing his letter by addressing it to others, my message was actually a form of prayer for him. Mark is our church's senior pastor *and* my very good friend. If you read my last book, *Connecting the Dots...*, you know that he was pivotal in my coming to Christ, that God used this man to help rivet my attention to Jesus through attraction, not compulsion. Ultimately, it was the Holy Spirit who was beckoning me. The Holy Spirit is also vividly at work in Mark's life, and some of that glow rubbed off and moved me, too. Though Mark could easily fit in several of my categories, it was no contest for me to settle on this month because Mark is such a generous giver. He frequently says that when he gets to Heaven, he hopes he comes in scarred and beat up for giving it all he's got to bring folks to Jesus. Mark is no hippie, let alone the type of evangelist you'd think of from what you've seen on television; he's a man who thoroughly enjoys life, loves to laugh and hang with friends and family, and it would be rare for you to see him not smiling. He's too cool to be anyone's fool, and he is also prudent as to whom he lets speak into his life. He's usually running late because he's always on the go, like he can't miss out on the next thing more to do for Jesus. Without fail, this involves his loving on people right where they are; I think that's the ticket and the key to the successes Mark has made. He knows that it's on God's watch and His will if the time is right for a person to come *or* to return to Him. As a pastor, Mark can speak with thunderous authority or with the tenderness of a broken angel equally well. God has anointed and enabled him to present the Word so personally and boldly that it "pierces as far as the division of soul and spirit...and [is] able to judge the thoughts and intentions of the heart" (from Hebrews 4:12). My friend has his own unique story, and I learned that from the age of four on, Mark's biological father chose *not* to be involved in his life, in effect, leaving him an emotional orphan. Therefore, I decided to inform his earthly father what he had missed out on and to thank his *Heavenly* Father for not only stepping in and filling that void, but making him feel complete and fine and loved just as he was. God came to his rescue, and Mark learned how to give from the One who can't be outgiven.

Let's read more about Mark. You will be inspired by this renaissance man.

"And we know that God causes all things to work together for good to those who love God, to those who are called according to His purpose."
— *Romans 8:28, emphasis mine*

December 2, 2018

Dear Mr. Jackson,

We have neither met, nor are we likely to, but I have known your son as my friend and pastor for the past five years, and, if I could, I would like to share with you some things about him that ought to make your heart swell with pride. No, I don't know you or pretend to perceive what impresses or moves you in life, but absence begets ignorance, and even if for this moment, I would like to reveal to you some successes of your namesake. I know five years hardly sounds like a long time to be acquainted with a person, but this period may very well be longer than the time that you have spent with him. Please understand that I have no malintent in writing this note; my words will not imprecate you, just educate you. You may rightly ask, who be I to speak to you, and what knowledge do I have of him that is of use to you? I may not be family, but he is my brother in Christ. An outsider's perspective can shed unique light for those who have imperfect recollections and tainted associations which mar the memory of a man you *only thought* you knew or may have heard tell of. I have written your son countless letters, hundreds of texts, and listened avidly to scores of his sermons; I have even walked with him and a couple of other friends in the footsteps of the Apostle Paul in Greece. No, your son is not my idol; we just worship the same Man.

As you read this note, you will no doubt wonder what my purpose could possibly be to contact you: it is to remind you not only of who your son is, but also to take this moment to speak of Christ. I can't talk about the one without mentioning the other. You should understand that I am one who formerly was not open to Jesus; at one stretch of time, I walked in pride and ignorance. After I'd heard Mark preach on one occasion, I am just glad I had a spark of curiosity and took a chance on asking to meet your son to talk about Him. He agreed to come! Mark briefly shared his own background and story of coming to Jesus; then he asked me about mine and who I thought God was. It was give-and-take, not push-and-pull. You should know that when recounting his youth, your eldest never cast aspersions on you; in fact, he is the first to say he has let bygones be bygones and that he has forgiven you. tMy intent in writing is *not* to recount things of which I have no first-hand knowledge; however, I *would* like to speak to the man I see your son has become, even if you may be disinterested at best or disappointed at worst. Above all, your son loves Jesus, and this love of Him radiates in the unique way he loves people. His passion for Christ led to my own coming to faith in Him and ignited a burgeoning love that continues to grow. You may think that charm, appearance, and intellect are essential ingredients he inherited from you, but what counts in life is how he has chosen to use the elemental stuff of which he's made. He gives it right back through serving the One who made us all. He pours himself out as a drink offering every day and spends himself on others with no thought of gain for himself. Most of all, he tries to be as real as rain with no fakeness, smugness, or pretense to those who are hurting or needing the hope and help that only Jesus Christ can provide. The epigraph above has me shift my focus on you. Why? *You, too*, are part of these "things" that God has worked together in your son for His glory. Even though Mark surely wasn't seeking grief, angst, or bewilderment as both a boy and a young man smarting from your absence, our Heavenly Father was transforming this experience into the good for your son. I'll bet there was a time when he would have jumped through rings of fire to have won your love, but that was not meant to be.

Thanks in part to you, Mark long ago learned how to compartmentalize his feelings, and this inadvertently has served him well at times, like an emotional buffer, without which he might have grown weary sooner, what with the demands his vocation prompts in him to commit to others. Giving his all yet conserving his core has made it easier for him to obey God's calling on his life to show Christ's love for his neighbor, and that's us *all*. Giving has become his *modus operandi*, and it is an engrained habit. Your absence brought about a people-pleaser in him, and this, in turn, produced a drive to go further, do better, and be all his Heavenly Father would have him to be. He challenges himself daily and looks down the pike so that he can be the better man *then* by growing in *today*. He's an avid reader, and he looks to push past norms or boundaries by trying new things. He carries no chip on his shoulder, and there is no self-pity smoldering. I'm glad that his decision to accept Christ was made in tender youth and got launched while eating fare from the Sonic on a Mr. T tray, no less. He committed himself to Jesus Christ, and his faith has grown and panned out to today to where he now feeds souls hungry for Him. Your son is a man who shows up for others, and so steadfast a one is he. I have no idea what quickens your heart, but beyond a shadow of a doubt, your son ushers in His greater good.

Did you know that by attending to the negative space and drawing *around* a particular chosen subject matter that an artist can have it pop into the foreground of a drawing for the viewer? Therefore, to see who Mark *is*, we can also look around and note what he is *not*. So, who is the man your son has come to be? As a bystander who has no other motive than to report the truth, I'll spell it out for you; it would do you well to set aside assumptions and hearsays. First of all, as a father, he is the dad you never were to him: he shows up and involves himself in his daughter's and sons' lives. They also teach him, and he duly takes note. He eats up all the joys, pangs, frustrations, and all the silly and mundane moments they bring, as if it were manna from heaven, and it is. They know who they are and where they come from, and he is leading them to become stalwart Christians with a purpose more significant than sustaining their daily lives. As a husband, he seeks to adore his wife with steadfastness and solidity that only a best friend for life can provide. He is an affectionate man, and though he doesn't wear his feelings of his sleeve, he also isn't afraid to show them. How refreshing!

Time and again, what stuns me is Mark's instinct for showing us the value of *mercy*, a trait sorely lacking in the world today. Your son "puts on love" (Col. 2:13) as he disciplines himself for Him; he is continuously "renewing his mind" (Rom. 12:2). The Apostle Paul says that "God loves a cheerful giver" (2 Cor. 9:7), and there's not one person who can accuse Mark of not being this! Our pastor leads by serving, and he places a particular focus on discipling men of our church. They bask in masculine pride and in the brotherhood and comradery of their being modern-day fishermen who choose to follow the Son of Man. They are all better leaders for having such a volunteer spirit. Your son has turned your absence into a pledge of his presence, and though he will be the first to tell you he is a "words guy," Mark is also a man of his word. With every fiber of his being, he tries every day to show up so He can show out. Oh, sometimes he may be late, but he'll not leave you hanging, and he is always right on time. He is a natural teacher: into his sermons, he weaves biblical stories, timeless themes, pressing social issues, not to mention stories from his own life, all to move us to change from the inside out for His glory. Gaining salvation is inestimably more valuable than earning a degree is one lesson I've learned. He delivers God's truth like some skilled surgeon performs an operation or like lightning striking a tree. It's that profound. He must provide in an hour what we who teach have the luxury of a week's contact to purvey, but where the professor disseminates knowledge, your son, so much wiser than his years, preaches the eternal truth of God's word. It is Mark's way to boost people's confidence by telling them *he is proud of them*, and mountains are moved. In fact, your son's encouragement of me has propelled me to do and be more than I could have generated for myself; the Holy Spirit saw to it. I do believe he is as much His pride as our joy.

Mark's drive and zeal for sharing Christ's truths and charity must surely be borne from an early period of wanting to know *why* this and *how come* that. Armed with biblical wisdom and the love of Jesus, he moves us all towards a greater depth of understanding Him. That he is powerful without being conceited and gentle while still being germane are traits that make Mark stand out. Regardless of how "hard" his word, which can sometimes cut us to the quick, he never leaves us without hope, humor, or joy. I suspect that this, too, is an inverse lesson generated from his youth. It's just got to be *real* for Mark. I am sure you are familiar with the story in the New Testament of the parable of the Prodigal Son. In this case, however, I think it may you who is the prodigal one, except that you haven't returned, and it is your son who has become the wise father. Who knows what your future brings such that one day, in recognizing the brevity of life, you might long to venture out and see him and his? My own dad used to say that *we grow old too fast and wise too late*, so I hope that this may not be the case for you and that you realize that "you are just a vapor that appears for a little while and then vanishes away" (James 4:14). Seize the day and mend that fence. Though Mark says you know the child by his father, in the case with you, I believe Mark has done everything in his power and through prayer to prove the opposite, so much so, I'll wager he now resembles *His* Son more than he does *you*. As an aside, I can't neglect to mention his stepfather, the man he calls "dad," who has shown him a lifetime of kindness and generosity, day inand day out. Mr. Jackson, no one is perfect, and everyone tries to make the best of things missed or gone astray. Forgiveness has already taken place within your son's breast long ago. Still, I *do* have a prayer for you: against all the odds, regardless of whatever accomplishments or accolades you have achieved in your life, I hope God would give *you* a heart and put a new spirit within *you*. After all, God "can take the heart of stone out of flesh..." (from Ezekiel 11:19). Out of sight doesn't have to mean out of mind; it only seems as such if you remain spiritually blind. God can heal fractures that are as wide as canyons; He can break the silence and lead your steps to where you can shake your son's hand before your last breath is drawn. Miracles still never cease. Meanwhile, life moves on and is blossoming beautifully for Mark; therefore, I'll turn my attention to "the man upstairs" who has abundantly provided for Mark and give thanks to *Him*. I do appreciate your attention thus far.

> *"I will give thanks to the Lord with all my heart; I will*
> *tell of all Your wonders."*
>
> — *Psalm 9:1*

Thanksgiving 2018

Dear Heavenly Father,

I save this supreme though second letter for You, God, You who have no beginning or end. Lord, thanks to your adopted son, Mark, I have come to know Your love and believe in Your Son. I have half-joked with Mark that one small crown I hope he earns as your "good and faithful servant" (Matthew 25:21 NIV) will come from his having led me to You. Though his father of the flesh may have been dismayed, I'm so grateful that he responded positively to Your calling on his life. Everything about Mark is one huge affirmation; to be with him is to feel like you're in flight. Do you watch him Sunday mornings, Wednesday nights, out at coffee shops, in so many a kitchen or living room, out on the field coaching, and in his office planning? I am confident You see him in his office streaming modern hymns as he pours over your Word, perhaps in private prayer and supplication, or maybe weaving the words of some sermon through which he hopes to move hearts and lives? Oh, do you sense Your Spirit overtake, possess, and provide him with providential truths which You ordain him to preach, yes, with that velvet touch of his? Do you like his modern-day parables? We surely do! Do you see how intent, sometimes even with cool desperation, he wants us to understand and crave You with more insight, clarity, depth, and accuracy, activated today more than yesterday?

I know each person you conceive and craft is done with intentionality and extreme specificity. Still, You broke the mold with Mark: he is a bundle of contradictions, yet the whole of this man is vaster than the sum of his parts: you have given him a brilliant mind and a spirit filled with joy and vigor, and he preaches to us with all of his heart that is filled with Your Spirit. He is a rational man and a quick thinker, but he has the soul of a blues guitarist and relishes the world You made. You have made him quite the dreamer, but his feet are firmly planted on the ground. Do you see the man sitting in his favorite beach chair staring out in childlike wonder at Your endless waves, like a balm to his brain? I'm sure you notice the quickening of his step on the golf course, where power and finesse unite on a field of green under a bright blue sky. He has a silver tongue, but he communicates more when he gets still and quiet. He knows when to leave well enough alone. He is a passionate man full of love and life, yet you gave him compassion for those who suffer in silence or have lost their wits and way. There is no indulgence of self-pity in others as he does not tolerate this in himself; it would be akin to being satisfied to idle in neutral. He loves his own flesh and blood, but he feels tenderness for the orphaned, and he adores his church family as if we were his own. You have made him a teetotaler, but he is a champion of the addicted and afflicted, and he lavishes his energies for their welfare and shows them a better drink, the cup that holds Your Son's blood. He is a man who seeks Your wisdom, yet he is not afraid to be thought a fool if it helps further Your kingdom. He understands the mystery that is woman and how she can suffer so long in silence, yet You have made in him a man's man who knows how to bring the best out in any beast.

Even though he admits to being afraid of the dark and mice, he is a man who is a warrior for our soldiers and heralds those who provide relief in disaster. He is a visionary and plans for our future, yet he is a man who calls himself "old school" and honors past pastors. Mark is such a one who, when committed to Your cause, he's all in and out front. To some, he can be elusive as a sprite; like a butterfly, he cannot be contained or held. His mind is like quicksilver, his sensitivity as fine as a spider's thread, yet his preaching can feel like dynamite when he gets moved by Your Spirit. You have graced him with an appearance that's easy on the eye, but like Paul, you've pricked his pride with some unseen phantom thorn that stings when he senses undue attention. You have made him a leader of men, yet a master of none because he belongs to You; he is Your bondservant; You're his #1. He may also say of himself, "Oh, wretched man that I am!", but just when he struggles or might second-guess this or that, he recalls the words of his Pepaw: "His grace is sufficient" (2 Cor. 12:9), and he is fortified. He has never met a stranger and has boasted he could sell ice to an Eskimo, so praise be to You that he spends himself by giving You away to those who would have eyes and ears. He advises many, but it's Your Spirit who counsels him; loyal ones are sometimes not so plenty. Like any normal man, he appreciates a pat on the back of affirmation, yet because he knows his gifts and talents are supernaturally endowed by *You*, he will say thanks and quickly shift the focus back on the *other* guy. He won't take personal credit where he feels it's not due.

It's only in writing that I can slow down and take a moment to thank him through my prayers to You so that my gratitude can be shown. Mark has done a whole series of sermons based on the premise that all the *what- ifs* we possess exist right now for the taking and doing; we are not promised tomorrow. Therefore, I must seize this chance, glance back as I step ahead into what You might have me do. Attention must be paid. When Mark first came to sit at my kitchen table with Bonnie and me, now over five years ago, he stepped into both our home and hearts. He told us that he is a changed man from when he started in the ministry, and, as odd as it sounds, though I *am* sorry for his dark days, whatever You did to get him to be the man he is today, he has come to be a stronger pastor and a better man for it. You took his power and pride and gave him passion and pain, his wealth and knowledge exchanged for wisdom. You turned a Saul into Paul and one with a heart like David. Mark is my brother, mentor, pastor, and Rocket man; he is my friend and a man I respect. I also know that the Thief works particularly hard on him, and he often advises us on how to be better at being battle-ready. I'm now going to pray with specificity that whatever dreams and means he has to further Your kingdom, that You help them come to fruition. As I speak about him now, I feel like I'm soaring in my mind, and in this upcoming month, when we give more to commemorate the gift of Your Son to us, Mark will be the first to say that *no one can outgive God.* So often, this man tells us that he just wants "to bust into Heaven, beaten up, bruised, with scrapes on his knees and back," worn out from having spent a lifetime of serving and bringing in hurt souls and "jacked-up" folks to You. Oh, I am such a one.

I'll end with a heartfelt thanks to *You* Who inspires Mark to challenge us all every day to live more like Your Son, our Savior. Mark has our hearts, and I'm sure he is a man after Yours. He is "faith, hope, and love" (1 Cor. 13:13) in the flesh for us. I pray that you protect, sustain, and fortify his mind, body, and spirit for all the rest of his livelong days.

Your daughter,
D.C.

12. Tanya

Meet Tanya. Should you ever encounter Tanya, you would never forget her. She is full of zest, and she's ready to go and do. She has been a friend and sister in Christ to me for over five years, but it feels like longer for all we've shared. There's an easiness about Tanya that makes it effortless and safe to confide in and do life with her. She is a happy person by nature, and God made her "all girl," as they say, so there's a sass, spice, and silliness about her that has you feeling light, cheerful, and sunny. She has both gumption and grace. Where she is, fun is sure to follow. I don't want to give the impression that it's all light and fluff and games with her; it's not. She is incredibly discerning, and in a glance, she can tell if you're down-and-out or hiding some pain, and she is ready to give or do you whatever she can to make things right. She is aware that everything she can offer comes from Christ anyway. She'll tell you quickly and outright that she has the gift of prophecy and will do battle with the wily one like she's a panther. Therefore, it is a no-brainer for me to call Tanya a giver because doing unto others for His good comes naturally for her. She'll be there for you when the chips have fallen where they may, and you find yourself in need of a hot meal some cold night, a ride to the hospital (*and* someone there waiting for you when you're done), or a steady hand ready to take yours when tears are falling down your cheek. She is that one. It's no wonder she has a passion for persons in the poorest place on the planet, Haiti. I am also impressed by the fact that she regularly opens up her heart and home for women to take part in Bible or book studies. You can rest assured that you'll grin, giggle, and cut up in the same hour she will share in earnestness with you what's in "*her* Bible," as she is want to say.

*Can you think of people in your life who have been there
for you through thick and thin? Who is that one in your
life who puts the simple but special touches on a gift that
lets you know you are cared for? Do you have a friend
who withholds judgment, knowing she, too, falls short,
yet she raises your spirits as she lifts your chin and has
you feeling better before you know it?*

Read on to see more of Tanya.

"But the fruit of the Spirit is love, joy, peace,
patience, kindness, goodness, faithfulness..."
—Galatians 5:22

December 9, 2018

Dear Tanya,

Bonnie and I have been attending the same church off and
on for the better part of five years, and when I think about all
the people that I have met and befriended there, you stand
shining heads and shoulders above the rest. Your smile, the tilt
of your head, your easy laugh, your close attention to others,
and positive spirit are all attributes that anybody could easily
recognize you by. In the early days, I'll never forget coming
upon you once in the park when Bonnie and I were taking a
walk. Bonnie had just received troubling news and had stopped
by a tree to pray for her brother *and* for herself, when, out of
nowhere, there you came! You told her that *you had had her on
your heart.* I would be hard-pressed to think of anyone I know
who is so in tune with and responsive to the Holy Spirit's
promptings and nudges. This would be the first of many divine
appointments of your appearing to us like some angel of God,
yet at the same time, you are a genuine friend, tried and true.

How can I not mention here that you came and sat with me in the hospital waiting room for hours, in fact, the better part of the day, while Bonnie was in surgery, yet we could also cut up and feel joy even in that cloudy time?

You call yourself a prayer warrior whose spiritual gift is prophecy. At first, I did not understand this, but I have surely seen such with my own eyes, and I know it to be true. I know that God uses you in a thousand different ways, I am moved to tell you just how much I admire you for being the hands and the feet of Jesus. You may have many other Bible verses that please or speak to you, but for me, the passage above from Galatians I now place in your palm like a small gift today because you exemplify all these qualities of goodness, and I smile in wonder at the woman you are. Your sass and brass delight me, too, and I love that we can be silly one minute and fully and seriously intent in Him the next. You have brought a smile to my face with your charm and disarming honesty. Bonnie has gotten much cheer from your steadfastness and positive energy. I am so grateful we can hang out and laugh together, hugging one other in times of sadness as well as happiness, be it after Sunday School or running into you at some random place like Wal-Mart. You are the first person through whom I came to understand what is meant by "church family." That we are His and speak of Him in everyday conversation means the world to me! In short, you give the fruit of the Spirit non-stop: you host a Monday night study for women; you volunteer to help folks states away to show them how Jesus shows up when life gets messy. I love that you are ready to go at the drop of a hat when people are in need, be it in L.C., Haiti, or a place that has experienced a natural disaster. You can cook —*and how!* — and you clean and work hard at *any* task you're given, all with the energy of a diesel engine and the sweetness of a saint. You are a powerhouse through your submission to King Jesus! You may be "country," but your God-given curiosity, bright mind, and desire to explore and admire new, beautiful, and wondrous things has you traveling to all sorts of places. Oh, the places *you* go! There is nothing too big or too small, too spectacular or ordinary that you don't note the presence and power of Him! You take your nieces to the zoo, enjoy a picnic in a local park, or get away with your husband to see the likes of America's castles and gardens at Biltmore Estate. You are ready to get up every day and go and do and be for the Lord, and I have no doubt He smiles when He sees you wake up each morning.

You are the epitome of the salt of the earth and the light He seeks to have us shine. Sometimes I can be moody or lost in thought, and I notice you keep a respectful distance, yet all the while, I feel your caring gaze. I see that you pay close attention to that which and whom He would show you, and, time and again, you discern His truths and promptings as to what needs to be done. Speaking of which, you are one of the Lord's encouragers, and you press into what He puts on your heart to say to others; I have been a grateful recipient of this myself. May I also say that I admire how much you have given to your extended family in ways that are healthy and righteous? You inspire me to be and to do the best I can, too. I also feel compelled to tell you that I admire you as a mother, and it is evident that your daughter has turned out to be a wellspring of generosity, in great part because of how much of Him you and your husband have fostered in her. Sometimes those who give the most sometimes don't know how much they are appreciated, and telling you is just what I'm up to here. Let me sing *your* praises! No, none of us is perfect, and we are a work in progress on this road of sanctification, but why not *also* speak about the awesomeness that God has put in *you,* tell you about it, and celebrate you, even if for a moment here and now in this letter? Why should we wait until a birthday to write someone just how much we love them? I am not, and so I say to you, Tanya, I am glad you were born. I am glad God sees fit to use you as He does, and I can hardly wait to see how He continues to do so in your future. I am grateful to be your sister in Christ and a friend who is just around the corner.

I love the fact that you are always up for something new; you have an adventuresome spirit, and it never surprises me when I hear you are off doing some task here at home *and* that you desire to galivant halfway across the world to learn more about Jesus. Your open-mindedness, lack of judgmentalism, desire to keep on learning and growing, and your warmth and depth of character make you such a great example to us all. Over the years, these qualities have done a number on your husband, too. A shining beacon of His love, you waited and patiently and stayed the course without being bossy or pushy, and this helped bring about the metamorphosis from how I imagine your husband *used* to be to the man, Christian leader, and servant he is now.

Tanya, God is using you mightily; you are one of His *Yes* people! No Dallas Cowboy cheerleader has anything on you, and so I wanted to stop, take note, and tell you all about it. I love you!

Your sister in Christ,

D.C.

13. Catherine

God broke the mold when He made Catherine! There's no one like her, and, likely, no one who would want to *be* her. Most would say that *the* most distinguishing marker about her is that she has thirteen children, but I can attest that she is no Jill Dugger parading what she provides. Catherine is my friend, and I love her dearly. You'll also come to learn that she is one of just a handful who went from student to friend for me, and I have known her well over twenty-five years. Her life is so full and on-the-go, that if you watched her hectic day in fast motion, you might notice only a blur of children whirling about the house, laughing and chasing one another around the yard, or eating on the fly while still in the process of dressing for school. The common denominator for any scene and every moment in Catherine's household and life is the outpouring of love she gives every day. No one sees how she does it, but I know that her patience, perspective, and pleasure are God's provisions for her. She will never not be a mother, and though she cherishes infants in her lap, there where she can make the world snuggly safe and warm for her babes, she avidly looks forward to when her adult children come back home to her hearth. The age makes no difference to her. I, too, have been the recipient of her lavish love, and our friendship means the world to me. Recently, she confided to me that the gift of quality time is what means the most to her. I can see why; that is *her* love language, and she dispenses it daily and freely; her love is in endless supply. Catherine is a liberal giver, and I pray that she may be blessed in equal measure throughout her beautiful life.

Do you know someone whose life is far from neat and tidy,
but one who would offer you any and everything he or she
has got without batting an eye in order to make you feel

safe or at home? Who is that person for you who lacks pretense and guise, the one with whom you can drink tea, horse laugh with over things others may find not so funny, or, in the blink of an eye, discuss the profound or pertinent matters of your heart? Do you know someone who celebrates life with the same enthusiasm as one who lives for football?

If so, then you're ready to read more about Catherine.

"While we try to teach our children all about life, our children teach us what life is really all about."
—Angela Schwindt, homeschooling mother

December 16, 2018

Hello, Catherine!

Goodness knows that for some time now, I have had it on my mind to write you a thorough thank you letter. Looking back over the twenty- seven years that I have known you, my heart is aflutter with love. Life is full, and we can get preoccupied with daily tasks and the needs of a busy moment — even if they are labors of love — to the point that we let days pass us by without telling those nearest just how much they mean to us. Therefore, today is the day that I would like to breathe in and take my time telling you how very dear you are to me. How could I have known way back then that a particular burst of laughter which came from the back of my classroom at the perfect time over some wry comment I'd made, would come from *you*, you who would come to be one of my closest friends?

A couple of background commonalities instinctively drew me to you early on: you and I are the eldest of three daughters as well as the product of an American and Mediterranean heritage. We are half this and half that and a one-of-a-kind whole! You, too, came to have an interest in Russia, but that was just the start of it. On our school trip to Russia, now over a quarter of a century ago, I'll not soon forget giving stern warnings about not giving handouts to strangers for wanting to protect you all from the groping hands of beggars. That made no dent in you, so it was with no surprise that I would see you handing a loaf of bread to a bent- over, haggard, and scarfed babushka one minute or candy and kopecks to eager hands of hungry children spiraling around you the next. It was as if they were rays spanning out from your warm sunshine. To our cores, we both love life and people. We have an appreciation for life's ironies and are ready to laugh on the spot when we hear it. There is a lightning-quick pace at which our minds travel, and we impose no limits on topics we broach, be they contemporary issues or the psychological underpinnings of why people act the way they do. Our conversations and conclusions lead to many a broad smile on your beautiful face. I love sharing ideas and life experiences, trying different cuisines on our double-dates, and so much more with you! In admiration, I notice that regardless of the swirl of activity and the ongoing needs of children, be it a rocking lap, a swat on the behind, or a hug around the neck, you don't miss a beat or the chance to have grown-up talk. Who else says in quiet confidentiality, eyes shining with wicked mirth, "Go ahead and get yourself a plate before the kids do," knowing that their onslaught will soon wreak havoc on the bounty you've set out? When I'm with you and we get lost in thought in some deep conversation, you make me feel as if there is no one else in the room you'd rather be talking to. Yet, all the while, you are orchestrating or attending to a thousand and one details around you. Not only this, but without fail, you check in about my coming to the next upcoming gathering. It is as if you never get your fill of doing life together, be it in small spurts or long afternoons, and I am agog at this. I cannot keep up with your heart's pace! You are a marvel to me, and I have a tremendous regard for you now that you are in the full-blossomed years of your life. Your ability to keep in the forefront what's *truly* important in life is a lesson in perspective I learn from you. Oh, you are a wealthy woman, and the precocity and vitality I saw in your mind as a maiden have become wisdom, strength, and the open arms and heart of an independent woman deeply in love with her husband and family. It overflows in your laughter, words, appreciation of life's inanities, your protectiveness, and ready compassion. With you, every day is like Thanksgiving.

Your love for your family knows no bounds; it starts here and spills out there. I understand now why you liked the town of M. so much: it is a village that was an extension of your family. That's just how much love you have in you! Now that you have come back to T. for reasons both obvious and yet not, I see you returning to embrace the fold of your flesh. However, true to your form, you ensure that your need for privacy and autonomy in the sanctity of your own primal womb — your home — is met. Though others buzz around and are welcome in your hive, you must be your own queen bee. Thomas Wolfe may say, "You can't go home again," but I beg to differ. For you, the return to this hearth, albeit in your house, has brought about healing in some, heroism in your husband, happiness of cousins, and new hope in you. When folks are dubious as to how you could have so many children, I let go of the world's ways and codes, meet them eye to eye, and say that you couldn't *not*, that you'd *always* wanted a large family. Though your family is far from looking like the Waltons, I see yours as the best America has to offer: real brotherly love, a love that is blind to prejudice and bigotry, a football team whose primal chants and cheers raise boys to men and girls into strong women. I can count on one hand, maybe a couple of fingers, the people I know in life who would take me in and put a roof over my head and food in my belly if the world came to a crashing halt. I know beyond a shadow of a doubt that if for any reason I would come to be in dire straits, I could call you, and not only would you come running (or send your boys to do so), but you would invite me to stay in your home. That kind of love is so uncommon, valuable, authentic, and precious. Eve as a teenager, who but you called to check on me when I was home alone, my mind reeling with all that could have happened from just having experienced a hurricane that barely missed hitting my house?

You are a woman of substance who *has* to have things *real* over what conventional wisdom might deem as being "right." I beg to plead your case: you are a rebel *with* a reason, and your being a doula, which, as you know, in Greek means "a woman who serves," *is* your life's calling, and many are blessed beyond measure for your innate capacity to be such. You have a lawyer's logic, and, like some a patient judge, you present your children with the ten commandments without having to lay down any man's law. You instill in them right from wrong and love felt deep in their bones which will nourish them for life. They may live as one-for-all and all-for-one, but each is valued and acknowledged for his or her unique gifts and ways. Not only do you celebrate each of their birthdays with flair, fanfare, and a birthday cake as big as a float, you bolster them for a life of knowing that *they matter*. Your quick wit and keen sense of irony have you being like Catherine the Great, ready to remark that "the world is full of strange situations." You are one who patiently stands at attention, ready to defend, help, or make much-needed ado or light of some particular predicament or prospect. Even though I may not understand the peculiar love for an infant, one fresh and fragile, so vulnerable and in need, I think that this touches upon the very core of who you are. You are such a one who would like to make the world stand at attention forever at that which is as perfect as it gets here on planet earth. However, your passion for the teenager I *do* understand: their morphing logic, intense emotions, lurchy teetering between prideful independence and utter dependence, and light-heartedness brings us joy. Your capacity for hope and faith is also vast, and you show it when, one by one, you release your children into the world as readied souls.

I want to mention one other thing I've always admired about you that was absent from my parents' marriage: no matter what argument, infraction, or misdeed that has occurred, you remain steadfast and devoted to your husband. You are not a quitter, and through your daily renewing good intentions and fresh commitment, you make a way to keep respect feeling alive and well throughout your marriage. You don't backbite or vent because fairness is your flagship. That is so uncommon today because the world tells us that we should get what we can for ourselves or that with three strikes, you're out, baby. Rather, it's "seventy times seven" (Matthew 18:22) that quantifies the forgiveness in your heart! Everything about you is a sacrifice without your being a martyr. The hour has recently come to envelop your mother with your own maternal love, and such an unexpected harvest has been bountiful. Despite a few frustrations, you will not regret this, and I, for one, I have been grateful to watch your tentative, respectful, and sensitive steps towards each other so that peace may reign and love flourish. Your mother treasures you with all of her heart. Speaking of motherhood, though it turns out that I have begotten none, you are the only person who has ever sent me a Mother's Day card, and as a result, if but for once, I felt the spirit of the daughter in you for me. To be chosen as godmother to one of your daughters seems only fitting in our full circle of love.

In short, *there is no one like you,* Catherine, and I, for one, am glad to be your friend *and* your family. I know I'm not alone. The complex, tangled, and messy loving relationships you have with your mother, your sisters, and, yes, with your dad, are nonetheless blanketed with a supreme love that transcends all. Heavenly day! You are *such* a giver that it cannot be contained. So today, tomorrow, and always, let me tell you with a full heart and open arms that I love you, and I am *so* happy we are in each other's lives.

Sincerely,

D. C.

14. Paige

Meet Paige. For almost ten years, she became what many would call my "boo" at my job. With our work carols situated right across from one another, it just so happened that we discovered that we not only share the same vocation and love of kids, but we are of the same mind in matters that count the most. Paige has a stunning wit, and she can have me belly-laughing in no time at all by some sarcastic or ironic remark she's just made. Cue her eyes rolling. They say humor is borne from pain, and I know this to be so for her. Our backgrounds couldn't be further apart, but as girls, we both experienced the same longing for love from our mothers when they were not in the position to give. Perhaps that's partly why I have put Paige in the category of givers: she gives 'til she's tuckered out and then gives some more. I care for her as my friend, and I respect her as my colleague; she is one who will be there for her true-blue friends above and beyond any sense you've ever seen. Her professionalism is not so prim and proper because her call of duty is savage, and you can always count on her to tell you the unvarnished truth. Honesty for her is indispensable. She wants things to be right *and* real. I know few who are as loyal as she is, and even though she has shifted her role from teacher to a counselor, her underlying sensitivity, care, and devotedness to helping those in need during their storms by her giving of self remains undiminished.

Who is that one person you can think of that you know you could call, day or night, no matter what, and he or she would be there for you, no questions asked? Who is that steady friend that lends a helping hand and gives a ready ear when you are down and out? Whom do you count on for no-holds-bar honesty? Who can read you

like a book without your saying a word and give you a
touch of affirmation you didn't even know you needed?
Who is the one who seeks what's righteous and will take
a stand to makes sure all is as it should or could be?
Who makes the difference for you at work by being your
"partner in crime," all the while doing her best at the
appointed task or duty at hand?

Read on, and you' ll meet Paige.

"If God is for us, who can be against us? Who
shall separate us from the love of Christ? Shall
trouble or hardship or persecution...? *No,* in *all*
these things *we are more than conquerors* through
Him who loved us."
— From Romans 8:31–27 (NIV), emphasis mine

December 23, 2018

Dear Paige,

The afternoon you told me, half-jokingly, yet in characteristic
raw directness that you'd like to have tattooed on your forehead,
"We are more than conquerors," was the day you confirmed
for me that you are wholly His. Oh, there is a still much of the
"Invictus" or unconquerable in you, but, unlike William Ernest
Henley, though you may be the "master of your fate," it is *Jesus*
who is the "captain of your soul." Therefore, today, this day of
your baptism, I congratulate you openly, unabashedly, and in
full celebration of your being my sister in Christ. As you said,
the decision was made *decades* before, but now is the day you
share your claim, that perfect little stake in Heaven's soil, which
confirms your identity for all eternity as being *His.* Oh, to feel
the power in His forgiveness and grace and love like no other.

So, on those gray days when you get upset by the thousands of little things out of place in the world, you *can* have the "peace which surpasses all understanding" (Philippians 4:17 ESV), knowing that, yes, the bad guys really *do* lose because the Good Guy has already won; we are just catching up to that then. I gently remind you to say, "Tsk, tsk," to the darkness because you *have* seen and know His Light.

It has been in my heart to write to you since well before today, so I'll continue with what I had on my mind to say. Around Christmas time, people are reminded that it is the time to give, but, my dear, giving is something you do of your own accord *all the time*. Life without Him would crush us, and if you didn't give, you would feel empty, so I thank you for the kindnesses *I* have received from you, be they in the form of a hug, an attentive ear and ready heart, that deadpan look that tries to hide due disdain, or even a slice of your delicious coconut cake. Like Lucy, we have had the "Psychiatric Help, 5¢, The Doctor is *In*" sign for each other too many times to count. You have made airport runs for me and watched over my home while I was out of the country practically annually; youeven replaced my bashed-in mailbox! Such a loyal and steadfast one you are! And then there's work...

Somewhere back at the beginning of every teacher's career, there comes that moment when we are just supposed to accept the fact that we cannot save all children, that, statistically speaking, some children *have* to suffer or fail, yes, even on our watch. I think someplace deep inside, you never accepted this, and I want to say that you are my hero for being such. In fact, that you have shifted your professional course may empower you to help even more teens to reach their potential! To switch from the role of teacher to counselor confirms to us all that you refuse to let kids fall through the cracks; this originates outside the classroom. You want for them to more than just avoid deleterious circumstances; you want them to survive and thrive. You seek for them to triumph, and that, my dear, is a testament to your character.

You may protest and counter that, in part, you desired to reduce your grading load. I think differently: you have been much put upon for butting your head against various forces in our educational system, which, as Emerson would say is a type of "society in a conspiracy against the manhood of every one of its members." You have exchanged the dissemination of information in the classroom for helping cloak the full armor your students need to succeed both in school and life. The love of the family-feel in the classroom that only a teacher understands you will transform into individualized compassion for both students and teachers alike such that they know to their core that *someone has their back.* When I look over your career, it has been *students* who have moved you, be it the odd girl who composed the story, "Who Be I?", or those who stayed back in your classroom long after the bell rang. They needed to talk to you in their quiet, tearful, yet expectant confidence. Who but you traveled half a day to attend a commencement ceremony from a military academy for a student you taught the year before? Students are like diamonds in your sky, and with you, they do not wonder what they are. Your protectiveness of and tenderness towards the outcast, downtrodden, disconnected, and invisible ones marks you as one of the few genuine guardians in this troubled world, and these recipients are all the better off for having felt your love and support. Blessed are *you*, Paige; because you hunger and thirst for righteousness, you shall be satisfied. Being one of the pure in heart, you shall see God (quoted from Matthew 5:6 and 8). Students aren't the only ones you protect.

I could hope for no better friend than you! Your brilliance, perfectionism, sensitivity, astuteness in assessing human nature, and desire to get to the crux of matters of substance are balanced with a down-to-earth practicality, humor, and authenticity unparalleled. You are a steward through how you have championed rescuing pits, so much so that three have become your children. Yes, your pit-bull, Jen, is your spirit animal, and to be loved by Jen is to know a fierce love. Speaking of which, how can I not mention the commonality we share of *not* experiencing this from our own mothers? Regardless of our different upbringings and backgrounds, you and I are two who have felt an impaired maternal love, and the result is that this ache has us stare out wistfully when we whiff out such essential oil in others. We may stand perplexed at the prospect of selecting a Mother's Day card because such banal messages expressing gratitude do not match the crinkled reality we recall. Yet, with wry humor aside and life's petals of hurt having long since fallen, we *can* do better for ourselves than repine! You and I help each other get on with the vital business of forgiveness as we ourselves become a kind of maternal force to be reckoned with. In like vein, you live up to your Biblical name. You abound in doing good things, and you are kind (from Acts 9:36), and you now nurture your newly-arise self. In this respect, you are more alive today than when you first set foot in this state. That you dressed up as the beautiful Snow White a couple of Halloweens ago is not coincidental: you have claimed a prince, made your own castle, and you still are the fairest one of all.

I would be a liar if I didn't say that I miss seeing you every day and walking out of the schoolhouse together as we laugh or lament over the travails of our day. So many trivial and mundane things happen as we work our magic, you know, changing lives and all. More than you realize, I am comforted in knowing that you are just around the bend. You have a permanent place in my heart, so, irrespective of the paths our lives take, I wanted to take a second in our busy lives and say *thank you* for the gift of you!

Much love and a little prayer said for you,

D.C.

15. Heather

Meet Heather. Like Catherine, she is one other person mentioned in this book who has gone from being a student to becoming my friend. I write about and to her here. No matter how much time passes between visits when get to hang out together, it's as if *no* time has passed at all. Heather is one who can make time stand still because if you are her friend, this is a state that does not change. You may have lost or gained weight, turned gray or wrinkled, gone from rich to poor, or moved to a different country, but you will always be the same to her, and by that, I mean you are in the category of a forever friend. This kind of person bears more heartaches than many because such devotion is not always reciprocated or maintained. I do not mean to imply that she would hold onto a toxic relationship or suffer abuse. She is too strong and self-possessed for that; she knows life is too short for loving haters or users. That said, when her heart has given her the green light, and you're "in," her love and generosity know no bounds. There is not a doubt in my mind that should I ever become feeble-minded or of little account to others, she would take me in and do her best to nurse me back to health or love me right where I was until the bitter end. Her heart is as big as Texas, and I hope to always visit her state. In fact, anytime I'm heading in her direction, a seventy-mile jaunt, I need only text, and there's an excellent chance that if she's not at her job, she'll drop other plans so we can work in a visit. She is a lover of animals and protector of the weak and defenseless. She is that blessed gentle one mentioned in the Matthew's Beatitudes. Heather gives generously with open arms every day.

Who is the "animal person" in your life? Whom do you
know that adores her pets, both large and small because
in their simple innocence, they love with a sweetness

*that gets soiled in their two-legged counterparts? Who is
one that loves you as a part of her herd, pack, or pride?
No, this is no odd "cat lady" who couldn't be bothered
with mankind anymore. Instead, she or he is the one who
loves life so much that she appreciates it in its purest and
dearest state, and she loves the beasts and the children.
How might you give back to one whose life is all about
dispensing love like there's no tomorrow? Do you have a
kind word or a morsel of chocolate on hand? She does.*

Please go on to read about Heather now.

"If you don't own a dog, at least one, there is
not necessarily anything wrong with you, but
there may be something wrong with your life.
Dogs are not our whole life, but they make our
lives whole."
—Roger A. Caras, Author of *A Dog Is Listening:
The Way Some of Our Closest Friends View Us*
(1993)

December 30, 2018

Dear Heather,

I haven't ever sat down to write you a warm note of thanks,
but it is long overdue; therefore, I have decided to close out this
year with a letter to recount for you all the wonderful ways you
mean to me! There are precious few students who stand the test
of time to become *this* teacher's friend, but not only have you
done so, now going on twenty years, but even more, I consider
you family. It didn't take me too long to recognize and admire
your acute powers of observation, extraordinary sensitivity,
undying devotion, determination, and steadfastness in the face

of adversity or obstacle. On top of that, you have a readiness to smile and laugh. I have gotten to see of these qualities in you unfold beyond the classroom into real life. Your capacity for loyalty and generosity I consider nearly unparalleled. You are one who is there for your friends for the count and through thick and thin; you are truly extraordinary in this manner. I have seen this time and again. In fact, your go-to response is always to consider the other guy before yourself. To be loved by you is to possess the knowledge that there really are still folks out there who have your back, will stay by your side, can lift up your chin, and make your spirits bright. This applies not only to precious people in your life, but to pets, too. Animals mean the world to you; they need so much from us, and we are called to be their protectorates. I'll turn my attention to horses and dogs now to demonstrate the best that's in you *and* to highlight how much you have come to mean to me.

Many a quadruped has benefited by your charity, steady hand, and tender loving care. I'll start with horses because in learning a bit more about them, I see that the best in them reveals qualities you, too, possess. It is common knowledge that the horse is a very sensitive and intelligent animal. In particular, horses "can sense the feelings of those nearby — particularly hesitation, fear, confidence and anger" (*www.equine-world.co.uk*). You are as adept at reading a host of facial expressions and body language as you are at knowing the clues that the flick of an ear or tail can transmit. Eyes speak volumes if you are attentive and fluent in their language; you are. You are wizened to emotional clues in us biped counterparts and can decipher and break many a code of our mysterious ways because you are alert and perceptive. Like horses, you estimate a person's alpha role, not by his physical strength or power, but rather by his tone and attitude; by this, you can quickly decipher if you've a friend or foe. I am so glad that I am a part of your "safe people" herd! I have observed your devotion and faithfulness to loved ones for whom, like horses, flight — not fight — equals life when they have had to outrun predators of the mind and heart to survive.

As much as I have come to see this free equine spirit in you, it is the love of a dog that most captivates your heart, so I redirect my focus to this aspect of you. Oh, there is many a dog lover out there, many a lady who clutches a tiny toy miniature one like it's some new purse to be displayed, and many who improve their overall quality of life by acquiring a dog. Still, for you, it's much more than that. The love of a dog reflects something deep inside you, too, which the rest of us would be wise to ape. As a groomer, you have your followers who have seen what a whisperer *you* are when you attend to their do 's needs. That you care for these pooches as much as they dote on us reveals your particular brand of love, one that extends beyond the critters in your care at work. I have benefitted by your attending to my pets while on vacation, now too many times to count. There is no one I would trust more to take care of my animals. You have welcomed dogs distressed, geriatric, and infirm to make a home alongside your three shelties, your own trio of wise ones. Your chihuahua named "Mousie" that peeks out from under your shirt is like a living appendage attached to you; he is guaranteed to a make you giggle with delight. This is such a happy sight!

Heather, when I see you, I know I am looking at one of the rare "gentle, merciful, and pure in heart" in this world (from Matthew 5). As the song says, "Bless the beasts and the children," and you definitely give them *and* us a safe haven when disaster strikes. Like the dogs you love, you, also have an emotional E.S.P. If you were a dog, you would be my pick for a service dog because being around you makes even the most anxious feel calm. Plus, I know who would fight to the death to defend me. With you, a loved one never would fear separation anxiety, and even if I were chasing my own tail, you would not leave me as if I were feral, rabid, lost, or stray. You would come to my rescue! Like the animals you love, you have a playfulness and a lightness of heart that is rare, and your capacity to work to please those you love is undying. You guard your chosen ones possessively, and your olfactory sense of sniffing out who is safe or not is quick and spot-on. More than any other innate trait of yours that I esteem, it is your capacity for empathy that is the most remarkable. Wikipedia tells me that "dogs orient toward their owner more often when the person was pretending to cry than when they were talking or humming." Isn't that amazing? That's no new trick for you because you are in a breed unto yourself! You stand ready at attention and do likewise, and we are all the better for it. I saw hints of this back when you were in my class.

These traits of constancy, loyalty, attentiveness, and a readiness to enjoy life have remained in you long past what I got a gander of in class. You made a mental record of words of wisdom and acts of kindness like other students do charts and diagrams. Beneath that big shock of long, wavy hair was a chivalric scout who would remain my tested friend for life, and over the years, I am glad to have become a part of your pack. As the adult who is garnering her own life experiences, I have looked on from afar and admired your willingness to get up and go at the drop of a hat for your dear ones. Why, you have zigzagged across the country to do so. I have also seen you turn more discerning and wiser as to where to put your eggs, and I want to tell you I am proud of you and impressed with your becoming selective in this respect. Some baskets are not capable or meant to hold the golden eggs you possess. You have grown better at guarding your gifts and protecting who *you* were fashioned to be. I consider your hearth, house, and property like a Ground Zero, like the center of a vast crossroads to come home to when the ways of the world are too much. Though I have half-kidded and remarked in passing that if I were hobbling along and on my last lap your life, I believe you would take me in because I will never be a stray to you, I hope you know that the same holds true for you with me.

In the same way that you carried that oversized box around high school which held inside two tiny calico kitties — one of which would become my cat — that were in need of a home, I have marveled watching you pick up the broken pieces of many lives. You held kittens in the palm of your hand and have helped your friends in need to heal and get stronger. You are a person who is never too far or too busy to pick up the phone or be open for a visit, so I stop right now to celebrate *you*. In short, I love the special way you love life and are over-the-top present and accounted for, especially for those you enfold in your heart. You are as sweet as one of the dark chocolate-covered strawberries in your fridge, and your readiness to go all out for your beloved ones amazes me every time. This letter is just my way of letting you know that...

I love you!

D.C.

January

Promise And Potential

For January, I decided to take an unconventional approach to celebrate the new year by asking myself — and *you* — what if I lived with the *end* of my life in mind? What would that look like? By the end of the first week of January, I had just returned from my first mission trip to Haiti. I will share with you one of the many lessons I learned there. Despite widespread poverty and a smolde ing anger people have towards a government corrupt, a stance which hung like a pall as thick as the smoke in the air from burning trash, by and large, you saw smiling faces and a carefree way among these people. In general, the Haitians are *not* downcast, and it struck me that it might be *we* who are the ones who are starving for not partaking of a steady diet of love. How could this dichotomy be? Perhaps it was because daily they stared death in the face. They really didn't know if disease, sickness, voodoo, or violence might snatch away their life as quickly as one can snuff out a candle. The collective result is that the Haitians really relish the small moments of their day, simple necessities, and their loved ones. What if *we* acted more like this? Despite the odds of us not falling victim to an early mortality, the fact is, we are *all* dying. As morbid as it may sound, one of the essay topics I give my students is to have them imagine that they are on their death bed saying goodbye to family and friends. Who would they choose to be there? What would they like to say? As it turned out, one Sunday this month, my pastor told us that he had just finished reading something by Bronnie Ware dealing with the "regrets of the dying." As a hospice nurse who provided palliative care, this woman had developed strong bonds with people during their last weeks of life, and they often got raw and real with her and revealed what they really thought mattered in life. Had they to do it over, these folks said that they would have pursued their dreams and not settled, spoken their mind more and held onto resentments less, worked fewer hours and spent more time with friends and loved ones, and finally, the dying wished they had said, "I love you," more. One other consideration, also prompted by Pastor Mark, was his suggestion that we *spend time with people who are going to cry at our funeral.* I hoped to have the courage to be the person God desires me to be. Therefore, for this month's focus, I take to mind the wisdom from above and choose the freshest and brightest young ones in my family to write my next parcel of love letters: my fraternal nieces and nephews. I want each of them to know what they mean to me, so I wrote them as if I were facing them on my last day. My charity begins at home.

16. Cindy

Meet Cindy. She is small of stature but big of heart, and often you will find her singing without a thought or even a definite tune. Her music within is on auto-pilot. Left to her own devices, you'll likely notice her drawing in her sketchbook a detailed rendition of some character or perhaps even her own hand. She is also an avid reader, and she's rarely without a book. Because I am more of the rough-and-tumble type of aunt and have spent countless hours for three years longer with her older brothers, to be honest, I feel like I'm just beginning to get to know her. She is on the cusp of her teenage years, so I'd better not delay. When I do spend private one-on-one time with her, I am often impressed by her astute observations and especially by how she describes what she sees, be it something in nature or the expression on her father's face. I believe she has a poet's ear for words and making comparisons. I love the dimple in her brow that pops up the second a question has come to her mind that she wants to ask but isn't sure she should. It brings me joy when she does venture forth to ask me my opinion or stance about something that's in her heart; it's good to have trusted ones to feel that it's safe to be exactly the way you are. Every time I see her, I tell her that she is the best hugger I know. In fact, she's like a koala baby affixed to me. No matter how grown she gets, she will always be my "strawberry girl."

What younger relative in your life are you aware that you
need to get to know better? How will you carve out some
time to discover who she is? What particular "thing"
do just the two of you have or do? What dreams, fears,
hurts, secrets, and hopes have you listened to from a
young one? Do you honor them and their trust in you?
How would you choose to encourage them and foster their

*dreams? How do you help your nieces or nephews in ways
that their parents cannot?*

Come with me now to learn more about Cindy.

January 6, 2019

Hello, Cindy!

Well, in the one decade you've been alive, I think this is the first time that I have ever sat down and written you a real letter! You know, typically, when people want to acknowledge birthdays or remember celebrations, they go to a store and pick out a card. It is very different when somebody personally writes and sends you a letter out of the blue and for no particular occasion. My reason for doing this is simple: I really wanted to surprise you and tell you all about how much I love you! I know I spend much time with the brothers, but as I am thinking of you now, I realize now that you are growing up, and I desire to share some particular thoughts just with *you*. Do you remember about three years ago when you made a long list of foods that you and I had in common we both liked? You put the list up towards the bottom of the fridge and held it in place with a magnet. When I would come and visit, I secretly liked going to the fridge to glance at and re-read it because it made me smile. Why, there must have been well over twenty-five foods on your list! Miss Strawberry Girl, to tell you the truth, I suspect that you and I will have many more things that we like and have in common in addition to favorite foods. As you continue to go through life, I will be happy both to discover and to share many more moments, experiences, and especially ideas that are dear to us both.

Recently, through private conversations that we have had together, I realize just what a special person you are! I want to compliment you on some specific things I admire about you by sharing several famous quotes that make me think of you. I hope you'll find them both pleasing and meaningful! My first quote was written by a woman named Louisa May Alcott, and she wrote a book called *Little Women*. She wrote of one of her characters, "*She is too fond of books, and it has turned her brain*." "Turned" in the quote here means to influence in a good way. It brings me no small delight to see you curled up quietly reading on the couch, so absorbed by what you are taking in that you may not notice this or that going on around you. When we are driving somewhere all together, I notice that you almost always have a book with you to read. This is really great because you are feeding your mind *and* heart! I want you to know that I think you have a vivid imagination, and even though you have not yet read my book, I believe that you, too, have the potential to write someday. Why do I say this? You have a curious mind, and you already have a way with words! When we were lying in the hammock together looking up at the stars, I was pleasantly surprised to hear you say that you thought it looked like we were under the mast of a ship because of how the planks of the broad deck above us lay. Last summer, when you and I took a rowboat ride together out on the lake at grandma's, you remarked that the deep yellow in the middle of the water lilies looked like small egg yolks inside starbursts on the water. That's how a writer sees objects in the world! When I visit, I see that your habit of reading is so much a part of your life that you own little light attachment so that even if it is dark out, you can read. You already even have your personal favorite author. Why else is reading so great? We can travel to distant places that are both real and imaginary to learn, be inspired, moved, excited, and ultimately transformed. If you were in my class, you would know that I read out loud to my students every day, so important do I consider this.

The next quote that makes me think of you is something that Jesus said regarding children. There were some people who were bringing little children to Jesus for Him to love on and say kind things to, but His workers criticized Him because they thought that He needed to be with grownups. When Jesus heard this, He got angry. He said to them, "*Let the little children come to me, and do not hinder them, for the kingdom of God belongs to such as these*" (Mark 10:14 NIV). A couple of times when I have come to visit, I have seen you ask your dad if we could all go to church. I've even heard you ask him about God, and I want you to know that even back in His day, Jesus told the men around Him to not stop the children from wanting to be near Him or talk about Him. Why? Because you are at the age when your heart is open, curious, and attracted to intense goodness, so, naturally, you want to be near that which you instinctively feel is the source of everything even though you can't put it into words. I want to tell you again that a couple of months ago when we were sitting together eating our frozen yogurt, I loved the questions that you asked me. They are so straight-forward and full of thought; it's not just about what's right around us. Sometimes I don't think grownups take children seriously enough. Although you may be small in stature, I want to tell you that you are quite a mighty girl! I know that you will continue to blossom and mature, and I, for one, am excited to keep on getting to know you year by year! No matter what, you can *always* talk to me about what is on your mind, and I will do my best to be there for you and encourage you!

This leads me to my next saying for you, and even though the author is unknown, it will be one that will hold true for you for the rest of your life. Here it is: "*Believe in yourself and you can do unbelievable things*." Sometimes when a child is the youngest, and especially if she is a girl with older brothers, there is a tendency to let the older children be the responsible ones or take care of business. Sometimes the youngest cannot physically or verbally compete with an older sibling, but let me be the first to tell you that there will come a day when you will not only be able to hold your own and defend yourself, but you will shine brightly and succeed in your own right and full measure in life. Your size will mean nothing compared to the power you possess within you and display. You already are "clothed in strength and dignity, and [you can] laugh without fear of the future" (Proverbs 31:25 NLV).

I have one final quote that reminds me of you, and it was actually said by Taylor Swift: "*Happiness and confidence are the prettiest things you can wear*." No matter what is popular, "cool," or what the brothers or others are buying and admiring, I hope you know that you already have all the awesomeness you will ever need within you! By focusing on the good you can do and be, you will continue to be the smartest, kindest, and most beautiful girl ever! Others' opinions won't change this fact. There is no one like you. I know you have much virtue because you sing all the time; the joy inside you is spilling out! And, as I tell you each time I see you, I think you are the best hugger ever. You involve your whole being as you tightly wrap yourself around the person. I am incredibly proud to be your aunt, so I celebrate you here and now!

I love you with all my heart, sweet Cindy!

D.C.

17. Vincent

Meet Vincent. Sometimes you click with certain people, and you can't explain why; it's just how it is. That's how things are for my nephew, Vincent, and me, and it has been this way since he was a baby. We have always taken delight in one another, and it doesn't matter if we are talking or just hanging out together; the feeling is always right. Our closeness doesn't diminish the relationship I have with my other nieces and nephews, but there's an eagerness to be near one another that's special with Vincent. He has always been full of questions, and with me, there's a no-holds-bar sense that he can feel free to ask away, be it about God or foreign countries or what it was like for me way-back-when. There's an old soul in that big boy, and he is getting closer to becoming a man every time I see him. One of the qualities about Vincent that makes him stand out in the crowd for me is that he really enjoys hearing stories from people's lives; he wants to know how it was and what you did. And, as if I didn't know it already, he's a people person and already a quick study of people's actions. He has an analytical mind that puts the puzzle pieces of life together, and stories add texture and richness to the people he loves. He's already attracted to those things in life that are considered "classic," and here I thought I was getting old. Though he doesn't know it, the very songs, feelings, and opinions of matters closest to his heart that he confides in me about are identical to those I hold dear. If it's a song, then it'll come down to the very parts of the songs that move us. He values family in a powerful way; therefore, the fact that my home and heart have remained unchanged in his life makes our bond all the stronger. There's *so* much more to look forward to in life with him, and I don't want to miss a beat. So, yes, I'll take that ride on the back of the jet ski and let him fly me around the lake, with a clear sky and the sun shining down upon us.

> *Who is a child or teenager in your life that has much*
> *in common with you, one whose similar impulses seem*
> *innate and not learned? How do you help this person*
> *grow his heart and strengthen his values when he's in*
> *the years when what his peers say is alluring and what's*
> *cool is king? How have you made yourself available in*
> *ways that make it easy for him or her to share his heart?*
> *Do your deeds match your words so that you know you*
> *have his respect?*

Let's go visit Vincent together now.

"There are places I remember All my life though some have changed Some forever not for better Some have gone and some remain All these places have their moments With loved ones and friends I still can recall Some are dead and some are living In my life I've loved them all. But of all these friends and loved ones There is no one compares with you And these memories lose their meaning When I think of love as something new Though I know I'll never lose affection For people and things that went before I know I'll often stop and think about them In my life I love you more." [Cue harpsichord]

—Taken from "In My Life," by the Beatles, from *Rubber Soul* (1965)

January 13, 2019

Dear Vincent,

Considering I saw you last weekend, I know it might seem odd that I would write you a real letter, but I have much that has been building up in my heart and mind to tell you, and writing allows me the opportunity to linger longer and be more precise. Many times, people go their whole life without sharing just how special someone else might be, and that is the purpose of this letter to you. I don't mean to be over- the-top or make you feel awkward, but I've not known anyone that couldn't use a word of encouragement, so I wanted you to have a letter in your hands to feel and to hold; it contains the thoughts and feelings from my heart to yours. Whenever you visit me, I see you inhale deeply and smile as you come up the stairs, taking in the aroma of my home, almost as if you were a dog that has found its favorite familiar scent; it is *that* secured in your memory. You are one who takes in the world with all of your senses, and your heart is loaded with tried and true treasures here, be it your decade-old personalized cup, the glow-in-the-dark stars over your head, the "formula" for our skin, or my Greek sailor's cap which awaits being yours when you turn sixteen. That you feel a sense of peace and order and "everything is in its place" when you visit me and that you can breathe a little easier because here you feel that all is right in the world brings me deep satisfaction. Oh, the many talks we have had in my office!

There's nothing more you need to acquire when you have the kind of loving feeling we have because you know that you already have it all, and *that*, my friend, is wisdom. It is no secret that you and I have a special relationship, and we have had such since well before you could even form words. I remember gazing at you in the hospital as you lay in the quiet of your infant bassinette. There were evening shadows around you, but your face shone out and had CHRISTAKIS stamped all over it. Even as a baby, you would smile and reach out for me, and it wasn't long after that that our relationship took off. I am grateful to your parents for understanding this. Fast-forward to today: as you are in the first footsteps of entering manhood, I want to linger on a few of the thousand memories you and I share from the past before proceeding to build you up in honesty, strength, and a full-throttle, V-8 love geared up for your future. It takes no effort for me to recall that when you were less than five, I'd make up "once-upon-a-time" stories for you and Robert underneath the blanketed fort, pretend to be your "mama bear" by protecting you, play "ice cream man" with you as my young customer, playfully toss you full-body right onto the couch, or vigorously roll the Bosu ball at you, all but for you to gleefully shout, "*Again!*" over and over. Then we move on to making Greek salad in the corner of your old kitchen with you standing on the stool, getting the taste of it down *just* right, and you knew if we needed to add more oregano. As a boy, you'd sit still on my lap to gaze at the pictures in the book on Crete. From the get-go, you've always felt at ease to ask me questions, and no topic or thought you had was out-of-the-question. Do you remember the weekend you came down and we went ice-skating? How about when I helped you with your "Where's Waldo" project? I will never forget that trip to Folly Beach and the balcony from which we took the selfie portrait of ourselves overlooking the ocean. There are only two such framed pictures in the world, and we have them. Every visit includes taking long walks, and you, Robert, and I have taken *dozens* of walks together, as if we were in our own private gang.

Years have passed since you were that little boy, but our closeness remains. What we have comes as naturally and effortlessly as our doing the "Bo-Bo" clap routine, as if we were one person, and I'm glad you sense this, too. Since you've become a teenager, we've come to share much music (and my albums) of *all* types, discovered each other's favorite bands, and listened to our favorite songs. Now when we ride together, *you* play DJ, and I love what you choose, be it bouzouki music, CCR, Hank Williams, or Johnny Lee Hooker. Who knows what's next?! I *love* piling up in the back of the theater, with you, me, and Robert quietly chatting before the movie starts, probably having just eaten out together. Now that we've been to Greece altogether, I got to see you come to life in Meteora when you took in that peaceful feeling of being at such a remote and sacred spot, and I was moved. I know you can recall at the top of Santorini the promissory knot we made of our interlaced wrist bands to commemorate our Christakis visit to Greece *and* it not being the last. I could go on and on about the many memories we have made and the traditions founded at the lake. They will be locked in my memory bank as long-lasting as some ancient temple. I'll always remember the first time you caught a turtle because you also chose a particular spot to release him. And look at you now! It pleases me to experience your joy by letting you practice driving my Altima or Rogue, slowly but surely gaining experience and confidence in driving on each lone road we go. Can you feel the heat of the bright afternoon? Can you see the miles of corn around us? I could continue with my recollections, but I'll get on to my main point. You may ask yourself, why am I recalling all these memories we have? Good question. It is leading up to my wanting never to hold back my support and feelings of love for you. As we get older, sometimes we don't say, show, or tell the ones nearest to us just how much we love them, and this is my small way of my reminding you of this. You can hold this letter in your hand when you are an old man; by then, we'll have done a million more things together, but this is a marker for you today. It is just the tip of the iceberg, with so much more beneath the surface of these few pages. I want to remind you of good things in the past as a means of proof we have a sure stronghold for continued goodness in our future, even after you are out and on your own. I want you to know I love you not for what you *do* or *have* or can *buy*, but for exactly who you *are*; that's enough. I always want to support you to help bring out the very best in you, even whether or not I'm with you in person.

So, just what are the things about you I cherish and see as some of your best qualities? First, you are an "all-in" kind of guy, and there's not one visit I have had but that you always bring up the *next* possible visit, so much do you want for our togetherness to continue. Even when you were little, you'd eagerly want to know how many "darks" I was staying because one was never enough. I love that you never get your fill and are hungry for more! Next, you have a curious mind and are eager to converse and share. What this says to me is you have both a strong sense of hope in the many possibilities, and, like Zorba the Greek, a passion for life. You are restless and ready to figure out and do more, whether it be learning about places in the world you haven't yet been to, hearing family stories, discussing human nature, or talking about the sections of songs we like, which makes them even greater. This hunger for life that goes to the core of your being also has the effect of making you observant about what's truly vital in life. I hope that you develop the habit of *giving* more than *getting* because this way of living will ensure you have a prosperous life, one full and abundant. I cherish the fact that when you were only six, you gave me a figurine of one of the three wise men (who you thought looked Greek) for a Christmas present. I'll also not soon forget the birthday present from you a couple of years ago which greeted me in the bathroom sink at the lake: a vial of good hair product bathed in a small flotilla of balloons you'd prepared as a surprise for me. Just so you know, most kids do not think about giving presents to others until they are nearly grown.

Thinking of the other guy is a sign of maturity and thoughtfulness, and I hope you keep this quality. Next, your devotion to family *and* keeping the peace is essential to you, too. I think you crave the rock-solid feeling of what's wholly holy, which goes *way* past religion. It is a pure love and goodness which you desire to your core, and this drives deeper than the fad being cool; it's what's gut *real* for you. Country strong, in and out. Speaking of religion, I'm not gonna preach to you, but I can say, I do love sitting beside you in church, too, because I feel you drinking up Mark's words of wisdom about *life*. Why is this so? First of all, you are growing up, but I think your essence is captured in the lyrics of "Good Feeling." Vincent, *you* "have the heart of twenty men"; *this* is what makes a man powerful! Another trait I love about you is your readiness to laugh. Life is too short not to seek joy and laughter!

I'll end this letter by having you look back at its beginning to the song I chose since it really makes me think of you. I picked it because in showing the speaker is looking *back* on his life, I'm hoping you may get a glimpse of what's *ahead* in *yours*. When it's all said and done, I know I will *also* be able to say that "in my life, I love you more." In the meanwhile, I'm looking forward to making many more magnificent memories with you. You can *always* count on me to be on your side because...

I love you so much,

D. C.

18. Robert

Meet Robert. He's the first-born of three from my brother's first marriage, and we share a unique bond and know the privileges and burdens of being the eldest child. As his aunt, I doted on him when he was a baby because he lived closer to me then, and I felt and feel tremendous pride in him; such trusting eyes and an open face he had. It came to be that he is an introvert, and he expresses himself best by deed rather than word. He has an incredible knack for not only figuring out how things work and fit together, but he has gotten so good at mechanics that adults seek his advice. Glancing at what's shown on YouTube is enough to figure out how to go about accomplishing the task. Currently, he's at the last year of high school when others expect him to know what he's going to *do*, even though he's still figuring out who he *is*. When he was a boy, he was taking care of younger siblings or doing this or that while his parents were not in a good way, and I have since seen Robert mature into a responsible young man who still does his fair share of caretaking. I know I can count on him for anything I ask of him, no questions asked, Johnny-on-the-spot, and come-what-may. He's *that* kind of guy. His shoulders are broad even if he is leaner than most. My nephew has the gaze of a hunter, and he hawkishly watches those around him to see if their actions are righteous. His moral compass runs due north, so when I'm with him, I sense an adult by my side even though there's not the age to match. He is no thrill-seeker and avoids conflict; peace resides in his soul. Robert and I communicate more through glance or grin or touch than I might others with paragraphs of words. We can read each other in mere seconds. When I take his now grown hand in mine, then I know the world is right.

*Which of your nieces or nephews is getting ready to
graduate high school? How is he or she special to you?
What could you say to validate and encourage him or
her? What have you seen him do that no one else pays
much mind to but that you admire? In the time when
many kids have no idea what comes next, how will you
take their hand and be there for them tomorrow and
particularly the next few years while they grapple with
identifying what might be their calling or vocation?
When will you spend some down-time just to let him or
her do the talking, let him confide in you? Hush. Listen.
You will learn more than you expected.*

Let me tell you more about Robert as you read his letter.

"Hey tomorrow, where
are you goin'?

*Do you have some room for
me?*

'Cause night is fallin' and
the dawn is callin'

I'll have a new day if
she'll have me. . .

'Cause I've been wasted
and I've over-tasted

All the things that life
gave to me And I've
been trusted, abused and
busted

And I've been taken by
those close to me.

"Saturday in the park

I think it was the Fourth
of July People dancing,
people laughing A man
selling ice cream. . .

People talking, really smiling

A man playing guitar
(play a song, play a song,
play on)

Singing for us all (singing
for us) *Will you help him
change the world* Can you
dig it (yes, I can)

And *I've been waiting such a
long time. . .*

Hey tomorrow, you've
gotta believe that *I'm
through wastin' what's left of
me* 'Cause night is fallin'
and the dawn is

callin'

*I'll have a new day if she' ll
have me.*"

— Taken from "Hey
Tomorrow," by Jim
Croce, emphasis mine,
from *You Don't Mess Around
with Jim* (1972)

Listen children *all is not
lost*, all is not lost. . .

People reaching,
people touching A real
celebration

Waiting for us all (waiting
for us all). . ."

Taken from "Saturday In
the Park," by Chicago,
emphasis mine, from
Chicago V (1972)

January 20, 2019

Hey, Robert!

I can't believe you are less than a year away from graduating from high school. Because I know that this is a milestone marker indicating that childhood is behind you and that "new day" is ahead, I wanted to take the time to celebrate and anticipate that a new future and fresh start awaits *you*! Oh, "she *will* have you"! How could she not? For most teenagers, the prospect of this next step proves a bit daunting, and for some others, it is exhilarating. I think that you belong in the second category. Beneath the mask you can sometimes wear, there is a longing for joy, righteousness, and the simple things that mean the most in life. I see in you a quiet optimism brewing about what it will mean to live freely and out on your own. I am not putting the cart before the horse, and I would never wish time away.

I relish all the moments I have had with you up to here and now. It's just that in your young manhood, and I see how your character is maturing, I can already imagine the visits I will have with you when you are an independent adult, and I get excited! That said, living on your own is not the same thing as living apart from others; man is not meant to be alone. I am *incredibly* grateful for the closeness you and I have, Robert, and I always want to be an active part of your life. Maybe it's because I've already dealt with death and seen a few severe sicknesses in my life, but recently, I got this idea in my head that I wanted to share particular thoughts with those whom I care for the most in life and tell them with exactitude and a generous heart just how much they mean to me. You are one. I decided to do this where I am right *now* in life and not wait until God-knows-when — not that this invalidates or discounts all the continued succulence in our future. That's why I'm going to linger a moment here and talk to *you*. Robert.

You are so real and can whiff out anything fake or hypocritical that I am grateful and glad for this chance here to reveal myself to you openly and directly. I want to pour out my heart to you and be one of those "people talking, *really* smiling..." Why? Because every time I am with you, it *is* "a real celebration," and, for sure, I know it is true that *you've* "been waiting such a long time." For *what* exactly? For feeling, receiving, and giving the kind of love that makes you want to "help change the world." You've got *that* kind of goodness in you, Robert, and I am impressed beyond measure! When the child becomes the man, as is happening with you, certain values and priorities become more evident and in greater focus. Such is revealed in your character as to what is of primary importance to *you*, and I would like to say that *I like what I see*; I admire that which gives *you* meaning, direction, and satisfaction.

You are the kind of young man who appreciates the *classic* in all things; it is evident by the music you listen to, the way you wear your hair, the movies you watch, and the motorcycles and cars that turn your head. What you like or enjoy reflects something more profound in you than meets the eye. You have a hunger within you that craves what is fundamentally sound, fine, righteous, and enduring in life, through the ages of all ages. I think you have a respect and regard for all that is *excellent* in life, and when things turn out to be fraudulent or fake or untrue, it bothers you more than it might others. How do I know this? I notice and love your attention to detail in all things, be it how you place in your fork, knife, and spoon *just so* on the surface of a napkin, how you caringly stroke the head of the snake you have just caught or fed, or how you photograph some bird in flight that has captivated you. Some might say *Quentin Tarantino* movies are violent; however, when I watch them with you, I see wrongs righted, fairness and goodness prevailing, and the *real* good guy, who may be the underdog, triumphing over who society considers top dog. I also appreciate in you that which I personally don't have: a mechanical mind, and I am in awe of your uncanny ability to figure out how things fit, operate, and work best together. That you take the time to show and explain to me how this or that part of your bike works is endearing and humbling. Sharing is caring, and I'll listen any day to *your* teaching me about all that's dear to *you*. Even though you keep a low profile, for me, your image is that of a young warrior with your full mane, your confident stride, and leather jacketed back. I respect your inner strength, loyalty, patience, and endurance. I think that your love of speed reflects something within you that craves a sense of lightness and freedom; you love the feeling of taking flight. Although speed can be exhilarating, full satisfaction in life comes from what I see that drives your character.

That which unhinges or even hurts us can sometimes actually contribute to making us more resilient, so my hope is that the frustrations and disappointments you've experienced in life will be transformed into what is essentially great. In fact, I already see this happening. Even though your brother and sister may annoy you in different little ways, when it counts, you, are consistently protective of them — automatically and without needing to be told. Sure, you may get in a tiff with your brother; after all, you are teenagers, but I know you'd fight *for* him out in the world. As a fellow oldest sibling, I am aware of the unique burdens and privileges that come with this birth position, but your sense of responsibility and protectiveness has now become a life habit in you, and I *also* see you looking out for the elderly or weaker ones. For example, in your family, you are *always* the very *first* to lend a helping hand, to wait back and see if Bonnie is all right, or check if I need any help. This does not go unnoticed. Not only do I know that I can rely on you for assistance, I feel I can *really* trust you, whether it be with my money, private thoughts, or burdens in life. Recently, it was *you* I thought to call to check and see if I'd left my wallet at your all's place. I always feel at ease when you are at the wheel driving me around.

You have a strength and sensitivity in your soul, and although you are capable of going under when you feel pain, hurt, or anger, locking your reactions under a mask of stone, let me say that it does not make a man weak for him to show his feelings. Our feelings should never be pent up or put on lockdown; we are emotional creatures, and there is no gain by what gets hidden. What goes in must come out, so rest easy: you can breathe with me, Robert. What I see in you and want to compliment you on is your transforming the bad to the good, be it turning the other cheek, taking the high road, or turning the page to what is better to come. You do not sulk or complain. You have developed patience, consideration, allegiance, compassion, and devotion. Freedom and goodness prevail in you. I love it when you feel free inside and are relaxed on the outside! Then I see you grin broadly, hear you giggle in delight, and witness your full-throttle readiness to "bounce" and live life to its fullest, be it making brownies (that is, "whities"), lapping up a plate of lemon-doused calamari, basking in the Mediterranean sun, or bounding on up to the back row of a movie theater to watch some Tyler Perry movie with your brother and me.

By now, we've already made *many* memories together, and these are treasures for me as surely as any*thing*. I will always remember our first turtle hunts at the lake as we silently glided along in the canoe. You scouted them out with your eagle eyes, ready to scoop up a turtle poking out its head just above the water's surface. Do you recall your avidly learning from Bonnie the secrets of fishing? At my home, you have happily sifted through and picked out an old album of mine that has caught your interest. I loved the first time you showed me your bedroom at your mom's, including telling me how you chose to arrange your room, your kingdom. These memories are all valuable to me! That you drove to visit me on your own last fall really rocked my world, and it makes me look forward to my hanging out with you when you have a place of your own someday in the not-too-distant future. Let me also say that our being in Greece together deeply gratified me, and I will not forget that, after months of admiring my Greek key ring, you moved heaven and earth to purchase your own. This ring symbolizes the blood and country connection you and I share, one we were born with and will die with. I also want you to know that whether it is you or I who is driving, I love reaching out to hold your hand and your readiness to take mine. I have felt your hand go from that of a boy to now a man, and I tell you with pride and joy that I will reach out to hold that hand for as long as I live! You are a man of few words, but the look in your eye always expresses more than a thousand could say. Please be assured that I avidly look for and read your expressions like I would some favorite book, and when you're in the way and place to *really* talk, I *always* want to hear all that you have to say.

It's at the point when you can put this letter down and away; hopefully, you will glance at it every now and again, even years from now. I hope you take that "new day"; she'll most certainly have you! This letter is just my little way of telling you just how much you mean to me and that I'm *so* proud of you, Robert. *I lerv yer* bigger than the ocean, from the bottom of my heart, and with all I've got.

Σ'αγαπώ —Sagapo! I love you!

D.C.

19. Abbie

Meet Abbie. From the time that I wrote and sent her *her* letter a year ago until today, Abbie has moved to another state, gotten a decent job, met a good man to whom she's engaged, and given birth to a son. These are the productive years of a life on track; Abbie's progress and successes are all the more impressive when I consider the trek she undergone up to now. They say that children are "resilient" and that we shouldn't worry if they have to deal with their parents' separation; I couldn't disagree more. Divorce and death are shockers and bring on stress, doubt, and pain kids don't really know how to deal with, so their frustrations get manifested in all sorts of ways, none of them ever pretty. Land mines are set, and you don't know if, when, or where there is a ticking time bomb ready to go off at any moment or in the distant horizon. Therefore, when the child becomes the adult — as my niece surely has, and we get to see poise, composure, accomplishments, and contentment through new love, then our hopes are resurrected, and we *all* have faith renewed again. "This time will be better for me; we will get it right this time," we hear them say. My niece and I have an excellent relationship, and much more than her brothers or sisters, Abbie inherited my brother's calm, so I feel at ease and at home when she's around, no matter where we are. She received help in the means and measure called for, and she has grown grateful and tempered in her manner. Also, more than any other grandchild, she received a concentrated infusion of my father's love; he was *her* papou. Our Greek circle is still unbroken. I know she has borne much pain, but she puts her best foot forward every day and carries on with her head held high. I admire her so much, and I swell with a maternal pride I never thought I had when I think of Abbie.

Do you have a young adult in your life that you have seen make it through turbulent times? Do you pray over one right now who is still engulfed in trouble? Have you told them that you pray for them? What can you do or say to instill faith as well as a belief in themselves? Have you ever taken them to church and out to lunch afterward? In what ways could you invest in them to let them know that you care and want the best for them? How can you show them that success is measured not merely by tangible markers? How has she or he rounded that corner into the world of grown-ups, and proven that she wears it well?

Come with me to read more about Abbie.

"He gives strength to the weary,
And to him who lacks might He increases *power*.
Though youths grow weary and tired, And vigorous young men stumble badly, Yet those who wait for the Lord *Will gain new strength;* They will mount up with wings *like eagles…*"
—From Isaiah 40:29–31, emphasis mine

January 27, 2019

Hello, Abbie!

I first started writing this letter after your visit from a little over a month ago; you were preparing to make your big move up to the city of brotherly love. Oh, to be young and independent and ready to take the world by the horns, to lasso and shape your future as you wish. Ah, to be free of spirit, steady of mind, and willing of body to follow your dreams and ready yourself for new experiences meant to further your direction, strengths, and aspirations. Praise God for His being with you always, guiding and protecting you with His Spirit such that you know *you are never alone* and that there is One far greater who cares for you much more than some who have proven *not* to be of sound mind, intent, or character. When I hear the news or about wintry weather from the area you're in, you remain fresh on my mind, and I wonder how you're faring. I got it on my mind that I wanted to send you a love letter so that when you are in the quiet of your own home after some busy day at work, you can relish and receive a much-needed boost in morale, a word of support, or a reminder as to how much you are loved. Therefore, I pen this note of love to you here and now, seemingly out of the blue. It never hurts to hear words of affirmation, so I want to hit pause for a second and tell you that *I have so much admiration for you and am proud of you*! You are a young woman on the mend, on the rise, with hopes in her heart, and the inner strength to step forward in faith and trust for better days ahead. They are already here! You have that power and strength! Yes, I will be the first to admit that I have not spent nearly enough time with you, yet when I am with you, it takes zero time to feel the deep familial connection we share. Do you know what I mean?

Even though there are many life experiences and things about each other we cannot understand or appreciate and which add to that the many miles between us, I trust and still desire for my heart's print to be indelibly stamped in your soul. Yours is on mine. You are your own woman now, but, of course, every child takes a little something from her parents, and I genuinely believe that you have gotten *the best* from both of yours. From your mom, I see that can-do spirit, a willingness and ability to work hard, and a keen understanding of human nature that makes it such that you instinctively know how to handle people with finesse, grace, tact, as well as a gentle firmness. I love how close you are to your mother and that she has been such a loving beacon for you. That you readily acknowledge her is a sign of maturity. From your father, you got your penchant for math and figuring out advantageous angles to pursue what you want; he has more of the marketing and sales approach. This remains to be seen in you, but I believe you'll find a way to keep on pursuing your academic goals so that you will be more prosperous down the line. You are a goal- setter and achiever. I actually think you are more like your dad than any of his other children in terms of looks, temperament, outlook, and a focus on the good that's to be gained ahead. You are both calm and persistent. The fact that you can whip up and serve food like it's nobody's business may be one job you have learned at work, but you come from a long line of those who have made it their livelihood to prepare food, and this, too, will serve you well.

It is clear to me that you are a generous person by nature. The positions of leadership and authority you've already held reveal your reliability, responsibility, and general capabilities. It was very purposeful that the last thing I gave you, intended as a house-warming gift of sorts, was that framed picture of your dad and papou somewhere in Greece. My hope was for you to have a visual reminder of your papou so you could reminisce on how much he loved and adored you, believed in you, and, truth be told, even if it was when you were a little girl, invested more into you than in all of his other grandchildren put together. Your recollections and frequent mentioning of papou are sweet to me, and I'm so glad that you had him in your life when he was still healthy; you both obviously relished one another. That this picture of them is in Greece is a reminder of your heritage and roots and a place where I hope you, too, can visit and see with your own eyes one day. You would *love* it there and recognize the confident and natural openness Greeks have that is in you, too. Plus, need I also remind you of your love for lemons and feta?!? LOL.

You and I not only share blood, memories, and the kind of outlook that exudes a spirit of freedom and optimism in life, but we also share the same faith, and for this, I am incredibly grateful. I began your letter with this particular Scripture from Isaiah because I know you have dealt with much that, at times, has given cause for you to feel anxious and unsure. You have survived the volatile teenage years and have learned life lessons to enable you to recognize those who ultimately do *not* have your best interests at heart. In your long-suffering, you have developed the art of keeping much mum and putting on a pleasant face; it doesn't matter that I do not know all of the details of the past. There is not a person alive who hasn't gone through tribulations. There is not one thing you've done or experienced that I can't *also* say, "but for the grace of God, *there go I.*" Precisely what you've experienced may be unique to you, but you can be sure that parallels exist within my life as well. You've my book to glimpse at to recognize this for yourself. Some people can get stuck such that their past continually follows them in their present, but I do not see this in you. Every step you take further into adulthood and womanhood shows me how strong, resilient, capable, trustworthy, bright, caring, loving, and awesome you are. I know I am just beginning to see the woman that you are becoming, and I'm in awe of your character, beauty, and abilities.

While I'm thinking of your God-given nature and life, may I also say thank you for asking to go to church with me, be it up and visiting our little church that, for a short while, was held in a high school gymnasium or sitting beside me at an Easter service when we had moved up on a hill. I'm glad He lives in your heart, and perhaps we can share more of this one day. Abbie, you have a good head on your shoulders, and though there has been much in life that has tried to knock you down, you take it in the chin and swallow your pain. I know that Jesus sees this in you and will help you bear *any* further burden. After all, in Him, we are "more than conquerors" (Romans 8:37 NIV)! As an affirmation of this, always remember your full name has embedded within it the word "*victorious,*" and this is not by chance! You are like Lady Liberty, and even if, up to now, you've chosen cats over kids, there is something essentially nurturing and compassionate in your nature. You give back in all you do. I have observed a sensitivity in your knowing eyes that you recognize those in need around you, and you *always* show you care. I, too, have received love and acceptance from you in my life, and for this, *I thank you.*

I have the brightest of hopes for you and an assuredness that you will continue to make strides and wondrous discoveries about yourself as you press on and give life your all. Not only are you my family and precious niece, but you are also a child of God and His beloved. Do you remember when you were a little girl, and you and I would giggle as we'd sing that goofy, made-up song called "Turkey head"? This takes me even further back to the first time I saw you, an angelic cherub in your cradle when your parents lived together in what they used to call their "love shack," now so many years ago. Since then, you have experienced more than many, and I view you as one wise beyond her years. You have come out on the other side, thriving more than other adults might have. You have already "been there and done that." The world is your oyster! When we become adults, we often search for that which was not provided or attained in youth. As you shape your destiny, founded on your sound and worthy aspirations, let me assure you that the love you seek, He will always provide the means and the measure for attaining, and that includes what and who is best for you. Always know and seek that. Anyone you choose for a friend, be the nature of which platonic or romantic, should be deserving of your respect and bring out the finest in you as much as you would in them. Let me also say that I'm glad you have tried and true female friends!

Meanwhile, as you hold this letter in your hands, hundreds of miles from me, know that, in my mind, I am hugging you in my arms, kissing you on the cheek, as I hold you close in my heart. I see *you* soaring like that eagle!

Σ 'αγαπώ τόσο πολύ! I love you *so* much!

D.C.

February

Loving On Thinkers

February is the month I view as being the longest *and* shortest of the year; most people associate it with Valentine's Day. In fact, the day after Christmas, candy and cards are already being put out on store shelves on ready display for us. I am going to mix and match air with water and focus on loving the *intellectuals* of my life. These are the ones you might dismiss as being the *last* folks you'd consider as lighthouses for the giving and taking of love. With primped pride, brow-arching disdain, or wicked wit, they may say that public displays of affection are overrated, puerile, unnecessary, vapid, or bathetic. Why state the obvious? Why wear your heart on your sleeve? Why go out on a limb if you've already experienced feeling loved, then lost? Many times over. Why participate in a mass marketing scheme? For us thinkers, getting in touch with our emotions, let alone putting them out for public viewing *or* private consumption, can be feel like we've chosen to flip on the Hallmark or Lifetime Channel; your brain might hurt from want. I get it. I ought to know; it takes one to know one, and I used to be one. Actually, I still am one except for one little fact: I've been changed from the inside out through my contact with Jesus, a reality that can't be denied though it defies explanation. I've had a permanent change of heart which you can see for yourself in a new spirit that's mingled with my same-old-me personality. I tell you, it's a bold- faced lie to believe the propaganda put out by one far more cunning than the media; evil is in camo, and it wins over your pride and can have you thinking you don't really need the touch of love. You do. Just watch what happens when a person has a train wreck in life, and you'll see them run for all they've got to seek love like there's no tomorrow. There may not be. This is the case for the physician who finds out she has a brain tumor, for the engineer whose wife is leaving him, or the A.P. student who suddenly feels suicidal. In these cases, and more, the only medicine that'll fit the bill and have a prayer to save a life will be love. All else are just supplements. Real love is an outpouring that should be reserved for *every* day of the calendar of your life. In His famous parable about the seeds and the soil, Jesus described the people who had heard about Him but were not moved by Him as ones who'd had His offered seeds snatched away. Maybe His offering got overlaid with thorns of distraction or pride. You may say, who be I to water dry soil, sand, or rock? If Jesus can change water into wine, heal the sick, and raise the dead, He'll bless my efforts here to talk to you. He's *still* in the business of performing miracles: you're looking at one right before your very eyes. Sand can be enriched, parched soil watered, and stone blasted so that His seeds *still* germinate. Lives flourish in ways unexpected, unimagined, and unforeseen. Deserts can become gardens of paradise for the brightest of the bright who only *th ught* they had it all figured out. It's like going from life in factual black-and-white to vivid technicolor. Therefore, I now address all my Prufrocks: "Oh, do not ask, 'What is it?' Let us go and make our visit."

20. Fellow Colleagues

Meet my fellow teachers, yes,the lot of them. Thirty years ago, when I was a new intern, I was invited to attend a retirement party for an administrator and supervisor who had been at it for well over thirty years. At the time, three decades sounded like three hundred years because such a span seemed inconceivable in my early days of overwhelming task and toil. Yet, there she was in front of us, veritably glowing and still looking so full of life. She was moved to be at a celebration with those whom she'd spent a lifetime of doing good unto others. Typically, the one due such praise and honor is on the receiving end, but not for this woman; she was prepared to give one more time. After dinner was winding down and the guests were taking bites of their dessert, our guest of honor became the toastmaster, and she stood up and faced us all. Forks were put down, and expressions of wonderment came over our faces. After she'd gotten our attention, she quietly and sincerely announced that *the honor and privilege had been all hers*, that serving through teaching was what she was most proud of, and so, she wanted to take a few moments to thank *us* for being a part of her journey. Eyes were welling up with tears as, one by one, she turned to face each of a dozen or so individuals who had impacted her particularly and profoundly. Glancing at remarks she'd written on 3" by 5" notecards beforehand, she spoke to each as if no one else was there, and, as a result, we all felt revered and rewarded. I will never forget it. Over the next ten years, when two teachers *I* adored were saying *their* goodbyes, I found myself writing a thank you letter to them; it was like a sneak preview of what you are reading here. One was my mentor and administrator, the other my department chair; they were power-houses to me. I read one letter aloud at a department Christmas party, and the other I read on the last day of school to the entire faculty with a microphone; I was as mortified as she was moved. Skip ahead to this month in 2019 when I decided to go public about taking early retirement. The short of it is that insurance money would be provided until the age at which I was eligible to receive Medicare. This incentive was available only for those teachers with enough years of experience, and it was an offer I couldn't refuse. I knew it was not likely to be given again, so I stepped out in faith. I used to think that retirement was a death sentence, but now my mind was aflutter over the possibilities of what might come next. As I began pondering, I found myself looking around at my peers at school in a different way; I become overwhelmed with the desire to properly recognize and thank them. This was three months before Bonnie pulled off a surprise retirement party for me, and because this gathering of friends, colleagues, former students, and fellow travelers came as a complete shock to me, it's a good thing I wrote what I did here and now. As fate would have it, God would see to it that this would *not* be the end of teaching, just a turning point in my career to ease into teaching half-time. How perfect, how golden. Please continue to read my goodbye letter.

Who at your work makes you feel valued and unique?
Who has gone from a colleague or co-worker to your
friend and one as indispens ble to you like family?
Whether you may be years away from retirement or
weeks away from quitting, can you think of some persons
who have made your days brighter and more meaningful?
Who are they? Try writing the kind of a letter that
follows, and you will see for yourself who is most
important to you; go tell them. You' ll learn much about
yourself in the process, and they will feel the love you
have but may have never told them.

"My long two-pointed ladder's sticking through
a tree Toward heaven still,
And there's a barrel that I didn't fill Beside it,
and there may be two or three Apples I didn't
pick upon some bough. But I am done with
apple-picking now... I keep hearing from the
cellar bin
The rumbling sound
Of load on load of apples coming in.
For I have had too much
Of apple-picking: I am overtired Of the great
harvest I myself desired.
There were ten thousand thousand fruit to
touch, Cherish in hand, lift down, and not let
fall..."
— Taken from Robert Frost's "After Apple
Picking" (1914)

February 3, 2019

My Dear English and World Language Colleagues and Fellow Admiral High Teachers, Typically, it is at the commencement of the school year when we faculty are sitting down in the cafeteria for one last gathering and finishing up our lunch provided by the Entertainers that we recognize those who are retiring. The roll is called, and these ones humbly come to the front to be acknowledged in a way they never have before, mere moments before they quietly exit the building one last time and take their place among the rank and file of those who have served their time with us. We who remain look on with wonderment, poignancy, a little curiosity, and reverence before we are released to go back and complete some hundredth task of the day. Today it is I who am among those retiring at the end of this year. Although I have taught thirty years at Admiral

High, I am still relatively young; therefore, some may be in querulous disbelief that it is my turn. So, out of love, respect, and consideration for you, I want to be the one to explain my decision and leave nothing to chance, rumor, or speculation.

You also may want to know why I am writing this to you all here at this particular time of year. Good question. With preparatory steps being made for next year's schedule now underway, I have just made my decision known to admin. such that modifications can be made accordingly; therefore, the time is right to let *you* know before word gets out, and the truth may get bent in a way that does not convey my reasoning. You're hearing it straight from my mind rather than someone else's mouth. We both deserve that, and I love you more than to keep my motives to myself. I'll start by telling you the practical considerations first. One of the most daunting aspects of retirement for me was to figure in the cost of health insurance, so when downtown admin came up with its proposed Certified Retired Incentive Program, which I shortened to "R.I.P.," my curiosity was piqued. After doing my due diligence of careful research, writing many an email to H.R. down at central office, and double-checking with my own financial adviser, I see that this proposal *is* legit. and one not likely to be offered again anytime soon, so this gave me serious pause.

Furthermore, I will have the opportunity to work half-time at a relatively handsome rate, and this is precisely what I intend to do. You may not have seen the last of me yet. If I had my druthers, I would come right back here by your side next fall, teaching half time! Indeed, I have high hopes and every intention of being able to honor my commitment to my current Russian 1 class of [20] stude ts such that they will be able to complete their second-year fall of 2019. Furthermore, I also have 9 students in Russian 2-3 who, in all likelihood, will want to go on to their next level, too, in my combined-level 2-4 class. I have no control over whether or not Admiral High School will be in the position to offer Russian after that, but at least I can finish this year's class. Should I be able to teach half time in 2019-20, my other three classes would obviously be English, most likely 10 and 11. I will make my intentions known and apply as I need to, but you are familiar with how these things go: I might not know until the eleventh hour. With this much clarified, I still have more to say.

If you will permit me, I want to share with you the deeper pulses of why I feel released from that which is *so* much more than a job. Some of you may know that I have come to recognize the brevity and preciousness of life by personally caring for those closest to me who have had a brush with death in battling cancer. Life may be snuffed out well before we are old and feeble. So, in not wanting to live a life of regrets or to miss out on any more time which we are not promised, I am going to honor what's *truly* important in life by giving more of my time and energy to those who mean the very most to me. There is one more reason that has made this decision easier than I could have anticipated; it is one that is less logical but just as compelling. For whatever reason, I feel like I have been in a slow-motion process of a psychological dissevering or relinquishing, a preparation of sorts, such that I can say, "*the readiness is all.*" I now have it, and that this sense of release coincided with admin.'s offering seems more than mere chance to me. As I take this next step, I am both at peace *and* excited about what the future holds in store for me. I consider this positioning a gift because I could not have orchestrated such a convolution of favorable circumstances.

Yes, teaching *is* my calling; I will never not be a teacher. I have shared with thousands of students my passion for all things Russian and my love of literature and language. Even more, I have simply loved *them*. In some ways, Admiral High School has been the love of *my* life. I have divested and invested so much of myself to my stude ts. Currently, I feel as giddy as a senior at wondering *what's next*. I know there are *many* more chapters in my life; therefore, I will take a leap in faith in exploring what is yet in store for me. As I stand at these crossroads, it is crucial for me to convey to you that my decision to retire is not based upon a reaction to any particular circumstances. I think in much broader terms than that: I have thrived and survived and remained fully alive under *five* different administrations. I have experienced the ebb and flow of various and sundry educational trends and cycles, not to mention, given my blood, sweat, and tears in both agony and ecstasy to this profession. That's what we do because that's who we are. Behind closed doors with our students in our little kingdoms is where all the magic (or madness) and meaning come to fruition, and, class after class, we hold this conviction deeply. Everything else is support that we can only hope to receive in some measure and for which we are grateful. However, regardless and ever regardful, long ago, I made a vow to myself that I did not want to go out like one particular teacher I knew who had taught well over forty- five years. Upon her retirement, she made her way out to her car that one last time, and, unseen by an observer who was watching her from the administrative perch above the cafeteria, she sat down in her car. Placing her hands on the steering wheel, she just *gazed* at our school — her very *life* — and did not stir or start her car for a full [30] minutes. She was not for all that long after she left. That is *not* how I want to go, and so I have decided to leave riding high in my saddle. Like you, though I have spent my life giving it my all for my students, there are students everywhere, and I refuse to leave my life here feeling spent, sick, or cynical. I will take the necessary steps to put my hat in the ring and hopefully remain here in a half-time capacity. Yes, the timing is such that "they made me an offer that I couldn't refuse," which, coupled with my readiness to *carpe diem* as well as serve and devote myself in a different capacity, I am ready to see what the next chapter in life holds.

You may be asking yourself why I am making much ado here? Considering this, our vocation and passion, how can I *not*? My fellow teachers, writing you here and now also lets me linger a moment so that I may praise *you*. We don't hear or receive words of affirmation or encouragement nearly enough; therefore, let me be one who tells you to keep your chin up and keep on fighting the good fight! What we do *matters*, and your contribution to your students' lives is phenomenal, invaluable, incalculable, and worthy. Don't let tribulations or weariness lead you to become disillusioned or take for granted what you do; our profession is *still* honorable, and it is what we who have responded to that higher calling do. There are no stats that can quantify the inestimable and positive impact we make on our students' lives. More than three- quarters of the staff that I started out with are gone, so I write here and now to you teachers who are so very dear to me. M.M., may I also give an extra warm shout-out to you who are of the same '89–'90 vintage as I?

This is not the winter of my discontent; hope *still* springs eternal, and my cup runneth over in wanting to share my joy with you. I will *always* be your comrade in arms! I stand at attention, hand over heart, and warmly applaud *you*! I am *so* proud to be who you are and what I am. Who knows? Hopefully, I'll see you for part of the day next year, but I did not want to wait until the very last day of school this year to say goodbye to you and to the life as I have known thus far. I leave you here with...

Much Love and Great R-E-S-P-E-C-T,

D.C.

21. Gertrude

Meet Gertrude. She is my sister's daughter and one whose birthday is two days away from mine, so no matter how far apart we are, I have an annual reminder that she will always be in my life. Though we couldn't look more different, we have much inside that's the same, not the least of which is a quick wit, active mind, and a leaning towards the logical. We get down to brass tacks because our brains cut to the chase; we like to tell it like it is. Sometimes mum's the word. This similar state of mind can have us butting heads sometimes, but more often than not, we soar together. Now grown and out on her own but still under thirty, my niece is at the time of life where she's making her mark on the world in her own place and at her own pace. Like her mother, she is one with whom I can guffaw and pile up on the couch for how in sync our humors and moods are. We are like homemade guacamole and chips together. She is one who has the wisdom of one far older than her years, yet I still see glimpses of the girl within; she is a free spirit. I love the fact that she's game for doing things with her aunt and mom that others might find bland, you know, like going to visit gardens and museums.She takes delight in this and in us, as if we were her dessert, but, the cake for her!

Can you think of a young adult who doesn't care what her friends are doing or what's hip because she's happy to spend some time with you? Have you ever found one who is so mature that you could even imagine him or her being your caretaker one day? If you have children, which is the one you'd trust and know could count on? Who is one who is quiet about her private life but is present and accounted for in yours, maybe when you least expect it? With whom do you share humor such that whenever you laugh together, it is a balm for your soul?

Read on to learn more about Gertrude.

"Be wise in the way you act toward outsiders;
make the most of every opportunity. Let your
conversation be always full of grace, seasoned
with salt, so that you may know how to answer
everyone."
— Colossians 4:5–6 NIV

February 10, 2019

Hello, my sweet Gertrude!

Ka-kaw! Surprise! For no apparent reason, yet with many bursting inside me, I couldn't *not* write you this impromptu letter. First of all, though it's already been quite a few months since you moved to C. and there are a couple of more months until I visit you, I felt like a letter to you was long overdue, at the very least, to congratulate you on your taking the next step in shaping your destiny by fine-tuning where you choose to settle yourself. Many folks hash over various critical considerations to the point where they can get stuck and stay right where they are. Not you! Did you know that your mother was in awe over your decision-making process by first choosing a location over the job? I think it shows a gut-level trust in your ability to survive *and* succeed because you know you are worth more than, for example, the birds in the air, and you *will* be provided for; therefore, you instinctively "make the most of every opportunity." Why *not* research and move to a location that meets your criteria and promises to be pleasing to you?

As odd as it sounds and as I have mentioned to you in passing, I found myself actually grateful for Hurricane Irma in that it brought us together under one roof, and we got to spend some *real* time together a year ago. No, I'm being neither morbid nor cavalier about the havoc wreaked on many. It's just that I've been struck with the thought that if it took a natural disaster for us to get together, the least I could do would be to write you a letter filled with evocations of my love for you " *just because.*" You know, I really like this phrase: we use it when life prompts us to do that which we would *not* typically or when we go out of our way for some altruistic aim. When I mull over the matter, don't you think that anything we do that's *really* worthwhile gets accomplished when we realize that there's more to life than just completing the tasks at hand?

I will share with you some of the many reasons for loving you because a generous heart doesn't hold back and doesn't withhold love; it finds a way to share its inner-most glow and heartfelt pulses for those whom it folds into itself. That's me for *you*! How and when should we express that which is *usually* held in because it is *understood*, yet which deserves open declaration? Just because I love you, just because I have only one life, just because we are not guaranteed the next month, let alone day, and just because I care so much for you, I want to count the ways. No, don't worry — I am neither sick nor dying, just bent and determined to break a tendency or habit many have — and I include myself — and that is to let months, sometimes *years* go without saying what certain ones mean to them. Some argue, "*It goes without saying*" this or that, but I beg to differ; if you can go a whole lifetime without uttering oaths of love, then where does that leave you? Old before you know it, likely with several regrets, and having amassed decades of silence and distance between you and yours. Such is not the case for us! Oh, no! you and It takes me no effort to think back on when you were a little girl, just a young she-wolf cub crawling around with glee inside the dog crate. I took delight in the fact that you had such a savage spirit within you, and though you now have your resting "cool" face down, *par excellent,* I knew back then what pluck and character you possessed. Who asks while still under ten years old to watch the classic horror movie, *The Wolfman*, scooched up next to her aunt? You did! Who took delight in piling up on a sled together as we whizzed down some snowy hillside which your mom took us to? You did! Who was thrilled that her aunt came to visit her elementary school during the middle of class to bring painted turtles just caught and still in hand for a personal show-and-tell, especially for her niece? Still you! Later on, one of my favorite times spent with you was when you and I were in the car together riding shot-gun with your mom and Bonnie as we trekked our way up to grandma's. You played DJ and, boy, howdy, did we get our bass and groove on! And these are just a drop in the bucket of memories I have of you, even if we then lived a thousand miles apart.

Admittedly, many revolve around enjoying the gusto of fun food times, but that, too, reveals connections between us. Do you remember the first time we boiled lobsters in your mom's kitchen, and one dropped and flopped on the floor, still alive? You squealed and about fell out yourself! How about when you all came down to hook up for a visit with us in Atlanta, and you ordered the molten chocolate lava cake at Galileo's restaurant which came wheeled to you at our table on a linen-covered cart, like some scientific experiment, and dry ice emanated from this decadent confection? Your eyes were as big as saucers! Do you recall that for your graduation, I sent you an edible bouquet? I was in delight to discover you loved fresh pineapples! If memory serves me well, you had your first sushi with me, and you made your selection like a connoisseur! Ah, and in Greece, the discovery of what a gyro should *really* taste like, and your contentment to daily devour one slathered with extra tzatziki remains fresh in my memory. I'm pleased we both can eat vats of holy guacamole or perhaps a container of frozen Cool Whip! I do not mean to imply our connection is merely familial or culinary — oh, no! I know we take a deeper delight in each other than this, and one of my favorite things to do with you precisely *because* it makes you giggle or gawk (or both) is to dive right into your personal space to land a few kisses on your cheek! Love at its best is something that can't be explained, it just *is*, and I am so grateful to have this with you, regardless of the space or time between us. What we have means the world to me because there are not many people in life that you can be utterly real with, no holds bar.

Allow me also to expand on a few unique qualities I admire about you; some are, in part, the result of being your parents' daughter, and other aspects are gifted to you, all of which is wrapped up in a swath that is 100% unique. From your dad, I see your keen logic, love of speed, and no-nonsense practicality. When it's all said and done, like your mom, you lean towards a consideration of others, and you also share her quirky sense of humor and love of what's ridiculous. Like her, I see that you have a natural curiosity and keen appreciation of how animals behave, which, I suppose, we could do worse than to learn from. Indeed, you are like a sleuth or some private investigator with your keen powers of observation. Ultimately, in this your second significant move as a young adult, I see that your dreams and goals are intersecting with your talents and gifts. Here now comes the remainder of the opening quote from Colossians that applies to you, that being "the way you act toward outsiders" and your ability to conduct "every conversation full of grace, seasoned with salt." You have an uncanny ability to see through to what's right, and this includes people's underlying motives, fears, and values. You quietly assess and act in a manner that swiftly resolves problems, diffuses angst or anger, or gently leads people to what's better in life. I also like that you have a natural way of seeing the best in people, all the while noting that which needs improvement. Whether you sharpened this skill from working at a job where you had to use a calm voice on the other end of the line, you have helped those you never actually faced by meeting their inmost need of assurance and masterfully steered them to the best route they needed to pursue.

Impressively, you remain nonplussed, dispassionate, and steady.

I, too, have benefitted by your precocity. Do you recall when you provided me with that second set of eyes and critiqued a response I'd written to an anxious parent? That was incredibly helpful! Long story short, you have a gut-level and uncanny understanding of people's motives, which will serve you and others well in life. Not only this, when you've smoothed some situation over, you *also* possess a healthy readiness to disengage from an adult's soul-killing seriousness so as to laugh, chill, or take delight in the moment. Relaxing and *ostensibly* doing "nothing" can be fortifying and restorative to the soul; therefore, "nothing" becomes an important *something*, and this I have learned from you. You are also a reserved person who doesn't broadcast her news; you keep your cards close, but I want you to know that *I see you* and love all that's in you. Let me repeat it: I admire you and totally think you've got it going on! Your sights are in laser-focus, and you drive through life with the accuracy and assuredness of an Indi-500 race-car driver. Your finesse, confidence, and wisdom will make you one to be contended with; you already are a powerful woman, indeed, a modern-day goddess or mermaid who allures and confounds, who beckons and yet remains in control. You have *such* a good head on your shoulders that I can say without batting an eye, though as odd as it sounds, I trust you with my very person. When you graduated high school, it was beyond suitable to gift you with Athena's owl as the chosen pendant on your necklace. Although you are supremely private, let me also be one to say that I wish for you in life an abiding love and respect from those whom you choose to be your closest.

I have no idea what you'll be doing five or ten years from now, let alone where you'll be living, but I hope you keep this letter tucked away in some drawer to glance at every now and again, so that if you are ever feeling lonely, alone, or blue, you can look it over and read how much your Aunt Dimi loves you. I treasure the fact that you and I have a special bond and affinity for one another, and when I look back at the picture of us sitting side by side in the restaurant at grandma's eightieth birthday dinner, talking about this and that, including my telling you in confidence about *Connecting the Dots...*, the whole world could have melted away for how we were engaged with one another. No matter how grown you get, rest assured that I will *always* reach out and take your hand, ready to hear your heart, or giggle together over some merriment. I am *so* looking forward to seeing you, thankfully, now much sooner than later.

I love you with all I've got!

D.C.

22. Persephone

Meet Persephone. She is my younger sister; it can't quite seem possible that she's in her fifties, the same as I; in some way, she'll always be the young teen who sought my big-sister wisdom in our formative years. Now I look to *her* for support when I need a council or an audience. Although she lived a decade in Europe and another fifteen years a thousand miles from me, we are as close as if we were one flesh. Our life experiences couldn't be more divergent: she's a mother, a lover of the northern clime, and one inclined to melancholy. She was and still is the artist in our family, but life has taught her many lessons and provided her with more than enough knocks such that often, *she* could use a dose of hope. I trust she knows she can always count on me for this. I'm afraid that in my early days as a super immature Christian, I frothed with much vim and vigor that she likely found off-putting and hardly holy. So, little by slowly, with humor and humility, over the past few years, I've tempered my extolments. I hope she sees it's still me inside, but I pray she also notices something new. I attempt to withhold judgment, turn off my tendency to be critical, and try to be gentle where formerly I was likely to be harsh, even if the object of my gaze is a common "enemy" to us both. My sister told me that the birth of a child is all anyone could ever need should she wonder if there's something greater out there. Ever the egalitarian, she would rue the day that she would ever pick *one* entity above all others as her religious mainstay. Her primal need for feeling a part of the greater whole is satiated by participating in a drumming group she's joined, which is really no different than her being in high school band way back when. We all need to belong. She and I will forever be a part of a gene pool regulated to just a precious few. She brings light, color, balance, and perspective to my world, and I love her with all I've got.

*Who is someone in your life whom you know like the
back of your hand, and not a word needs to be spoken
to understand what's on his or her mind? Who is your
go-to person that will give you an honest opinion or fresh
perspective every time you need it, but may not want it?
Who can you count on to be there for you unwaveringly
throughout your days? No matter how much has passed
since you last saw them, who is that one that, when you
do get together, in no time at all, you find you're back
in sync with them? Who is someone with whom you
share a similar sense of humor, taste in things you like to
see and do, and fundamental values, but with whom you
might not see eye-to- eye regarding politics or religion?
How could you build a bridge of grace and choose love
to take your relationship to a deeper level?*

Hark, listen, and read on to meet Persephone.

[1]"'Twas in another lifetime, one of toil and
blood When blackness was a virtue the road
was full of mud I came in from the wilderness,
a creature void of form Come in, she said, I'll
give ya shelter from the storm

[2]And if I pass this way again, you can rest
assured I'll always do my best for her, on that
I give my word In a world of steel-eyed death,
and men who are fighting to be warm Come in,
she said, I'll give ya shelter from the storm

[6]Now there's a wall between us, somethin'
there's been lost I took too much for granted,
I got my signals crossed Just to think that it all
began on an uneventful morn Come in, she said,
I'll give ya shelter from the storm

[10]"Well, I'm livin' in a foreign country but I'm
bound to cross the line Beauty walks a razor's
edge, someday I'll make it mine If I could only
turn back the clock to when God and her were
born Come in, she said, I'll give ya shelter from
the storm."
— From Bob Dylan's "Shelter from the Storm"
on *Blood on the Tracks* (1975)

February 17, 2019

Dear Persephone,

As I write to you now, in my mind, I am talking to you; it
feels as natural as if I were sitting beside you on a comfy couch.
I recently shared with you a parting letter I wrote to my fellow
faculty members expounding on why I decided to retire and
that I felt compelled to say goodbye to them. My reason for
writing you is not dissimilar in vein: I want to take my sweet
time and write *you* a love letter, but not because it's anywhere
remotely near the time for us to part. I selected the above song
for both obvious and obfuscatory reasons. Though you love
poetry and are a poet yourself, how could I not choose Bob
Dylan to launch my letter to you, considering that he, along
with e.e. cummings, first stirred those fragile and sensitive
impulses within you? I felt a tiny clap of internal thunder in my
instinctively knowing that this was the right selection for you.
As a matter of fact, I looked up several online interpretations of
this song to determine if any seemed applicable here. None did.
You can discover for yourself suggestions that Mr. Zimmerman
references the Vietnam War, the divorce from his wife, and
even his burgeoning fascination with Christianity, but, if I might
propose, I would like to apply some of his lyrics here and now
to what you and I have. I hope we will always find in one
another *shelter from life's storms*. The first stanza I view as the

epoch of "blood" and "mud" during mom and dad's divorce. Ironically, it blurred together with the period when you and I were growing closer, perhaps in part because you were entering adulthood and were rife with those questions which have no neat and tidy answers. We would come to know in our gut that we could trust each other when life came untucked or undone.

The second stanza has me fast-forward three decades to where we have recently stood together. You and I stared death in the face when dad died, standing like steely soldiers when cancer came upon him like some stealthy sniper. Walt Whitman said, "Agonies are one of my change of garments, I do not ask the wounded person how he feels, I myself become the wounded person." Though your son lives in intentional silence some three thousand miles from you, without asking, I know how much you ache, hoping he fights to keep warm. The sixth stanza best explains the impulse behind my writing to you: I do not want for there ever to be a wall between us, for signals to be crossed, or for either of us to take the other for granted. *I don't you*, and I'll very soon shower you with particular praises that only *you* are deserving of. The final stanza proves particularly poignant for me because in my coming to faith in Jesus Christ, at times, I have felt like a foreigner in my familial country because I speak a new language and have a different basis of belief; it is beautiful on this razor's edge.

I cannot turn back to some point in space and time which no longer exists, but, Persephone, I *can* pledge my love to you, and, coming full circle, reaffirm that I still and will always give *you* shelter from life's storms. Yes, we both have our homes, purchased and paid for, too, and numerous times you have said with staunch conviction that you don't want anyone to have to take care of *you* in your elder years, but I believe that this is just pride and fear talking. No one wants to be a burden to anyone at any time, but if we are blessed (or cursed) to make it to a century, the likelihood of falling to our final sleep without experiencing a single hitch or glitch along the way comes with no guarantee. If I am able, I will be there for you; the willingness is already there. You may say, "Well, that's just fine and dandy, but we each have our own lives, and I don't see either of us moving." Maybe not, but that need not be required for visiting. Just for this moment, I want to make time stand still, write you a love letter, and send it to you in this bottle of an envelope so you can have and hold in your hands a token of my love. With me, you need never feel alone or afraid.

Speaking of which, Bonnie once told me that when both her parents had died, it made her feel like she was an orphan. That sense we do not know yet, but between mom and dad, our relationship with mom is infinitely more complex; therefore, grappling with *that* loss will be all the more daunting. I will take your hand then, too. Just the thought of this, coupled with our pledge of late to be frank and sober regarding our health and finances, compels me to share myself with you in a different way here than a ubiquitous phone call could provide. That said, I *do* want to thank you for your considerable efforts and more frequent attempts to reach out to talk and, even more importantly, to suggest ways we can spend real time with each other. I'm already stoked about our visit in a couple of months! I don't know about you, but as a result of not seeing you more than once a year, when I do face the whole of you, I am as powerfully drawn to you as steel is to a magnet; I feel *such* joy and relief when we embrace! Seeing you is like beholding a mirror image of myself or looking at that picture of two ancient Greek youthful boxers facing one another who have come to life today. You are one of only two other Adams in the world who has the same genetic composite, all the more so because you are a woman. I feel the passage of time more in glancing at you or Stephen than with anyone else; the result is kinetic and stirring.

What does that mean as far as my relationship with you goes? I will be brave and say I love you in a fierce way that's almost desperate. Though we belong to one Christakis prototype, we are each distinct in our own way, a unique blend with irreplaceable gifts and traits. You were our "flower child," our artist, and poet. No one batted an eye to discover that as a little girl, you had an imaginary friend named Trixie, who lived in a nearby antebellum mansion. You loved horses, unicorns, and possessed a bevy of stuffed animals to protect you as you lay you down to sleep. Who else but you had a hutch of rabbits, a clutch of banty chickens, more parakeets than one could count, a tank full of Bubble Eye Goldfish, and wandering cats that found a home with us through your surreptitious feeding? If you had had your druthers, you would have worn dresses on Saturdays and eaten big bowls of chocolate ice cream for your three-square meals — certainly neither meat nor peas. It wasn't lotions and potions and makeup *you* placed in the cubbyhole shelves of the pine-paneled bedrooms at the lake, but Maraschino cherries! When one is a child, every year can seem like a decade; therefore, my being four and a half years older put us at quite a distance from one another during *that* span of life. It seemed to me that even by age ten, you had never misbehaved. There was never any call for you to be spanked; for sure, one stern look would have done the job.

Considering our upbringing, I found it curious that, once in your elementary years, you attended a local Methodist Church with a friend of yours. At the time, I think I chalked it up to the likelihood of your seeking some semblance of normalcy because our family was such an alien lot compared to those around us. You and I had no in-depth discussions then; I considered you adorable but more under the influence of Gwen, what with taking part in all that was of sugar and spice and Barbie-doll nice. Our universe tilted on its axis when mom and dad's world fell apart: you were at the precipice of entering high school and found yourself floundering and with little direction. As your self-appointed guidance counselor to help with your scheduling, we forged a new path in our relationship, and it became one of substance, respect, and affection in a manner that hadn't existed before and which hasn't stopped since. What talks we had as we walked around our neighborhood! We would stop at this or that bench on the golf course, intently contemplate the meaning of life, the existence of what lies beyond what meets the eye, or discuss the reasons behind our parents' irrational or dumbfounding behaviors. These topics were the stuff of that which made the tolling of our hearts beat sure. We listened to one another, and in the process, we buoyed each other up. When you visited me in college, you were starving for affection, but we satiated one another then; our bond today is sure, and we continue to sustain one another. Once, I remember coming home to discover a copy of *Crime and Punishment* in your bedroom and a journal of poetry you'd been working on. I was moved and impressed! That you dressed up and went with a friend and me to the B-52s concert was a pivotal marker in my mind of your being "grown-up." Look at us now!

My intent here is not to write a sketch of your life, but because *vita brevis*, I do desire to take a moment to celebrate the underpinning of our relationship, one which is steadfast and sure. The decade that followed ushers in a story unique to us each, and it is neither my place nor intent to tell your story. I don't pretend to understand or appreciate both the exhilaration and the agony you must have felt in the epoch of your new motherhood while in D., and though it may have flummoxed us at home, your own adulthood was forged. When you would write me letters on the back of Erik's sonograms, I inhaled your news, clutching each note the way I would have wanted to have held you. Suffice it to say, regardless of the chaos that ensued in our family as each picked up the pieces from the rubble from a marriage gone awry, we all underwent a journey that had us traverse from murkiness to a new light. Through it all, *we each and all missed you terribly*, Persephone. You need to know that. When you came home, only then did it feel like the sun could begin to shine on us again.

What I *can* speak to now is my perception of you as a

woman and human being, and these are not merely the remarks of a big sister. Though I've said it before, it merits repeating: regardless "the time that goads between," as Dickinson would say, rest assured that there has been nothing that wrests away the sweet familiarity and tenderness that grips me each time we meet face to face. How can this be? You have a way about you that is attentive, gentle, accepting, and soundly present. The protectiveness that was developed in you from maternity gives me the sense that no harm can befall us; you jealously guard your time with me. You possess a residual precociousness that has ripened into wisdom that radiates where matters of the heart and your understanding of human nature go. For example, for you to discuss what delights and stirs you regarding *your* students moves me. Everything you do for them is done to promote the good nascent in each which life has not robbed or diminished. You have a disarming way about you, and it not only feels safe and inviting to talk to you because no criticism is looming on the horizon, but the questions you generate say *you care* and that you want to hear more.

You put people at ease, and they can bask in your attention. Most folks I know secretly seek to be the star of the conversation — not you. You are a quick study of the human heart, and not much escapes you, but what does is intentional because you put things in their proper perspective and differentiate between the inane and pertinent. To discuss your taste in aesthetics, cuisine, and music, reminds me that the little Miss Suzi the Squirrel within you who reclaimed her own idyllic and cozy treetop home on a street in V., as it turns out, has become quite the sage! So, whether you serve tapenade, rustic soup, or a homemade and delectable dessert, all of what you do stems from your desire to celebrate the best and purest stuff in life, that which has *not* been profaned by corruption, be it pollution or man's wayward ways, like greed and hate. That you have taken up drumming makes total sense to me; your heart longs to beat in unison with the primal beat of life. We can get so out of step because of the cacophony we've caused in our cosmos. Another quality which few people possess but which flows naturally from your humble heart is the ease at which you empathize with others. You are swift to volunteer or acknowledge your own weaknesses, be it something you can't help, like a lack of a sense of direction, to that which you and I *both* have to fight, that is, our being brusque or dismissive if something seems distasteful or untrue to us.

Persephone, though we may not desire to keep up the frenetic pace so as to be sturdily cool, and we may not be able to remember what street we parked on, *I never feel lost with you!* The trail of crumbs we drop for each other in the form of sweet reminiscences, a ready ear, and a steady pledge to be there for each other translates to us *always* having a home with one another; no magpie in life can snatch this away from us. May I also confess I long for your innate equilibrium, that internal compass always pointed toward balance, peace, and harmony. I love your bursts of laughter that come forth when your spirits are light and gay, usually when one of your now-grown children has said something witty or silly or bright. Sweet sister, the private world you have created with them is sacred, and I adore how you cherish both it and them. That you had the bravery to step out in recent independence was radical for you, all the more so because it wasn't prompted by how you were treated. Instead, the tipping point and line-in-the-sand for your not continuing on that path was how another — your father-in-law — was disregarded. This point segues to our paternity and the particular gifts we have been richly endowed with through *his* code, and that also includes being bypassed in inheriting the disfiguring huntingtin gene. I'm sure you also still thank God for being spared that affliction, that slow decay of the basal ganglia that triggers the performance of such a horrible choreography.

Instead, I'll relate a characteristic you share with dad that leaves me breathless: your sense of wonder in the world. Who else but you in youth would take an interest in biophosphorescence, the behavior of sloths (including their rigorous sleep schedule), or the echolocation bats utilize? You know the scientific names and traits of perennial flowers like children who have found favor with you. I remember the first time I broached the topic of God with you, and you enthusiastically told me that conception, the gestational processes, and the birth of your children testified to the fact that you knew something infinitesimally greater and vaster than you created them. I couldn't agree with you more. From whom else but God do we get the miracle of one plus one equals three? And then there's cell division that brings about a multiplicity of systems functioning harmoniously.

I respect the sanctity of your private reverence in God as you understand Him; after all, you have that freedom and right. I am also grateful that on one of our long walks at the lake, you permitted me to recite some Bible verses I'd recently memorized, two of which particularly struck you. I will recall them here: first, "do not be conformed to this world, but be transformed by the renewing of your mind"(Romans 12:2) and second, "the Spirit also helps our weakness; for we do not know how to pray as we should, but the Spirit Himself intercedes for us with groanings too deep for words" (Romans 8:26). Though we may not see eye-to-eye about the Son of Man, I take comfort in the fact that I believe we have more in common than we give ourselves credit for. I will never forget that it was your soothing voice — with no faith faltering there — that softly read prayers aloud to our father, the trinity of his children haloing him as he departed his life.

Even though there has been much in your life that you have come to experience for the first time in your middle-aged years, I see you hold your own as you grapple with new and raw emotions that both mystify and humble you. More than anything, I wish you love and a reassuring peace. You will always have that with me. As we well know, no man can provide all, and no one is without flaw, whether in thought or deed. I have to remind myself of this daily, but let me tell you that, from a thousand miles away, you still inspire me. Experiencing loss has also made you fiercely protective, and I, for one, am amazed at the strength you often aren't aware of in yourself. You have an instinct for gratitude that shores you when darkness tries to assert itself. Your exquisite sensitivity enables you to swiftly assess any situation, and, in genuine appreciation, you give thanks where thanks are due. This has become a life habit for you. I remember that when I was in the midst of the madness in caring for dad, there was no other voice I heard than yours expressing thankfulness, and I gulped up your encouragement. I enjoy reminiscing over the time when you and I consigned ourselves to cleaning cruddy bathrooms in dad's house. In the meanwhile, he was reclining on his loveseat like some king, toes wriggling in delight, while his daughters toiled to the backdrop of Greek liturgical music. I took such relief in hearing your peal of crazed laugher at this apropos irony. We were of one mind and mood.

Let me also say that I have been grateful for your patience with me because in the unfolding of my own life, I have had seasons where I was far from my best, yet you showed me patience and kindness until I had made it to clearer skies. You once sent me a bright card in acknowledgment and celebration of better days. The best in life that has happened to me has involved a supernatural or divine intervention. Having you as my sister, I count as one of these. And though you are a thousand miles door to door from me, in my way of thinking, you are a mere hair's breadth away. In his poem, "The Second Coming," W. B. Yeats wrote that "mere anarchy is loosed upon the world, the blood-dimmed tide is loosed, and... innocence is drowned." Let me counter that notion by testifying to the adoration, respect, and love we share. Let me not be shy in showering you with affirmations. Time is fleeting, and a conservation of love or withholding affection compounds no interest.

We both possess a hope and lightness that beats steadily within our breasts. It is for certain that we are *not* leading lives of "quiet desperation," as Thoreau dubbed it. No, all is not for naught! Every day that you wake up and go to work to enrich your students' lives, that you pray for your son's well-being, that you admire your adult daughter's confidence and independence, or that you take a chance on new love is a day leading to the next one that will fill your life with courage, gratitude, and grace.

Still yet, there is always room from improvement, don't you think? I am much more selective in what and whom I choose to hold onto and to relinquish. The scale of relativity as to what truly matters is constantly getting fine-tuned and realigned; I wish to be more like you because you are so sensitive to life's clues. You focus on the *who* and not the what, the *manner* more than the matter. Intentionality and awareness are key. We cannot afford to bear the burden of bitterness, can we? It shackles the soul. I cannot hold your hand right now or laugh (or roll our eyes) over some inanity to reassure you of my good will. Therefore, I will tell you that as we get older and continue to bare our souls to one another, I am super grateful for having a sounding board, a mirror, and a truss in *you*, and you have the same in me.

Please consider this letter a way for me to hit pause on the cassette recording of my life so I can say, *I love you, Persephone,* and I am *so* proud you are my sister! No, I am not a mother and have never birthed a child, but I have long considered you similar to Persephone from Greek mythology. In that sense, it is I who have felt like your mother, Demeter, she who treasures you and looks for you just as the winter longs for spring. With you in sight, life is in balance, not hanging in the balance. I close this letter with a hug, a smile, and a sprig of fresh basil; after all, "basil" in Greek means "king." You are an artist, a mother, a poet, *and* a courageous soul who happens to be my sister *and* a princess reigning tenderly.

Love and such,

D.C.

23. Emily

Meet Emily. She may look like the girl next door, but for me, Emily stands above the masses. She is not only a dear friend, but she is one who embodies kindness, tenderness, and mercy in her everyday life. Such is axiomatic and natural in all Emily does for the other guy, be it for her darling daughter she adopted from China or broken ones she has patched up and put back together during therapy sessions in her office. She has a poise and a softness about her that makes it easy to approach without caution, especially for those outcast and troubled. Your heart instinctively knows she cares. I have not seen her in well over five, maybe seven years, but we have no perforation in our relationship. Emily comes from the era of my undergraduate years and was one of the few that also majored in Russian. Though we were not quite in tandem at that time, we absolutely were so in graduate, a.k.a. "gradual" school. We both started out in the Russian department, but within a couple of months, we made the fine-tuning adjustments that set us off on our respective paths of life. I was a master to her doctorate degree. These were troubled times that also brought us joy, energy, and laughter for how much we helped each other out. On many a rainy or snowy afternoon at school or during any of the many road trips we made back home for the weekend, much was illuminated as to what was essential through the conversations we had. Mainly, we figured out what we did and did not want to do in life; we let our souls do the talking while the radio blared behind us. We've now five- hundred miles that separate us, but that is a trifling when I consider the fact that the next time I see her, it will be as if no time has passed at all.

Whom do you know from college (or some other specific period) that you still have an unbreakable bond of friendship with? Is there a friend you have that pops into your mind and who lives miles apart whom you haven't seen in a while who is particularly dear to you? Who is that gentle lover of life who quietly helps those in her world, and in everything he or she does, you can't help but notice an embodiment of intelligence and T.L.C.? Do you have a friend with whom you can giggle and get down to the nitty-gritty and talk about whatever is on your mind or going on in your life? I hope you'll consider reaching out today. I did.

Read on to read about my sweet and savvy friend, Emily.

"Follow me, reader! Who told you that there is no true, faithful, eternal love in this world! May the liar's vile tongue be cut out!
Follow me, my reader, and me alone, and I will show you such a love!"
– Mikhail Bulgakov, *The Master and Margarita*
(1967)

February 24, 2019

Darling Emily,

Как мне не стыдно! Давным давно я тебе не писала, дорогая моя! Как я скучала по тебе! Shame on me for not having written to you for so long! How I have missed you! Oh, we let a year or two slip by, and then, before you know it, there's been a decade or two that is the space between. By now, your daughter must be a teenager, and I still would love to meet her! I do hope life is treating you well! Before any more time slips away from us,

I thought I'd send you a time capsule in this bottle of a letter and take a moment to share a few memories that only you and I possess. Why would I do this? *I want to celebrate my friendship with you*, so I will tarry a moment in a time and place that was pivotal for us both. I, too, "will show you such a love"!

Traversing one's mid-twenties can prove to be one of the most baffling, exhilarating, humbling, and empowering times of one's life: you don't know how your life is going to pan out, where you'll end up, what you'll soon be doing, let alone with whom you'll spend your life. The world may be your oyster, but at the same time, you are never more aware of how powerful and vast the ocean is. By the end of our first semester, as graduate students, you and I found ourselves looking to switch gears *and* directions, all while still driving down a byway we *thought* had been the right one. There was no GPS at that time, and we had to navigate by trial and error, making wrong turns and U-turns until we, indeed, found our way. I don't know if there's any truth to Robert Frost's remarking in retrospect that he "took the one [road] less traveled by." Still, I *can* say that being your friend during the transitional period between our final days in undergraduate on through our brief stint at graduate school "made all the difference" for me. Yes, we ended up back in our home town, each on a different career path, but now that you are in W., if I may, I'd like to reminisce with you so that ultimately, I can shower you with a love I *still* hold for you, now over thirty years past our maiden voyage.

We are part of the precious few who fell under the spell of the triune, Dr. F., Dr. F, and Dr. R. Though you and I were out of step as to when were the classes we took there, we were in sync because we shared a passion for all things Russian, so much so, that by then, you, too, had studied in Moscow one summer. As it happened, we were to enter graduate school at the same time that fall of 1986, not even six months out from when the nuclear plant disaster occurred in Chernobyl. I'm not sure if our malaise came about (a) because we were two states away from home, or (b) because we were disappointed that the Russian Dept. in graduate school hardly held our heart's attention as did the one in undergraduate years. It took us no time at all to figure out that (c) the Ph.D. track we'd eagerly sought had gotten derailed somewhere deep in our directional core. Maybe it was due to (d) all of the above. We just knew we wanted out! That we carried on with the initial courses we had committed ourselves to, all the while knowing we would have to revamp our best-laid plans that had gone awry, was primarily made possible because *we found support and strength in each other*, and, boy, we did bare our souls to one another!

Looking back, it's not surprising that we were in shock because we were stock sprung from the Germanic and Slavic Dept., a tiny, close-knit nucleus housed in a few rooms in "the Tower." Anyone who was a Russian major there was part of the motley crew of the few, the proud, the misfits who looked past the Soviet mantle to find an enduring "eternal love" in Russian culture and history, literature, and language. Contrast this with the two long corridors in W. Hall, each lined with offices for professors with specialties of every possible slant and focus imaginable. You were tracked for literature and I for linguistics. Of all of the erudite professors in this graduate school, only the soft-spoken Pole and the enthusiast of Gogol, the dissident from Leningrad whose elderly mother we visited, and the keen-witted and brilliant linguist stand head and shoulders among this broad array of faculty. These people were as valuable to us as Russian malachite and amber were to the tsars, yet they and others proved impotent in retaining our attention. We got lost in the cracks because our hearts knew before our minds that this ivory tower was not for us. You and I both wanted to determine the lot of our lives differently than could be found in the lyceums of academia. That said, *we did not bail*. Instead, until we formally had switched our programs — for you, the Ph.D. track in psychology and for me, the terminating M.A. program from the Russian and East Europeans Institute, we survived through weeknight study-break treks getting a bagel, catching a foreign or alternative film at the local pub, or chatting with other graduate students in our favorite lounge. There it was so full of foreign exchange students that it felt like we were taking part in the United Nations Security Council.

We also hankered to head home on holidays. With Janet Jackson or the Judds blaring on the radio, we would speedily drive south and get back home, glad for a chance to drive through a fall fantasia of hectic red and yellow foliage, for this or that break, or for no particular reason at all. To me, it felt like we were Thelma and Louise breaking away. We were relieved to have a reprieve from the burden of shifting the course of our lives midstream. We arrived at your home, and it was usually late at night. One time, your mom greeted us with still-warm, homemade cookies as your dad stood nearby, hungry for our news. I learned that your ease and readiness to giggle or squeal in delight comes from your mother. And, that you are the youngest of four and I the oldest of four helped make our connection a natural fit. Although we'd done only light socializing in undergraduate school, in graduate school, the depth and breadth of our chats took us to another stratosphere. I innately knew that I'd gained a sister in you; I felt this clinched whe we visited your parents.

Those three years in graduate school forged a bond for us for life, and though I would with affection call you "old woman of the woods" for the wisdom you possessed then, I am sure it still holds true today. Yes, I am still the same Dimi who adores you, but I also hope and pray you might discover in me "a new creature" (2 Corinthians 5:17). It is not my intent here to chronical the steps of your career or the moves you've made in life; however, it *is* my desire to shower you with affection and reminisce our shared recollections and terms of endearment. You are an *incredibly* special person, Emily! Your readiness to take delight in life's farcical *and* tender moments is matched by your intellect, depth of perception, and capacity for getting to the crux of something of great gravitas that *so* merits our attention. It could be it a fractured spirit or a young maiden halfway across the world in sore need of a mother. When I first met you, I encountered one with an unflappable expression, a genuineness, and innate goodness and sweetness of which all belie a heart that not only cares, but is ready to shoulder life's burdens. Your placid and peaceful expression conceals a fiercely keen mind that can solve life's mysteries as adeptly as some master locksmith. Should some emergency arise, like quicksilver, you move from mirth to solemnity. Your beauty is marred only by the furrow in your wizened brow, which is the tell-tale sign of a perspicacity not to be discounted or dismissed. Throughout your career as a psychiatrist, you uncracked the code for many of *non-compos mentis,* ones who were too wounded to swim among the mainstream. When I experienced my first heartache, caused by one who had abandoned both God and me to enter divinity school, it was *you* whom I called from a payphone at the Cracker Barrel. Like some EMT, you speedily drove to me right then and there to help me begin to put back together the pieces that had me feeling shattered. There was not even a thought, and, as usual, we were in tandem both in ways and wit then, too. As a mother, all that you've gleaned and gained — and then *then* some — has expanded even more into the robust and rich woman you are today.

I'll now catch us up to speed past both graduate school and your time abroad in M. with the Peace Corp — a decision of yours I still marvel at — to the period when you and your husband moved back to this neck of the woods. You had completed your education and had moved to the states of M. as well as G. Though it wasn't for too very long, upon occasion, you and your husband and Bonnie and I would get together to eat out and chat about politics, education, beautiful places we'd visited, or share new dreams and plans. It was a natural kinship, and we felt it. I loved that your husband adored American lit., and I was envious that you'd recently visited Flannery O'Connor's estate in Milledgeville. We delved into more than literature; we revealed longings for what else the future might hold, including parenthood. By that time, you had recently done battle with and defeated cancer, such a formidable and dispiriting opponent, a circumstance I have borne witness to with Bonnie's recently waging war with it. To that end, let me also say I admire your tenacious spirit and resolve to ingest only that which is pure or free from carcinogens. This morning, I asked Bonnie if she remembered a particular meal that we four ate together — one I'm fairly certain involved us eating mimosas at an Indian restaurant. You two had just then announced you intended to move to China so that you would be able to fulfill the stint of time required for Americans who intended to adopt a baby from there. We were so impressed and in awe of you! Plus, that you gifted your daughter with your mother's namesake is such an honor. I'm sure your mother is beaming radiantly from Heaven over this. Since you moved near to our nation's capital, the time has gotten away from us, and, to my discredit, as of recent, I've even not managed to send you a birthday card. I see your daughter and you only through snatches of pictures posted on social media, all of which I avidly take in for wanting to hold onto a few pieces of your life.

Since you are one of my favorite persons, I would like to share with you my own news of late, and that is that after thirty years, I have decided to retire. With requisite paperwork completed, I've but to finish out this term. I have also vocalized that I want to continue in a half-time capacity next year, but it will be months before I'll get word on that. You and your family drive this way infrequently, and, when you do, the time is naturally filled with seeing immediate family. I understand that it is impossible to do much more than land and rest and go; I get this. At a time conducive to us all, I would like to propose that Bonnie and I come and visit you there were you are. I've no particular date in mind; after all, when I started this letter, I had no other purpose but to sing your praises and to recollect a time only we two share. It was that in-between stage when we were past official youth, yet not quite thirty. We were groupies of local musicians and followers of Russian literary giants. We drank in pagan milk and were uncertain of where life was leading us; the vision of what lay ahead blurrily came into focus. I am grateful it did and that we experienced this together.

Oh, Emily, what a bright star you are to me. How could I not send out a little lifeline, a gingerbread cookie crumb, a filament more real than an electronic note, and write you a real letter with pen and paper? Please consider this unexpected love letter, one a long time coming, like a delicacy for your soul, one which is served neither at The Flame nor The Spartan Horse.

I love you with all my heart!

D.C.

March

Those Full Of Hope

March is the month which is known by its familiar idiom, "in like a lion, out like a lamb," because it straddles two seasons. I, too, have friends that straddle two realms, be it the sacred and the secular, this and that job, or a couple of seasons in their own life that are in flux or transition. March is also the marker that announces spring officially begins, and with a flutter of anticipation, everyone's thoughts turn to longer days and more sunshine, even though we are well aware that there will be plenty of blustery days in between. We don't mind. The friends I wrote to during this month are all ones who have placed their hopes in some dream, project, vocation, or destination; *they are living for something greater than themselves.* Each in his or her own way is taking steady steps to go about making their vision come to fruition. Without fail, this involves taking a leap of faith as well as having the mettle and resolve to see the plan through. It requires grace, too, and I see they give and partake of it regularly. Another idiom that suits these unflagging ones here is that they are not deterred by the fact that "the devil is in the details." They rise to the occasion. Without exception, my friends here are meticulous, thorough, and precise, be it evidenced in their passion, project, work, or play. I admire my friends because they possess the courage and resilience that helps them get through trying times which might cause others to pause or quit. Not them. There's also a levity about these people that makes them like skylarks, and life is better when they sing, in whatever form that takes. These folks keep on makin' the donuts, and it is my hope that their reward will be greater than anything the world can offer. Oh, sure, they earn their daily bread. Still, my focus here is more about the sweet intangibles that they attain you know, the inner glow of a job done well and *just so*, of sticking to one's guns, of remaining staid and dependable despite hardship, of making a difference in someone's day or life, or knowing that by staying His course, they each will hear the words, "Well done, my good and faithful servant" (Matthew 25:23 NLT).

24. Jimmy

Meet Jimmy. I greeted Jimmy at the onset of school in the fall of 2007; after all, he was to be my intern that year, a fact in itself that was unremarkable. A little over halfway through my career, I had mentored some half a dozen student teachers, but when I met Jimmy, I could tell that there something was unique about him and that the year would hold exceptional promise. First of all, he was already pushing forty and had recently left a successful career because he felt the call to teach. I saw in Jimmy's eyes that he sought the intrinsic reward only altruism in action can bring, and he was gung-ho to go. It didn't take me long to let him take over my class. How could I tell he was ready? From outside my classroom door, I could hear the spontaneous eruption of laughter, the shuffling of papers during the sound of silence in test-taking, and the volley of questions coming from students during a lively class discussion. Jimmy was a quick study of classroom management and rarely had to excoriate his students; gentleness and respect proved to be his best weapons. There were other unanticipated moments of growth for him as well, and the organic give- and-take between the two of us went above and beyond the call of duty; we became friends. For this reason and many more, of all my interns, it is toward Jimmy that I now direct my loving gaze and attention. Thirteen years later, I don't have to hedge my bets to know he is a successful and effective teacher, and, yes, a very happy man. Good move, Jimmy.

Do you know someone who changed his or her career midstream? Have you witnessed a friend go through a midlife crisis? Has your friend or sibling had the bottom of his life drop out such that he found himself back at square one? Did she realize that it wasn't too late to follow or explore her dreams? It was now or never, and she couldn't not try. What about someone whose drinking or drugging got out of hand, and this friend lost control of his life? Were you there to give support, lend a hand, or offer words of kindness when everyone else was playing judge and jury? How about the man or woman who is stuck in indecision, but she knows something needs to change? Will you listen to and be there for her? What about the man that has undergone a metamorphosis in a career such that now his life is teeming with successes you might not think he deserves? Will you congratulate him and share in his gladness?

Read on to meet Jimmy.

"Momma sewed the rags together Sewin' every piece with love
She made my coat of many colors That I was so proud of.
As she sewed, she told a story
From the Bible, she had read
About a coat of many colors
Joseph wore and then she said
Perhaps this coat will bring you
Good luck and happiness
And I just couldn't wait to wear it And momma blessed it with a kiss My coat of many colors
That my momma made for me
Made only from rags
But I wore it so proudly
So with patches on my britches
And holes in both my shoes

In my coat of many colors I hurried off to school
Just to find the others laughing
And making fun of me
In my coat of many colors My momma made for me
And oh, I couldn't understand it
For I felt I was rich
But they didn't understand it
And I tried to make them see
That one is only poor
Only if they choose to be
Now I know we had no money
But I was rich as I could be
In my coat of many colors My momma made for me Made just for me."

— Taken from "Coat of Many Colors, "by
Dolly Parton (1971)

March 3, 2019

Dear Jimmy,

Surprise! It may seem like this out-of-the-blue letter was written on a whim; therefore, I need to explain that I've embarked upon a journey whereby I'm writing a select few who are or have become particularly precious to me. You are such a one. Even though we don't see each other with regularity or frequency, you have long since become like a brother to me, and I wanted to take the time to relish what you mean to me and to tell you how much I admire you. The year 2007 will be forever emblazoned in my memory as the year that I had to take over my father's affairs when he began his swift mental descent. That it was the year you became my student teacher is no accident. Although, I did not acknowledge it nearly enough, you went above and beyond in every mean and measure: there was never any task, burden, or favor great or small you didn't fulfill with willingness, full capability, and good cheer. When I became my father's durable power of attorney that year, a whirlwind of frenetic activity skyrocketed, what with so many new obligations, responsibilities, and obstacles coming about, and all of which needed my full and immediate attention. Truth be told, though I was your mentor, you became my rock. All the while, as a budding teacher, you could not have known that you already had that indefinable "it" that only exceptional teachers possess, that is, an equilibrium maintained balancing expectations and standards while guiding with gentle firmness. It is a compound formed from the essential elements of compassion, intelligence, earnestness, and devotion to bring about the improvement and advancement of our youth's welfare, academic *and* otherwise. Oh, and that's aside the subject matter we teach and *way* past the degrees, certifications, etc. we've earned.

The life lessons you "scaffold" into your lectures I'm sure are brimming with wisdom, and I've not a doubt in my mind that your students can write and think *much* better than when they first entered your class. You are such a one who stepped out in faith and did a complete mid-stream career switch as a result of your listening to those never-ceasing stirrings in your soul that beckoned, yes, prompted you to take *this* path. It is no wonder then that you sang the praises and anthems of Emerson and Thoreau because you knew what it is like to "hear a different drummer. Let him step to the music which he hears"! Many dismiss or ignore such cues and miss out on much in life. That was not the case with you. Look how far your choice has positively impacted not only your own life, but, like the ripple effect, it has touched the lives of so many students! That you were captivated by American literature, in general, and the Transcendentalists, in particular, struck me, and I felt a glow within. You were a quick study of the literature we taught and an even swifter one of the sometimes maddening, always captivating mystery that is the teenage brain. Although one might not know by the poker face you can maintain in class, I know your students bring you no end of joy and, yes, sometimes sorrow, should you come to learn of some private plight. You are sensitive and show both compassion and joy readily and easily. Students live for that knowing look that says, "I care," and they can find this in you. You are such a thoughtful and generous person! I'll never forget your giving a particular student several chances in his attempt to recite from memory a few lines from Thoreau's "I went to the woods because I wished to live deliberately" so that he could gain a few points of extra credit. I recall privately chiding you to *be fair over nice*, but it was you who were right and I wrong. It should be the other way around. Why *not* give a child a second or third chance when he shows initiative to go past what is just expected? In the end, the child will not remember the quote, but he *will* remember your kindness, and I'm sure he did yours. Now twelve years since working with me, the breadth of courses you teach as well as your being a respected faculty member where you currently work, I couldn't be more pleased. Please consider this letter as a way that I can tip my hat in respect and recognition of you.

Oh, but we are more than colleagues. I'm not sure if it is because you are the youngest of three girls and a boy and I the oldest of the same birth- order construct, if it is because we both adore this beautiful little corner of the country, or if it is because we are more family than one measured by blood. Any way you slice it, we are more kith than kin. That you and yours have reached twenty years together makes my heart swell with pride because every year that passes, you break the mold of a stereotype that says such a "lifestyle" is superficial, silly, or fugacious in nature. In fact, I think these anniversaries should be measured in dog years for the endurance and fortitude required. To that end, you have sanctioned your union by making it legally binding, and that you did so in our nation's capital is both capital and splendid. Thank you for inviting me to your reception afterward to celebrate your momentous occasion.

Reflecting back on our year teaching side by side, I am compelled to relate another bond you and I share that got launched that year. When we met, I was already seven years abstinent, a fact which I decided to get vulnerable and divulge to you. Sometime during your term at Admiral High, something within you clicked such that you, too, recognized your need to take hold of the banner of that white flag of surrender, which, in reality, is *so* empowering. No, this was no light and transient affair for you. From a distance, I marveled at your level of participation and depth of commitment, intersecting in a way that renovated the who you *had been* to the who you intended *to become*. The proof is in the pudding, and you are still at it. Hurrah!

Through glimpses of you on social media, I have observed

a metamorphosis in you that has been impressive; not one stone of your life hasn't been turned over and positively impacted. I can't keep count! In your pledge of allegiance to the Serenity Prayer, which has us take *one day at a time*, I have also seen you honor the temple by transforming your physique all without making a god of yourself, and I have no doubt that you are healthier now than you ever have been. Working out helps you to work in the values of the twelve steps and traditions by rewriting a script into one that keeps us alive and vibrant in a way unimaginable before. Next, I don't know to what degree you were a performing musician, but now I see posts of you doing gigs and playing in a small band, singing and playing your guitar for all you're worth. And to think that we couldn't imagine figuring out what to do with ourselves if we hadn't a drink in hand! Turns out, there's quite a lot. And then, having a clear head on your shoulders, your capacity to wonder and take a chance on an entrepreneurial enterprise like owning vacation rental property is mind- blowingly impressive! Your cozy cabins in the Smokey Mountains and your recently-acquired beach houses speak to your honoring the soul's more profound need for respite, for admiring Nature's beauty, and for a time of renewal, reflection, and restoration. You're making this possible for others, too! How could those who rent from you possibly know that, in paying for a short get-away in some pristine spot, they are securing a piece of the peace you've made for yourself?

Just this past fall, you and I came full circle concerning our oath of temperance because in your reaching out to ask me to share my story at a Friday night speaker meeting, we were together again, partners of positivity. Your invitation showed me that, no matter how far or near we are from one another, regardless of what we're doing in life, you and I can always pick up where we last left off. I didn't anticipate I would feel as moved as I did by hearkening back on that part of my past. Revealing this portion of my history that eve ing made it such that the legacy of Bill W. pulsed in unison within all of us "in these rooms" who *still* want to *let go and let God* so that we might live like we never did before. Oh, the power of feeling like *we are in this together*! Teetotaling fits us to a tee. We don't want to squander our precious gifts, do we? Jimmy, let me repeat it, you have *so* many! For this and everything, *I thank you.*

You may wonder why the reference to "Coat of Many Colors" launches my letter. How could it not? You are past fan to being a true aficionado of Dolly Parton, and anyone who knows you recognizes that it is because the East Tennessee boy in you *also* has an enduring spirit and a great capacity for joy. Her songs speak to the native son in you. Paradox is my favorite literary device, and I don't need to tell you that this song contains lyrics that put the iron in irony! Not only this, but Dolly's alluding to a story in the Bible inserts a valuable life lesson that might otherwise go unnoticed or unheeded in our world today. Therefore, I chose this song because it teaches us that which many eschew: wealth is not based on what glitters. Gold is determined by the value of one's character. Not only one's existence, but one's earthly circumstances are God-given. In this song, those who are unduly scorned and wrongly ridiculed get the final word. Joseph, whose father gifted him a colorful tunic which would have indicated a position of future leadership within the family, was abducted, abandoned, and left for dead by his jealous older brothers. He survived and came to be a great leader; you, too, are such a one with a resurrected life. The story of Joseph demonstrates that through the sufferings of a righteous person, blessings *can* come to many. For those of us who have the privilege of knowing you, Jimmy, our lives have also improved due to *your* generosity and goodness. In short, let me say that I am so glad to be your friend, colleague, and *much* more. You can be sure and know it in your bones that...

I will always love you!

D.C.

25. Kostas

Meet Kostas. He is the attorney in Greece I employed to help me sell my father's properties, and two years after my dad died, he also assisted my siblings and me in acquiring our dual citizenship. The former was such a tedious undertaking, what with my having to provide nearly twenty documents certified and apostilled *before* he could get down to the business of his representing us, that I felt like I would never get done all I had to accomplish. The personal relationship I developed with this man came about because of the care he took while performing his charge and officiating all his duties. He was the consummate professional, and he became my mainstay. My focus on Kostas is not due to anything *he* went through. Oh, no! It was I who was being stretched and pulled apart as I juggled all I had *and* desired to, all during the two-and-a half- year span of taking care of my aging father who lacked sound mind. For much of this time, my petulant dad fought me tooth and nail. All the while and behind the scenes, I dealt with a litany of doctors and lawyers and made reels of decisions and phone calls so as to maintain his well- being *and* secure his cumbersome estate. More than any other person outside my own home, including family, it was Kostas I relied on to accomplish my tasks and goals; I got real encouragement to boot. Every time I found myself facing some new enemy, obstacle, or challenge, he was there in my corner, advising me what to do next. He crossed every *t* and dotted every *i* for every *p* and *q* I had to mind, mend, or make.

When I felt broke or overwhelmed, it was he who rallied me from across the ocean; I may have had the final say, but we were on the same page and team. To celebrate his indispensable and invaluable help, I took the liberty of using the language and the parlance of this field — Latin, so throughout this letter, you'll notice I sprinkled this jargon known primarily to litigators.

During a specific crisis or challenging episode in your life, who was there by your side and ever at hand to help you accomplish some herculean task? Whose unflappable and unshakable presence did you come to depend on for a specific function only he or she could perform? Who was present for you and never cast doubt, aspersion, or dismay, but rather, got down to the tasks at hand and helped you knock them off, one by one, with perfection, perseverance, and pertinacity? Who was your hope, hold, or harbor during a particular storm?

Read on to see how I celebrate Kostas.

"Neither by nature, then, nor contrary to nature do the *virtues* arise in us; rather we are adapted by nature to receive them, and *are made perfect by habit.*"
—Aristotle, emphasis mine

"For you were formerly darkness, but now you are Light in the Lord; walk as children of Light (for the fruit of the Light consists in all goodness and righteousness and truth), trying to learn what is pleasing to the Lord... *All things become visible when they are exposed by the light,* for everything that becomes visible is light... Therefore, *be careful how you walk*, not as unwise men but as *wise, making the most of your time...*"
—Taken from Ephesians 5:8–16, emphasis mine

March 10, 2019

Dear Kostas,

This year and month mark the anniversary of my father's death ten years ago. As a tribute both to him and even more so, as a token of gratitude to you for the alliance we set in motion back on Jan. 17, 2007, the day you replied to my (desperate) query for help handling my "Matter in Greece," I have decided to write you a letter. You may consider it my laurel leaf presented to you. Furthermore, that you have recently opened your own office in Athens merits celebration, too. You know, when you completed the undertaking of selling my father's four properties some thirteen months after this date, I felt like we had run a three- legged marathon together, so arduous and steep the path, so fulfilling its conclusion. The thoroughness, meticulousness, and τελειότητα — perfection — with which you handled the granular details of this arduous task was done with diligence, finesse, good cheer, and such υπομονή και επιμονή — patience and persistence. The degree to which I experienced your effective completion of all tasks and undertakings was made dearer to me because you held me in respect and regard. Such was palpable, and I never felt alone with you even as I was losing my father.

When we had all of the necessary paperwork completed and after I finally arrived in Greece, I'll never forget coming to see you face-to-face in your office; I was so relieved to meet you! You even permitted me to move a chair so I could sit side-by-side next to you as we strategized and looked over our list of tasks and plans. I was filled with hope. Do you recall our having to deal with the treachery of Medusa L.? Your selling these properties for me/him I consider a major accomplishment, one that honored my father by disallowing his property to be squandered or lost. The reason I am still able to come back anytime I please and stay at the small beach house my papou built in Skala O. is because we sold it to the deserving ones — my good and righteous relatives. Since then, my relationship with them has flourished and grown stronger. I thank you for this as well. I would like to say that I wish the circumstances would have been different such that you could have met my father. I have often described myself as being a mere pinky nail in comparison to his arm of Zorba-like energy and passion. In any event, after all was accomplished and behind us, I put a gold star on what you'd done by writing a letter to the U.S. Embassy singing your praises. I confess I learned a new word I had found to describe your work: *nonpareil*. I exclaimed to myself, "Eureka!" Continuing in this vein and because I didn't want to merely repeat previous praises to you here, I decided upon a novel approach to laud you. Since Latin is the language of lawyers, I looked up some of the more common terms that proved both *apropos* and *sine qua non* in depicting our journey and mission together. So, if you'll indulge me, I'll attempt to use some such parlance with and for you; believe you me, my motive is *bona fide*.

I write *ex tempore* about what you did for my siblings and me *ex post facto*. Action speaks louder than words, and what you accomplished was ultimately realized through *facta non verba*. In all humility and gladness, I say to you that I am *still* beholden and grateful for what you did! Unlike so many others whose talk is cheap, you remained not only the consummate and capable professional, I witnessed a man of truth, kindness, courage, and one good to his word. I write to you here and now, you who were *in loco* my father in Greece; my intention is also *de mortibus nil nisi bonum*. *In medias res*, you and I were of one mind and accord as we walked *manus in mano*. My own Greek tragedy proved to be no play: my father had been declared *non compos mentis*, such that in no way could he understand or appreciate that my every thought and deed were, in fact, for his good. Sadly, he treated me as if I were his *persona non grata*. In my mind, had I *not* done everything that God gave me the strength to do to protect what was his and preserve him in his wobbly and often maddening decline, it would have been tantamount to my bearing the stamp of *mea (maxima) culpa*. You and I faced obstacles and perfidies *ad nauseam*, but speaking honestly just *inter nos*, I will look back on this time as one of the most potent and poignant times of my life. You taught me that *vincit qui patitur, videlicet;* we were successful in finishing what was set before us through your tireless work. As a result, today, *in memoriam* of my father, you and I can exclaim, "*Veni, Vidi, Vici!*" *ad vitam aeternam.* Yes, indeed, *tempus fugit*, but to you I will remain *semper fidelis.* And then, even after my father died, you rallied my brother, sister, and me to *carpe diem* to stake our claim and right to dual citizenship. After all, we do not live *in vacuo; vita mutatur, non tollitur!* You next helped us obtain our Greece passports which, when renewed, will be good *ad vitam*, yes, *in perpetuum!* That, too, proved no small feat. With each time I come to Greece, I hope that in learning more and more of the language, I will be able to chip away at the marble stone of fluency such that it is no longer the case that *omnia mihi lingua Graeca sunt.* As I turn the page from this paragraph, I say to you, my dear Kostas, *Deus vobiscum!*

At the opening of my letter to you, I chose two quotes, which at first glance might seem incongruous or unlikely to be positioned next to one another. I'll tell you how such a juxtaposition couldn't be more on the mark. In His infinite wisdom, God chose the country of *our* forefathers as the stage that would prepare the world's minds and hearts for wisdom and a hope heretofore unfounded by mere mortals. Through the philosophy of the Greeks, he cracked the skulls of many a Cretin and showed that there is a beacon of light that throws itself upon us for our good. There is substance beyond the mere shadows that we make for ourselves. The Aristotelian virtues became articulated and were brought into clearer view as being "*goodness and righteousness and truth.*" Our predecessors knew that it was through practice, practice, practice that we can stay ourselves on the path of perfection; when the kosmos' light switched on from B.C. to A.D., Paul took up His Way and charged *us* to walk as ones of the Light. That's just what you and I did together, and, my, did we make much of our time both serving my dad's interests *and* ultimately honoring Our Father's values.

Such pedestrians we were and are! It pleased me to no end to meet, chat, reminisce, and look to the future over a cup of coffee together a couple of summers ago. I bask in the easy comradery I have with you, the one with whom I served shoulder-to-shoulder in *our* tour of victoriousbattle. Know that I am always happy to hear your news, and I hope to see you again soon — this summer even — or whenever I come to Greece! In the meantime, please consider this letter my paean to you, you who came to my rescue in a time of such critical mass. Like putting a bow on a present, you topped this feat off with the attainment of my Greek citizenship, a relic of my identity lost and found. "Potato, potahto, tomato, tomahto," *–akis, –akos,* we *can* call the whole thing *done!* Kostas, you are *still* the best, and I am *so* glad to call you my friend *for life*. Keep up the good work, the good life, *and* the faith! Know that I stand smiling before you, with olive branch and hand extended in love...

Et quantum amare et revereri tenemur,
D.C.

26. Lilith

Meet Lilith. She is a colleague of mine who is a couple of decades younger than I, but because she is an old soul, we mesh well; in fact, we make much mirth daily. There are others at my job with whom I confer directly and efficiently about this or that problem or situation, but Lilith prefers a more oblique route for the giving and taking of support. We share in common a love of looking at pictures of her young nephew or her pooch. For a few moments during a frenetic or hectic day, we can escape the travails of the world, the inanities of students, or other irritations that may vex us, but aren't worth the bother to fuss over. We peer into these pics and videos daily because they sustain and soothe us when we get our feathers ruffled or need a boost to fortify our mind or moment. We interpret this or that glance, gesture, or subtle nuance in each child or dog because we take delight in the unaffected. What is it about them that enchants us? She and I both crave an innocence and goodness, so, when the world or our morning has been filled with the insipid, inane, or irritating, she and I still have hope that springs eternal, and we know just what the doctor would order to fit the bill. The pure at heart and untainted in action give us wistful glimpses back at a simpler time, and we are filled with the sense that "*it is good.*" Lilith is one who shows restraint of pen and tongue when a student's behavior is awry; I admire her light touch, finesse, sensitivity, and poise, but there's also a part of her who appreciates the pure and primal. When we encounter the unaffected, unadorned, and genuine, we ourselves have no pretense, guise, or falseness; it's like sitting down to a homemade meal that is delicious, nutritious, wholesome, and filling. Where there is hope, we feel no ache or void. Lilith is like a lavender macaroon for me.

*Who in your life do you sit down with and get lost in
pictures of grandchildren or pets? With whom can you
really be yourself and share intimate moments when
you are feeling fragile or vulnerable because that person
is there to give you a boost or shot of hope? Who is
your go-to person when you need clarity, honesty, and
impartial judgment one moment, but who is ready to take
five and escape in a playful or frivolous moment the next?
If you can name that person, you are ready to read my
letter to Lilith's young nephew, Teddie.*

I will report to Teddie all I appreciate about Lilith.

"Among other things, you'll find that you're
not the first person who was ever confused
and frightened and even sickened by human
behavior. You're by no means alone on that
score, you'll be excited and stimulated to know.
Many, many men have been just as troubled
morally and spiritually as you are right now.
Happily, some of them kept records of their
troubles.
You'll learn from them—if you want to. Just
as someday, if you have something to offer,
someone will learn something from you. It's a
beautiful reciprocal arrangement. And it isn't
education. It's history. It's poetry."
— From J. D. Salinger's *The Catcher in the Rye*
(1951)

"If one of us likes anything, there must be
something to like in it — and the other one must
find it. Every single thing that either of us likes.
That way we shall create a thousand strands,

great and small, that will link us together...
And our trust in each other will not only be
based on love and loyalty but on the fact of a
thousand sharings
—a thousand strands twisted into something
unbreakable."
— From Sheldon Vanauken's *A Severe Mercy*
(1977)

March 17, 2019

Hello, Teddie!

In all likelihood, you are a tyke whom I am unlikely to meet in person, but there's hardly a workday that goes by that I am not afforded the joy of seeing a new pic or video of you or hearing of some new exploit of yours. "How?" you may ask. I make my acquaintance with you through your Aunt Lilith; we call her Lily here at school. She shares these emblems of you with us, and they help us keep comity (and sanity) in our particular little corner of the department. Not only is she my colleague and fellow English teacher; she is my friend, and we are like-minded in many ways. Through revealing that which brings us delight by beholding you, I aim to capture for *you* some glimpses of precisely what touches your aunt's heart and thereby show you the preciousness of *her*. I am blessed to see this daily. It is only a matter of time until you two become better acquainted; maybe one day you'll read this letter and come to know more fully what stirs her heart and moves her mind. Oh, I could describe her many gifts, talents, and eclectic interests. Instead, you can actually learn more about her through the private revelations of a few select people and worthwhile activities that bring *her* delight. So, sweet Teddie, I begin with you.

More often than not, my first footstep in the department each morning leads me to your aunt. With a smile on her face, a twinkle in her eye, and a quickening of her step, she is pleased as punch to inform me, "I've got a new one!" or "I think we need to see the one of Teddie where..." There is any number of possible images of you that we both know by heart, like some favorite passage we adore. We often bookend our day with you, too, and again, her step quickens to come over and show me some new exploit of yours. You bring us such glee and laughter, that I sometimes have told her that perhaps I should be paying you for therapy sessions for all the relief and entertainment you bring. After all, laughter *is* the best medicine. "For what?" you may rightly ask. In the realm that encompasses our work, what a teacher does in her classroom is only the tip of the iceberg for all that is involved in educating her students. I need not digress too much.

Suffice it to say, although Lilith and I would have no other job than this one, we *can* grow weary from barely camouflaged disinterest, unending excuses, or just plain old sloth. Sometimes it is not due to *students'* lack of initiative or interest that's the source of the problem. Rather, we can look to parents who either do *way* too much *or* nothing at all for their bundles of joy. I know it's not easy there, either; what a different world we live in, especially considering how greatly technology has both connected and isolated us. The extreme range of parenting styles is staggering, too. Achieving academic success is only one step on the path to becoming a well-adjusted and contributing member of society, but it takes *sustained* help and *consistent* training *early* on for kids to be students who *really* excel. We who teach A.P. students bear witness to this. Smarts won't get you too far without self-respect and self-discipline; this is fostered by parents who put their faith in gear and love into action. Therefore, little Teddie, when Lilith and I gulp in glimpses of you, we get a shot of the *best* that man has in his primary steps: joy uncontained, hope unblemished, wonderment pure, creativity bursting, and a double scoop of love from your parents. In you, we see man's reaching out to the take hold of the life that he's been given and engage with all his little might.

By now, I've collected a bevy of snapshots of you in my memory that warm the cockles of my heart. We could go back to your infancy, when you were more like an amoeba than a man, what with the spasmodic movements you made, as if even then you felt trapped and were trying to wriggle your way out of your little infant's sack. You are so attached to your grandfather that you don't mind being tethered or tangled in a jumble of his green tubes which shuttle in life-giving oxygen to him. A sight of this brings *us* fresh air as much as his love sustains you. When you don your bright tangerine-orange toboggan and wear dinosaur jammies complete with footies as you start your day, we see no pretense or guile. Whether you arrange bottles of spice along the window sill — stacking some as high as you possibly can, position animals in their barn *just so*, or place your French fries upright in a holder, you show us you are open to possibility through your clever construction and order. There are no mistakes there, and we would do well to learn from you whose merriment, laughter, and purposefulness merge into many meaningful moments. It matters not that you trip full-on over some threshold, that you dance and twirl until you fall out, or, in some moment of contemplation with your fingers moving to match the frenetic activity in your little problem-solving brain, you give it all you've got. We — your aunt, another colleague, and I — take this in like it is an elixir of life, like ambrosia still left over from the Garden of Eden, when we were uncorrupted and in a brief state of inviolability.

Teddie, if I might, let me say to you, regardless of the grown-up world in which your aunt now resides, yes, the one that daily chips away at truth and tries to knock down building blocks of hope, she has preserved within her a wealth of strength, grace, dignity, and righteousness, and she would protect you like a wild mountain lion. Oh, you will love her as I do! She refuses to be accustomed to any mendacity, and, like you, she puts things in place so that when much else is faulty or amiss, at least her spot is in order. Your Aunt Lilith has a readiness to giggle over some goofiness or shenanigan, and she insists on things being as real as can be. Life is too short for pretense; if we can't be who we are made to be, what's the point? She is exquisitely sensitive, and her soul finds a safe harbor in acts of creativity, including her own drawings that render ones who try to connect with or date her, valiantly, but also in vain. Sometimes she takes refuge in rich literature to help her stay the course. Many a time, she has dashed over to share with me some passage in which an author has brilliantly worded a truth, has hauntingly rendered the harvest moon, or has positioned the protagonist in a way that touches her. William Wordsworth had it wrong: for your aunt: "for this, for everything, she is *not* out of tune; [God's own heartbeat] moves her." And so, when we catch glimpses of you giving it all you've got with your whole little being, *it is we who learn from you.* How could your aunt not be stopped in her tracks and exclaim, "What a guy! He's just the best!"

While I'm on the subject of those who touch some spot in your aunt, she who craves authenticity, there are two other beings that I want to tell you about. They, too, possess an air of assuredness and a righteous refusal to compromise and be brought down by the feckless and foolish. Your aunt has taught every grade and every level, and she has become one of our solid advanced placement teachers, but it is not about them that she comes to share some situation with me in between classes — oh, no. It is a young lady, Miss Anne. Although this student lacks full mental capacity, she delights your aunt with uncultured pearls of wisdom. This Miss Anne always cuts to the chase and assesses a situation with swift accuracy, be it the merit of a movie or whether or not a person or circumstance is "dumb" according to *her* standard. Under the aegis of some protective and guiding hand, Miss Anne's self-esteem is sure and intact, and she is not easily dissuaded or brought down in the doldrums. Your aunt draws strength from this maiden who, like Holden Caulfield, refuses to settle. Do not think that Lilith elevates herself above others; she is acutely aware of her own awkwardness while living in these muddy waters; therefore, she all the more clings to the few who do not receive or deserve opprobrium. More often than not, she and I interact in a mode of subtle irony; this both delights and buffers us so we *can* remain calm, cool, and collected, no matter what may come our way. This groove of ours is undiluted, unfiltered, and never prosaic.

I know many a tale of her youth, and what that she would write about these for you someday. She's also embarked upon a graphic novel, devoting pages to prurient lads who seek to wrest your aunt's attention through selfies and brief introductions that would hardly inspire a passing glance of interest, just the rolling of eyes or an emission of a sigh. She is loath to join those who grasp at straws and unabashedly vie for her attention by turning a glaring spotlight on themselves. What tomfoolery! What agony! With *you*, we see one absorbed in *life*, not self. Daily I also receive texts from your aunt that include pix of her own woman's best friend: Miss May, her black lab mix with a velveteen coat of sable fur is the one who always brings a satisfied smile to her face. Let me say that, if we go by what the *world* dubs normal or fine, then there can be no greater compliment than your aunt saying of her pooch, "She is such a weirdo!" This term of endearment is bestowed upon May because *her* canine tastes and priorities are irreproachable. Why *not* bask in unapologetic indolence settled up next to the most important person in life while sharing Wasabi peas in a moment of blissful quietude? Oh, and that we should *ever* have to get up from that to attend to more mundane matters like "earning a living" brings a disdain and hauteur from May that delivers to your aunt no end of delight. May will stand statuesquely in some corner like a "creeper," hoping your aunt will just *please* come to her senses. Eventually, sharing a pillow, throw, or forbidden section of the bed will bring swift forgiveness, and for a few blissful moments, all is right in the world again. Teddie, I'll close this note to you by explaining why I chose those two quotes at the beginning of your letter. The first is one your Aunt Lilith shared with me, and it happens to be her favorite. In the moral morass we live and breathe in every day, your aunt takes pith and pitch from all that is untarnished and eleemosynary and sends it back out, be it in the hospital where she quietly volunteers, in her classroom, or with her close- knit circle of true-blue friends. Because I have had a "privileged glimpse" into *her* heart, I have been given the gift of *her* poetry, and I am all the better for it. We at school who know and call her Lily treasure her, and although she would recoil at having such attention drawn on her, you will want to bow down to the queen that *she* really is. There is something in her both regal and yet simple, sophisticated yet primal, austere but — like you — capable of surges of vitality. Her dulcet smile belies a depth and peace within, that, should you come to know your aunt even more than I do, you will discover that there is *so* much to appreciate in her, and you will find yourself with a trust, love, loyalty, and mercy in her *like no other*.

Here's to *your* having thousands of unbreakable strands of sharings with her. I remain...

Your fan,
D. C.

27. Jan

Meet Jan. She was an administrator of mine for ten years; before this, she was a special ed. teacher. Though I hadn't known about Jan's own plans to retire before I gave her this letter, I am so glad I did. In hindsight, the timing seemed fortuitous for us both, providential even. We teachers look on those who have chosen "sped" for their area of certification as a special breed of educator. First of all, you have to have the patience of Job because you know from the get-go that any progress made will be done in infinitesimally slow increments. Yet, these steps can be as great and grand a leap as any accomplishment earned by another in a conventional setting. Jan will be the first to tell you that the whole scale of what's essential shifts when you operate under this paradigm. You look at the heart, the motive, and the moment like others would view a score on a test, quiz, or essay, and what you will discover is that these gentle lambs will change *you*. Jan is one who is in tune to children's whimpers, whispers, and touches, so when she became an administrator, her training and intuition went into gear, and she applied her skillset on us teachers. Of course, she did all the many duties that an administrator must in dealing with the discipline or extenuating circumstances of students, but I am shining a spotlight on an area that is not technically part of her job description: loving on teachers. Jan knew that if she gave *us* a safe space to air our fury or frustrations, she would have a better crew renewed, ones ready to take up their pickaxes and head back to the salt mines rather than to head for the door. Many a teacher can languish; she longs for the same kindnesses, encouragement, and consideration we give to our students. Jan is that rare administrator who dotes on us, shows us respect, and takes the time to celebrate us, and we are all the better teachers for it. In short, we love to feel loved by her.

Read on to meet Jan. I' ll bet you know one, too.

"The LORD is my light and my salvation; Whom shall I fear?
The LORD is the defense of my life; Whom shall I dread?
When evildoers came upon me to devour my flesh,
My adversaries and my enemies, they stumbled and fell.
Though a host encamp against me,
My heart will not fear;
Though war arise against me,
In spite of this *I shall be confident.*
That I may dwell in the house of the *LORD all the days of my life,*
To behold the beauty of the LORD And *to meditate in His temple.*
For in the day of trouble He will conceal me in His tabernacle;
In the secret place of His tent He will hide me;
He will lift me up on a rock.
And now *my head will be lifted up* above my enemies around me,
And *I will offer in His tent*

One thing I have asked from the LORD, that I shall seek:

sacrifices with shouts of joy; I will sing, yes, I will sing praises to the *LORD.*"
From Psalm 2:1–7, emphasis mine

March 24, 2019

Dear Jan,

Months before the possibility of early retirement came up, I started to write a letter to you to thank you for all that you do for us teachers and to tell you what you mean to me. Now that I've crossed that line in the sand and made the decision to depart, it is all the more imperative for me to finish and share with you this token of love. Initially, I couldn't even count back to know for sure how long we had worked together as the days and years here stack up more quickly than anyone might imagine. It turns out that it has been a full decade that we have been colleagues at this high school. My, but we pack a lot of life into our day! I want you to know what a difference you have made not only in countless students' and teachers' lives, but mine personally. You were part of the "dream team," a vintage administrative from a bygone era comprised of five folks who would do whatever it took to get us curmudgeons and much put-upon teachers — we who take ourselves *so* seriously — to feel support, appreciation, and a lightening of the load.

You put things in proper perspective with laughter and a hint of silliness, knowing all the while and even more than we, that there are parameters, policies, and practices that we *all* must abide by, which can keep our hands tied and frustrations high. When we "in the trenches" face restless natives who have become disrespectful or disobedient, or worse, hostile, apathetic, or defeated, it is *you* who are our next line of defense.

There is *always* a back story that we are not privy to, but you make sure we know there *is* one, that their being incorrigible has an impetus. I hope you know how relieved we are for the support you provide. You bear the burden of knowing troubled kids' backgrounds that would break our hearts. There are tragic tales that are not fiction, and though you are bound by law to keep confidentiality, you would not have told us what you know anyway because you are sensitive to what we bear in the classroom. You are mindful of the swinging of the pendulum that keeps going higher and higher toward the side that ostensibly protects and provides more for those lacking ability or support. The net result is that we have less available for the average student in our hallowed halls of public high schools. I well know this keeps you running fast and furiously for all those who have fallen in the gaps, cracks, and pits of life and find themselves propped up with the likes of IEPs, 504s, SpEd accommodations, and a plethora of other codes and cues. You came to us with the background as being a special ed. teacher; therefore, you are uniquely qualified and able to empathize with those who are especially trained to care for those students with particular needs. As an administrator, who more fitting than you to better guide us regular ed. teachers in order to better serve them? We also know that for the good that they do, these policies can be but Band-Aids. They are not the be-all, end-all, let alone a panacea; in fact, they have also given rise to many an entitlement and other woes the public doesn't know. In spite of all you have been privy to, I see you as one who still remains hopeful, optimistic, and positive, and this mode of yours is not Pollyanna-ish; such an outlook comes from an abiding faith and trust that *all is well* even when things ain't right. You keep us grounded when matters are unsettled or up in the air, and together we make strides to keep the light shining in the dark. Our students are all the better for it. Not only do you serve, steer, and discipline students, but even when we teachers get blamed or blasted by many a frustrated parent, you are a protectress of us. You are a beacon of hope, a ray of sunshine, and guiding light for us *all*, and even when you are unbelievably busy, I am aware you are shouldering some burden that eases a troubled student and helps make the classroom run more smoothly for us. Oh, it takes a village, doesn't it?

You would be quick to say that you are not the only one doing this, and you are correct. Still, I shower *you* with praise because for us teachers, there is no safer place to vent our frustrations, bare our weary souls, and share laughter through the tears than with you in your office. There we find a home base to come to get centered if we get addled or rattled, and you don't judge or hold it against us. You know that the hurt and bile must come out, and, like burping a baby, you let us have this place to cast out our demons of despair. Countless times, I have sat in your office — my makeshift "tabernacle" — baring my soul or yowling in frustration, all but to leave with a smile on my face and my posture a little straighter knowing *you have my back*. Beyond a shadow of a doubt, I know what gets said in your little corner of our schoolhouse stays there. To be clear, it's not your office; it's *you* we come to. Despite your ability to commiserate with us by offering to share parallels in your own career, you maintain your professionalism and do not dog or rag on anyone else. Never.

Your office is not only a sanctuary and a refuge from a world of noise and frustrations, a private corner we teachers go to for restoration, a spot in our school where it is safe to curse or cry; it is a place where we laugh and celebrate. In a job and a time when we are more than ever likely to be questioned, accused, or called on the carpet, we can always count on you, Jan, to help us turn the other cheek, to keep our spirits bright, and to hold our heads up high. How? In a manner that suits us each, you remind us that we *do* "fight the good fight of faith" (1 Timothy 6:12), and even if we can't fix or solve the problem of the day, we *can* "do all things through Him who strengthens us"

(Philippians 4:13). In short, *you believe in us*, and we feel this in our core. Should someone who is not in our shoes read what I've written to you, he or she might be unprepared or surprised that the little cherubs we teach can also bring a world of hurt, but that is because we care so deeply. No matter what stats or data or facts or figures we use to measure our students' growth, they are flesh and blood with a mind and heart, all of whom need our T.L.C.

With you as my evaluator, I have had only positive experiences, and whatever there is that needs adjusting, improving, or tweaking, you are the first to help us brainstorm or look for ways to fix this or that, and not just for the sake of looking better on paper. When you are in the classroom, a teacher can relax and know that you are not there to sniff out the wrong but to look for the good, and we know you will affirm this to us. Nowadays when I teach Langston Hughes, I recall the pleasure I saw on your face when you watched my students unpack some of his poetry, which pointed to the fact that racism that still persists, and *we need and can do better*. For me to discuss the reasons behind Prince Hamlet's toying with the notion of "self-slaughter" in a still room full of seniors, listening intently with bated breath, was made all the more poignant because you and I lived through the anguish of that pain for real. When things get that real, you are really there. Your go-to mode is always *joy*, and I love the fact that even though some folks may be a bit intimidated by my teaching Russian, you always find a way to make me feel grounded and humbled. How so? You give me a dose of down-to-earth, homespun country-speak and interpret for *me* just how an East Tennessee hillbilly redneck might phrase this or that notion or highfalutin fancy phrase. I become the wiser *and* happier for it! You have the inner strength of a Viking, but you are as sweet as sweet tea or a Georgia peach (or a Big Gulp fountain drink of Diet Dew), and this Greek girl loves you for the broader perspective you bring to the table.

It is crystal clear to me that you have your priorities in righteous standing and good order; it shows in all that you do. There's not a doubt in my mind our Heavenly Father uses you for *the* good — *His* good — and daily. One more thing I wanted to speak because I, too, have walked in your footsteps, and that is your taking care of your mother in her last years and days. This can be alternately a frustrating, amusing, disturbing, and fulfilling experience that drains you *and* fills you at the same time. It is all the more the case because of the giving that is required in this labor of love. When I came to your mother's funeral, I realized that you come from a race of giants, and I witnessed a rapture radiate from you even in that time; your heart knows no fear because it sings praises to our Lord. You have never been afraid to be vulnerable and show yourself willing to laugh, be silly, and do whatever it takes to keep our moods raised, feathers unruffled, and pride praiseworthy. Yet I know that beneath your optimism resides a strength borne from trials and tribulations through which long ago, you made a decision to look and keep on the sunny side of life even when things aren't so. Anyone who comes in contact with you surely knows this, and I am glad to be such a one.

No matter where life takes you after Admiral High isn't a part of your immediate world, I want you to know that I hope your life is full and satisfying. I know that whoever spends time with you, be at your grandbabies, children, or folks in your community, there's not a doubt in my mind that you will make their day brighter! I couldn't leave without letting you know of my love and gratitude for you who are *so* one-of-a- kind! I wish you *many* blessings in your life to come. Please remember that I remain respectfully and...

Warmly yours,
D. C.

28. Josh and Candace

Meet Josh and Candace. They are husband and wife and my brother and sister in Christ. You read about Josh in my last book; he is Bonnie's brother. My walk in faith would not be the same without these two because through the multiple visits I've had with them over the years, I have gotten to see up close and personal what a life in Christ looks like, and by that, I mean one where He's involved in every thought, deed, and word each day of the week. These are real people with real struggles, challenges, and obstacles just like anyone else, but they have shown me that with grace, humor, discipline, and persistent prayer that Jesus is always right there and ever at-hand. He surely hasn't left or forsaken them! We have developed an ease and an intimacy among one another, and I look forward to our visits because our conversations run the gamut. We learn much by being together, and it's evident that God blesses our friendship. It's a celebration every time we meet! They are both in the medical field of Ob/Gyn: Josh is a retired physician to his wife's being a nurse practitioner. Their vantage points and contact with thousands of women promotes life itself and sees it through, starting with the moment after conception. Though these two couldn't be more different individuals, they each and both have had a significant impact on me and my journey in Christ.

Do you have a friendship with a couple? When you visit them, does the totality of what they bring to the table convey more than any two other individuals you know? Have you ever felt a persistent presence and the joy of Jesus in your interaction with two like-minded ones with whom you share your faith? Does He season and lead your conversations such that you are inspired to do more

*for Him? Do they make you smile and laugh for their
being genuine and open, and you find them neither stuffy
nor judgie? Have you recently realized that this type of
Christian fellowship is as precious as a pink pearl?*

*If you have a friendship with a couple, please read on to
meet Josh and Candace!*

"Oh, sing to the Lord a new song!
Sing to the Lord, all the earth.
Sing to the Lord, bless His name;
Proclaim the good news of His salvation from
day to day.
Declare His glory among the nations,
His wonders among all peoples."
— Psalm 96:1–3 (NKJV)

March 31, 2019

Dears Josh and Candace,

Since I did not use any actual names in *Connecting the Dots...*,
you didn't get to read my original Acknowledgment page.
There you would have found your names among those ones
who helped me grow in my faith and understanding of Christ.
You two supported me in my earliest steps as a young pilgrim
when I felt like I was trying to catch up for what seemed like
was squandered time. Instead of an acknowledgment, I'll give
you a letter. Often in life, we don't fully thank or recognize those
who are nearest and dearest to us; usually, we are prompted or
reminded to do so on holidays or other noteworthy occasions.
Though celebrating you has been on my mind for some time,
the moment for doing so is now; in fact, He compels me. We
may visit only quarterly, but we surely pack a lot of life during

our time together. In fact, it almost feels like there's no time in between these visits for how natural and easy is our flow; it doesn't matter if we are catching up in the living room, as we usually do, or are driving by and gazing at the best of gaudy, bodacious, or august yards decorated for Christmas.

I mention this closeness of ours because I have also experienced the inverse becoming true: the more I spend time with my brothers and sisters in Christ, the more I can feel alien or ill-at-ease around my own adult blood relatives. I do not avoid them; I am just aware that my walk around them can bring hints of discomfiture or mental distance. Though I love life, I concur with the Puritan poet Anne Bradstreet who wrote, "Let me no longer love the world!" I know any antipathy is actually directed toward Him in me; from you, I've learned that even and especially if my tank is running low, I must love them with His love. I am on call for Him. James tells me that "mercy triumphs over judgment" (James 2:13), and I have seen this lived out in you.

I also want to mention a couple of things that you both have brought to the forefront of my attention: the first is the sanctity of human life. I found a quote from Scripture to capture this: "A woman, when she is in labor, has sorrow because her hour has come; but as soon as she has given birth to the child, she no longer remembers the anguish, for *joy that a human being has been born into the world*" (John 16:21 NKJV, emphasis mine). That you both have spent well over half your life caring for those who bring new life into the world creates a remarkable energy to be around. I love to hear you describe this and that birth you've witnessed throughout your careers; evidently, no two births are alike. You are both good teachers, each in your own right and way. You have explained many an unknown procedure, surgery, and medical term to me so I can better comprehend the miracle of life and birth and the various processes involved in ensuring both mother and child survive the nativity. In your world, the sacred and the secular overlap daily, and you never tire of it. Josh, I have seen you demonstrate via "air surgery" how you might perform a procedure much in the same way I would draw a Russian letter in the air for a student.

Candace, your insights as a midwife, most assuredly one of *the* most ancient of women's professions, are as visceral for me as if I were actually in the delivery room. Both of you get in the zone as you describe "catching" a newborn, like it is some baseball game God has invited you to personally in order to bring forth yet another homerun hit, another miracle that is never commonplace to you. I now better appreciate how you could never imagine taking for granted each swaddling bundle by terminating one for any reason. We are His long before we are our parents, aren't we? And speaking of which, I also admire the hardy relationships you form with these mothers and/or couples. Your putting them at ease keeps the needs of the infant at center stage. That they request you for their second or third birth and that you have delivered babies of women you've brought into the world speaks volumes. I have known you long enough to have also watched you wait in quiet readiness and anticipation for when your own children would have children. That day has come, and I have seen the grandparents' glow that can only come from witnessing the cycle of love and life come full *Lion King* circle in your own family, and I am ecstatic for you. God has lavished upon you the gift of five healthy, happy, and vibrant grandchildren. They are your babies as much as your sons were unto you.

The second realm that you've both spent countless hours at is mission work. Candace, as of recent, that you have come to graciously bow out and work more so as to enable your husband to continue leading mission tours in the international field during his own so-called retired years isn't lost on me. You, too, have your own tales to tell, and those ones in particular from Romania I am riveted by, what with these people's displays of generosity as well as their old-world superstitions and suspicions which you have described to me. Before I met you both, I simply didn't fathom what it meant to be "mission-minded," let alone what all was involved for those having a heart for mission work. Now I do; such has been spurred in me and even more especially within Bonnie. I used to think if a person was Eastern Orthodox or Catholic, then, as a follower of Christ, this person need not be saved or helped. Now I know that adhering to traditions, participating in sacraments, and resting on the laurels of one's historical proximity to Jesus in no way measures one's personal intimacy with Christ. We need to know Him in a way that is closer than one's breath or the beat of our hearts. I used to wonder why a person would go *abroad* to help denizens of destitute places when there are plenty of unbelievers here at home in the U.S. of A. Now I get it: you are being obedient to His command to "Go into *all* the world and preach the gospel to *all* creation" (Mark 16:15, emphasis mine). Anyway, for the most part, in the States, the *name* of our Lord and Savior *is* known already. He *is* familiar to us; therefore, we can claim no excuse of ignorance. Unfortunately, we are lured off-course by pride or distracted by Satan's trappings of ease and luxury. Meanwhile, time's a-wastin', and there are plenty of folks in the rest of world who either have not been exposed to Him or they live in areas where it is dangerous to live openly as a Christian. It is a sin of great gravity, irony, and consequence that familiarity has bred contempt for Him here at home in our beloved nation and even in the homes of our own relatives. This is not the case with you. I sense such a bedrock of solidity and fullness of Him in your lives, it's no wonder I already feel at home when I'm with ya'll. Why? *You abide in Him.* If you'll permit me, I would like to say a few words to you each individually, and I will start with the queen of the house.

Candace, if ever there was a mother earth type, it is you. There could be no other profession than obstetrics that better suits you; delivery may expend much of your energies, but ultimately, it is a labor of love that gives back to you. You have *such* a passion for life, the delivering of it, the nurturing and protecting of it, and even the getting down and dirty with it — be it bodily fluids or planting bulbs in dirty, fertile soil — that your stamp and bearing on life makes us all the richer for it. You are the best of what woman was meant to be: mother, guide, and lover of life. I envy your grandbabies for their having such a one as you to follow and jump into magical sidewalk drawings and into the realm of the imagination, endless possibility, and wonderment. I love that you are a kinesthetic learner; mere facts and figures leave you high and dry. And your wisdom is wiser than words can convey. You breathe in and deeply feel the air about you as if you were some living barometer for any room's emotional atmosphere or spiritual bearing. You aren't squeamish about touching that which people only read about, and the pulse of life in any object fascinates or interests you. What you behold can become a part of you; it is as if you absorb its essence through your fingertips, be it the pain through the Wailing Wall in Jerusalem or contentment felt through the smooth skin of a newborn. Though usually buoyant, bright, and happy, I know you are one acquainted with the dark. When I catch a glimpse of melancholy, it makes me appreciate all the more your ability to shore yourself up with faith, family, and friends who mean the world to you. Your home and hearth are like a divining rod that points us to the good life.

It is no wonder you love nurturing your own small garden of Eden on Forest Walk. For me, your laughter is a song of praise to Him, and you bring Him glory with your beautiful smile and full guffaw, the kind that involves your whole person and beckons those around to join you in your joy. It brings me particular happiness when I spontaneously laugh along with you the moment when something has tickled us both. You have a powerful intuition and feel things before they are known, and I admire the mamma lion in you that defends your own. This protectiveness of yours I have personally experienced. At one of your grandson's baseball game we once attended, I unexpectedly caught sight of a middle-aged man who was obviously afflicted with the same debilitating disease my father had. Upon reading my pained expression, you quickly put your arm around me and ushered me off for a walk through an adjoining wooded path, diverting my attention to better things before I could get stuck in grief. I love riding shotgun in your ride because you crank songs from the sixties and seventies that bring you as much glee now as they did in your youth. More than most, you know that reveling is a form of exaltation, too. Even more, I appreciate the fact that we always have no-holds-bar conversations because with you, one feels free to ask questions a child might ask or to share an intimate moment or provocative thought that only the best of friends can express.

Speaking of which, in my early days of faith, when I related some of the details of my eclectic background that had proved a temporary road block to coming to faith, it was *your* voice I heard that said, "*Write a book*," so that my atypical story could be heard. The Holy Spirit used you to strike that notion within me, and I am forever indebted to you for this. It does not matter that our experiences and background are different because we have a shared and common future, don't we? In celebrating your sixtieth birthday at the Tea Room, I got to see slides pictures from your childhood, family events, and trips gone by. I was moved by your being in awe of the stunning beauty of Alaska; your display of patriotism at the Memorial at Pearl Harbor brought shivers down my spine. I loved learning about how your ambition, drive, and intellect burned within the young woman you were and about the women in your life who made such a difference for you. It's hard to turn the page because every meal and moment with you is like taking communion, be it pho at the Tai restaurant or fowl at a steak restaurant. I know if I up and called you again to ask if I could turn back around and stay one extra night at your place, the answer would still be an immediate and enthusiastic, "Yes!" My heart overfloweth with love and gratitude to you, Candace...

Josh, as I now turn to you, let me start right off the bat by coming to you in prayer. As new life enters your family, with your latest grandson barely weeks old, we come to the Great Physician again and ask him to eradicate a malignancy in your prostate. Who says there is no such thing as miracles? They still occur, and you are my proof. I firmly believe that your kidneys were declared free of multiple masses is the direct result of answered prayers from all over the world. Our Father listens to us when we cry out to Him; He is *so* good. I owe you a debt of gratitude I'll not soon repay. Though it's only been six years since I came to Christ, I have you in great part to thank for my greater understanding of Him, not that we can ever wholly have such this side of Heaven. Your passion for His Word is unrivaled by many I see who call themselves Christians. Your obedience, self-discipline, and perseverance drive you to your personal office — your sanctum sanctorum — and there, ultimately, to your knees. Here you study, pray, and pour over His love letter to us. I'm sure you ask yourself, "What more may I do for you, Lord, to serve and bring You glory?" As Bonnie and I got more involved in church, and the questions started to tumble in, I was so thankful and appreciative of feeling free to be able to turn to you with my questions, no matter how seemingly trivial or esoteric. You not only didn't dismiss them, you even asked others how to help you answer me, be it about the Holy Spirit's staying power, the relativity of time, or the fickleness of the people in Jesus' day. I still cherish your first gift: Henry Blackaby's *Experiencing God*. When I first saw its cover, I was shocked to think someone was trying to depict God, not recognizing the man to be Moses. Using it helped me to jumpstart learning how to approach reading the Bible. This workbook had me lucubrating even when I while on bus duty at school early in the morning. Your own sustained passion for learning about and growing in Him inspires me; indeed, you are one who breaks to mold: to your core, you are a man of science *and* of faith; they are indivisible.

More than any other person I know, you have shown me

that the two worlds, that of the rational and spiritual, the mind and the soul, the finite and the infinite *can* coexist peacefully *and* logically. Such a hybrid state may be a no-brainer to you, but your frame of mind, which is both brilliant and bold and yet humbled and awestruck, is not such I'd ever encountered. Regardless of how hard you or I or anyone could ever try, we all miss the mark, and efficacy crumbles because, as your favorite hymn attests, "the love of God is far greater than tongue or pen can ever tell." You have shown me we can take the Bible both literally and figuratively at the same time, that the symbolism of the one does not nullify the reality of the other! "'*All* things are possible to him who believes'" (Mark 9:23). The whole of its mystery is verified through the sum of its parts; although there are many writers, we find one Author. Not only this, when we come to visit and I directly face you, as Bonnie puts it to me, I am looking at "the boy version of her." Your duck feet, familiar mug, crooked smile, and sturdy fingers make me blink twice for their familiarity, but even more, you have the same yearning to build, to fix, to heal, and to sing and "to declare His glory." Such leaves me breathless and nearly moved to tears when I see it in double.

Your passion for mission work is undoubtedly *the* hallmark of your faith, and, without a doubt, the Lord is proud of such sweet fruit. I can't count how many times I've looked at your power-point presentations abounding in pictures of new converts from all over the world who have received His blessings and help through the hands and feet of *your* team. When I observe your assembly stations downstairs, what with all the dozens of vials and types of medical supplies, stuffed toys for children, and medicines you risk taking across the border, I feel like I am witnessing Christmas presents lined up and overflowing from under the tree. You are giddy from wanting to give. You prove to me that love does not have to be transactional; Jesus' love is *not* a business! You give something for nothing because it is what is needed, period. I shake my head in wonderment and am likewise inspired to put my faith into action. Just as moving is the look of deep satisfaction and joy on your countenance when you are aiding the destitute, downtrodden, or diseased. It is the look of His love that cannot be falsified or duplicated in any way other than through Christ-like action. No wonder you live for such trips abroad, where you can help save lives and dispense hope in Him.

Though you are technically retired and not receiving a living wage, you are surely earning nods of His approval by also helping those here on the home front through serving at your free clinic. Even though you live in chronic pain, with cracks and chinks in your clay pot, you still give it all you've got. Plus, now you've got your own grandbabies who slumber peacefully in your protective arms or lap. Not only do I want to thank you for opening your home and heart to me, and I also have you to thank for my first meal at Chick-Fil-A and that memorable and delicious spread you prepared one Thanksgiving that boasted of being practically carb-free! What *can't* you do? Finally, I smile to myself as I see your pride and joy come out in the form of bulldog statues in the lawn, the Georgia red that colors your walls downstairs, and the array of UGA insignia on many a personal item. All of this speaks of your desire to be a part of something bigger than yourself, and you celebrate the connections you create founded on Jesus. In fact, you are a living mascot for Him as well as a fan of your state team.

I could go on about you both, but I will put my pen down here. I'll end with the first passage I came to memorize from the Blackaby workbook because I see this is who you both are and what I now am, a branch having become engrafted as of late: "I am the vine, you are the branches. He who abides in Me, and I in him, bears much fruit; for without Me you can do nothing (John 15:5 NKJV). These words are now written on the tablet of my heart. I love reflecting back on when we watched in reverential wonder the sunrise that Easter morning along the Charleston harbor at the Battery. Not too far long from now, we shall meet Jesus, our bright morning star. Along with being your loving friend and family, know I am glad to be...

Your sister in Christ,
D.C.

April

Faith And Resurrected Lives

April is the month we typically celebrate Easter. This year on Easter Sunday, Pastor Mark revealed the architectural blueprint for our new church, which is to be launched and ready for worship in roughly a year. In this day and age, the likelihood of our or any church expanding, let alone relocating in anticipation of further growth, is astonishing. Our church is one that is not suffering from palsy or shortness of breath. We are thriving! We have a vision that includes wanting to give back to the community in a host of ways. There will be obstacles and pushback, so faith on fire is what is required. Whether it is a church or person whose life is being moved to the next level, there will be a birth of some sort on the horizon. Therefore, I have decided to devote this month to those who remind me of Christ in that they have experienced a resurrection in their lives which has renewed them in ways no one could have anticipated. They are not just survivors; they are "A CHOSEN RACE, A royal PRIESTHOOD, A holy nation, A PEOPLE FOR *God's* own possession" (1 Peter 2:9). No one seeks trouble, and God doesn't *cause* it, but when He *is* involved, pain can stretch, grow, and refine you. Even Jesus asked of His Father in the Garden of Gethsemane to take the bitter cup away from Him; He knew what was right around the bend, and, for a few moments, He would have to go it alone for what He'd chosen to bear for us. What love! Often times, it's in life's darkest moments when God is the closest to you. The women from this month have undergone trials and tribulations, which might make the hardiest of men faint. No one is left unscathed by the bumps or bruises in life, but we cannot sequester ourselves! Taking step after step in faith and overcoming trepidations and fears of the unknown, each woman here has arisen like a phoenix. One even has a colorful tattoo of this bird on her calf. Time and again, all have risen from the ashes to become stronger, even more beautiful, and more generous. These ones here have shown me what an extraordinary life looks like in real-time when you choose Christ as your mainstay, best friend, and savior. I'm here to testify to you that collectively, they have found, cling to, and continue to "have confidence before God; because [they] keep His commandments and... love one another..." (from 1 John 3:21–23). Each of the following women has been changed from the inside out; you'll see.

29. Mary

Meet Mary. She was a colleague of mine for over two-thirds of my career, but when I think of her today, what comes to mind is hardly the subject we taught or how we were both fellow teachers in the same department. She has been my confidante and one whom I continue to look up to for her wisdom, humor, and all she has been through. The quick version is that she is a survivor of cancer and not just any cancer, but pancreatic cancer, which has one of the lowest survival rates of any type. Did you know that to be considered a "survivor," you have to have been free from cancer for five years? Yes, I know that we each have an impending date with death, that, as they say, we are living in the dash that precedes an hour and year already set. When we walk alongside ones who have encountered a roadblock or some mudslide which has wreaked havoc in their world, we passersby can feel like we are rubber-necking. However, with Mary, I am so glad she shared her drive and will to live by letting us in on the process she had to undertake to get back to wellness. We in the department all knew her doctor by name, and we got a crash course as to how he was going to keep that bad thing from happening to her. No, I was not one of the five hundred who witnessed Jesus walking around during the forty days after He was killed by crucifixion. I did not put my finger in the gash in His side or in the hole in His palm as did Mr. doubting Thomas, but I *have* seen Mary make it, when, by all accounts, she should have been another statistic. Our will to live is also God-given. We who love those that have been stricken with affliction root them on. We know He is still in the business of performing miracles and resurrecting lives; it makes much of Him. So, when I see Mary today, be it is at Panera's to grab a bite for lunch, on FB to see what new adventures she's taking across the country or the globe, or in school when she happens to be subbing, I hug her for all I've got. She is such an inspiration to me for her strength and resolve, and I love her dearly.

> *Do you have a friend who has shown him or herself to be so full of faith and fight that even a brush with death that put her life on hold or in a tailspin couldn't keep her down for the count? Have you witnessed someone get up time and again, like a beat-up Rocky Balboa in the boxing ring, and it left you shaken and stunned to see such a will to live? Isn't it time you embraced her and thanked God she's alive? What inner resources has God provided you with?*

Read on to learn more about miraculous Mary.

"To be an artist includes much; one must
possess many gifts — absolute gifts — which
have not been acquired by one's own effort.
And, moreover, *to succeed, the artist must possess the
courageous soul.*"
"What do you mean by the courageous soul?"
"*Courageous, ma foi! The brave soul. The soul that
dares and defies.*"
— From Kate Chopin's, *The Awakening* (1899),
emphasis mine

April 7, 2019

Hello, Mary!

Surprise! Like catching an oldie but a goodie on the radio, I decided to write you a good old-fashioned letter. I can't believe it has been some seven years since we were working together side by side; time flies, and here I am within mere months of joining the rank and file of those consecrated ones who are in their active retirement years. Before any more time built up and the space goading between our points of contact turned into a decade, I decided to send you a post; hopefully, soon, an actual visit can take place. It did my heart such good to see you recently at school, and I took encouragement by your involvement in teaching the little ones, those who are openly, avidly, and unashamedly so eager to learn. As of recent, I have somehow had it put to my mind to stop, catch my breath, and reflect back over special ones vital to me, and you stand out like a bright beacon.

I remember when you first transferred to Admiral High; this was near the tail end of the first decade of my teaching, and I knew you then were a force to be reckoned with. I was not a little anxious to have your daughter in my class, and what with your divorce impending, it was no surprise she was out-of-sorts and stumbling, yet you were not upset with me when she faltered on my watch. Those chips fell where they did, and you did not clean up her spilled milk. In the long run, this made your daughter learn accountability and gain resilience, a life lesson many youngsters today are robbed of for their parents wishing to soften growing pains. You are both the kind of parent *and* teacher who gets right in the thick of life and *become* the change you want others to see. As always, our mantra is "*I do, we do, you do,*" and you showed your daughter what you told your students, that they are the kings and queens of their destiny. That said, should one falter and make his bed and lie in some lamentable place, she or he doesn't have to *stay* in it. You encourage growth in all whom you know: you lead by example and start with yourself. That's leadership! It is this quality of yours I'd like to celebrate now.

As my colleague of well over two decades, you and I have experienced triumphs and agonies that only we working day in, day out in the classroom intimately know. We have been privy to the "ah-ha" look of epiphany in a student's eyes who finally understands some particular point or nuance, the unaffected quips of wisdom that come from the mouths of babes, and the love that arises when we grow into a family. You are a champion of the underdog who suffers private pangs, injustices, and wrongdoings and can whiff out these ones like a bloodhound in order to get her students the help they need. You also have challenged many a freshman in your honors class, and they master and make connections between what they read on the page with life right under their noses. I love watching you teach because your presence radiates confidence, care, and intense personalness; you always respond with real regard and refer to your students by name as if they were the only ones who could rivet your attention. Indeed, by making a concerted effort to call them by name, you make children feel they are worthwhile, valuable, and unique, even while they sit among a group of often over thirty. There's no need to perseverate when you've already gained their respect.

To say you and I are "old school" could convey no greater compliment; we are of the generation of educators that puts stock in the classics, tried and true foundations of grammar, and the "practice-makes-perfect" process of learning to write. We know that to take English amounts to *so* much more than gaining snippets of our literary heritage or the foundations of our native language and its grammar. We also recognize that these aspects are golden in their own right, regardless of the public's perception or students' opinion of this or that course. No one will ever *not* need what *we* dispense, that is, the ability to give and take what's on our mind and heart with accuracy, depth, clarity, and pith. Indeed, our ability to communicate and reason is what separates us from the rest of living creatures. To gain what we give is to add wisdom and craft beyond skills, grades, and credits earned. Oh, we crave to have our students speak with the "tongues of men and angels" with love and *not* to be a "noisy gong or clanging symbol" (1 Corinthians 13:1).

Never satisfied with the status quo, you have also been one to model growth and improvement in yourself. You earned your master's degree in administration. Plus, you have taught us teachers how the teenage brain works and that the body-mind connection is absolutely fundamental to what we do. You introduced a system of writing whereby — thanks to you — literally thousands of students do not fear the often-daunting process of putting pen to paper by your introducing to us all the "Six Plus One" writing (and grading) approach. For once, a child's *voice* could be recognized as one deserving of as much attention or praise as her skill (or lack thereof) in conventions did our criticism. Much that we attempt to do in education seems to be a superficial and short-sighted approach to fixing the woes of even vaster social problems that afflict our country. We have seen a lot of changes in education, now haven't we? The tweaking of this or that standard and trying to impose a common core of curriculum can't succeed if at home standards are diminished, dismissed, or discarded. In this fast-paced world in which our children are brought up, often they are given shiny trinkets and end up possessing a warped sense of values. They mistakenly think quantity trumps quality, breadth is greater than depth, and substance replaces spirit. Oh, but we know differently, don't we?

Speaking of meaningful encouragement, yours is not limited to what we dole out to our students. Who else but you made sure *this* teacher attended graduation one year so that she could obtain her crystal apple in recognition of being awarded Teacher of the Year? Who but you made sure that vertical teaming had some teeth in it and found a way for us few who taught A.P. and honors to solidify our vision, approach, and sense of unity and purpose? Do you remember with fondness as do I when we the core four A.P./Honors teachers went to J. for our training? Such a trip promoting collegiate bonding and goodwill seems unfathomable and impossible now. Who but you held numerous pool parties at her own home to keep our department's spirits refreshed? Like me, you, too, have beheld many beautiful places and shared with students the wonderment of trips taken abroad. Yes, what merit *this* type of show and tell has! Pictures from scenes in the Mediterranean you've seen now decorate your walls at home.

I also shake my head in awe of your desire to keep abreast of the latest trends and policies in education. You not only don't shy away from change, but you also embrace it head-on, often stepping out in front of the pack, as was the case where, for example, being tech-savvy was concerned. As my department chair or our "queen," as we affectionately dubbed you, you walked the tightrope as the liaison between teachers and admin., and I got to see up close and personal what a thankless yet paramount role this is. Perhaps for the first time, through your eyes, I appreciated how the management of teachers fits into the mechanism of operating the whole school. As occurs within any family dynamic, you and I have been no strangers to conflict at work, and you have borne my mercurial nature. Do please know that I have felt and appreciated your patience with me as I was unraveling whatever mental knot I was in; not one of these particulars do I now recall more than your abiding faith in our friendship, and in the final assessment, a relationship like ours that has gone through a few glitches becomes the stronger for it. How could I not but admire you professionally *and* come to know you as my dear friend? I have also enjoyed many moments of humor and cheer, noticing the many ironies in life, and we have broken into hearty laughter more times than I can count. I love your laugh! Only the demands and impositions of a career and calling such as ours, that which is ever so more than a job, could temporarily impede more frequent contact.

As a woman, I would be hard-pressed to know one in my life who has been another of such resilience, pertinacity, and positivity; you represent our sex well. I'll never forget that you and I had neighboring and adjacent carrels. I would pass by yours every day and catch sight of those thick notebooks on your desk teeming with evidence against a man, your spouse, who had, among other transgressions and hurts, wronged your daughter. I knew I was witnessing a modern-day warrior. Oh, no, you weren't going to leave yourself a damsel in distress or permit your own princess to be treated as scullery maid or strumpet, and so you fought and conquered. For some reason, we are made to think that it is man who is to protect woman, and maybe this is the way it was intended, but down here in this most imperfect world, I have seen you rise to the occasion, and, time and again, provide refuge or asylum for those who need it, ironically including even those who have done you no good, and I include your own brother as one. How you handled your brother and his affairs, with such patience and grace, gave me the prototype to follow when I found myself in a similar position to have to do much the same for my father. You are also a guardian of the disenfranchised and disregarded. I have seen you stand up for those both in school and out who society, as well as the church, view as undeserving of rights and rewards, and when I came to Him, you expressed your concern for me, knowing that ostracism can also come in the form of condemnation. Your wisdom and experience at school had us calling you "life coach," and when practical matters such as dealing with this or that entity, including the Charybdis we call health insurance, we knew we could count on you. Speaking of health and being such friends as we are, I want you to know that, in spite of *and* because of the darker days you've endured, I know you to be a woman of great capacity and endurance.

The fact that, to your core, you love Kate Chopin's short stories and *The Awakening* is because you appreciate the ironies in her stories. After all, they reflect experiences and parallel core values you possess. We are ones who apperceive that the most profound truths and paradoxes to be pondered often come through seeming twists of fate. Mary, *you* are the artist who possesses the "courageous soul," and I have witnessed you endure your own dark nights, managing to keep afloat with your head held high even when you feel down at heart. Not even a diagnosis of pancreatic cancer could crush your brave spirit; if anything, it brought out even more the will to not only live, but survive and thrive, and now that you are past five years out (which seems to me to have gone by in a blink), that is precisely what you have done. The Race for the Cure you trained for and ran was more than a symbolic gesture; you ran for your life and won! There could be no greater triumph and gift for you than this new lease on life. Every detail that you were enabled to attend to as you navigated your way back to health, I believe, was God-given. Starting with *not* accepting a bleak and flawed diagnosis and seeking the very best care you could possibly find, you took the initiative, time and again. You made your own way out of the maze! Even I know the name of your hero and specialist: "Foxie," he who treated you with dignity and respect as he found a way to extirpate the corruption that is cancer. What you underwent, including the aftermath that followed, I do not pretend to understand; such cannot be captured in a sentence or a paragraph or in a book. When I think of your experience, bravery, and recovery, I recall something Flannery O'Connor said: "In a sense, sickness is a place, more instructive than a long trip to Europe, and it's always a place where there's no company, where nobody can follow, ...and I think those who don't have it miss one of God's mercies" (*The Habit of Being*). I am one of many who is grateful for His mercy in healing you.

Whenever I see you now — as I did just a month or so ago — I smile and feel the love we still have for one another, and I am gladdened that we can pick right up where we left off. Such is my clue and proof of an honest and genuine friendship. I see posts of you visiting your adorable granddaughters, going out west to bask in the warmth of the California sun, reveling in the pride and joy of a restored relationship with your son, your continuing to contribute to our school system, and even gallivanting off to Dubai. I know that your life is precious and full. I'm also sure there's many a cup of coffee poured and books read in the delight and comfort of your own private womb of a home. You remain that lifelong learner, a fiercely protective friend, a stalwart woman of strength and substance, and my friend whom I still and will always love. Now that it's soon to be my turn to join those whose time is the r own, I close this note and with an open heart and look forward to a visit with you in the near future.

Much love and affection,
D.C.

30. Bonnie

Meet Bonnie. Once you meet her, you can't forget her. In fact, you are now getting ready to read the longest letter in this bunch because she has meant more to me than anyone else here breathing. No label suits her; in fact, I am reluctant to call her anything but my bestest friend ever; Bonnie and I do life together. She is my miracle worker, and Jesus holds her in the palm of His hand, so we are both blessed. She and I have witnessed births and deaths and experienced tragedy and triumph together and think of one accord. Since it is true that "where two or three have gathered together in My name, I am there in their midst" (Matthew 18:20), she and I live in good company. Every day. My *Connecting the Dots...* is replete with mentionings of her. I think if Bonnie could tell you one statement that is important to her, she would want to say, please *do not mistake kindness for weakness*. Since Bonnie has experienced brokenness in life, she both appreciates and offers a lighter touch; gentleness works more wonders than the world would like to think. Like Mary, whom you just read about, Bonnie, too, was recently diagnosed with cancer. She is in year three of five of becoming that "survivor," and it is a hard row to hoe for having to endure additional aches and pains that are the gift of chemotherapy, that poison which gave her a new lease on life. In Bonnie's six decades, the list of trials and tribulations she has experienced are enough such that she suffers bouts of PTSD today. Most folks just don't get it because they can't see it. Her default mode for shock is fear, so when she is fortified by Jesus and can "sing for joy in the Lord" (Psalm 33:1), I see the miracle of faith renewed in her, and I am beyond grateful. You don't have to be a son, formerly profligate or prodigal, to see that in Bonnie, you'll find another one "after God's own heart" (adapted from Samuel 13:14). She is one you cannot take for granted.

> *Whom do you know that has experienced a lineup of calamities but claims no martyrdom or victimization? Who is one that is a beacon of hope and a prayer warrior but never seeks attention or the limelight? Who loves with no agenda or ulterior motive other than meeting a need where she sees it? Who is as indispensable as air for you, the wind beneath your wings, the one you need to shower with love today? Who is one who listens so well that she doesn't miss a beat, especially if she hears the beat of a broken heart? Who is one who shows us, time and again, that because <u>He</u> lives, she can face tomorrow (from Bill Gaither's "Because He Lives")?*

Read on to meet Bonnie.

> "A poor widow came and put in two small copper coins, which amount to a cent. Calling His disciples to Him, He said to them, "'Truly I say to you, this poor widow put in more than all the contributors to the treasury; for they all put in out of their surplus, but she, out of her poverty, put in all she owned, all she had to live on.'"
> — Matthew 12:42–44

Easter Sunday, April 21, 2019

Dear Bonnie,

As I start this letter to you, there's a little less than a week left until Easter. With the most recent CT-scan results attesting your being declared free and clear at this two-year marker, my attention hovers between being excited about Easter *and* brainstorming about a special way to say Happy Birthday to you on your sixtieth. To tell you the truth, my mind has been dictating a letter to you for some time now; thoughts of you command my attention. When a person meets another whom he knows is going to be "the one," the desire to express one's heart's joy, passion, and gratitude for a once-in-a-lifetime love can become overwhelming. If and when two lives cleave into one and the days turn into months then to years, the earliest pulses of the first *this*-es and *thats* experienced in doing life together turn into a steady groove, and, before you know it, you look back in wonder at just how quickly the time has passed. Often, we miss the boat and fail to say how precious are those ones who are nearest and dearest to us, those whom we cherish more than others, primarily for their uniqueness, realness, and faithfulness, to count just a few of the many ways. You are this for me, and I do not take you for granted or what we have lightly. Your steady love has girded my life; moreover, we share the same Cornerstone. Though you are as sure as a flame that shines from a single taper, the kind one can see from the road at Christmas time, I know you shy away from the spotlight and do not seek attention. Therefore, for this momentous birthday, rather than try to find the perfect card, I decided to write you a love letter to read to yourself and, hopefully, feel a glow within. My intent is to celebrate you while you're very much alive.

I will start with your own love of life. From the first walk we took down Apple Lane together, gazing at wildflowers you called out by name, I could tell you appreciated Nature and all her splendor. Though you lamented leaving the hustle and bustle of city life, the one brimming in A., I marveled at how you both designed *and* built your own home, a feat not many can boast of as an accomplishment. It all started with your choice to buy your trailer; the land you inherited became a part of you, and you treated it with sound regard. Like a beautiful garment one might wear, your yard had the look of love. Who could have known that the house and grounds you festooned would become a home for so many? Before I met you, I never had a garden fund, and you soon transformed my back yard into a small park, the whole of which got started up when we had to put my dog down. You hoped to boost my spirits, so you commenced with this undertaking. Since then, many trees have been felled to ensure the safety of the house; plus, more light now falls on many a perennial you've planted. Hostas, elephant ears, lantanas, clematis, and wild roses adorn our azalea-filled yard, and verdant grass now grows where there was merely moss on a lawn expanded to twice the size of what it once was. We watch in wonder on our back porch at the red-tailed hawks announcing their return home, at a small fountain you erected which offers refreshment to many critters, and a variety of familiar birds that come to any of the five feeders we put up. Robin redbreast frolicking in the fountain, the bright and bold hummingbirds preparing to kamikaze at his competitor, and the bluebird twittering with his inimitable song all delight your heart. There s not an inch of this land where you haven't left your mark. However, you are no average earthy flower-child; you are full of praise for the splendor and sustenance *He* has provided us.

Some might say that because you are not gainfully employed that you have little income. In the earthly sense, this may be so, but I would disagree because your pennies saved means dollars earned; your banking savvy in financial matters has boosted our welfare even more than if you brought home the bacon. It was you who encouraged me to speak to my father with respect and kindness that broke the ice and started the flow of income that relieved me of my hefty student loan. It was through your observing that interest rates were falling that lead me to refinance and save thousands. You also quickly encouraged me *not* to spend a dime of my uncle's life insurance inheritance, so that I might put it towards the principle of what I yet owed on the house. In every detail of how our household is run, all is good, and our life has never been more comfortable. The *survivor* in you not only put a roof over her own head, but she has also constructed and helped me complete many a house project, including a finished basement, a safe and beautiful master bath, replacing carpet with Australian cypress hardwood floors, expanding the back porch, and installing a radon fan. There are many more. When we travel down some highway or byway or if you happen to spy an attractive camper in the next lane, you get in the zone, and your brain goes a mile a minute in the flurry of imagined preparations being made for homesteads built in the pathways of your mind. Your longing for some modern-day covered wagon trek is due to this strong survivor instinct.

I have seen you in action, and there seems to be nothing you can't fix! I sit in helpless wonder as I watch you do anything that's needed, be it building, setting up camp, or making a fire upon which to cook the fish you likely caught! There has been no one more supportive in my life than you, and I thank you for all the encouragement you've gi en me behind the scenes. I am *so* grateful, and I, in turn, want to flood you with words of adoration. Time and again, you keep your promise to always be honest and say what's on your heart, and even though the truth can sometimes sting, we are always the better for it. Long ago, you came to know you could not depend on mere man to put bread in your belly or a roof over your head. However, since your youth, you have worked hard and have come back full circle to find one man, the Son of Man, who spoke softly in your ear, "Take My yoke upon you and learn from Me, for I am gentle and humble in heart, and you will find rest for your soul" (Matthew 11:29) and, despite yourself, *you have*. This quiet bending of the knee and a raising of the white flag has led to your settling into another calling that makes use of your ability to not only survive, safe-and-sound *and* sober but also to help others thrive.

This unique gift you've been given is that of healing. No, I don't mean you are a miracle-worker, but there *is* something built into your system that desires to take away pain and infirmity when you see it. I first witnessed this near compulsion and capability of yours to nurse ones in sickness through your caring for Kimberly, but that was only the beginning. Though you are no physician, the nurse in you possesses keen powers of observation, intuition, and attention, and when you see loved ones aching or those whose health has gone awry, you do whatever needs to be done to put them on the mend. You have described yourself as having an "emotional barometer" to assess the mood in any room, and this enables you to determine whether it's safe to come out of your shell. Still, you will turn this master switch off to move heaven and earth to aid those who are downtrodden, bedridden, or forsaken. You also now live with chronic pain in your feet, like some phantom ghost in the machine that cannot be pinpointed, and yet you remain optimistic and say, "Maybe *today* things will work themselves out." I ache for your pains. Your readiness to mend hearts or hurts is interlocked with your concept of what it means to be a friend. Oh, to be a friend of *yours*!

To be your friend is to experience steadfast devotion in a helter- skelter world that operates by here today and gone tomorrow. Not with you! You are that friend for life, through thick and through thin, for better or worse, yes, even in spite of the times you might wish you this weren't wired this way. Your credo is *"you must do what you can live with,"* and such a philosophy is one that will leave you with a life of few regrets. You came to watch Kimberly when you weren't even well yourself, and then it was my father you helped me tend to, he who in the throes of his decline would call you "Nurse Bonnie" with a simpleton's gratitude. We went from there *much* too quickly to your mother's aid. Despite mere weeks that you had left with her, you brought her comfort and assistance like no other, and, in turn, His Holy Spirit came to your emotional rescue by helping you recall and whisper to yourself, "It is well, it is well with my soul." It will take many more moments before "faith shall be sight," but it shall surely come.

Who else has been touched by your healing hands and loving heart? There are quite a few, but I'll start out with your big sister, who is closer to you than words can convey because "tomorrow and today, [you're] beside [each other] all the way (from Bread's "If"). In fact, you'd think you were next-door-neighbors for how attached you still are. I envy this. You both know and relish the value of *really* being there, come what may. Your sister has the kind of fierce protectiveness and undying devotion that is hard to find these days. I have experienced this care and consideration from her. I think that the kind of loyalty you two have for one another is stronger than any iron link known to man. You've more shared memories from youth than one can shake a stick at, and your sister happily recalls them all as if they occurred but yesterday. Plus, when we three get together, it's like we are having a slumber party or like we are on some personal episode of *The Golden Girls*, be we eating out or laughing together on the couch. Bonnie's sister is light and air and quickness to Bonnie's warmth and ground and steadiness, and they complement one another, especially when laughter and tears are to be found. They both have endured much and provided one another a lifetime of buoys. All these things and more, our Heavenly Father sees. Several of your close friends of well over three decades, each broken in their own way, has received your steadfast diet of love, moral support, and ready wisdom for the taking. Time and again, you put your money where your mouth is, and these ones have not only received support in the form of an attentive ear on the phone, but you have shown up in their greatest times of need. Through you, He shows out, even and especially to those who are reluctant to recognize Him. Your pledge to say, "Yes," to anything that comes your way shows your faith and commitment to Him and furthering His kingdom. Like David, you put yourself in

His hands and have said to you Father, "Try me and... lead me in the everlasting way" from (Psalm 139: 23–24). Often this readiness requires the patience of Job, all the more so, since many times you yourself have been down and out. In fact, you have been like some soldier of misfortune who has been stricken repeatedly, yet guardian angels protect you so that you can keep on keepin' on.

It's not only loved ones but complete strangers who have been the beneficiaries of your help; that's because you asked Jesus to *break your heart for what has broken His*. Even if you need propping up to do so, you heed His words from over two thousand years because they still ring loud and clear and true today: "Truly I say to you, to the extent that you did it to one of these brothers of Mine, *even the least of them*, you did it to Me" (Matthew 25:40). If that's the case — and it is — you have come to the rescue of King Jesus countless times! You have helped a stranger get out from under his wrecked car, checked on an elderly diabetic man who drove off the road, stood up for a fragile little girl who suffered abuse at the hands of her father, baked homemade birthday cakes for dozens of women who left abusive homes, and provided homeless ones prepared bags of food and hope along with a slip of Scripture. Why do you do this? Because *you can't turn a blind eye*. You don't give up just because someone gave out; you never promised to change the world, just to help the guy next door.

In short, you stop your ears to the sirens of cynicism and plain ol' *give*. Like the poor widow Matthew recounts, you hand out your two coppers whenever you get them. As a result, people in China you'll never meet will receive Bibles, and a poor and illiterate older woman right around the bend got her door fixed and now has a way to listen to the Bible on tape. Not only this, you helped provide an orphaned girl in Haiti food and education. Plus, there is a bright young woman from there, also the recipient of your time, love, and resources, who calls *you* "Mom." When you smile at some elderly woman in a store who is obviously alone, she is no longer invisible; she is beautiful. And because you said, "Yes," to a friend who found herself with child in her middle years, you have cared for a little boy twice a week for the better part of two years. He smiles broadly for feeling your sure love, has come to learn table manners, knows the name of Jesus, and calls you "Liefa," a name that breaks your heart for its sweetness. Indeed, I almost feel like an intruder upon your good works!

In addition to the philosophy of you must do that which you can live with is your maxim, *fail to plan, plan to fail.* Your preparedness for each day also helps keep our house in order; peace and tranquility blanket our home. I know I sometimes joke about "the covered wagon girl" in you whose purse, backpack, or suitcase are ever-ready for any contingency, emergency, hardship, camping trip, Y2K or, perhaps even the Apocalypse, but this has caused me to adopt such a stance for myself. I think of you every time I've been equipped for some unforeseen problems. For all the many trips we have taken abroad, it is *you* who have come to the group meeting with your suitcase neatly and efficiently packed, showing all that, yes, it *can* be done. Somehow you seem to place an entire pharmacy in your first-aid kit; it's like watching the feeding of five thousand when you dispense what's needed. Though we rely on Him, we use the faculties He's given us to ensure security for our nest and other little pockets in the world. I only hope you know how much I've come to trust, rely, and depend on you. Your foresight has brought about both sound financial planning and prudent legal decisions, and because of you, we have our ducks and affairs in order. Your mindset of looking ahead makes it easier to enjoy the day and to live in peace, and not only that, it leads to really living and not waiting until the so-called golden years to do things we haven't yet done. We have that now!

Of course, we can't foresee all ill-tidings, but we can make sure we get to explore what we want while we can. Going back to 2005, it was *you* who suggested the idea of not only taking students to Russia as I'd done for nearly a decade; you also promoted my going back to Greece. Since that year, we have globe-trotted our way to well over a dozen countries, showing dozens of students the value of traveling, and that's not including our own four summer-long stays in Greece. When I reflect on our life together, it's natural for me to see that we are "two drifters, off to see the world... after the same rainbow's end." Bonnie, I *am* your huckleberry friend! After my dad died and all of our hard work of taking care of him was finished, you sealed the deal and promoted a way for me to have no limitations as to how long I could stay in Greece. I give *you* full credit for my attaining dual citizenship in Greece. Not only this, it was you who saw to it that I even consider my *eternal* destination and gently got me to open my mind and heart, first to the possibility and then to the imperative of salvation. Now *that's* love!

Thanks to your looking beyond the horizon where the sun dips down and is extinguished by the ocean's cool breath, *eons* past the here and now, I know we have that blessed assurance that our Heavenly home awaits us. Before I became a Christian, I never knew, let alone heard the term of "prayer warrior," but now I know I live with one. On Saturday mornings, while many are out shopping or have their nose stuck in social media, you have an ongoing list of people for whom you pray, and our Father hears you loud and clear while you quietly talk to Him at the kitchen table or in your private chambers of the nearby water closet. This worn scroll of yours holds no rote or static formulaic approach; people are added and taken away, some stay on for years, and when others' needs have been fulfilled, they're replaced. That you have experienced fear and trembling is, in great part, the result of mischance, mistake, and misguidance from the past.

Please know I now pray for your courage! We have a Savior who will come to our defense because He doesn't go back on His word or His promises. You bare many scars, some seen, most not. It's no wonder you exalt in His healing like you do!

Why? You know that no one but our Lord raises the dead, offers fresh mercy daily, knows and loves you like no other, and gives us reasons for hope even when pain remains. I look over at you in church when you hear your sentiments echoed in song, and you can't *not* raise your hand, tears of joy streaming down your cheek, as *your* heart cries and *your* bones do sing, "It's Your breath in our lungs, so we pour out our praise to You only." You have told me that *songs are like prayers to you.* I have no doubt He sees His daughter's faith and her countless acts of compassion and is pleased. You may not be able to imagine what Heaven looks like, but we have "this hope ... as an anchor of the soul, a hope both sure and steadfast" (Hebrews 6:19). Therefore, you *can* rest assured that Heaven is not only real, but beyond vaster than a recently taken photo of some mysterious black hole, which is reportedly billions of times greater than sun and is devouring the insides of a galaxy millions of light years away. *Heaven is no black hole!* It is "the city [that] has no need of the sun or of the moon to shine on it, for the glory of God has illumined it, and its lamp is the Lamb" (Revelation 21:23). Until that time and place come to be, no matter what's going on with us or around the world, we will bask in love and "blessed peace with our Lord so near, leaning on the everlasting arms," as the enduring hymn attests.

I know and deeply respect that you have wanted to *get it —* your salvation — *right*, but that's why our faith is the only prayer we have, and you have never not had faith in Him. After all, it is not you or I, but *Jesus*, who is "the author and perfecter of faith" (Hebrews 12:2). For all of us who have been touched by your generous nature, I become amazed when you ask in genuine wonder whether or not He's disappointed that you don't evangelize. All great things begin with small things. Your actions speak louder than many with eloquent speech. Since that's the case, your hands and feet do more than many a mouth. Do recall that "it is much truer that the members of the body which *seem* to be weaker are *necessary*" (1 Corinthians 12:22, emphasis mine). I take comfort in reminding you that I may know and teach truths, but you possess *wisdom*, and you ought to know this fact by the countless times I've asked you for *your* take or impression of some particular interaction, behavior, scene, or nuance of expression we see, and in turn, for the holy way we ought to respond.

Speaking of gifts, though this isn't explicitly biblical, you possess that innate sense of direction, that inner "grid" we kid about all the time, that which keeps *you* from ever feeling the panic of not knowing where you are. I am so jealous of this! Even in the days before GPS, you helped me find my way out of a many a paper bag, neighborhood, and state of confusion. I have counted on you to help me navigate from point A to B more times than I can count. Your ability to know how things fit and work together transports your reliable bearings from 2 to 3-D, and you can design, construct, and build with the best of them. Who else but you have been the one to put together many a Christmas present that required assembly? You know the language of the builders we've hired, so in your giving assistance to them, I would be hard-pressed to know whom to give the credit for a job well done. I marvel at how your brain works, but even more so, your heart. It, too, has a keen and righteous inner bearing to know how to treat people, how to show respect and kindness, and how to silently guide ones so that they never take offense, let alone notice that you are gently steering them to the better life choice or a wiser decision.

When Jesus gave us the commandment to love our neighbor, it got stamped on your heart and is played out in your life. Your beneficence towards our friend and neighbor across the street, sweet B., scarred by tragedies in life, undoubtedly appreciated your friendship more than most. As time went by, your acts of kindness towards him were hardly random. My mom's husband, who, for all intents and purposes, is blind, has been the recipient of your help and consideration. You make sure he knows he hasn't been robbed of his dignity or your respect. Most people are nearsighted or prove unable to cast aside their ego to allow men like these to have the gift of a brief upper hand or the satisfaction of believing that *they* were the ones to come up with the idea, which, in fact, you had planted in them all along. As I sing your praises, I also know neither of us is the person we'd like to be yet, but now that we are living in The Way, yes, *His* holy way, as we walk this straight and narrow path together bound for glory, I need no map to know we'll both be there.

There are so many facets to who you are, that, like a jeweler inspecting some diamond, I could spend hours peering through a loupe and not do justice to praising your clarity, beauty, and priceless value. Your first words uttered were, "Do it myself," and due to your staking independence at a relatively young age, I have come to witness what I have long dubbed as the "Survivor girl" in you. Your own mother spoke of your resilience that actually helped bring you into the world; today His mark is evident in your life. Though long ago you may have thought you had reason to run from Him, you could not hide because He promised, "I will be found by you, and I will restore your fortunes" (Jeremiah 29:14), and He surely has. Despite your break, coronary infarction, cancer, lobectomy, and all the many other injuries, hurts, and surgeries you've endured, you are not only a Survival girl, but you "a new creation" (2 Cor. 5:17 NKJV). Victory is yours!

Life ain't easy, and you have borne more than many, yet for all the gentleness in your nature, there's still a fighter in you who is hungry for more in life even if you are on a diet. This is no fad, and, as you have said, *"I am not done."* More than once, you rightly chided me about the sands swiftly falling through the proverbial hourglass of time. That you have become hyperaware of the brevity of life has caused me to reevaluate my priorities. No, we cannot see into a crystal ball and predict the future, but neither can we bury our head in the sand like an ostrich. Yes, you can be Chicken Little at times. Nature and nurture have done a number on you. Still yet, you do not bear your scars like a flag; you keep them hidden and take it in the chin all without losing your composure. You are no Humpty Dumpty waiting on horses or men; King Jesus has put you back together time and again. You radiate a sweetness that is invisible to the naked eye but is discernible to any alert soul. It takes no time at all for others who ache to sense the balm in your spirits. That's why, for all who can weigh you down, many seek to drink from your deep well as they mourn their own struggles.

You tell me now that all you want now is *sweetness*, and immediately, Otis Redding's sage advice, "try a little tenderness," comes to my mind. All too often, in my imperfect flesh, what comes out of my fountain is not fresh, but bitter water, and the last thing you need is salt (from James 3:11–12) on your wounds. This letter is one such stand, a token of my love and allegiance that you can take to the bank and hold in your heart. I may not have your grandma's hands, but my own hope is to hold yours. I instantly feel love with the touch of your hand; it is a warm and grounding force. I am moved to see how our sweet Lord loves and lives through you; His light shines when you rock babies, when you sing His praises, and when you take joy in life's simple pleasures like laughter. I also want you to know how proud I am of your sticking with Him *and* me. I realize that this journey with Jesus has not been an easy one, and it's precisely *because* He is apparent in your walk that you have dealt with demons who desire to put you in darkness or despair. No wonder you turn away and try not to watch the wicked ways of the world!

Turning to the realm of song, the "Lyrics-dot-com" in you is always on point. I marvel when I observe your uncanny ability to recall words of songs while other memories can sometimes fall out of the sieve. How can this be? Simple: a poet resides in your breast. Even neglected lyrics, like those from the third and final verse in "Silent Night" still stir you, regardless if it's Christmastime or not. With great gratitude, you know you have received "love's pure light, radiant beams ... of redeeming grace." There's not enough softheartedness of the kind you possess to wrap around us all! You may *also* serenade us on your guitar.

Bonnie, I hope I have lifted your spirits with these words of truth and praise. You have proven to me that it is both wise and true that *kindness should never be taken mistaken for weakness.* In fact, the kindness I see you showing others *is* the fruit of His Spirit: "patience, goodness, faithfulness, gentleness, and self-control" (from Galatians 5:22). Though I have listed many whose lives you've touched, there can't be many more so than mine. Life is better with you in it, and I thank you for loving me. I may only have known you for a little over nineteen of your now sixty years, but I hope and pray that there are still *many* more decades left. For now, I'll end your Happy Birthday letter by having you recall the lyrics of a song which has become like an anthem for us: "For a friendship with me, you see, F-R-I-E-N-D special. You are my friend; you're special to me. There's only one in this wonderful world. *You are special.*"

All My Love,
D.C.

31. Sveta

Meet Sveta. She is my friend from Moscow, Russia, and I've known her since the winter of 1988, the semester when I went to school there, and she was one of my teachers. Since then, she has become my friend and one who imbues the Russian religious spirit for me like no other. I've been to her apartment in Moscow and had a homecooked meal with her husband and her. Another year, when she taught here in the States, I drove to visit her on campus; likewise, she has also been to my home. There have been numerous, albeit sporadic visits in between then and now, but each time we meet, it brings our souls respite and renewal. Sveta is one who has suffered particular hardship in her domestic life, and her patience, devotion, and the honoring of her word to God and man keep her steadfast and strong. I have seen her pick up and bear a cross that was not even hers to carry, and she does so without complaint. Her faith has sustained and provided her the courage, compassion, and patience that comes from above more than within. All I can do is admire her from afar.

The letter that follows is going to be different in that I am *not* going to translate it for you. No, it is not that I do not want to share its contents, but rather I want to highlight here the various gifts and talents God provides us each with that become the means by which we love others. After all, God uses people in a million different ways to reach people. For me, one of the means He has endowed me with is language; I translate. I am fluent in Russian and am learning Greek. Do not be impressed; you have your own gifts, talents, and ways that would amaze me! The Apostle Paul tells us that "God has appointed in the church, apostles, prophets, teachers, miracles, gifts of healings, helps administrations, and various kinds of tongues" (from 1 Corinthians 12:28). And then there is the brilliant analogy of the church being like the body, "one and yet [having] many members" (1 Corinthians 12:12), and each part is indispensable, especially the less visible or "presentable" (v. 23) ones. I may be a mouthpiece using my lips and tongue for spiritual service, but you may be His hands and feet or lap or open arms, and we are all the better for it! In Romans, Paul instructs us that because "gifts that differ according to the grace given to us, each of us is to exercise them accordingly: prophecy, service, teaching, exhortation, liberal giving, diligent leadership, and cheerful mercy" (adapted from 12:6–8). That covers everything; no one is without excuse!

What is <u>your</u> unique way of giving or doing or providing for others that shows you care? Oh, He dwells among us still!

<u>"Давайте восклицать!" — Булат Окуджава (1978)</u> Давайте восклицать, друг другом восхищаться.

Высокопарных слов не стоит опасаться.
Давайте говорить друг другу комплименты

—Ведь это все любви счастливые моменты.
Давайте горевать и плакать откровенно
То вместе, то поврозь, а то попеременно. Не нужно придавать значения злословью -
Поскольку грусть всегда соседствует с любовью.
Давайте понимать друг друга с полуслова,
Чтоб, ошибившись раз, не ошибиться снова.
Давайте жить, во всем друг другу потакая,
Тем более, что жизнь короткая такая.

28 апреля 2019

Дорогая Света, родная моя,

Мне кажется, что столько лет полетели до того как я последний раз видела тебя. Как я по тебе скучаю!! Ах, как у нас вместе хорошая, близкая, и прочная дружба. Между нами не существует такого недоразумения —только блестящая доброта! я хочу тебе знать, что ты для меня такой милый, близкий, душевный человек. В прошлом году когда я так сильно хотела тебя видеть в Москве, это было из за того, что бывшая поездка, к сожалеиию, мы не смогли встретиться. Ты единственная учительница и подруга души которую я больше ^{30} лет знаю, и так, я решила тебе писать настоящее письмо своей рукой от моего сердца твоему -- не просто через e-mail или Facebook. Да, конечно, это здорого, что мы можем видеть такие фотографии и статьи которые нам интересно; я благодарна за эту связь! Разве, я не знаю когда будет следующий раз когда я могу смотреть прямо на твоё лицо и слышать твой голос, и так, я сейчас вспоминаю несколько моментов в нашей жизни вместе. Я такой сентиментальный человек, и я так тебя уважаю и ценю нашу дружбу. Когда я была студенткой на твоём уроке разговора русского языка в Пушкинском Институтете, ты помнишь когда мама твоя умерла, ты вошла в комнату и решила объяснить значение корня слова "жизнь"? Ты была тронута и решила пригласить любого, кто хотел поехать с тобой в Загорск. Я была одним из немногих, кто пошёл с тобой, и я это никогда не забуду, насколько святым и особенным был этот опыт. Я чувствовала особую связь с тобой на протяжении всей моей жизни в вопросах сердца, жизни, Бога, и веры. Мы оба тоже встречались друг с другом в наших домах, и я надеюсь, что ты знаешь, что каждая поездка, которую я совершила в Россию, была направлена имена на то, чтобы увидеть тебя, даже если это только встретиться в холле такой-то гостиницы пить чай и разговаривать пока окруженна моими драгоценными студентами. Я поделилась с тобой своими самыми глубокими мыслями о вере, страданиях, и надеждах жизни. Я знаю, что мы продолжим поддерживать контакты друг с другом, но я хочу почтить нашу дружбу и выразить тебе свою благодарность и любовь здесь и сейчас. Мы с тобой оба верующие и знаем, что жизнь часто нелёгкая пока она ещё красивая. Когда моя маленькая помощь была отправлена тебе несколько лет назад, я действительно хотела отправить себя к тебе. Ты многострадальна, сильна, и мила в своей душе, и я очень восхищаюсь тобой. Я также хочу, чтобы ты знала, что твои Витя и Саша для меня тоже как семья. Позвольте мне сказать тебе снова и всегда, что я тебя так люблю. Нашему сердцу полезно слышать твой голос и говорить с тобой, как много мы значим друг для друга; ты для меня золото. Мы не должны терять одинокий момент, пока у нас есть время. я не знаю точно когда мы действительно можем видеть друг друга ещё раз; честно говоря, это мне горько- сладко объдумать. И так, пока мы шаг за шагом проходим через и танцуем в жизни, позвольте мне высказать, что я тебе желаю на всю жизнь счастья, здоровье, мира, и доброжелательность. Пусть у тебя будет доброта, нежность, искренность, смех, радость, и полная любовь. Я не могла бы не рассказать тебе все эти вещи в моём сердце, разуме, и душе именно для тебя. До тех пор мы снова встретимся, я посылаю тебе всю свою любовь, крепко обнимаю, и тепло целую тебя, Света моя. Я закончу своё письмо, сказав, что Христос воскрес!

Твоя близкая подруга и сестра по Христу навсегда,
D.C.

32. Natalia

Meet Natalia. She is another Russian woman I met who went from being one of my guides to becoming a close friend. I worked with her twice between 2009 and 2013 when I took two groups of students to Moscow and St. Petersburg, Russia, and, most recently, I sought her services as our guide when a trip was organized for a Footsteps of Paul in Rome Tour for fifteen members of our church this past June 2019. I freely admit that I do not know the intimate details of her life, but because she has a happy, open, and welcoming aspect; a love of travel that remains fresh and exciting; and a buoyant personality, we bonded easily and readily. She takes care of her *group* like she's its mother duck, yet she is also sensitive and responsive to the needs of the *individuals*, so all feel attended to and fussed over. There is an intellectual curiosity, free will, and drive within her that resonates with me. The year I requested her to be my guide on yet another prearranged tour to Russia and discovered that this could not be because she had moved to Italy, it left me speechless! I was filled with wonderment, concern, and questions for her. Would I see her again? What prompted such a move? How could we reconnect, work and/or visit together? The long and the short of it is that she fell in love with Italy, and she took the leap of faith by moving to her new home-away-from- home. Evidently, the spirit of the Italian people matched and aligned with something deep inside her, and she was emboldened to start her life anew there. I cheer her on every day!

Who is someone in your life that followed his dreams and heart and made a daring move to a new place or position? Whom do you know that has gone out on a limb and taken a risk because to do otherwise might make her feel like she died a little on the inside? Contrastingly,

*who is one that has remained ever- faithful, steady, and
on your side, yet during a time when you had wanderlust,
she or he was content to stay at home? When you came
to discover that you traveled the world but to end up next
door, did you meet them with new eyes and appreciation?
Who is someone you adore that loves people and doesn't
know a stranger; therefore, they are home no matter where
they hang their hat?*

*Read on to learn more about a soulmate of mine,
Natalia, who, time and again, has followed her dreams.*

"Who can turn the world on with her smile?
Who can take a nothing day, and suddenly
make it all seem worthwhile? Well, it's you girl,
and you should know it
With each glance and every little movement
you show it. Love is all around, no need to
waste it.
You can have the town, why don't you take it?
You're gonna make it after all
You're gonna make it after all!"
—Taken from "Love Is All Around," better
known as *The Mary Tyler Moore Show* Theme
Song, written and performed by <u>Sonny Curtis</u>
(1970)

"I believe there are some natures too noble to
curb, too lofty to bend..."
— Abigail Alcott, Louisa May Alcott's mother,
said while referring to the *Little Women* (1868)

"Trust in the Lord and do good;
Dwell in the land and cultivate faithfulness.

Delight yourself in the Lord;
And He will give you the desires of your
heart."
— Psalm 37:3–4

"Луч́ ше один раз увид́ еть, чем сто раз услыш ать."
                    — Russian proverb

April 29, 2019

My Dear Natalia,

Please forgive me! It has been nearly seven months since I last saw you, so I know that this letter is *long* overdue. I have much to say, and it's hard to know exactly where to begin, so I'll start with an explanation of the quotes I've handpicked for you. I'm not sure if you have ever heard of *The Mary Tyler Moore Show*, but it was one of the most popular sitcoms of the early 1970s and one that ran for seven years; I watched it faithfully as a girl. The show became an anthem of sorts in that it showed how a liberated and independent woman might live happily and successfully. There is an unforgettable moment at the show's opening, its theme song playing in the background when, at the end of the sequence, as the central character is walking among the bustle of people at the Nicollet Mall in Minneapolis, she spontaneously tosses her hat way up in the air. *She'smade it!* Every American of my generation can remember this iconic image. For me, this recollection still makes us smile, knowing that her spontaneous show of freedom, of taking life by the horns and throwing caution to the wind to follow her dreams, is met with sweet success and a sense of personal triumph. There was something so sturdily regular, fresh, and unassuming about Mary that she was our every girl, and if she could do it, so could we! Natalia, you have that same grace, goodness, cheer, and resolve in you, and, truth be told, when I picture you in my mind's eye, I am mentally singing this song. I imagine your broad smile while you, too, toss your beret in the air. You have followed your dreams!

The Russian proverb that says it is "better to see once than hear a hundred times" rings true, and by now, you have amassed so many "onces," that I am sure that you could write your own guide book for travelers. Quite recently, I saw the film adaptation of *Little Women*, a nineteenth-century American novel written by Louisa May Alcott, and I was struck by the quote uttered privately from mother to daughter. Mrs. Alcott recognized her daughter's adventuresome spirit, bright mind, and bold nature and realized there would be no compromise or containment for who she was at heart. I don't know if you had such a mother, but if you did, let me say that, like her, I would want to say that I am incredibly proud of you! You have not only gone out on a limb, but you have also flown the coop and moved to a country whose people have the same sunny disposition and merry temperament as yours. Though Mother Russia will always be your native soil, I'll bet it felt like coming home when you found Rome, the Eternal City; she became the capital of *your* world. And though many eschew the topic of religion, I know that you and I share a deeper bond than most; in our faith, we are sisters — *family* — and there is a place within you where your soul abides that gives you heavenly resources unknown to mere and mortal man. You are instinctively and respectfully obedient to the commands of the thirty-seventh Psalm mentioned above, and the beauty and bliss that radiate from you is a testament to His Holy Spirit dwelling in you. It is apparent that He has given you the desires of your heart, and for this, I am elated!

You might not know it, but when you and I met in 2009 on my then sixth tour with students to Russia, my father had died three months before this; Bonnie's mother had barely been buried two months prior to our departure. We were then weary, but you brought us a cup of cheer. Your kindness, generosity, and attention to detail are not just aspects of how you are as a guide and teacher; these qualities are an intrinsic part of who you are. Your joy, optimism, and caretaking make traveling with you at once easy, engaging, and unforgettable. Though it is always pleasing for me to be in Russia, the land my soul adopted when I was just nineteen because it fulfilled a part of me that yearned for a geography and culture that my father had *temporarily* forsaken — his own heritage, this particular trip brought about a resurrection of my spirits, in great part, because of *you*. In no time at all, you quickly went from tour director to friend for life, and for that, I am grateful.

Maybe you wonder why I love Russia so much. Like you, I was baptized Orthodox, and the faith of my father courses through my veins. As you well know, like Rome and Constantinople, Moscow is also placed on seven hills, and she is referred to as "Muscovy"; centuries ago, this made her synonymous with Russia itself. Every time I have come here and even though I know it is not actually factual, I get reminded that this city is the repository for safeguarding the Christian faith. One of my favorite quotes proclaimed by a Russian monk in 1510 to Grand Duke Vasiliy III is that "Two Romes have fallen. The third stands. And there will be no fourth." It may not seem to hold true any longer, but I do associate Russia with this sacred charge, and it stands as at least a partial truth in my soul, where I also carefully guard my faith. All that withstanding, my rational mind and confidence sharply correct me: our love of God and Son and Spirit is *not* based on geography or culture; the living God does not occupy a place but a holy space within us believers. He resides inside those who love Him. It's a love story made in Heaven that dwells in the saved soul — *our* souls!

I return to our link to another place in Russia. That you still hold keys to your apartment in St. Petersburg is not lost on me, and when we talked about your having a dual residence (and I, my dual citizenship) this past summer, I can't tell you how many times since that I have thought about coming to visit you there.

St. Petersburg is attractive to the westerner because it shows thoughtful and systematic city planning, logical organization, a familiar grid of streets and city blocks, and a charming neoclassical architecture. Warm shades and pastoral hues of pink, butterscotch, and coral not seen elsewhere bring the buildings to life. I can't help but imagine what it took to build this city atop a swamp, this city "built on bones." Therefore, for me, Dostoevsky best captures her essence when he describes her as the "most abstract and premeditated city in the whole world." The bronze statue of Peter the Great, gifted by Catherine the Great, stands out as a haunting testament to her sacrificial beauty on Senate Square.

I'll tell you a secret: I wish that this Venice of the North, this City of White Nights, was *not* the "window to the west" because what all Russia has taken from this direction is hardly the best. With the collapse of the Soviet Union, I have seen with my own eyes that the worst of the west rushed through the open window and blighted Russia with greed and materialism. Of course, such occurred because human nature is the same everywhere; we want what we want when we want it. I do not idealize the atheistic state that robbed Russians of individual initiative and centuries- held evocations of her faith. For this alone, I would not go back in time. The complexity and depth of this country become the fertile soil that became your home. Those from southern climes do not understand the value of a blanket of pristine white snow and the purifying effect it has, the goodness that penetrates one's soul by gazing at a grove of silvery birch trees or a strength gained by riding the rails and looking out onto a clutch of dachas or some ancient cemetery with a golden fall foliage as its backdrop. The Russian language I adopted is your mother tongue, and when I speak to you, my brain enters a different mode and claims an identity that satisfies. I know you understand what I'm talking about. I've heard that the study of this mental shift known as psycholinguistics investigates what happens to our brains as we enter into an esoteric region of cognition, association, and emotional texture through the words, idiomatic expressions and grammatical constructions we use. They impact our self-concept, and we need no passport or visa, just a calling within. You and I possess that alter ego and therefore are kindred spirits; for all I know, you are quad-lingual, going beyond Russian and English to speak Italian, and perhaps even Georgian.

It was the end of my seventh trip to Russia in 2013, and my second tour with you that, again, we saw and did much more than was listed on the itinerary. I learned that, like me, you, too, have a split identity: your mother is Russian and father Georgian whereas my mother is American and my father is Greek. Our fathers are the wild card in the mix. I realized that this was yet another reason for clicking the way we did and do. I know next to nothing more about your background, but based upon what resonates between us, I extrapolate and believe I understand your nature relative to my own stock and store. I wonder: do you have more than your father's dark eyes and hair? Did he pass on an energy and passion that comes from his home of majestic mountains, monasteries, and fortresses? Does the optimism, enthusiasm, and reverie that sprung from an ancient soil known for its wine, spectacular Caucuses mountains, its chivalric people, and horseback riding find itself residing within your breast? I think the answer is *yes*. But the capacity for endurance, patience, and suffering in the Russian soul that is manifested in your inner quietude, care, and sensitivity, I speculate comes from your mother. No, I do not know this to be so, but what I can say is that there is no one like you, Natalia. You are at once beautiful and sophisticated, genuine and joyful, all in one complex and serious and wonderful person. I celebrate who you are and what you've done with your life. You share your love of travel, your wonder of the world, and, most of all, your love of people everywhere you go, and I am so glad to be one of these!

Another aspect of possessing two cultures in one frame is that you search and seek a place that matches your nature, and

I appreciate the fact that for you, it is Italy that has captivated you. She is the incarnation of your warm nature that lives to love, to explore, to act, and to sing. Your laughter comes easily and is a delight to all. All the finest that Italy is known for is an intrinsic part of you: a renaissance of art and music; a reverence for what's holy; and a spirit that is free, light, and merry. I'll wager that there are those there who do not appreciate the extent and expanse of your character; they may even be capricious or careless, perhaps even occasionally leaving you feeling like a clown who cries on the inside. I do not know this to be fact, but I can tell you that I feel protective of you because even a people-person can feel the pang of loneliness or disappointment when she tries to find a secure harbor or safe haven to attain rest or comfort, far beyond harm's reach. Not all supports are made of steel; therefore, let's you and I recall that we always have our faith, "this hope... as an anchor of the soul, a hope both sure and steadfast and one which enters within the veil, where Jesus has entered as a forerunner for us" (Hebrews 6:19–20).

I have no doubt that it was a divinely ordained decree for you and me to work together this past year as we plan and prepared a Footsteps of Paul in Rome trip for a small group from my church. Most had never traveled to Rome, many never to Europe. You and I worked like a hand in glove; let me compliment you again on the perfection of your bringing my plans to fruition, down to organizing the last details and then some so we could see with our very eyes where Paul stood and what he did during his final days in Rome. And don't you find it fascinating that the greatest missionary who ever lived, this Saul-turned-Paul, a Pharisaic Jew, was also a Roman citizen *and* one who spoke and wrote in Greek, all to reach the Gentiles? We are his modern-day recipients and ones who appreciate such a dynamic identity. So many more things fell into place in our short stay that I'm sure you would agree that He had His hand on our plans! We did it all, from seeing the Vatican — yes, even downstairs where Peter was buried — to the Catacombs, from hearing the thunderous peal of a grand organ inside Saint Paul's Basilica to standing in the immensity that is the Colosseum. We connected the sacred with the secular. And that you and I got to work together as professionals, as believers, as fellow guides and lovers of travel, and most importantly, as friends, made this one of the most special tours I have ever led. There is not a week that goes by that one or more of these folks doesn't speak fondly of you, and they are still in awe of what they saw. When the final tour I'd planned to Russia in '18 got waylaid due to security restrictions, who would have known that, as it turned out, I would still get to see and work with you? Therefore, all that is near and dear to us — our love of the Mediterranean clime and people, the fidelity to our faith, and the mutual admiration and affection we have for one other — God saw fit to bring together in this profound way. We left too quickly for my satisfaction, and so I take my time here writing to you, Natalia.

May I say again that I admire you incredibly for taking the leap of faith and being courageous enough to cut the strings that kept you in the security of your home in Russia and that let you fly to the place that matches your spirit? It is commonly thought that Icarus scolded Daedalus for flying too close to the sun and that, in his folly, his son dismissed reason and paid the price. However, I think just the opposite: if we don't follow our dreams, which sometimes have us brush perilously close to the sun, we might die from staying put and letting hopes lie dormant. Therefore, I lift you up and applaud you for following your vision; it shows in your bright spirit. The day before the group arrived in Rome when you and I got to catch up and spend some solid one-on-one time together, I asked you about whether or not the Russian in you had anyone there who truly understood you; perhaps you hungered for such contact. I, for one, appreciate the bittersweet price for freedom that brings both gain and loss. May I also confess that I am not a little envious of you because I only spent four months in Moscow, and though I have been to Greece four times just a week shy of staying two months each trip, I have not yet taken the plunge like you so as to bask and bathe and bide in a land that brings new life. You inspire me!

I will put my pen down to embrace and kiss you three times, Russian style. Let this letter be a small token of my love and affection for you, my sister, friend, and fellow globe-trotter. Maybe the next time I see you will be back in St. Petersburg, Russia or in some sunny spot in Greece. Until then, I thank you for your friendship.

With much love and a thousand smiles,
D.C.

May

Mothers Of Life And Joy

The American transcendentalist, Ralph Waldo Emerson, once penned, "What potent blood hath modest May," and the Austrian composer, Gustav Mahler, echoes our sentiments when he wrote, "With the coming of spring, I am calm again." Still, for me, I choose to usher in this month's chosen ones by celebrating a few women who are ardent mothers to their core. To be a mother is to possess a role so deep that it never stops; it's as invisible as air and indivisible as flesh and blood. You don't need me to tell you that everyone from grown men to little girls dotes over their moms on Mother's Day. Some gloat, others gush, and some guard their display of love. I hope you, too, shower your own or one like a mom with your well-wishes, words of love, and demonstrations of gratitude. After all, she is the single-most person in the world with whom you have the longest and most complicated relationship. She may or may not have given birth to you, but she is the woman you call *mom*, *momma*, *ma*, or *mother*. Bar none, there's no one in the world like her. Yes, of course, our fathers are in our hallmark hall of fame! I absolutely adored mine! Many consider men to be the ones who ought to be the spiritual leaders of their home; however, this is not always the case. In fact, many men are not in charge, and some aren't even at home. More often than not, I would say that it is our mothers who are the ones wholly involved in the mundane details and who remember all the significant markers of their children's lives. It is they who inculcate us with their core values, honor us with their spirits, and fill us with a backbone of love. Mothers introduce us to our nebulous and nascent understandings of morality, ethics, and spirituality; they implant us with their religion or leave us with their void. We record them with our souls. In fact, they know our core before we can speak a word, will recognize our voice from among a sea of children, prove time and again ready to come to our aid or rescue, and will prop us up even if we are middle-aged. I still recall looking at my mother in wonder when she told me *she already knew who I was before I was born*; she knew what my name would be. My mom needed no ultrasound to feel the heartbeat of love she had for me. Our Heavenly Father saw to it.

We expect *so* much of and from our mothers. As a result and in large part based on what they have done to or for us, they get more praise *and* more blame than anyone else in our lives. Perhaps we resent them for an emptiness or chasm they've left within us due to a time in their own life when they were emotionally or otherwise unavailable because of some human weakness or despair, but I would contend that we are not scarred for life. I also realize that not all women who are mothers embody nurturing and selflessness or fortify their children with words that uplift and validate. Not every mother's default nature compels her to support us unconditionally; maybe nurture stepped in somewhere and marred her sense of worth so that *she* was left a little off-kilter. Perhaps she was catered to for so long that she herself is like a spoiled child, or maybe the case was that her parents were harsh or exacting that now she can be demanding. Conversely, she may have gotten hurt to the point where her esteem and worth became so damaged that she is a ghost or shell. She may feel invisible or unwanted. *Give what you want to get* and no one will be the worse for wear; that's a promise. There are also plenty of women who have never given actual birth but who provide more for their stepchildren or adopted babes than the women who delivered them ever did. Most moms give 'til they're all tuckered out, and then they give some more. Sure, at times, some play the martyr, but I've come to learn that it's the ones who say the least who have sacrificed the most.

I take the time to touch upon the complex gamut of what we can find in many a mother. The ones on my shortlist here are a group of women in my life who prove that soft and bold can coexist; their love doesn't fail, and they never seem to give out, even and especially if *we* feel like giving up. Each of these women is endowed with a reflex to give, and, as a result, they remain involved in their children's lives even though they are adults and parents in their own right. I owe them a personal debt of gratitude because I, too, have fallen into their orbit of love, and my life is all the richer for it. I hug them here for all I've got.

Oh, do not wait for Mother's Day to come around!
Please take a moment and thank your mother for who she
is. For no apparent reason and for every possible cause,
tell her you love her today. I know I will!

33. Hannah

Meet Hannah. She is the mother of four children, three of whom I have taught, two of whom traveled with me on tours to Europe as a part of their family vacation, and one of whom I taught in two different courses and who accompanied me on four trips abroad. Hannah makes sure her children see the world — preferably alongside her; her zest for life and generosity spill over into her children's lives. Even today, she sees to their needs in ways and means that are less direct but still as potent as when they were little. If you met her, you would be drawn to and instantly like her. In Hannah, you will find one who has a hearty laugh, an open and curious mind, an earthiness, and keen intuition that makes her at once familiar, comfortable, and wise. I can't imagine life without her in it. Though she may sail the seven seas, you will spot her right by her husband's side, and he is a rock and anchor and gentleman in his own right. They are well-suited and perfectly matched for one another though they couldn't be more opposite in manner. She is as garrulous as he is quiet, and she finds words — many of them, which he communicates through eye and gesture. Hannah's maternal strength and sense have been heavily tried with a tragedy no parent ever should have to bear: not too long ago, she had to bury one of her beautiful daughters, and it nearly knocked the breath out of her. Nonetheless, I find in Hannah a kindness and consideration that still knows no bounds, and every time I see her or have dinner with her husband and her, it is like a new adventure has begun again.

Who is a woman you know that has a passion for
what's rustic, real, and a little unkempt? Who is a
woman you admire one who "thinks on these things,"
that is, the "true, noble, right, lovely, admirable,

excellent, or praiseworthy" in life (from Philippians 4:8 NIV) and celebrates them in many bright ways? Who wears her heart on her sleeve but guards her own with her life? Who is united with her husband where it counts and appreciates the differences that make them each tick? Who with everything she does makes you feel special and loved and appreciated? Who will laugh with you as readily as she will mourn with you?

Read on, and you' ll meet Hannah.

"Now this *I* say, he who sows sparingly will also reap sparingly, and *he who sows bountifully will also reap bountifully*. Each one must do just as he has purposed in his heart, . . . for *God loves a cheerful giver*.
— From 2 Corinthians 9:7–8, emphasis mine

May 5, 2019

Hello, Hannah!

With the world newly green and lush during May, we celebrate everything coming back to life *and* honor our mothers who give us so much. Many mothers love more than their own children. Therefore, of the women I know who are particularly strong mothers, I naturally think of *you*, Hannah. If I may, as a way of showing my love and appreciation for how much you have impacted my life, I would like to count the ways and think on the bountiful good *you* do, day in and day out. I'll start with your children, formerly my students, who are now adults. It has now been close to twenty years ago when I taught your oldest daughter, she who had an intentness and passion for learning and stood tall in strength because her pitch and core were shaped by all that is joyful and righteous. I knew even before I met you that this young woman was being groomed and encouraged to become a wise, caring, and capable person and mother. As just a symbol, she was and is as beautiful as the Fabergé eggs she spoke so knowledgeably of and shared with our class.

Years later, when I taught your youngest daughter and then your son, I realized that this was no fluke or one child wonder, but that your brood ate a steady diet of cheer, confidence, and substantive character-building qualities. I saw this in the classroom before I witnessed it out in the world. Children are their own persons, but they inevitably reflect those from whom they spring and who raise them, so when I see the best in them, I know it is your brand of love I see in living color. You say your youngest daughter is more like her father by noting the fact that she is attentive to detail and likes things just so. Her eye for beauty, her precocity, and her instinctively knowing how the puzzle pieces of our lives fit together come from you. Still, on her wedding on a day, when all others should blur behind the most beautiful moment in a young woman's life, she made it a particular point to come over and embrace and sincerely thank me for coming. I knew she meant what she said applied to my being a part of her life and not just the evening. Gratitude is a learned stance, and she emulates this quality which she observes in you. At her nuptial ceremony, we witnessed your daughter express her gratitude for *all* of those who helped her arrive at this point, including her knight to whom she gave *her* heart as well as her father who gave *his* away in giving *her* away.

When I turn to your son, now halfway through his third decade, I still see the avid student in him, the kind of kid whose attentive gaze and stance stand out in a classroom for his apparent desire to soak up the kind of knowledge which transforms, not just provides facts for a test. He is no mere sponge; this young man mulls, questions, and chews on what he learns as if it were cud, so much so that what he ingests becomes a part of him, and he can recall this or that fact as it relates to the vaster landscape. To have taught him in both American literature and the Russian language further fastens him to my life. That *both* of your youngest two have musical souls is noteworthy, and although talent is something one is born with, how that talent gets fostered, developed, and grown is due to countless hours of lessons, encouragement, and facilitating. So, when I hear your daughter sing some gutsy blues or poignant torch song or witness your son's robust voice booming through the choir, I am seeing a part of *your* spirit in song, and I am doubly moved. On one of our many trips, I will never forget sitting down next to your son, both of us in awe and relief for *finally* having found the source of what we were sure to be angels singing. He and I simultaneously heard and were drawn beyond our volition to quickly seek unseen Russian liturgical singers up in the heavenly portions of a church. We silently sat in reverence and felt as if, in hearing them, we were facing God. And that he and I couldn't *not* climb up, up, up in tower after tower to behold the full expanse of some city or panorama of even more exceptional beauty surely springs from your desire to partake of more from this life you love. His ease, readiness to laugh, and primitive impulses I believe come from you. You have an uncontainable joy and a keen mind that takes delight in irony. There is something within your son that is atavistic, that has the stamp of your Nordic print on his being that cannot be denied no matter how enlightened he becomes. His appreciation for that which is traditional shows he yearns for what is time-honored, meretricious, and of substance; though this runs deep in the veins of your husband's system, your inner compass magnetically aligns with these enduring values as well.

You married a man who could not be more of a gentleman, he whose heart is kind and honorable, humble and reliable. You and your husband balance one other organically because your center of gravity leans towards what's unaffected, righteous, and elemental. After all, sophistication, class, and education are arid and dry if we don't experience them in the flesh!

We have touched the naval of life with our fingertips at the Omphalos of Delphi! Your husband is the perfect yang to your yin; he is the sure, steady, and quiet type to your support your energy, passion, and overflowing cup of love and verve. At the moment a compliment comes your way, your lightning-quick wit will deflect and spring forth a decoy via some humorous or earthy statement. It is as if you have an instinct that *we must remain humble in life* and not take ourselves too seriously. Oh, you know the blows of real pains borne, so where lightness can be grasped, you are there for the taking *and* giving of it. Your hearty laugh, your open heart, your analytical mind, your depth of understanding of human nature inspire and, at times, overwhelm me. You know that to *really* live, we must see all we can *and* with those who mean the most to us. Why? Life is best when we share and travel through it *together*, and you make this happen time and time again.

I want to celebrate the archetypal explorer in you. Like the geologist who investigates the dynamic physical history of our earth and like the archeologist who sifts through the rubble to excavate and examine the lives of early peoples, you are a modern-day pathfinder. Truth be told, with all the traveling you have done on my watch and have toured with your family on your own, I wouldn't be surprised to find you standing etched among those famous navigators in Lisbon's Monument to the Explorers! I attempted to look up apt quotes on traveling to perchance find one that would capture your essence, but as there were so many good sayings, unsurprisingly, not one was sufficient to fit the bill, so I will take your lead and choose *more* as my launching pad. How could I possibly be conservative when there are so many moments and memories *you've* birthed, created, or orchestrated? I do not pretend to know the width and depth of your life, so let my pen serve more like a Polaroid than a Nikon to chronicle more of the fabulousness that's you! I am still sore at and therefore, won't quote Bourdain because he snuffed short the best journey of all. As it turns out, Rick

Steve's was right: travel is "intensified living," and the ultimate souvenir is "a broader perspective." Following are several more fitting expressions.

> *"Like all great travelers, I have seen more than I remember, and remember more than I have seen."*
>
> —*Benjamin Disraeli*

Our first trip abroad to Italy and Greece in 2010 undoubtedly has been one of the best tours I've led, and I have you in great part to thank for that. Such energy, passion, and love we packed into that trip, be it during the first days in Rome, when our guide became our own private gladiator who with great pride showed us both the sublime and profane. We took in the grounds of Capri as if *we* were the celebrities, initially not knowing on which syllable to lay the stress, but thrilled to take in the illustrious grandeur, what with her turquoise grottos, limoncello, pizza Margherita, and sumptuous estates on clifftops belonging to the stars. In Florence, we in wonder took in Michelangelo's *David* — this after having beheld his *Pietà* and ever so much more at the Vatican — and we walked among the centuries-old cobblestoned streets with architectural, historical, and religious wonders literally bounding around every corner. Among dozens of other recollections from this trip, I am smiling to myself, remembering dancing in Delphi and then cruising the Greek Isles, which, as you well know, proved to be a trip within a trip, and, oh, we lived larger than life! I could never have imagined the that as we perambulated at the Acropolisin Athens that nearly a decade later, such would lead us straight to the Parthenon in Nashville to celebrate your daughter's wedding in a swank and remixed classic fashion. Your selecting this venue proves what we all who love you know: your love is Olympic in size and scope, and you would move heaven and earth for the rapture of your children.

Our second trip took us to new corners of the world, and your stirring photograph of the candles from Montserrat Monastery makes my study feel like a cloister. I love that you marvel at things like cork trees, and your creativity knows no bounds. Who else would afterward utilize slices of pine tree stumps to serve as rustic trays on which to put candles at some wedding? The Castle of the Bones wasn't creepy, but a curiosity and fascination to you! And how can we not laugh at my choosing a Fado concert over letting the kids dance at a hip club right around the bend? We can cross that off our list. That said, gypsies dancing to flamenco music was commanding and entrancing. Though an odd moment for you, we were all struck by a regality captured — not dampened — by the garb you wore in Morocco. And my, weren't we mesmerized by the eastern beauty at La Alhambra?! And that *you* scouted out where the bulls were kept at Seville was not surprising to me; our trip contained your subset adventures within! How can I not pronounce "Barcelona" without a lisp and laugh? Who else but you can stand in line to take respect at Montserrat's famous smoke-laden *Black Madonna* and then chuckle at the world's only depiction of *Our Lady of Expectation*, making suggestions as to what Mary's thoughts likely were? Your readiness for levity as well as your natural wonder of the *hows* and *whys* keeps you young at heart, nimble of mind, and vital to our lives.

Wherever you go somehow becomes a part of you, and I have vicariously tagged along through photos and got to witness your whirlwind worldwide tours with just your own family. Why? You "live your life by a compass, not a clock," as Stephen Covey has said. I will never forget your calling me while I was in Greece to have me speak to your son who was also abroad about a grievous loss and a place no parent would ever wish to visit. It created *saudade*, the Portuguese word we learned that means "missingness," and candles were lit to show we honored your daughter's memory. "If life is a journey, then let my soul travel and share your pain," said one Santosh Kalwar. Over the years since these travels, when you, your husband, and Bonnie and I gather together and go out for a meal, time stands still as we catch up on the latest. Although some might say we haven't bound about since then, I would beg to differ. Nowadays, we travel in the inner recesses of each other's minds and hearts and share our lives as if they are new islands to discover. That we have grown more rooted in our friendship as a result of partaking of the more tenuous, fragile, or even challenging moments in one another's lives means the world to me. I love sharing both our dreams and plans as well as our concerns and heartaches. That we have hooked up inadvertently and purposefully at many an Admiral High football game, not to mention Greek Fest, brings an *Opa*! to my heart! Another connection I have with you is that we adore our fathers, and we have a complex and sometimes trying relationship with our mothers. We look like and act like our dads, and sometimes this can put us at odds with our moms. This and much more we muse over. In short, I feel we four are a natural fit, and I love it in particular when you and I get tickled over some farcical moment in life, and many a time, we don't leave until we close the restaurant out. Oh, and I haven't even mentioned your tireless work setting up fundraising banquets for Juvenile Diabetes or that you are always on-call to help your husband with his work, seamlessly taking up the slack and joining him where needs must be met. The list could go on and on!

Like Athena holding the goddess of victory Nike in her palm, let me light a flaming torch of liberty with this my penned gratitude for *you*! We have done more than travel the world altogether. You have welcomed me into the depths of your heart as we trek through life, and for this, I am forever indebted to you. Let me take a moment and share these warm recollections and my admiration for you this way. I love that we give and take both laughter and tears, that we possess a common faith, and that we believe that life is for the partaking to the fullest. We do not squander this gift! Hannah, I love you bigger than a 40-oz. steak and look forward to more adventures and hearty gatherings with you and yours.

With love, kindness, and affection,
D.C.

34. Debbie

Meet Debbie. As is the case with Hanna, I also have taught Debbie's children multiple times in both English and Russian; I have twice traveled to Russia with her and to more than half a dozen other countries as well. As a matter of fact, it is now pushing nearly a decade since her two children graduated high school, and we have plans to tour both this summer and next. It doesn't matter how much time passes from one meeting to another; when we get together, we are locked and loaded and in sync, ready for laughter and learning. Like Hannah, Debbie, too, has experienced trials and tribulations in marriage, but where Hannah found it necessary to sever her first tie, Debbie's resilience, resolve, and faith have provided her the strength to stay the course. As a result, life has had its way of turning back around to the good again. As a mother, she had to help her children overcome auditory issues, and that they both took Russian, even when pronunciation proved difficult, is a testament to how she shored them up with confidence. Through her, I have come to meet her favorite traveling companion: her sister-in-law; she is the Ethel to her Lucille, and I love them both. A nurse at work and to her core, Debbie can assess any situation or person with accuracy and aplomb; in mere moments, she intuits if the person is on the up-and-up and one truly to have and to hold. Now a grandmother to two little granddaughters, I am overjoyed for these girls to have Debbie in their lives. Oh, the places *they'll* go!

Can you think of a mother whose life is wrapped up
in her children's worlds but has learned the delicate
balance of letting go while being available? Do you
know a mom whose kids love on or hug her, even though
they're well into their thirties? Have you a friend who

*considers her daughter one of her best friends and her
son still the apple of her eye? Do you know a woman
who is independent yet the best support a husband could
hope for? Do you have a friend who is both beautiful
and poised, but can have you snorting in laughter for her
readiness and ability to find humor in all things? This is
a mother who still seeks to see the world as she tends to
those nearest to her heart.*

Come and read more about Debbie.

"She is clothed with *strength and dignity*; she can
laugh at the days to come.
She speaks with *wisdom*,
and *faithful instruction* is on her tongue.
She watches over the affairs of her household
and does not eat the bread of idleness.
Her children arise and call her blessed; her husband
also, and he *praises* her:
"Many women do noble things,
but you surpass them all."
— From Proverbs 31:25–31 (NIV), emphasis
mine

May 12, 2019

Dear Debbie,

For some time now, I've had it on my mind to tell you how
much I treasure you, so during this month when we honor
mothers, I stake my claim and celebrate all that's *you*. In fact, I
am grinning from ear to ear in eager anticipation of writing to
you. Oh, it's easy to send a card or a note of cheer, but you are
the kind of person who deserves to be lavished and showered

upon, not only for all you do, but *who you are*. You seamlessly tuck in the corners of our lives in such a way that no one feels a wrinkle, sees a smudge, or knows the hours of tender loving care, attention to detail, and shouldering of burdens that it takes to make our lives and hearts light and gay, our spirits bright and hopeful. You make it all look so easy! Your children view the world with optimism, and how you radiate joy, strength, and a readiness for anything translates to me as a woman of substance, vibrance, and cheer, the likes of which I'm not likely to encounter again anytime soon. Every person whose life you touch feels at ease, like they're at home when they are with you. You have a light spirit, and your quick wit stuns and delights. And yet, your smile, charm, and beauty belie a keen understanding of the ways of the world, including her sorrows and disappointments which have produced the effect of your choosing transcendence, that is, the higher road. I close my eyes in awe at your readiness to make many marvelous memories with your dearest ones by sailing the seven seas or flying the (hopefully) friendly skies. Traveling with you always promises to be an adventure, so as I collect my thoughts, I've decided to write you out of the blue because there aren't enough Mother's Days to celebrate a woman like you! We can tell a tree by its fruit, so let me focus now on your son and daughter because they reflect your guidance and stamp of love. This will lead me to revel in and reveal the incandescence that is you.

Long before I knew you, when I was teaching your son, I realized that he must have a very special mother for the sweetness that was evident in him. I thought to myself that it takes excellent caring and a superlative nurturing to preserve an innocence and essential goodness in such a boy who I had no doubt would retain this on through manhood, and I still witness purity in him time and again. From day one, your son was enthusiastic about all things Russian, and he had high hopes and dreams about experiencing up-close-and-personal for himself this country he'd taken up studying, and so he did. Martin

Buber said, "All journeys have secret destinations of which the traveler is unaware," and no words could have become more accurate than when you accompanied your children abroad on my watch. I've led seven trips to Russia with students, and you are the only parent I've had to accompany not one, but both of her children there. In inviting your seemingly innocuous sister-in-law, I would have had no idea what adventures, glee, and laughter lay in store for us! Can you believe it has been thirteen years since we went to Russia on 06/06/06, a date we chuckled over and prayed there would be no evil lay in store for us?! I was overjoyed for your son to be able to see the country that he had fallen in love with. I watched him translating everything his eyes could gulp up that our bus passed by, and he would seek to find my face, noting if I were beaming proudly at his ability to read this or that. So much of what he'd done in his culture presentations and more were coming to life! That said, I could never have guessed what a dynamic duo you and your sister-in-law were and how much I would laugh when Bonnie and I would join you two. What a perfect blend we made, each of us complementing something in the other, which enhanced the foursome of us exponentially in our exploits within the tours.

Your unique sense of humor disarms; your ability to make silly faces with ready ease spawns hilarity, and your eagle eyes of discernment don't miss a beat, moment, or gesture. This teacher has learned many a lesson from *you*, and my life is all the grander for it! I may have shown and explained the art and architecture of a particularly dear-to-me Russian church in Moscow, imitated the goose step of the changing of the Russian guard, or shown you some sumptuous jewels and furs from Imperial Russia, but you were my scout and informant of errant children or perhaps an inconsiderate adult or leader. Without missing a beat, you helped me better guide them without losing respect or confidence in me. I think one of my favorite pictures of Russia is the one of just the women in our group when we stood by a thicket of slender birch trees; all of us were donning our bright shawls and flowered scarves, ready for whatever church came our way to enter and pay our respects to God. We could have passed for peasants were it not for our giggling countenances. Still yet, there was something of eternal womanhood captured and on display that day, don't you think? To visit the huge Hermitage, traverse canals in St. Petersburg, and eat borsch for lunch were all par for the course for a ready "Boris," the Russian name your son chose for himself in our class, and you were on-call and all-in for good times and great fortune.

It was also then you made the discovery that though fluent in Russian, I couldn't find my way out of a paper sack, and your sister- in-law, like Bonnie, with a 3-D map of the world built into her system, made me feel that we were always just where we were supposed to be. In fact, I still have the small compass on a keychain your sister-in-law gave me in thoughtful jest because I know with friends like you, I'm right where I'm destined to be. As J.R.R. Tolkien says, "not all those who wander are lost," and our paths crossing and re-crossing attests to this deep connection we have. Since his graduation, I have unexpectedly run into your son several times, once in Townsend during my winter break, another at the DMV renewing my driver's license, and most recently, at church. That he bounds toward me with a ready smile and an eagerness to share what is going on in life shows me he's still got the best of intentions, an earnestness, and a readiness to give of himself, a quality rare in an adult. Showering him with love did not spoil him; it preserved him, and he has you to thank for this, what for all life does to tarnish or make us feel dull. The joys of parenthood are touchingly evident in him, and that he has brought you a beautiful baby granddaughter I can tell is beyond gratifying, all the more so since there couldn't be a better father for a daughter!

On this first trip to Russia in 2006, our wheel of fortune to become friends was made clear to me on the train ride from Moscow to St. Petersburg; I came to know part of the back story behind your maternal strength and character. You are disarmingly light-hearted and seemingly carefree, but you keep some cards close to your chest as to what you have borne in life, so I would not have guessed at some of your life's trials until you chose to share a few with me, and for this, I thank you. When I look back on this particular trip, I remember us sitting Indian-legged on the upper bunks across from one another in the same berth of the train. The sound of train riding the rails, cha-chuck-a-chucking along, was rhythmically audible beneath us. You opened up and shared with me the discovery of your son's hearing impairment and all that was involved in getting this addressed and rectified. If memory serves me correctly, this happened again with your daughter, or "Maria/Masha," as she became known to me in Russian class. Forgive me if I have this mistaken. What I remember is the look you displayed as you were recounting this; such stems from an emergency mode most women sense when their child's welfare is threatened or at stake in *any* way. Your intent gaze revealed how you walked this tightrope, fiercely doing whatever it took to *make things right* for your babies so that they could regain their damaged auditory sense. There's too much to experience in life than to miss out in *any* capacity! I love your raw determination; your children possess it also. That both of them chose to study Russian, a language which necessitates learning another alphabet *and* that they strove to pronounce it well despite what could not have been easy for them, makes me want to bow to *you*. Their confidence is a testament to your influence.

At your job, even if the doctor is in, it will be the nurse in you whom sick ones do not forget. That you also dispense good cheer, kindness, and a loving touch is sometimes just the medicine we need to restore us back to health. Your charm and beauty are held in equilibrium by your generosity, and your core self is buttressed by fixing your eyes on what is "unseen [and] eternal" (2 Cor. 4:18 NIV). Little did I know then that I would be able to say, "But wait! There's more!"

And soon, it was your daughter I would meet and teach. Quiet, precocious, sharply observant, and fiercely determined, there is nothing that escapes her scrutiny. That I came to teach her fewer years in Russian than her brother was made up by the fact that I also taught her in English. Perhaps this was much to her chagrin because neither was easy, and I know she endured much by having to do double duty under my tutelage. That said, I would be hard-pressed to meet a student who communicates more with her eyes, and I came to read her mood by whether I was given her classic deadpan stare or a gaze that indicated whether I'd hit or missed the mark as to where we stood or what she understood. Her rich peal of laughter and her head thrown back in pure delight were also revelatory of some delight or success. Every now and again, I'd catch a full second or two of her full and soft brown-eyed gaze, which I knew few might notice, but one which clearly communicates her soul has been touched or moved. It is the look of love, and I know you know it well.

Your second trip to Russia in 2009 and first with your daughter may not have started out smoothly, what with your luggage arriving later than you, but that trip, too, added another layer to our friendship. I love how affectionate you are with your children, and when I see you and your daughter hug, you become like one person. The goodness that has been planted in her childhood is revealed by her ever-readiness to embrace you. It's like watching a child running to home base, knowing the world is safe and right there. How you were able to get her to laugh when she might have felt shy, insecure, or perhaps even momentarily miffed was like watching a conjurer pulling a rabbit out of a hat. You raised her spirits so swiftly that it had her giggling in a way that took even her by storm. And yet you also know when to step back and let nature and time take their course in order that your child can become braced by standing on her own two feet; not all do this, let alone well. Though we visited many cathedrals in Russia, including the iconic St. Basil's in Moscow, it was the *Church of the Savior on Spilled Blood* in Saint Petersburg that captivated you three. Your daughter's poster with actual photos of this staggeringly beautiful place with over 7500 square meters of vibrant mosaics is a testament to this and has adorned a wall in my classroom for well over a decade, and I shall return it to her. This church resonated with her because the holy sense there cannot adequately be rendered in word or pictures; being there with you three captivated my heart all the more.

I think more than anything, traveling with you makes me realize the power of the imagination and positivity that is at the core of your being: You say, "Yes," to laughter, to hope, to adventures, to learning, to love, and to life. That we've been twice to see the circus in Russia is just another of the greatest shows on earth for us! Whether you marvel at the beauty and brilliance of buildings established centuries ago or fuse the religious with the regular, you are always ready to make merry at many an odd moment life presents to us. Why? Because you miss nothing: you are one whose *eyes see* and *ears hear* (from Matthew 13). In fact, the powers of your imagination readily transform the mundane into the miraculous. Do you recall our meandering to the end of a corridor in the hotel which was out in the boonies past St. Petersburg? There we chanced upon a storage area full of an odd array of tall potted plants which became a pit orchestra of "students" that I was mock conducting. We laughed until it hurt (or needed a restroom)!

Even our fourteen-hour flight back to the States, which for most is the least enjoyable part of the trip, proved fortuitous, felicitous, and beneficial for us. In our being seated next to one another, you and I took a mental flight to another sphere as we entrusted one another and discussed private challenges in relationships we'd had and told how our faith sustained and strengthened us. None are exempt from tribulation. The give-and- take of baring life's trials and transgressions reveals stamina, loyalty, and a determination to walk through and survive trials and fires. Sharing some times of trouble led to discussing our faith, and there, thousands of miles above the earth, I welcomed the heavenly news of our being sisters in Christ. I bore my soul to you about my own past indulgences and the steps leading to my own coming to Christ, and I was grateful to discover that what steadies your spirit is the same as for me. It is *His* Spirit! That you shared with me the sleuth-work your daughter, like the detective *MacGyver* showed me that she, too, possesses a protectiveness; this time, it was the daughter looking out for her mother. Even now, she chooses to defend and advocate for the weak in her chosen career. The girl became a woman, but I still refer to her by the nickname I affectionately dubbed her; four years later, on our next trip, I saw just how much your daughter had blossomed into a capable woman, one of substance who remains ever- close to you. I was appreciative to have come full circle as I got to sit next to your sister-in-law and witness your precious daughter's holy matrimony at the enchanting Redbird Hill. I even got to meet your merry mother.

Hans Christian Anderson pronounced, "to travel is to live," and Anaïs Nin touted that "we travel — some of us to seek other *states*, other *lives*, other *souls*," and that surely is the case for us. For me to have the opportunity to travel with you, your sister-in-law, and your daughter again, I knew such would involve more than seeing new sites. I chose the 2014 tour to Austria, Germany, and Switzerland with you three in mind. There would be the rich history for your sister-in-law, the grandeur of classical Europe and sheer variety for you, and the chance to witness Dachau for your daughter, a request of hers because she, like you, has the sensitivity and stamina to bear witness to others' suffering. Speaking of which, though on a lighter level, to watch a group of teenagers take lessons in waltzing in some high-ceilinged, old-world ballroom, was a scream, and yet, also touching. We adults were privy to some valuable life lessons taught, and we hoped that they would take! Awkward boys learned how to lead young ladies. Our young ladies were baring the blush of beauty and yearned to be led with poise and respect. In stepping lightly

one-two-three —young gents can behold us floating and glide us right into their arms and hearts. In fact, such careful contact can only come from an unspoken trust when one abides by a higher and harmonious beat. No, not all are poised or ready, but we adults witnessed the miracle of manners and gentility that day and knew they'd gained more than a dancing certificate. The last memory I wanted to share that transported me occurred when we went up, up, up by cable-car to the top of the cloud-enshrouded Mount Pilatus. I saw you and your adult daughter embrace one another as if frontally communicating you *had* climbed every mountain. For me, you two show the absolute best of love a daughter and mother can have for one another.

I interrupt my writing to tell you that I *just* saw you and your sister-in- law and your daughter ay my surprise retirement party last night!! What joy! What jubilation! And how extra fortuitous in the writing of this letter, which, in several days, you'll come to know. As I perused the memories and pictures your ever-thoughtful sister-in-law chose to commemorate in binding, I said to myself, "Soon, she can revisit some of these memories here with my words." You can tell her that great minds think alike, and lingering over these pages confirms in my heart just how connected we are. *Travels with Dimi* would not be the same, let alone complete, without traveling with you and your family. And yes, after our upcoming trip down under to Australia, just right around the corner in 2020, we shall surely plan yet another trip, this time one of our own choosing. Who knows? Maybe we'll kiss the Blarney stone!

Debbie dearest, my life is so much better for knowing and having you *and* your children in it, and I am very glad we live in a familiar southern corner of this great country. I know we will have many more conversations that will run the spectrum; truth be told, I don't think there's anything I can't tell or might hear from you. What joy! What an honor! In short, I am beyond grateful that we are a part of each other's lives. Simply stated, I thank you and I love you.

Always,
D.C.

35. Betty

Meet Betty. She is Pastor Mark's mother and a *tour-de-force* of a woman, the likes of which I never knew up close and personal until I met her. It's no secret that she is her son's greatest admirer and advocate. I will be the first to tell you that I do not know but a few facts about her, but I am pleased to say that over the past seven years, she has gone from being a marvel from afar to a woman I look forward to hugging weekly. In fact, I sit right behind her every Sunday morning. I, too, am now a part of this female "Amen" corner. Betty is my sister in Christ, and I love her very much. To be honest, before I came to Jesus, I judged women like her; I did not understand that this kind of amazing faith, powerhouse femininity, southern charm, and high hostess at family gatherings could be for real. I was in awe. Betty couldn't have been more different than my own mother. Little by slowly, as my faith grew, I recognized that we had same "thing" inside of us, and it wasn't a thing but a living force whom I came to know to call the Holy Spirit. I saw what she and I had in common rather than how much we seemed different. Just like me, she had been gifted with His Spirit; the Holy Ghost had transformed and come to her rescue, too! I was getting to witness what *decades* of His indwelling Spirit looked like in a woman who had worshipped in church her whole life. Jesus was as vital to her as air and water are essential, and she spoke of Him like she He lived right down the street from her. Her faith in Jesus makes her fearless because she knows He took away the reality, the "sting" of death (1 Cor. 15:55). Just as love doesn't fade because we may not *physically* be with a dear one, the fact that we can't see Jesus doesn't make Him absent. We who believe in Jesus won't *really* die; only our frames expire. He Who sits at the right hand of His Father lives on, and so will we. It's this ability to transform every person who comes in contact with and accepts Him for Who He is that makes Him ever-relevant. How He manifests Himself in Betty is as unique as it is in me. I may not have been privy to the gestation of Jesus growing in her from when she first surrendered herself to Him, but I do see a woman so saturated in Him that her personality, charm, humor, intelligence, and strength exude Him powerfully and sweetly. "Rejoice in the Lord always; again I will say, rejoice!" (Philippians 4:4) are words spoken by Paul, but they also radiate from Betty's core. This no show; Betty is for real. That's what God, a *living* God, can do. It is through faith in His Son that we can ride on the coattails of His mercy, and this is a reality that never ends. No wonder Betty has no doubts! Because of her early recognition that her son was divinely anointed to be a spokesman for Christ, this led to his becoming a pastor and *our* shepherd. Betty, too, has been equipped to be a mother who supports her son in every way, and that's for life.

Have you ever met a woman who knows how sacred and special is her charge of motherhood?

Read on to meet Betty!

Let us ... put on the breastplate of *faith* and *love*, and as a helmet, the *hope* of salvation. For God has not destined us for wrath, but for obtaining *salvation through our Lord Jesus Christ*, who died for us, so that whether we are awake or asleep, *we will live together with Him*. Therefore, *encourage one another and build up one another, just as you also are doing.*
— From 1 Thessalonians 5:8–11

May 19, 2019

Happy Sunday, Betty!

It's unlikely you would anticipate getting a letter from me, but for some time I have been meaning to take a moment to thank you for being you, and this is the perfect month to do so. Let me encourage *you* who are such an encourager! Why? You already know our destiny! You *do* live together with Jesus! My father once remarked that *it takes an extraordinary mother* to raise a child who becomes a physician. I consider the same no less true for one bringing up a man of God. From a casual glance, you and I would seem to have little in common. For starters, unlike you, I was not raised in the church, I have not birthed or raised children, and our backgrounds couldn't be more opposite; resultantly, I often feel like one of the vineyard workers who got a late start at working third shift. Yet we both have a big love for Jesus, pride in our precious church, and a steadfast devotion to our pastor — your son and my friend. These commonalities unite us in a way I could never have imagined before; it is now standard for me to speak the same language as you because our values, vision, and destination are in harmony. We are ones who know that the world is fractured by spiritual warfare, but more importantly, that King Jesus has already claimed victory for us. Although all is already known by Him, there could be no more critical accomplishment in our lives than to walk every minute of every day, holding fast to His hand, stepping out in faith and not by sight. I clearly see this in you, and you are such a beacon! Mark may be moved by the last words his peepaw quoted, that is, "His grace is sufficient" (2 Cor. 12:9), but everything I see in your life is a testament that God gives grace in great abundance! I do not pretend to be familiar with more than a smidgeon of your life, but I am old enough to know that it's not only cats that have nine lives, and I am sure you have survived your fair share of life's trials. The passion Mark has for the Lord got deployed at home under your helm; yours is the kind of faith that is founded on a solid bedrock with Jesus Christ as its cornerstone starting in your own home.

I do not know what Mark's biological father was like, but I can tell that you more than compensated for this man's deficiencies and absence, in part, due to your having remarried a loving man we all adore. I would be willing to wager that your husband is the polar opposite of your first take. He is steadfast, sweet-natured, generous-hearted, and devoted, and such a man was the perfect dad for your son, who would not know the love of his father. This is a credit to *you*; your brand of deep love knows no bounds. Our Heavenly Father saw to it. Now that Mark has his own children whom he is pouring into, he models what he expects and parents in the same vein as you did: to their core, they are sure of his constancy, support, and love. He is cultivating a sense of destiny in his own sons, now on the cusp of manhood, so that they will be able to press into the darkness and live for Him, too. Even from the outside looking in, I can clearly see that your love spills into every nook and cranny of your children's and your grandchildren's lives; their life would not be the same without you! You are not one who says you're done when they're grown. It is clear to me that you are a hub, the Grand Central Station, the matriarch of the family, all because you've got that overflowing kind of love, so much so that Jesus could have told His Disciples to fill their baskets with your loaves of love for all the surplus there is. With no disregard intended toward my own mother, I can only tell you that not all women are created equally in this capacity.

For all your inner strength, you know that the best leaders serve, and you are ever-ready for this charge within your family. Your son soars higher and leads his church better, in part, due to your ready ear and shrewd counsel, even if now in his adulthood, this may occur in a more diminished capacity. With your having raised sons, it seems to me that you have an uncanny understanding of how the male mind operates. You know how to adore without adulating, make a fuss over without spoiling, remain firm without breaking spirits, and build up their sense of can-do without stealing their thunder. That said, you can tell that since he was a boy, Mark has long been your right-hand-man. His sensitivity, readiness to laugh and cut up, eye for style, and ability to listen to what's *not* spoken all speak to a mother's guiding hand as opposed to a father's tough touch. You are quintessentially southern, to your core feminine, always perfectly coiffed and colorful and beautiful. You are stable and strong, but you also know how and when to let your men roar. How can I not add that through your sons' wives, you have also gained daughters, and I see the kindness, respect, and abiding attachment you have for them and vice versa.

These past six years for me have flown by, and I am grateful to have gotten to know you. You and I had discussions on biblical topics and real-life dilemmas, and I've been privy to the goings-on in your own life, including how much you miss your mother. You have also shared snippets from your son's youth, too. You are still the expert on him, even if he is his own man. One commonality we share is how we adore our fathers. It would seem that this gives us an edge and undoubtedly has helped give us an inkling of the love of our Father Who art in Heave . I love that you are ready, not only say "Amen," but when Mark shares his nuggets of solid- gold wisdom as well as piercing truths spoken in the Spirit, you reflexively exclaim, "*That's right!*" It's as if you are a living, breathing exclamation mark that accentuates some profound point or pearl of wisdom he's just uttered. You know the gospel when you hear it! The recollections of our youth may not always be accurate, but they are nonetheless valid, and this is the case with the formation of Mark, what for the indelible imprint of purpose and calling instilled in his heart based upon the Holy Spirit's prompting. You watered and weeded the mustard seed that God planted in him, and, merciful heavens, how that it took!

With such a sharp mind and quick wit that Mark has, I'm sure you had your hands full with him as a youth. His humorous anecdotes about such confirm this case. You made him toe the line, but at the same time, you never withheld your love. Before I understood what the gift of prophecy was, in meeting you, I was introduced to one living and breathing with such powers and insight. I have heard you say that, early on, you knew Mark was headed for ministry, even if took selling cars and going through a few other twists and turns to get there. With the burden and blessing of this knowledge, you fostered what became his calling, and even later, when the chips were down, you helped steer with invisible hands until his sails came back up for him to stay the course. That he remains secure and confident having borne his own tribulations is, in part, a testament to you. However, do let me be the first to acknowledge that you *both* give God the glory; it is *He* who is the promise keeper. In like fashion, the encouragement Mark readily lavishes on us is a quality and capacity he inherited from you. You two both may have the gift of gab, but you've both got nerve and backbone, flesh and blood, and hearts of gold to align your deeds with His word. Jesus is your guiding light, and your son now helps *us* see the light. He has a sense of perspective, alertness, ease, and presence of mind that helps him know just when and how to dispense guidance and love for any soul. All who receive Jesus' love through your son's loving touch are all the better for it. Though he may start out with his own personal parables or dispense some old- school or country nostalgia, he won't mince words when salvation's at stake. He cuts to the chase with wisdom that can cut like a knife, and if we hearken closely enough, we can hear trumpets summon us to our Lord and Savior. Mark dreams all the bigger, better, and brighter because of his being grounded in Christ *and* his mama's belief in him. Yours is not the kind of love that merely props us up; it is a foundational love that supports through thick and through thin *and* allows one to run like the wind when God's timing is right. Mark is a natural leader who scans the horizon and views the present with the end in mind all to do more for Him. Glory be! You, too, have that presence of mind and assurance that no matter what, *God's got this*. Come what may; we are *so* blessed! How can this be? To your core, you have that coveted rock-solid faith that communicates to all who are near you that our Lord has "plans to prosper us and not to harm us, plans to give us hope and a future" (Jeremiah 29:11 NIV).

Everything that you do says you care and you love big. Why, even the name of your favorite radio station is W-LUV! I remember the first time I saw you, it was not your face, but your bedazzled hand shooting up nearly twenty rows in front of me at church that I spotted, obviously done beyond your own will. Having gotten to know you better from when our campus briefly met in L.C. to now coming back home to K. (and not too far off, to our dream-coming-true new church), I look forward to seeing you every Sunday! Now I sit in the row right behind you, right on up front, and though we are first and foremost followers of Jesus Christ, we are also fans of your son. We just can't get our fill of His word through Mark's positive preaching, can we? I love to see you write in your Bible; it's as if you're writing to God when you are taking notes from Mark's sermon. I'd recognize your Good Book anywhere: such a thick tome it is, well-worn and marked up cover to cover, protected by a cloth cover decorated with now-faded pink paisley flowers. I believe it has gotten thicker not only from constant use; the very ink from your markings has magnified and underscored His words' weight. Who could know the life-changing, earth-shattering power held in that jacket? You do! You inspire me because this teacher duly notes that you never stop learning and soaking in more of His Word every day. It's like a jeweler admiring all the facets of a priceless and brilliant diamond in his possession.

For always being in your Sunday best, you are a down-to-earth woman whose love is as real as it gets, and your actions speak louder than words. I love your hearty laugh, your straightforward approach, and your readiness to be assuring or compassionate in a moment's notice, even if you yourself might be suffering pains. This is what a woman of substance does; she understands the ways of the world and carries on, head held high for the knowing who's *really* in charge, no matter how often the wily one comes to pester. You have the kind of love that delivers, day in and day out, and, like some better version of *Everyone Loves Raymond*, you are a mother who relishes her sons and lavishes on their families, but you are *also* one who loves those who come in your sphere. I will never forget that cold winter's eve, after a long day at work, you came to my home with homemade potato soup and cornbread, all prepared with love for Bonnie. She was too weak to even raise herself to thank you as chemotherapy was still at work, coursing its way through her system. I also showed you where Mark sits in our kitchen, now so many times, and in a second, I could see your swift mind capture the conversations we must have had. You are always right on time, knowing full well all is accomplished on His watch.

I may not be blood kin, but I am a member of His family with you, and I do not take our sisterhood for granted or lightly. In the short bursts of time that we are in each other's company, you are always ready to give a word of encouragement or to share a story from your or Mark's past that relates to the moment at hand. I would like to take to say here that I know your heart grieves for various goings-on in your family, and your family is no more perfect or different than anyone else's in this respect. Therefore, humility and patience bide in you that makes it easy and sweet to approach you. *Thank you* for always having open arms and a readiness to talk. I, too, pray for *you*! You are a force of love to be reckoned with for all your warmth and giving. Your kind of love is hands-on and tangible; your loving touch for your family is as much an essential nutrient as is our daily bread. Every day is Thanksgiving with you!

I don't have to ruminate for one second to know your slant on life: everything about you says, "*Rejoice!*" The Lord *is* near — right here! I love the fact that you are ever-ready to scoop up your grandbabies, regardless of their age, and one could write a separate volume of the special kind of grandparent's love you hold for every one of them! Such affection, spoiling, and adoration of your precious grandchildren is the gift that keeps on giving. Whether they indulge in your red velvet cake, relax in your home and hearth, seek without asking for your advice, or swim in the cool blue of your pool, complete with our lake and mountains as the backdrop cresting just on the golden horizon, what a difference you make in our lives!

I love you very much!
D.C.

36. Josephine

Meet Josephine. This woman is Catherine's mother; she has three daughters, two of whom you'll meet later in the category of June. Any girl would be lucky to have a mom like Josephine because she is in it for life; motherhood is not a role that ceases just because her babes have reached twenty-one. She has made her daughters strong by endowing them with confidence, and she continues to encourage the quality of independence in each. Some say that being a stay-at-home mom isn't a "real" job. Not for Josephine. Oh, no. It is an identity that one dons and wears with honor. In fact, Josephine still assumes this role with as earnest a sense of responsibility and zeal as during the days when she was changing her infants' diapers; cooking, cleaning, caring for them in childhood, or watching them as they left her nest to start their own families. She will proudly tell you that she has twenty-one grandchildren; for her, being a grandmother is an extension of motherhood. Okay, admittedly being a grandmother or "nana" involves a slight diminution of power compared with the mother, but in the paradigm of power and influence, she deftly makes use of her position to orbit around hers with love, order, and affection. She is always in-the-know and on top of things. You can't slip anything past her — or not for very long. She appreciates the fact and from personal experience realizes that it really does take a village to raise a tribe, and she is ready, willing, and able to do and be there for hers — yes, *all* of them, the likes of which few women are. Any other way is unthinkable. To tell you the truth, she's the only other person I know who is like my father in the degree of devotion and desire for family togetherness; they both would beg, borrow, or steal to take care of theirs. There is one difference, however: a mother's love has no bounds, and I have seen Josephine take in the wayfaring stranger, the castaway child, and the widow when such individuals' sense of feeling loved is in want or when their well-being is at stake. She is still at it today, and for this and much more, respect is due. Her brand of selfless love and readiness to be present has been indelibly imprinted in all of her daughters. Her loyalty is fierce, her optimism bright, humor quick, and smile infectious, and though I am her friend — one less than a decade apart in age, her maternal sense has me feeling like a daughter, even though I have my own, many miles away.

What woman in your life is as active and involved in her grandchildren's lives as she was in her own children's? Whom do you know who helps take up the slack in her adult children's lives when the presence of others may have waned or proven insufficient? Whom do you know that perseveres through her own ills or troubles in order to provide for others? What mother have you witnessed disciplining and scolding one minute, but hugging, holding, and forgiving the next? She has eyes that show tenderness, a face that smiles, and arms open for an embrace — and not just for the first eighteen years, but for a lifetime!

Continue on to read more about Josephine.

"*Put on love*, which is the perfect bond of unity...
and be thankful."
—From Colossians 3:14–15, emphasis mine

Mangia bene, ridi spesso, ama molto. —Eat well,
laugh often, love much!
—Italian expression

May 26, 2019

Hello, Josephine!

More than most, you know the sacredness of time spent with loved ones *and* the imperative we have to share, to "*put on*" love with others. Therefore, in this month containing Mother's Day, as a gesture and token of my admiration and appreciation for *you*, I will write you now! Day in and day out, you continue to provide for your family. There's never a wrong time to say, "I love you," and, frankly, we need no occasion to celebrate *you*. Although we see each other fairly frequently at various events and family get-togethers, I never get my fill of you; quite the opposite: I wish I had more time with you! Amidst the whirl of children bustling about, of teenagers coming in and out of the house, or your daughters attending to this or that, it is you who are ever-present and constant. Your all's lives are intertwined, enmeshed, and pulsing with love in considerable measure because you involve yourself to such a high degree. No picture is complete without you in it!

To capture what and who you are for the *body* of your family, rather than to choose an organ, I would select the largest vein a person has: the *inferior vena cava*; it carries deoxygenated blood from the lower half of the body back up to the heart. Why this one? It runs such an impressive length within us, and we couldn't live without it. Though your daughters are grown, it is *you* who makes sure a trenchant love courses throughout their systems, exchanging the gift of time and aid and moving out that which isn't beneficial to our systems, be they worries, troubles, or dilemmas. You do *whatever it takes* to ensure your daughters and, by extension, your twenty-one grandchildren and one great-grandchild, are happy, safe, and content. You shoulder the burdens others often avoid — *volunteer* to do so — all so that life can continue less impeded and ultimately flow more smoothly, fully, and healthily. How else could there exist such a "bond of unity" among you? Even husbands step back when you step up. Day in and day out, you give; it's what you do and who you are, and so I just wanted to take a breath and take my time in recognizing just some of who you show yourself to be. Though I seek to be thorough, I can't even begin to complete the picture of the magnitude of your impact. Quite simply, because we do life together, I am going to count the ways I see you embodying the Italian saying above that hangs as a framed expression on your wall as much as it does a banner in our hearts.

Who would have known that nearly twenty-five years ago when a joyful, beautiful, and bright student in my Russian class who entered my life and captured my heart would lead to my becoming a part of her family and getting to meet you, the mother who started it all? I recall your attentive and courteous stance towards me, be it at some PTSO Open House or at your own home; you are of the generation and culture that shows respect toward its teachers. My voice mattered as to what and how I spoke into your daughter's life, even if your husband couldn't grasp why Russian language and culture in particular had captivated your daughter. In fact, I have no doubt it was you who ensured that when she desired to travel across the globe to see a little piece of the place she'd been studying, she should get the opportunity to do so. That year was the only time I invited my travelers to my home for a meeting, and I was pleased to have you come there. Your husband was curious and alert, you were warm and attentive, and Catherine, all adoration and smiles.

If I were pressed to choose, I would say Catherine has your type of titanic love, and with every child she has birthed, more than most can figure, you take each to your chest to cherish. Her quick wit, acute powers of analysis, readiness to ponder what makes us tick, generosity of self, and strong desire to have her children orbit around her come from the gravitational pull of the hale maternity in *you*. I think that is why light strife can occasionally occur with her; she is the matriarch in *her* family, the concentration of which is rivaled only by you. Though still entrenched in the nitty-gritty details of our daily living and raising her family, she, too, will soon enough possess the wisdom of one who sees the vaster picture; this is a grandmother's privilege. Your Catherine is intent on making life matter, and I am the beneficiary of her living love; it helps ensure the vitality of our friendship *today*. That she invited me to witness the birth of one of her children is eclipsed only by you reaching out your hand to hold mine so that we could sit side-by side-and watch this miracle of life. It was you who comforted me as I watched first in horror and then in wonder as excruciating pain transformed into tearful joy when mother met babe with a mere push. You also well know that life gives us lessons in shock and grief not only to build character, but to have us acknowledge that there is more here than meets the eye. What that we might humble ourselves more often and side our souls with our Savior! The tongue often reveals the state of our spirit, and for all the mirth that can come from careless mouths and carefree minds, I know it grieves you, as it does Him, whenever *He* is disregarded. Man may flinch and disappoint, but God is unfailing and boundless in His love; He waits in expectation for due deference. I know this is a lesson you hope for your daughters to fasten to their core and model for their children.

While I am on the subject of strength, how can I not mention that of all the parents I am acquainted with and way more than any of them, it is you who remind me of my father for the possessive love he had for us? It is a kind of love that is old-world, intensified in the same way the Mediterranean sun ripens sweet grapes into potent wine. No matter what, if we happened to be vexing or delighting, we were sure that dad would *always* be there for us; we felt this even more than we knew it. Truth be told, he wanted to be with us *all the time*! You are like this, too, so when I watch you on-call, yet unseen, ready to scoop up and hug a child in need of attention, affection, or admonishment, I feel a potent love for you that is reminiscent of what I had with my father and what I longed for from my mother, and it moves me every time. When I was young, I felt a sense of wholeness or completion when the rest of the puzzle pieces of our family were present or accounted for. Our wants became his wishes. That said, my mother was the reliable and calm one, and she surely helped cultivate many of my dreams.

Your vows taken in holy matrimony, though sullied by the flaws of the flesh, extend and transfer to commitments you make to your daughters and your progeny. You, too, have that kind of staying power, the type of love that indicates when you promised, "I do," you don't get to say, "I won't." Day in and day out, they receive your gift and sacrifice of time and immediate attention that are more valuable than rubies, yes, 'til death do part you from *them*. Any loneliness you may feel is put on the altar for the good of *your* chosen ones. How could they not realize that they are *your* beloved as much as I pray you take comfort in knowing that you and yours are *His*? Somewhere down in my gut, right or wrong, I knew that my dad would kill *or* die for us; I recognize that same primal impulse in you, and it makes me both pine for him and appreciate you. Your love is hand-on and heart-felt, so whether they get a swat from your shoe, spoon, or back of your hand or catch "the look" that says more than words could, they all know to their core that "your love never fails, it never gives up, it never runs out" (from Brandon Heath's "Love Never Fails"). All of your children get to know a taste of the love of Christ through how steadfast and full of joy *you* are, Josephine! And yet, your brand of love is not reserved for just your flesh and blood; it spills out like some broad ripple effect onto all those who come into your galaxy, be it a young widow, your geriatric dog, fatherless teenagers, or teammates and friends of your own *famiglia*. I am such a fortunate one.

Speaking of being a part of something greater and though it will seem humorous to you for how little knowledge I possess, I am going to attempt to make an analogy to football. I'll preface this by thanking you for indulging and engaging me in many a conversation, even while your Gamecocks were playing. We have had some of our best private talks while the rest of your brood was fanned out in front of the TV, fully absorbed in a play, so much so that they dared not move for changing a team's luck. Meanwhile, in my ignorant bliss, you allowed me to take advantage of some time when grading wasn't on the forefront of my mind, and, like referees of life, we discussed the moves of a family predicament, politics, or the wicked ways of the modern world. We are also optimistic by nature, and we look to what the future holds and talk excitedly about upcoming plans for members of our family. You have a survival instinct that enables you to land on your feet, to put a positive spin on *any* situation, or, at the very least, to appear that all is right and fine. In a sense, you can nearly *will* the good into being, and yet, you know God is in charge, and you always take a knee for Him, undoubtedly on your own as well as in public. For all your openness, positivity, and liberality, I also know you to be an extremely private person who bears her pains in her own inner private locker room, where it's just you and our Savior.

I may not know football, but rest assured we are both on Team Jesus. I see you as the owner of your own football team, and though each of your daughters has signed onto another team of her own choosing, you take dibs and rights as their first coach. Though the center of the solar system and the queen bee within her own hive, Catherine, is actually a quarterback. From the couch, she throws the ball out to encourage hers so they can make big plays in the game of life. She is always ready to rally and huddle and love her team in the middle of any scrimmage or practice; they all count and each matter. Next, I see your youngest daughter, Brittney, as one on the Offensive side, perhaps as some sort of receiver. When God orchestrates events and provides opportunities, she's on the ready alert for taking them, and, time and again, she has scored and scored big for *her* team. Look at the successes she's had! Brittney's willingness to take up the challenge, all the while showing no fear — be it dancing with a stranger or assuming the risk so as to advance her career and showcase her free spirit, determination, and ambition. Her motive is classic: she wants to provide more for her family *and* remain true to herself. To win, the offensive must advance *and* gain, and Brittney continues to do just that!

On the other hand, I see your middle daughter, Gabriella, as part of the Defense. No, she is hardly one you'd picture as being some bulky defensive end or linebacker, what for how beautiful and enigmatic she is, but more than your others, she has taken some hard hits in life, and she keeps on getting up. Of your three, she is the first to doggedly fight and defend her own receivers and kickers, and she will do whatever it takes to shield or block so that they can make their own touchdowns in life, and each of them shows his or her own unique promise and potential. In a certain sense, you and she have forged your own team, and, day in and day out, you are there for her, even if you are out in the backfield so as to make sure life doesn't encroach further or blitzkrieg her. You are ever- present and ready for practices that lead to playoffs and championship bowls, and you wouldn't miss a play or move, even if you have to sit in the rain or cold. You know that it would be a shame, if not a sin, for you not to pledge allegiance and be there for your team; why, it's unthinkable! To *not* play is to lose; therefore, every day you win.

You may have sprung from the country that brought the likes of Julius Caesar, Pavarotti, and Sophia Loren, but to your core, you are patriotic to our own U.S.A. I see this whenever the mention of our men and women in arms is announced; you display obvious reverence and respect, and such a response reminds *me* of the sacrifices made so we can enjoy the freedoms we do. I ought to know; I've seen otherwise elsewhere, so I thank you! I also like the tiny homage to your birth state, a Hawaiian palm tree tattooed on your ankle, a reminder of the daring in you. Speaking of sacrifices, without thought or expectation of compensation, you give grandly to your family, so much so, I'm certain they don't realize you are as fundamental to them as the earth is beneath our feet. Time and again, you lead us to look past the surface, past the predicament and problem at hand, so that we see the need of the human heart. You are honest and direct, and you also let it be known when it's time to recharge your batteries, to take five, or to enjoy an evening relaxing on your own, but then you are right back at it again: giving, loving, and being present rinse and repeat. You do not draw attention to yourself; you see the need and fill the void where and when you can, be it a ride to a game, a room in your own home, or ready arms for hugging and holding. A friendly pop and pointing of the finger mean beans and business, and in a split second, even teenagers are stunned and reminded of *your* score to be minded where the rules are concerned.

Much fluctuates in life, but not the constancy of *your* love. Sometimes we glance at one another at a poignant moment when we both know right when a child's character is being shaped. I quickly catch a knowing look in your big eyes that communicate full cognition for what's happening in the mome t and knowing how it will pan out down the pike. You are one who appreciates the value of time, and you intend not to squander a minute. You'll regulate your blood sugar as best you can to ensure this, all while cooking or preparing some vat or tray of deliciousness for yours. How could you not possess such an awareness, with your having years ago undergone and completed treatment for thyroid cancer? It does not go unnoticed or unappreciated that, as Bonnie's own friends have fallen by the wayside, you, in particular, have been there to reach out to her in times of need and want. Yes, you and yours have become our surrogate family, but I want you to know that it was *you* whom Bonnie first called when she found out she had cancer and you from whom she sought assurances when she was scared. Even now, when she posts clear reports, you are always one of the first to cheer a hooray of relief. Speaking of family and football, I would be remiss if I did not repeat that Bonnie and I appreciate our open invitation to come and gather with y'all at any football gathering, be it at home or on the ballfield where one of yours is playing. We are family! Though less practical to arrange, when you and your nearby daughters once did come to have dinner at my house, the honor was all mine! During the years that Catherine lived in M., you and I got closer by doing life together *here*, and for that, I am also so glad.

I also want to thank you for inviting us to your 60th birthday cruise. The scope of that idea was spectacular, and I am flooded with memories! I recall us all sitting out on your balcony, laughing at the dinner table, and basking in the sun out on the deck, while you drank in the beauty of your daughters, your most prized possessions. Your girls joke around with you, sometimes laughing at your expense, but this, too, is a sign of their love and affection. And most recently, you and your girls were a part of our two surprise birthday gatherings, back-to-back, as it turned out. I saw you shake your head at the irony and sweetness of such an occurrence; I hope you know that neither would have been complete without you! We are grateful to have been a part of the gang at countless birthday parties. For just a moment, we turn out the lights and make time stand still, candles aglow, and well over twenty of us sing in unison to the birthday boy or girl who is grinning from ear to ear for his or her special moment. Speaking of special, I would be remiss if I didn't mention that our bond is further solidified by going to church together. Your own religious heritage is one that reflexively has you recite a prayer in humble supplication, a habit from your Italian lineage steeped in Catholicism. But now we stand side by side in our little church, ready to drink in biblical truths from the pastor we adore and trust, and I note our being deeply moved time and again. In fact, although I do not believe in predestiny, I cannot help but be in a state of wonder and gratitude that God used *your* family to draw me close to Jesus by simply inviting me to church to watch one of yours get baptized. Yes, the Greek in me will always have a special affection for the Italian in you, but we are both daughters of the King, and it doesn't matter to Him if we are from Naples or

K-city; we are His.

If you are still wondering why I am writing, know that because life goes by fast, nowadays it is often through a text or Facebook that sentiments get expressed. So, for me, with pen put to plain paper, straight from my heart to yours, I wanted to suspend time and privately celebrate you this way. I am happy we are friends for life, sisters in faith, and family through all the mundane *and* magnificent moments. Imagine me now reaching out to you, giving you a big smile and ready hug. Keep your light shining! Your love radiates out in concentric circles, and all who know you relish you without end. You are the icing on our cake, and life is all the sweeter with you in it.

All my love,
D. C.

June

Family Of Choice

We live in an age when it is more likely than ever that when you become an adult, you will *not* be around the family you grew up with. Therefore, it behooves you to make friends who can be like family for you. If you do have family nearby, as in less than a thirty-minute drive, visit them with regularity. Many kinks can get worked out in person as much as bonds can be strengthened. (Of course, I concede some hurts warrant special help.) Our American culture promotes the posture of "I can do it myself" or the credo, "I'll go it alone"; after all, we tell ourselves, *"If we want a job done right, then..."*; you know the rest of this statement! There is an exhilarating sense of possibility, empowerment, and potential in our nation; we produce workers with a can-do spirit. In general, we are not bound to the past, beholden to tradition, or broken by war. Any call of duty we have comes from the inner self which compels us; sometimes we can get a false sense of security. We may brag that "the buck stops here," and we may feel as if we are the masters of our universe.

Entitlement ultimately leads to impoverishment. Like those who built the Tower of Babel, when we make much of ourselves, we become distanced from God. We get too big for our britches; troubles surely follow. Resultantly, the fall is all the farther and harder. The Enemy's method of destroying us is simple, predictable, and effective; I'll tell you what it is so you can be forewarned and forearmed. He seeks to divide and conquer. He will disrupt your life by paralyzing, bamboozling, seducing, dulling, or maiming you. If you go for what glitters rather than what is gold, it makes it all the easier for him to pick you off. You may ask me why I am talking about Satan. It's because many folks wonder why God lets bad things happen to good people. First off, not one is all-good, and nothing is relative with God. Holy is as holy does. Rest assured that God is in the business of turning curses into blessings; such is His love in the making for us. When the going gets rough or when life seems impossible — and hard times *will* happen — He wants for us to draw near to Him. My pastor says we are either heading into a storm, already in a storm, or leaving a storm, so do you really want to be in choppy, turgid seas *alone*? Our Lord "neither slumbers nor sleeps" (Psalm 121:4). Unlike people who can let you down, God is ever-reliable and intimately near, and the way we turn our knowledge of Him into wisdom is through living righteously, but not sanctimoniously, and trying to be better today than we were yesterday. This can take form through two outward acts: first, through prayer, and secondly, by coming close to those we love and who love us. It all goes back to Jesus telling us, "You shall love your neighbor as yourself" (Matthew 22:39), and by "neighbor," He means *anyone*.

Enter to center stage the dear ones of *your* choosing. Cultivate love with them and make this your life's calling as much as you do your passion or vocation. There is no greater investment you can make than giving your *time* and *attention*. Oh, take it from one who has had to work at it. These two ingredients and love are what you need to change a life; plus, you never know when *you' ll* be in need. Flannery O'Connor had it right when she wryly quipped that "the life you save may be your own." The family of your choosing is one that might spring up from your church family or from a group with a common interest; they may grow to be close enough to be there through thick and through thin, for better or worse. At the very least, they can be your immediate go-to folks. I am certain God also says, "*It is good*," when we spark up or rekindle friends who become our family. Our precious flesh and blood need not mind; it takes nothing away from them and adds more love to everyone's pot. I'll bet you'll find you have an ever-expanding and unbroken circle.

You' ll now meet some who have become family for me.

37. and 38.
Ted and Brittney

Meet Ted and Brittney. Sometimes you make friends through friends, and this couple showcases just that. Brittney is Catherine's youngest sister, and Josephine is their mother; Ted is Brittney's husband. I've been to more kids' birthday parties and football gatherings at Ted and Brittney's than I can shake a stick at. They would chuckle at my mentioning football because they know it's not for football I visit. Nope, it's for that coming-home feeling I get when one gathers with family. The real deal is, it's all about pilin' up together on the couch, catching up about this and that, rooting for your favorite team, sharing food and laughter, and a million other little things when you do life with friends. They mourn your losses, and you celebrate their victories, and next month, it'll flip. This is a couple with a family who open their hearts and home to me, so I celebrate them here with you. Ted and Brittney have been "movin' on up" the ladder of success, and since I have known them, their family size has grown to six souls and their income level to six figures. I mention this because how we handle our successes matters as much as how we deal with our failures. This couple has had to turn over a new leaf many times, to forgive and forget, and to choose love over logic. The scale matters not, and they are no different than you or me. Of the three sisters, Brittany hunkered down, hit the books, and catapulted herself to the highest level of education and income. As one who works in the medical field, I see her as a healer and a giver; she cares with intentionality. She balks at challenges that would deter many, not the least of which is balancing work and family. This is where her husband, Ted, steps in. Within this couple's state of equilibrium, it is Ted who has been the one to support and sacrifice to make it possible for his wife to go back to school. I am riveted by the give and take of each for the other because both are dreamers, particularly Ted, and I have seen Brittney defer to her husband when he has had a yearning to make his vision a reality. My relationship with each is as different as the sun is to the moon. Since both of them are the youngest in their family of origin, in terms of family dynamics, it is a natural fit for me, an oldest, to be with them. Evidently, I've still got a lot of big sis in me. That said, each has passion, potential, and purpose in his or her own right, so the topics of conversation I have with them cover the spectrum. With Brittney, I discuss the likes of child psychology through what is going on with her children, and I relish her lightning-quick wit and astute comments; her faith grounds her more deeply than she lets on. And Ted I adore for our no-hold-bar conversations; our topics of interest span the globe from religion to history to politics with no sense of fear of reprisal; we have genuine respect, curiosity, and affection for one another.

> *Do you know a couple with common faith, values,*
> *and pride in their family who demonstrate respect,*
> *understanding, and commitment to help and encourage*
> *one another as they each explore their unique purpose?*
> *Have you watched one put his best foot forward and*
> *extend a helping hand at a time when the other might be*
> *faltering or flailing? Can you think of a couple that are*
> *united and made stronger by their differences? Anyone*
> *can see that they're crazy for each other! To whose house*
> *can you go without a thought because you are welcome*
> *any day, any time? In fact, everything about them says to*
> *you that you are home in their house.*

Read on to see just how much love I have f r Ted and Brittany, each in their own right.

"America was built on courage, on imagination
and an unbeatable determination to do the job
at hand."
— Harry Truman

June 2, 2019

Dear Ted,

Although there's no way you could have anticipated getting a letter like this, for me, it comes as no surprise as I embark on a journey to take a moment to write a letter of appreciation to those in my life who mean the most to me, and you are such a one. Yes, we are friends to the point of being family, and I know this clan's code is to laugh, joke, and cut up because that is clearly a mark of being an insider. Teasing is a way for us to keep one another in check and balance, to make sure we are as authentic and honest as we can possibly be in a world that often promotes pretense and guise for the sake of preservation or promotion. I adore the wit, the readiness to laugh, the wicked delight in making double-entendres, and an eagerness to celebrate birthdays, holidays, and life markers with candle-covered cakes, burgers and dogs, open arms, and an inviting home. Yes, I know it takes a team effort to provide what you and Brittney do for your family, but if you will indulge me, I'd like to take five and praise you for the best I see in you. The only way I know how to do this is to write because our conversations usually take a usual turn toward politics, history, and ethics.

Folks say not to discuss politics or religion, but where you and I are concerned, I balk at that platitude. I remember when we first met, amid a swirl of frenetic family fun, right from the start we hit it off. If I recall correctly, I took a chance in trusting you and revealed my former penchant for alcohol, and you judged me not; in fact, you shared how the topic hit home with you. Though our political persuasions tend to gravitate toward opposite poles, time and again, regardless of the subject we sort through, I take fresh delight in our finding common higher ground; this reveals that our core values are aligned. I typically gain the details of current events from you, and you listen and glean the unique perspective I provide from my travels and knowledge of different cultures. We have respect and affection for one another that goes beyond the surface of party lines. That's why I look forward to chatting with you about the latest going on, be it in our county, capital, country, or beyond! There are not many people who would eagerly engage in conversation about topics where differences of opinion are sure to spring up, let alone really listen for more than five minutes. Not you. We truly learn from each other every time.

Above and beyond this, we are family. Having begun well over twenty-five years ago, my friendship with Catherine continued to flourish after she graduated high school, and this put me in direct contact with her family and thus, your wife, then a girl. Perhaps because of something innate and familiar to us all, like some distant Mediterranean strain or gene, but more likely a readiness to seek what's real along with a no-holds-bar love, we collectively adopted one another. It took and grew. You have welcomed me in your home too many times to count, and we have broken bread and partaken of many a birthday cake and much football fare. Even if I don't know what's going on with the game at hand, you always make sure I'm comfortable and fed. There's never a time when you and I don't find some corner to catch up on the ins and outs of our private life. It could concern the health of your parents, an issue with one of the kids, a world or national event, or something in my world of teaching. We linger and listen to each other's dreams and or topics that captivate our hearts' attention. I also appreciate the fact that you have a risk-taking explorer inside you. Although occasionally the best-laid plans go awry, you are one who knows it is better to have tried; there is a success even in that. The world needs more people like you who jeopardize for the greater good as well as for self-betterment; you are that team player seeking more. This takes me down another mental avenue that I particularly appreciate about you. You are both a dreamer *and* a doer! Probably because my mother was an interior designer who shared with me many a home improvement project, I love visualizing and discussing how you transform houses and how you see the potential for beauty and then make it happen. It could be it painting your kids' rooms the color their hearts desire or updating older houses to give them majesty, modernity, or more space to utilize. The times that you've asked me about this or that color, texture, or idea, I can see it right alongside you, and more often than not, we have a similar choice, taste, or approach.

Our talks are not confined to politics or aesthetics, but also to the values that underpin the way we deal with children, be they your own ones or my students. You are a rich family man, and that you care beyond the confines of your yard to what is going on in your community and how this may impact your own dearest ones, I really appreciate. I also want to tell you that I admire you in particular for the role you've had in raising Brittney's eldest. It is not my place to judge her biological father, but you have more than made up for any failings and/or inconsistencies that her father may have displayed. As a leader of youth myself, I esteem fairness, accountability, and respect. I notice you, too, are trying to instill these values in your children. Why? You well know how things can pan out later on in life; therefore, discipline, consistency, and righteousness dispensed with affection and a generosity of spirit are what's on the daily docket for you to ensure all of your brood flourishes. We know what the child can't: that the seeming hurt of the moment proves to be loving and beneficial in the bigger picture, and that Brittney's daughter has matured and displays grace now is, in part, a testament to your role as her dad. You have also been there and done similarly for Gabriella's kids when a paternal force was void in their lives. Not all men man-up to do what you have done, and if you haven't been told recently, I notice and want to compliment you.

Speaking of being supportive, I also see how much you encourage greatness in your wife. As I mentioned before, I realize that in this family, ribbing one another is a sign of affection, intimacy, and a way to keep one another humble, but where it counts, you are unwavering in support. For example, where Brittney has had aspirations to do more to live up to her own potential, you are all in. I know it's not easy to be alongside a spouse who is compelled or driven to change, to advance her career, to return to school, and to go out on the limb of self-actualization. It can be risky business. Support and sacrifice are what's required, and you have been a generous leader in your family. I wouldn't know about the many private talks you must've had, but I mark a man who supports his wife — the mother of his children, so that she can stake her claim to success and become a more significant asset to her family. How can this be? It takes a strong and confident man to be there for his wife so she can achieve her ambitions, and I see that your allowances have made this possible. I commend you.

You, too, decided to leave the security of sales because of a robust entrepreneurial spirit beckoning within you to be your own boss. You have the kind of passion for improving the sight and structure of houses because not only does it bring profit, but because to your core, providing home, hearth, and security is what is sacred for you. Plus, you are a natural salesman with a winning smile and attentive stance, and you put people at ease in the way you let them know you are there for them, whatever the need or request. In short, you are a generous man. You are present and accounted for when the chips are down, as well as when it's time to celebrate because you are sensitive to life's cues and markers.

I've also witnessed how you cared for your own father during recent health problems, and you have been that unfaltering friend to friends and neighbors who have been down on their luck. For some, you've put a roof over their head and food in their belly. You never make a big deal over it because you are glad to do so. Often whe you've had folks and family over for football, there is usually one or two present I don't readily recognize but whom I've come to learn you've lent a helping hand. And if you aren't up and about or watching the game, it's because you're downstairs grilling. Many a time I've seen you cut and pass out cake and ice cream to never less than a dozen, and it was likely you who filled your home with the goodies everyone delights in. You are such a provider! What you give is more than our daily bread. I also appreciate that you're ready to dream *and* do! Whether it's taking a spontaneous road trip like we did to the Biltmore Estate or it's investing in intimacy by taking your wife on a romantic outing, you are one to say, "Yes," to making life special. You will sacrifice time and money to do so, be it camping in the yard or going to Disneyland. Springing from your protective side, I also quietly admire your desire to prepare and stockpile for the unforeseen, be it Y2K, a nuclear fallout, Armageddon, or some natural disaster of biblical proportions. Indeed, I am compelled to stick close by; were anything to go south, I believe you would gather me in your fold as well. Your house is a homestead; therefore, be it today, tomorrow, or a decade from now, I know you would offer me assistance, favor, and shelter.

Because you are the youngest son of three girls and a boy, our birth order dynamic is complimentary and a natural fit. I am the oldest daughter of the same number in my family, so it's easy to talk to you, and I find you an attentive listener. You are like a brother in blood *and* faith, and that says it all to me. There's nothing I don't feel ill-at-ease in sharing with you, be it troubles and trials or distant dreams. No, we have neither daily discourse nor regular contact, but when we do catch up, it is like no time has passed, and I find myself gravitating towards you in our family gatherings to share snatches of the latest news. I love it that no topic is off the table, and I've had more engaging conversations with you on a greater variety of issues than with about anyone I know. You also check on me out of the blue when you know something of gravity is going on. I thank you for that, too. Your passion for history is arresting, and I hope someday you get to bring to life and see up close and personal all you've read and ingested about our world. Speaking of which, the fact that you are an aficionado of history and a patriot is what beckoned me to launch this letter with a quote from one of our own leaders, and the qualities President Truman hails are all hallmarks of *your* character.

I'll end by restating that one of my favorite things about you is your readiness to smile and to take a humorous or witty slant to something said; such speaks of your desire to help make spirits bright. So, all joshing aside, let me encourage you to continue being the protective and providing man you are and to keep those homes fires burning and dreams alive and well among your loved ones. I am so happy to be your friend and family.

With love, joy, and respect,
D. C.

"Focus on your strengths, not your weaknesses.
Focus on your character, not your reputation.
Focus on your blessings, not your misfortunes.
Don't be pushed around by the fears in your mind.
Be led by the dreams in your heart."
— From The Light in the Heart, by Roy T. Bennett (2016)

"She is frequently kind And she's suddenly cruel She can do as she pleases She's nobody's fool But she can't be convicted She's earned her degree And the most she will do Is throw shadows at you But she's always a woman to me."
— Taken from "Always a Woman," by Billy Joel (1977)

June 9, 2019

Hello, Brittney!

Surprise! Amid our fast-paced and dizzyingly busy lives, I wanted to hit pause, or, more accurately, gift you a slo-mo verbal snapshot of all that I see that's best in you. Why? It has come to my mind that I do not want to wait for some calamity or misfortune, let alone for time to pass to share with you private thoughts that merit voice from which you might benefit or appreciate, even if only during the time it takes you to read this. The good I note will hardly be exhaustive. In searching for a quote to set the stage for your letter, I wanted something both biblical in essence, but secular in tone; imperative in intent, yet gentle in mood; and emboldening for the soul, yet wizened in outlook. I found all this conveyed in "The Light in Your Heart." I see such a dialectic in *your* heart.

Knowing you stretches and challenges any person to seek to become more like you: you are passionate, principled, and, at the same time, fiercely loyal, all wrapped in the enigma of your disarming and quicksilver wit. Though long ago, Catherine wrapped me into the fold of your all's family, it has been through my contact and interactions with you in particular that has changed my life forever. I will start out by recalling the time — now years ago — something that I quietly whispered to you in church. After I had moved alongside you in the pew, red carpet under our feet, and the sun drenching our faces from the expansive windows off to the side, I made a mental connection between my having accepted Jesus as my savior to your first finding and following Pastor Mark as the shepherd of our souls. His manner of preaching the Word inspired you to attend church with regularity, so spot-on was his exposition of Jesus. Because of this, you not only influenced your family to follow suit, but you blazoned the trail for me to do likewise. I, too, fell under his spiritual spell, which ultimately culminated in my salvation. He is now also simply my friend. Though the moment was divinely ordained, I still owe *you* a debt of gratitude for pursuing Christ on this particular path for yourself! A couple of years later, at the L.C. campus, I was stirred by your being moved. You shot forth like a cannonball after Pastor Todd urged anyone to come to the altar who felt like he or she needed to renew his or her pledge of commitment to Christ. At the moment you came forward, we saw the adult in you "turn and become like [one of His] children" (Matthew 18:3 CSB), so pure and natural was your response, and I think we were all a little envious, humbled, and elated. Though you appreciate the message and delivery of Mark, you sacrificed this preference to attend a church closer by in order that your children can experience Christian fellowship with ones with whom they are surrounded by on a daily basis. Where you go to church is secondary to the fact *that* you attend, and, more fundamentally, that your core values are based on His ideals. No matter what temptations or trials life throws your way, you and Ted possess a united front through Christ, and such will continue to make your marriage *and* family robust and healthy. Your faith is not the only area that rivets my attention.

In many families, it is often the case that the youngest child of the family can remain "the baby" even well in adulthood, and this can translate into prolonged dependency. Not with you. Of the three, you have the highest ambition, drive, and yearning for success, and you have steadily climbed the proverbial ladder while keeping your feet firmly on the ground. Please know that the teacher in me mentally gives you a gold star for having eclipsed all of your family in terms of educational level and vocation. I also have had the privilege of seeing your confidence blossom since the days of youth when you hadn't come into your own yet, and now I know I can come to you, woman to woman, and talk about matters of substance, be it vital to my heart or head. Speaking of birth order, I know that one of the inside family jokes comes from your dad's second wife, who, after proclaiming her love for your two older sisters, said with mock generosity that she loved you "*three*," confusing "too" with "two." Still, I want to tell you a place where you have been number one. No one but you lived alongside your mother and witnessed her dazed and confused and crushed after being left for someone half her age and practically across the globe. She had to pick of the pieces of her life and survive in a way she could not have foreseen. It is no one's fault that the chronology of your older sisters was such that they were already out of the house and making their own nests, but you were there for her. You witnessed your mother's loss first-hand, and such created a steely survivor in you, a princess warrior who would defend to the death her precious loved ones and a loyalist to her core. No one crosses you or yours without witnessing a mama lion come out to roar. Though the youngest, I have come to see that it has often been through *your* generosity and capabilities that you have been the one to provide for others, sometimes for your nieces and nephews who clearly cherish you. Knowing the mysteries of motherhood and what all it means to be a woman, you have the guts and grace, spunk and spirit, pluck and passion, leather and lace, and quick reflex to help in just the right measure when people are in need. Sometimes bearing others' weight can lead to a weariness, but you have a light spirit, and to be around you is to feel the joy, spontaneity, and a readiness you possess, whether you announce that you are learning to box or that you are reviving your energies on an evening out with friends or on a date with your husband. At other times, you say nothing and just up and break into dance with a stranger on a cruise ship!

You have a no-nonsense way about you that enables you to sift through what life gives us and to separate the wheat from the chaff while not batting an eye, and, no doubt, juggling much, too. And where others may conform or do what is expected, I think you follow your heart to feed your soul by accessing your brain and His brawn. When it's all said in done, just as Jesus told Martha that her sister Mary had done right by preferring to listen to Him rather than make a fuss about tending in the kitchen, you, too, time and again, *"choose the good part"* (Luke 10:42). Your knowing what is really important is expressed by your being one who mends much in life. For example, when we get together and your tribe is sprawled out watching football, some of whom are milling about in the kitchen to get another piece of this or that, you may be sitting and catching up on your phone. However, if a child or any of yours has an injury, infection, or issue, you are ever Johnnie-on-the-spot and on-call: you triage the crisis at hand, never losing your cool. And this your conduct applies to tending to our neighbor as ourselves: an unsteady man who passed out in the park at our most recent gathering has you to thank that he didn't pass away. Oh, no, you are no alarmist, but when Nature calls or real trouble is at hand, you are there quicker than Jack flash, and your calm and expertise steady us as much as your wit delights. It is because of this incredible centeredness that your children come a-running to you when they find themselves in a hot mess, seek your favor or approval, or need to come in for a quick hug that only a mother can provide. Though demonstrated uniquely, each of your children has your free spirit, and being a mother never diminishes the more fundamental part of your being your own woman. I echo Mr. Joel's sentiments of your also being "always a woman to me," and a complex one at that. I am glad that such a strong woman as you is raising independent daughters; your three princesses are all mighty and capable, each with a certain wildness and inner poise, too, just like you. Your son (and mini-me), obviously adores you, and I love how you can get to or through to him when language is not adequate. Yet you are that friend who always has just the right word to say, yes, long before Words with Friends came to be.

Speaking of which, I think you have the quickest wit of the bunch; your words can pack a punch, and without batting an eye, your wry comebacks and unvarnished truths can rightly sting or make us all burst into laughter. You have a unique inte sity and seriousness about you that pleases and engages me, and in matters of substance, you are there, ready and able for any conversation. Whenever I dive into a topic with you, it is no longer Catherine's younger sister I chat with, but a woman who has come unto her own. You have wise assessments about serious topics, and you are ready to discuss all matters of the heart. We have discussed raising children in a world gone mad, remaining true to oneself all the while toeing the line for the ones you love. You and I both keep physically fit to keep our inner spunk *and* expend our hyper energies. I have so much respect for you! Though we can get absorbed in our own private pow-wow of seriousness, you invariably say something keen or absurd that has us both laughing, rolling our eyes, or shaking our heads when we land on a particular crux that we both evidently needed. Like some Magic Eight Ball shaken in my brain, I know I can trust that the answer with you will always be "Outlook good" or "Signs point to yes."

You are an optimistic person to your core, and the fruit of your spirit is an abundant harvest for all who interact with you; never doubt this. Sometimes in adulthood, we strive to overcome the adversities, pains, or issues that haunt us from childhood, and though I don't pretend to be acquainted all of with yours, I see you have taken strides to heal and grow. You are exquisitely sensitive, sharp as a tack, cool as a cucumber, principled, and steadfast as they come, and I have seen you fight for what is right. Indeed, you are the kind of person everyone wants in their corner, so let me also assure you that though I am not frequently by your side, I will always have your back. Thank you for always having an open door and an open heart, welcoming me like family, be it at a football game, a birthday party, or even that dinner date you and I once had. I feel welcome in your home, and I can make my way around your kitchen as if I resided there. To sink into a comfy couch in your sitting room leads my soul to sigh from bliss. I am grateful to be in your beautiful home and surrounded by friends who are family, so near and dear to me. Your walls are adorned with mottos to motivate and pictures of your children — the trophies of your heart — to celebrate, and where style is concerned, you know less is more, so you have more than most.

I hope you take it from one who has watched you mature from maiden to mother, from follower to the leader, from shy to bold: I see a woman of substance, pitch, and resolve. I am proud of you, and I love you. I'm sure there's something funny or silly you could think of right now that would take away the spotlight from being on you, but His light shines bright in you and all you do; it is inextinguishable. You are the sprinkles on our cake and, undoubtedly, one of life's most special treasures!

Love, laughter, and a kiss on your cheek,
D.C.

39. Gabriella

Meet Gabriella. She is the middle sister of Catherine and Brittney. Gabriella would be the first to tell you that throughout her adult life, her mother, Josephine, has been like a significant other to her. Some might say she has been unlucky in love, but that's because when she takes you in, she has a heart that gives with all it's got. There are takers out there, and in my opinion, not all have been worthy of her affection. Thankfully, she recently found one who loves her and holds substantial promise. If you met Gabriella, you would instantly be taken in by her beauty, but, in no time at all, you would learn that it is more than skin deep. Should she allow you in her life, it's for life, and she would say that if you are in need, she would give you the shirt off her back. Gabriella's four children range in age from twenty to four, and, like many women, she is on her own and goes it alone. Yes, her mother, Josephine, sometimes steps in to take up the slack or to provide much-needed support so that the day can go off without a hitch and run as smoothly as silk. In turn, Gabriella is both grateful to and protective of her mother, and she is always the first to be there for her. Gabriella stands her ground and provides for her children, even if to do so might cost her more than she's got. There's no sacrifice she wouldn't make for them, and, as a result, the kind of relationship she has with her children would be the envy of all for how close they are to her. In fact, the one son of her three who currently is graduating high school and has garnered an impressive college scholarship has on social media attributed his successes to his mother for all she has done. Gabriella and her daughter share a language of gesture and nuance that few are privy to or would be able to crack its code. Whenever I see Gabriella, be it a day, week, or a month since our last visit, she greets me with a hug and kiss and warmth that lets me know how special I am to her, and I am smitten by her sincerity and sweetness.

*Who is the single woman with children in your life?
What do you admire about her? Have you told or shown
her lately? Can you tell that her children have been fed a
steady diet of confidence and tenderness? Do you marvel
at how she can discipline with authority one moment
and show her vulnerabilities the next? Who is one you
can feel in pseudo-conspiracy with and are indebted to
because you can share your secrets with her without
fear of judgment or the cold shoulder? She has been
there, done that, and doesn't forget what it was like.
Who discerns truth and motive and offers a smile and
hand, never missing a beat, so that you never miss out on
love?*

Read on to learn more about unforgettable Gabriella.

*³Do not let kindness and truth leave
you; Bind them around your neck,
Write them on the tablet of your
heart. . .
⁵Trust in the LORD with all your
heart
And do not lean on your own
understanding.
⁶In all your ways acknowledge
Him, And He will make your paths
straight. 7 . . .Fear the LORD and
turn away from
evil.
⁸It will be healing to your body And
refreshment to your bones.
From Proverbs 3:3–8, emphasis
mine*

*"She's got a way about her I don't
know what it is,
But I know that I can't live without
her
She's got a way of pleasin' I don't
know what it is,
But there doesn't have to be a reason
anyway…
She's got a light around her And
ev'rywhere she goes
A million dreams of love surround her
ev'rywhere…"
From Billy Joel's "She's Got A Way"
(1971)*

June 16, 2019

Dear Gabriella,

Hello! If it is okay with you, I'm going to take you on a trip, but one that is neither a vacation nor a fantasy. Instead, let's you and I time-travel to fifteen years from now, making it the year 2034. The details will be fuzzy and imperfect, but the mood and images will be as real as if you were holding a Polaroid snapshot in your hands. In fact, I'm going to have you sit in the stands of the stadium where your baby, your B., is down there among a sea of his fellow seniors getting ready to walk across that stage and recei e his high school diploma. Your heart is swelling with maternal pride, and you are waiting patiently as the order of events and the ceremony itself are unfolding, seemingly in slow-motion. Can you see him now glance up to search for you, and upon spotting you, you see his broad grin with that intent expression that still melts your heart? As you smile reassuringly back down at him, you wonder where the time has gone. This is the point where I whisper in your ear so as to share the goodness I have witnessed in you over the past three decades or so. As I reflect on your life and note your accomplishments, Gabriella, I am full of wonder, and I feel compelled to remind you how richly blessed you are. I know Jesus sees *your* kindness, truth, and trust! Your beauty still stuns, and your core nature is ever-mysterious, alluring, and generous. Yes, you, too, "have a way about you." There's no telling how many persons have felt the rush of power and privilege in having received a wink from you or a tender touch, some gesture that promises *you love us more*.

Let me start with your children then, the treasures of your heart. I recall a conversation you and I had well before B. was born about how sometimes — and for no apparent reason — you felt a rush of fear for your children's physical safety. At the time, you were glad that they were past those early years of such vulnerability. Who knew you'd be given a little boy who would bring out bravery in you? Looking further back though, what a courageous young woman you were, living in Japan when your husband was stationed there, across the globe with no other familiar face to reassure you that everything was going to be alright. Coming home ended up with your marriage coming apart, but you held your head high and your family together. Did this mean you felt all grown-up and secure? No, but those were the days when, perhaps unbeknownst to you, the Lord was (and remains) near, not only providing, but shoring you up with a strength and resolve that you didn't know you had or were capable of possessing. Anyone who has witnessed you snap your fingers, heard the shift in the tone of your voice, or has spied the quick eye-locking gaze with one of your children, knows that mountains *can* move and children, growing or grown, *will* toe the line. I love how you pass on the gift of love, and that your children are so affectionate and loving of their own accord shows just how much they have learned from you, their mama. Your flow of warmth, your terms of endearment — in particular, the unique nicknames you have for your children, and the sacrifices you have made behind the scenes have created sons who are both sensitive and strong and a daughter who is confident and capable. I realize life has not been easy for you, what with your often having to go it seemingly alone. I also know that you are both prayerful and appreciative; you have made requests known to your Heavenly Father when your earthly men have let you down, and you are grateful for His provisions. A woman indeed needs a little tenderness, but when life gets out of order, and the strength she seeks from man or mate turns out to be as dicey as a house of cards, it is God who, time and again, guards and gives you the resources and resolve you need to keep your chin up when you are down on your luck. You are too special to pass by, and I am sure God must nod approvingly and smile when He catches a glimpse of the light about you.

May I go back a few more years and note the day you went from being just Catherine's sister to a friend with benefits for me? Now, before you wonder or burst into a giggle at that expression, I want you to know that what *I* mean by this is that I feel like *I hold a privileged spot in your heart*; you surely do mine. In fact, I'll always remember the first heart-to- heart talk we had on the front porch of your family house on V. Drive at the gathering held for you after your high school graduation. Apparently, school was still in session for you because you asked this teacher a thousand and one questions. You came to me as a trusting and curious child, an open book; therefore, how could I not share with you pieces of my life and the ways of the world that were yet a mystery to you? You possess the kind of intelligence few do: in a fraction of a second before there is even time to formulate a thought, you can size a person up in a glance without saying a word. Like some private eye, you study a person's expressions and body language and can accurately discern if that person is genuine, trustworthy, honest, or for real. It is clear to me that you can interpret my expressions like others read a book, and should you gauge sadness or see silence masking some distress, you immediately come to check to see if your hunch or gut feeling is right. Such is the brilliance of your intuition.

I think some folks may not give you credit where credit is due for the kind of powers of perception you possess, but no amount of training or formal education can teach a person to give the way you do. It's true that when the chips are down, you are the first to offer to move heaven and earth to put a patch on a hurt, even if you don't have a dime in your pocket! Often you keep your cards close because exposure to and trust in ones who lack backbone or brawn has left you vulnerable; not all have proved worthy, reliable, or credible, and so I say, shame on them. And yet, you are patient and biding; somehow you instinctively know that there's a bigger picture and believe that *better things are coming*. Gabriella, you are beautiful inside and out! You are one who makes life superlative, and amid many an ordinary day, you have made me feel cherished. For example, every time we have one of our gatherings, and later, when everyone is spent and it's time to go home, it is often *you* who gets up to see me out. Your wave and blowing a kiss goodbye assure me I am loved in the same way a child is when her parents tuck her into bed at night. She feels all is right in the world. Why, even the stars come out to twinkle a little brighter in the sky when they see you coming by. You have a way about you that when you lock in on a person, she or he feels there's no one else in the world that matters more, and this is as rare as finding a gem. What a simple and profound gift, and so I thank you. You give what you crave: respect, and this merits its own attention.

Even though it may seem like life has you cornered, leaving you wanting to disappear for a moment, like water changes from liquid to vapor, you remain standing, boots on the ground (though you're likely in heels), a woman of enduring faith and hope. Time and again, you prove to be as even-keeled as she comes. And related to our faith, may I say how much I have relished the frank discussions we have had out on your balcony about religious matters as pertain to our core values? Sometimes I speculate that because you have not advanced in your career as much as others, you might suspect that this diminishes our estimation of you. Let me assure you that it does not! If anything, I view you as a friend's best booster and the most forceful advocate your children could have. Such is a state no degree or promotion can give. Each of yours receives from you precisely what she or he needs in the right proportion and measure. Even if they do not make the grade, you always know the score, and the deal is that what is *most* important in life for you is to show up and represent. Your kids and your friends can feel the love.

Thanks to you, your children have learned to love abundantly, and they pass it forward. They have seen you provide shelter to a friend of theirs in need when you could have stood more help for yourself. Unlike many teenagers, yours prefer family to friends, or, even better, to bring their friends to hang out with family, and then *their* company feels like family. Your B. is showered with love and affection by his grown siblings such that he doesn't feel any paternal void. Your mother has helped shoulder some of the burdens you bear, and you are quicker than others to defend and deliver the respect *she* deserves as well. There is no generation gap in your family, and your pulse of love and support do not wain just because your eldest has left to start his own family or your two in high school are getting ready to leave the nest. They will always be your babies. It is evident by the affection and adoration they show you that they know who has been there, day in and day out, and who remains on and by their side. You skirt no responsibility. There's never a doubt as to where you are Friday evenings and Saturday afternoons throughout the fall. Come what may, your children know beyond a shadow of a doubt that you are out in the stands, attention riveted on them, your voice shouting support and your hands clapping instinctively, as if they, too, are cheerleaders. I also love that you are always quick to laugh at some not-so-funny, but still humorous moments — perhaps even a tiny calamity — and to share this mirth with you is to feel the privilege of being in on some great secret. How many times have you and I broke into laughter simultaneously at a moment that others would probably have missed out on, not even noticed, or thought inappropriate or indelicate? Too many to count! For the record, I accede that no parent is perfect. Perhaps you might think of a thousand incidents when you wished you might have done this or that differently or made an alternate judgment, but this is not a Monday morning quarterback type of note; I praise you for who you are, not for what you didn't do.

Speaking of some things you *did* do, I want to round the corner to the last quarter of my letter and mention a couple of decisions you made that have changed my life forever. The first is that I want to thank you for inviting me to church to celebrate your oldest son's getting baptized because, without this, I might not have come to know the love of Christ, let alone gotten saved. Then after my first attendance, you were swift to respond to my asking you if this pastor was for real. You enthusiastically assured me that you were sure he wouldn't mind if I contacted him. You were not willy-nilly in your response, but you audaciously took the initiative for me so that contact between us could be made; with permission attained, you gave me his email address. It turned out you were more than right about Pastor Mark, and the rest is history! God used you to help secure my salvation! Wow! For this and more, I am forever grateful to you. Next, the summer after Bonnie and I got home from one of our extended trips to Greece, per your invitation, we came straightaway to visit you. The discovery of learning that you were not just "a little bloated" but pregnant, gave birth to not only the reality of your precious son but a chance to let Bonnie have a brief taste of what it was like to be the grandmother she had always envisioned for herself. Those two years of her watching him were sacred, sweet, and secure. We've seen hundreds of pictures testifying to the happiness they both felt in being with one another. Such a radiant reciprocity! In short, in sharing your bundle of joy with us, each of them got to spend time with an angel, and I've no doubt God was smiling down on their pure love.

Finally, I love that you like to make ordinary things in life special. Whether you have candles aglow in your house, you've put up your Christmas tree and decorated it earlier than most, or you've arranged things invitingly in your cocoon of a living room, *you are one of the magic makers in life*, and we are all the more blessed for having you in ours. By now, you may wonder if I'm dying or something. No, I'm not, and neither is this note an elegy; I've just been dying to tell you this for some time. It hurts me that some folks in your life have not been as surefooted as you needed them to be, but no matter, you have your sisters around you like statues of Roman goddesses in some ancient garden. And though you have never set foot in Italy, believe you me, when I look at you, I see a Paisano. It is as if your mother's mother birthed you back in the old country, as if Italy itself was missing one of her native daughters. That same intense love for family that is such a classic characteristic of Italians still courses through your veins. Therefore, it doesn't matter if you are order takeout pizza from Little Caesar's, drink your coffee from a straw, or prefer potato candy to cannoli; this passion for your own did not get lost in translocation. I am grateful to be among your chosen ones as well. To be family with you is to feel the same love, passion, and commitment that any soldier feels for his band of brothers on tour or a football player for his team. Why? It's that same assuredness that God promises us to us that you say without using words: "Never will I leave you; never will I forsake you" (Hebrews 13:5 NIV).

I started out in this letter having you take a peek ahead. As I reflect on your past and present, and I have one last irony to tell you that seals the deal and speaks to our unique bond. On 11-28-18, the very day I started writing this your letter, out of the blue and for no particular reason, you sent me a text. I have to share it here so you can witness this well-house of love that we have for one another. Goodness! We were literally on the same page! Here it is:

> Hello, my beautiful! I hope you are having a
> wonderful day and this text brings a smile to
> your face. I met someone the other day and
> as we were talking and getting to know each
> other I was talking about you. It turns out, he
> was one of your students years ago. He said
> that you were one of his favorites... It made me
> smile thinking of how special you are and how
> you might not always realize it, but you make
> such a difference in people's lives. You are
> so special, and as he was going on about how
> awesome they all think you are, I got to say,

"She's my family!" What an absolute honor that
I get to be part of your life, and I get you call
you family. I love you with all my heart. Thank
you for being you.
☺ I love you more ☺

Gabriella, the honor is all mine, and I love you with all my
heart! May you forever find "refreshment [in] *your* bones"!

Always,
D.C.

40. Lewis

Meet Lewis. He is Catherine's husband of twenty-five years, and for the past five, he has been a colleague of mine. Lewis is also my friend, and no matter what is going on at school, when we see each other, he's sure to hug my neck and kiss me on the temple. Regardless of where I am, when Lewis steps into my view, I feel like I've just slid into home base. I'm safe! I get the sense and know from experience that "neither sleet nor snow nor rain nor the dark of night" would keep him from coming to my aid should the need or an emergency arise. No, he is no postal worker, but the kind of love and support Lewis delivers is always right on time. Doing life together has shown me what a hero he really is, and I am so proud that we are friends and family. He's the kind of man who is down-to-earth, spare of word, and prepared for the giving, correcting, and encouraging that only one born to be a combo of coach and dad possesses. I have seen young men cry and confide in him, and young women look up with hope and assurance from the encouragement he's given them. He instills faith and promise. Where the disciplining of children goes, Lewis and I are of one mind, so when we talk shop, we nod our heads and finish each other's sentences because we are in agreement as to which skeleton key to use to solve the riddle of some wayward child or student. Whenever I visit Catherine to enjoy a not-so-quiet cup of coffee, partake of an all-over-the- map conversation, and make much merriment together, there's not a doubt in my mind that not only is Lewis glad I'm there in his home, but that he wouldn't mind if I stayed. He would take me in in a minute because I'm in his heart's classification of family, not merely friend or coworker.

Who is a coworker that has become a real friend to you?
Whom could you turn or run to if you found yourself
in dire straits, no questions asked? Do you know the
spouse of a close friend of yours whom you also consider
family? Are you acquainted with a man who was born
to be a father, in part, because he leads with love that's
both tough and tender? Is there a man who is a pillar
of the community and a rock for his loved ones? Are you
grateful to be in his good graces? What man dreams of
going on a tropical island vacation but in the meanwhile,
grills and barbeques in his back yard, and we all get the
feeling that we are on holiday?

Read on to meet Lewis for yourself.

"Do nothing from selfishness or empty conceit,
but with humility of mind *regard one another as*
more important than yourselves; do not merely look
out for your own personal interests, but also for
the interests of others.
—Philippians 2:3–4, emphasis mine

"Treat a person as he is, and he will remain as
he is.
Treat him as he could be, and he will become
what he should be."
—Jimmy Johnson, coach

June 23, 2019

Dear Lewis,

It is a rarity to get an actual letter in the mail, you know,
one that isn't a bill, notification, or solicitation. Plus, in our

line of work, the news a letter brings can make or break a person's future, let alone mood and mindset, as he learns of acceptance or rejection, some award or loss. I'm here to tell you that this private note, just from me to you, is one of admiration, appreciation, and encouragement. I ask you to indulge this English and foreign language teacher who, unlike most of our students, not only likes to put pen to paper but deeply desires to "count the ways" she thinks *you* are incredible. You know as well as I that we don't hear enough of the good. In fact, somehow, we are supposed to outgrow or get beyond craving praise; I beg to differ. Like good food fuels that the body, words that affirm strengthen the soul. You ought to know: you are such a caring man whose action speaks louder than words. In fact, your love and support are as elemental as meat and potatoes, and no one starves on your watch. As a result, you are surrounded by loved ones at home and at school, grown and growing, who, in their bones, have come to know they can count on you because you have their back, be it in the ordinary moments or in times of trouble. Children are more overt in showing their desire for affirmation and acknowledgement. Yet even though adults ought to be selfless and not self-serving, it never hurts to hear what we mean to others; therefore, I call time-in to tell you what kind of a king of a man I think you are.

There was no way I could have known that way-back-when, when you were the object of Catherine's affection in high school, that I would get to bear witness to the devoted husband, adored father, and respected leader of your own and our community that you would become. Many pledge allegiance to you because they know from experience that you have the strength of character and stamina to help shoulder burdens. I am one of many who feels blessed to have you in my life. Though Catherine and I enjoy a special bond, it is no longer just her I come to visit: I seek to see you, and more often than not, we two get carried away by the much we have in common, both in vocation and in vision. We see more than meets the eye.

We know that above and beyond the stats, plans, modifications and accommodations that are in place for special students, they need adults who can help them toe the line and grow to the greatest of their potential. Often that is achieved through good old-fashioned dedication and sticking to sound principles. There is a real freedom that comes from such a mentality. We see no possibility for plausible deniability where the formation of character is concerned; therefore, I see you do your darnedest to ensure kids don't sabotage their own successes and that adults are aware of the indelible marks that *they* are making. Such a credit you are to your profession and to your calling as a father! Standing by kids' sides and working with them one-on-one to help them master the basics of math or essential life skills — like how to treat your mother or brother — is on the daily docket for you. When nature has not dealt the cards fairly, you help stack the deck so that the odds can be more in a student's favor and so that he or she might have a fair shake at attaining the good things in life, not to mention the better from themselves. Your type of nurture trumps nature.

Do we get frustrated when kids don't reach their potential or heed our voice of reason and perspective? Daily. Do we shake our heads in frustration or exasperation as we read the writing on the wall that spells out t-r-o-u-b-l-e for an anxious, delinquent, or damaged child? Yes, but time and again, phone call after email after meeting, I see you go above and beyond daily and nightly. There is no modicum of discretion in what *you* are willing to do for others. Whether you meet with a hysterical mother at her wit's end or drive to the hospital or house of some young man in dire straits, it is evident that God has given you "a spirit of timidity, but of power and love and discipline" (2 Timothy 1:7). Some call the kind of leadership we bring to the table "tough love," but you and I know we are building a reservoir of inner strength and self-respect, which is nothing short of *real* love and service with a smile. You are a family man to your core, a father to many, a coach both on *and* off the field, a king to your queen at home, and a brother who epitomizes brotherly love. Over the two decades I've known you, I've witnessed repeatedly where a word from you, a shift in your tone and stance, or a grin can make your babies' heads turn to find you and children seek to please. Minds grow and hearts swell in your love. When they sink, you swim; when they fumble, you don't falter, and when they triumph, we all win. The world doesn't have enough men of constancy, consistency, and commitment like you.

Often you spread yourself thin, and you, too, need your batteries recharged. Therefore, although you sometimes fantasize about a getaway vacation in Belize, it's usually a trip to Wal-Mart with a few of your bunch that can make it feel like taking five as you hunt and gather meat and manna for your home and hearth. Your providing doesn't stop with physical provisions: you bring the bacon home *and* cook meat over a fire, like men of caves and castles have always done. More importantly, you fill your young with emotional sustenance, a nutrient more filling than food. As an aside, I, too, am one who prefers the taste of wild goat to the tamer meats, and sometimes I feel like you and I at one time might have belonged to a clan or horde of nomads, with the exception that you can and actually like to camp, and I am more of one who would choose to "glamp." That said, I see your brain engage in wonderment when I speak to you of travels because you have an open mind that is hungry and curious to learn how people from different parts of the world live and do. And speaking of restoring ourselves, may I say here how much I relish our date night for the four of us? Whenever we find a way to make time to dine out together, the conversations we have nourish more than the food we eat, though I admit it's always fun to look forward to the restaurant we've chosen, be it for wings or sushi or gyros! What you bring to any table is rich and real.

You may be a man who more readily gravitates towards math, logic, and physical science, but you have a way about you that inspires those around you to have faith and hope in the bigger and better things that cannot be quantified. I have heard it said that we get our concept of God from the relationship we have with our own fathers, and if this is the case, your children will undoubtedly be at an advantage! Although your hands may dispense discipline, they also carry, caress, and comfort and let your babies know they are cherished by you, you who stand above *and* beside them through the peaks and the valleys, 365 days a year. In a day and age where instant gratification is coveted like fast food to be gobbled up, you break the mold of many a man and remain tried and true.

Another misnomer you dispel is the idea that chivalry is dead. I would be hard-pressed to think of any man more solid in this department than you, and I'm not merely talking about opening doors or carrying heavy parcels, which you and all your boys do. The kind of consideration you display towards women is not condescending. It's as if your inner man knows that man's role is to protect women and defend the defenseless because you have been created in such a way to do so; to do less would be to shirk your responsibility and God-given capacity. Your shining armor may come in the form of a jersey and your steed, an extended van, but whenever I see you, I always feel a sense of safety and protection wash over me, yes, even if we are talking shop or checking in. With the dangers that we in the trenches at school face today, I have told not a few people that if there were an actual threatening situation occur (and not "just" bomb threats), my mind would race, and my eyes would search for *you* because I know with all I've got that I would be safe and secure with you. I also believe you would seek and rescue me as a family member and a friend were bedlam to arise. Because I am unused to gallantry in my life, I am extra appreciative of your kind of kindness, be it in the form of coming over in the hallway to hug my neck and kiss my head, changing a flat tire in a darkened parking lot, or paying for my meal on the down-low. Your wife may sometimes have a quick wit and wicked tongue, but you are more careful with your words and roll your eyes and smile when she speaks loosely; a man cannot afford this type of indulgence. Your brand of love never tarnishes or diminishes because you see more than meets the eye, and your eyes often say more than your tongue utters, so to catch your words is like reading some playbook on discernment. Each point is salient.

You lead by taking action where it counts; we'd be wise to emulate you. That you are such a committed worker, often taking on a second job or doing what coaches must in their free time, has paid off more than materially. Your three oldest sons have also followed in your footsteps and stepped up in their own right to get a job and to be independent. I remember a few years back when you were applying to teach here, I could hardly wait to give my vote of confidence and inundate you with praises to the administration. Since then, I have seen you not only succeed, but you have become indispensable for us at school. I hope you know how much our staff respects you for what you bring to the table for our wayward or special ed. students, and that's not including our football players and coaches. Oh, you do your *alma mater* proud! In fact, I believe that the move back here, though for reasons not anticipated, has brought about a sense of deep satisfaction that has exceeded your expectations. I can appreciate raising a family the size of yours has its unique challenges. Time and again, your aptitude for fatherhood and the mighty love you have for Catherine makes me understand the reason behind the expression that a man is the king of his castle: you surely are of yours for how you lead and serve and give. You don't just settle: time and again, you tell me in private of your desire to improve, especially your health, and I know you mean it because you've got so much at stake. Much to our loved ones' chagrin, we can't be more than one place at a time, and time is always running in short supply for you because of the many obligations you keep; regardless, yours all gravitate toward and ecstatically run to you, their rock.

Sometimes a man does not realize even a tenth of what he gives to others, so I tithe this letter to you in hopes you can sense how incredible you are. Coming back home to K. doesn't mean you don't appreciate your time in M. or other places you've lived. You are a native son who *has* been able to come home. When I see you, I get a celebratory wish to give a spectacular homecoming parade for you, an American veteran, a fellow Admiral, and a Vol, yes, even among your spirited family of rival Gamecocks. Keep on keepin' the faith and bringing about the best in others, whether it is on the field or in your family. You are loved by *so* many people, and that certainly includes me.

Much respect and more love,
D.C.

41. Kevin

Meet Kevin. This is a man who grew on me quietly and one I didn't see coming into my heart as he was becoming my dear friend. Kevin is our "computer geek" at school; actually, he is one of only a few of these gems in the district that we have come to rely on heavily. For me and many others, Kevin is a miracle worker. It's as if he has a magic wand and knows just the right way to say, "Abracadabra!" and our computer glitches and technical woes vanish into thin air. My jaw drops in amazement as he walks down the hallway, nonchalantly as ever, to another teacher's aid. Not only is he one of our superheroes at school for us who deal more with flesh and bone and get stymied and stuck with technological travails, but he has made many a house call to help me with such issues at home. Slowly but surely, by steadily sharing each other's minds as we have waited for some process or file to complete its download, we have become fast friends. Kevin is definitely like a sweet onion for me, and by peeling back the layers, I have come to love the core of this man. Over the span of a decade or so, we may have met just a couple of times a year. Yet when we do, it's necessarily so for hours at a stretch. I have come to learn of his past vocations, pivotal life experiences, personal beliefs, and private opinions on any number of topics. And he mine. He is a curious and caring soul, the tortoise to my hare, and I am the richer for the give and take and mutual respect we have for each other. Many persons are propped up by platitudes and don't even realize it. Kevin is a discerning man, that quiet Christian soldier who operates under the guise of being just your average guy who loves baseball and happens to know a thing or two about technology. That's not the case as to how I view him; he is *so* much more than that. Whether I'm at my wit's end, ranting and raving at my frozen computer screen, or should he and I sit together quietly at home, my ailing computer between us, Kevin brings me calm to any storm. We take delight in fruitful conversation. He and I are more than colleagues: we are brother and sister in Christ, and I feel the fullness and joy of our being friend and family.

Who is the "computer guy" in your life? This person might be your accountant, attorney, advisor, or consultant who has come to your rescue in some way and therefore feels a little like a savior for the assistance or expertise he or she has provided. Have you gotten to know a person you might not usually rub elbows with because he or she ostensibly has little in common with you? When you did break the ice and got familiar with the crooks and crevices of his soul, did you discover that this was not only a person you had befriended, but one you had come to love?

Read on to experience Kevin.

"The plans of the diligent lead surely to advantage, but everyone who is hasty comes surely to poverty."
— Proverbs 21:5

"When you give to the poor, do not let your left hand know what your right hand is doing, so that your giving will be in secret; and your Father who sees what is done in secret will reward you.
— Matthew 6:3–4

The Masonic Mission is "to promote a way of
life that binds like-minded men in a worldwide
brotherhood that transcends all religious,
ethnic, cultural, social and educational
differences by teaching the great principals
of *Brotherly Love*, Relief and Truth and by the
outward expression of
these, through its fellowship, its *compassion and its
concern*, to find ways in which to *serve God, family,
country, neighbors and self.*" (Emphasis mine)

June 30, 2019

Dear Kevin,

It's hard to believe that a dozen or so years have flown by since I first sought your help with a computer issue or technology emergency. Back then, my father was still alive, and I was taking care his affairs; you also helped me with his antiquated machine. Like some old-fashioned doctor toting his black bag, you have made no less than twenty house calls. Whether it was to set up a new computer, to complete a routine maintenance check, to fix some technical error, or to eradicate a virus which put me in a state of panic, you have turned out to be one of the most reliable, steadfast, and capable men I know. There are too many times to count for how often you've availed yourself to help walk me through some step-by-step recipe of instructions over the phone in order to put right what was impairing my laptop, hard drive, or Outlook email. In the meanwhile, do you realize what happened throughout this time? *You became my friend,* and for this, I am very grateful.

Looking back, I can now say I appreciate all the time that was spent waiting for a zillion files to copy, for rebuffering to take place, or remedying some digital ailment. Why? It gave us precious time to converse, and over this span, we got to know each other. This prudent use of our time led to an inadvertent meeting of the minds, like some think tank that got launched. Although you and I are private folks with entirely different backgrounds and varying political stances, who would have known then that on a more fundamental level, we possess similar baseline values? We both have a passion for life, a thirst for learning, and opinions ripe for the sharing. The sum effect of our stints together produced mutual admiration and affection. We have eaten together, shared life stories, and laughed over the folly of the foolish and the faithful — and that includes ourselves. Though such a letter like this is uncommon, dare I say unorthodox, if I may, I seek to take a few moments and count the many blessings I have in a friend like *you*, you who are my *Braveheart* hero.

You break the mold of what a "computer geek" is supposed to be like. Though you are a logical man who prefers the rationalism and symmetry which comes with territory of computer technology, I have discovered that you have one of the biggest hearts I know. You are up-to-speed where the latest and cutting-edge technology is concerned, but in your soul, you are old-school. Yes, I know, your job for our school district is a thankless one, what for all the computers that come your way to be fixed, cleaned, updated, or resurrected, and I'm sure you continuously encounter much wailing and gnashing of teeth. Speaking for those around me, we feel indebted to and thankful for you; therefore, for you to go the extra mile and come to my home *and* my rescue is all the more moving to me. How many times have you been on-call and answered my texts of agony, day or night, about some digital crisis? I am loath to say, it has been too many times to count! Simply stated, you are an officer and a gentleman. In general, people do not have the kind of "compassion and concern" woven in their moral fabric as do you. When I was taking care of my father's affairs, I was running on fumes much of the time, so I'll never forget your volunteering to go to a store with me to help me get the item I needed. Right then and there. You are an "all in" kind of man. At that particular time of my life when I felt like I was running up against the world, you were an oasis in this storm. And your consideration for privacy and security is readily apparent: you physically turn your chair away every time I have had to enter a security code or password. If you ever make a mistake or prove to be in rare error, you are the absolute first to admit it and bend over backward to rectify the wrong. Little by slowly, as we passed the time while waiting for various processes to take place in the brain of my computer, we had the space to chat, and I have been astonished at the breadth and depth of the topics we've covered. Our natural curiosity and fascination with various and sundry topics have kept our conversations flowing, so much so that we sometimes pick up where we last left off. Not only that, but in a world where one more readily gravitates towards like-minded folks, we transform our circumstance, and, thanks to you, I have grown.

In one sense, we couldn't be more opposite: you are a republican in a quasi-democrat's home, a homebody with a world-traveler, a gun-toting former policeman facing a trigger-shy teacher, and a Christian with a then skeptic. Though no one could confuse me for being your Doppelgänger, in the core where character counts, we have much in common. As Walt Whitman would say, we are "curious, not judgmental." In the giving and taking of opinion on any number of topics or controversies, we present the facts with no agenda, guile, or affront. Be the subject politics, world events, local news, or the goings-on at work, time and again, we share a similar compassionate conservative stance that has us settling on the same side. How we assess human nature and man's motive proves to me that you and I really do see eye-to-eye. I would be remiss if I didn't mention what I have newly come to appreciate from you, that it would be best for me to keep a ready rifle behind the front door. I need not fear firearms; indeed, you even volunteered to take me to a shooting range! As a former policeman, you've seen too much to know that one would be wise to possess this ready defense. And that you openly embrace your being, as you self-diagnose, "OCD," makes me feel affection for a man who likes things done to perfection, be it clearing the clutter from your real or virtual desktop or dust from within the tower. As you run checks for viruses and bugs in the hard drive or a thousand other little things, you also arrange your life to maintain order and keep the peace.

Had our topics been relegated to what was going on in the world, perhaps we would have maintained a "business as usual" type of professional relationship. Still, the ease, trust, and honesty with which we broached all topics — none have been off the table — also unwittingly led me to share my own life with you. Little by little, slowly but surely, over another decade of coming to my home and to my rescue two or three times a year, we shared what was going in each other's personal lives, both the highs and the lows. I mourned your losses as you bore witness to my trials; I celebrated your life's triumphs as you heralded my vindications. We were there for each other and on each other's sides, even if from the sidelines. You are the tortoise to my hare, and you fight the good fight and win the race every time. It's not how fast we go, but how far we come in life that matters, isn't it? In those early days, I confess I recall scanning quizzically over your business card the words, "Proverbs 21:5." At the time, I did not look this verse up. Only recently, it occurred to me that other than through your actions, you neither proselytized nor evangelized to me; you had no agenda and needed no high-sounding words. You were not at all like how I'd envisioned "them." Eventually, I searched for this verse and understood with soul stirred that your *diligence* led to my benefit and *advantage*. I consider you one of God's guardian angels who tiptoed into my life and enabled me eventually to say, "Yes," to Him. Now that I've come to Christ, you are more than just "my computer guy." You are that quiet Christian soldier, a brother in arms, my compadre at work, and a friend for life; indeed, I consider you family. Plus, may I insert here that seeing pics of a big man who delights in his small dogs makes me adore you all the more.

For a man who is naturally humble, reserved, and stays out of the spotlight, it isn't easy to find a way to compliment you, but let ye know, I sing your praises! A couple of months ago, you recounted the background of the Masons and how its heritage, traditions, and noble purpose moved you. You are now a link in this centuries-old chain. It may be a mystery to many that this band of brothers keeps mum about the good they do, but these values are in keeping with what Christ asks of us, that is, to put a lid on broadcasting our service. The focus is on the deed, not the doer; that way, God gets the glory, and a needful one gets help. Win-win-win. You don't trumpet your thousand acts of generosity, but I'm here to tell you, your planned and random acts of kindness place you head and shoulders above the mass of men around you. It is easy to see that you are a living example of the Masonic Mission to which you subscribe. That you told me about an elderly neighbor lady you check on with frequency is just the sort of work you do silently behind the scenes which shows your noble nature, one I know is noticed from the One above.

May I end with my telling you how happy I was for you and your wife to go to Greekfest with me? How natural was our flow of conversation! How enjoyable it was to partake of lamb, try new dishes, and delight in pastries. I was pleased to explain some of the Orthodox beliefs and show you the interior of the cathedral. Like a student of life, you marveled at the multitudinous miniature tiles comprising the mosaics around and above us in the dome. It reminded me of your sharing with me the historical details authenticating Christ's cross at the base of the Church of the Holy Sepulcher. I smiled inside to see how taken you were by the panel with the icon of the wild-eyed and scraggly John the Baptist on the iconostasis. This Greek girl is impressed that not only can you make moussaka, but after our big fat Greek dinner, you bought your own icon of the Last Supper!

I believe that the core bond we share knows no bounds because we are confident where we're headed, so we enjoy the ride all the more. I'm well-aware that you desire to go to Austria or drive through the Alps in Switzerland. Still, in my mind's eye, I see you in a plaid kilt, standing tall and proud in the Scottish Highlands, ginger hair in contrast to the blue-green mountains off in the distance; it would not surprise me at all if you could play "Amazing Grace" on the bagpipes! And though I know next to nothing about baseball, I am as big of a fan of you as you are your Chicago Cubs. You are *my* MVP! I will probably catch my next glance at you at school, working as quiet as a mouse and busy as a bee, performing curative feats on our confounding computers, like some wizard. I am confident that King Jesus hears my prayers for you, you who never seek any fanfare for a job well done. I've no doubt you'll be exalted because you humble yourself every day. I laud you here now. As they say down in this neck of the woods, "*You's good people,*" so I hope you know how grateful I am for you, my hero *and* my friend. I'll leave you with a traditional Gaelic blessing:

> May the road rise up to meet you. May the
> wind be always at your back.
> May the sun shine warm upon your face;
> the rains fall soft upon your fields and until we
> meet again, May God hold you in the palm of
> His hand.

Sincerely,
D.C.

July

The Greek Spirit

Every summer, hundreds of thousands of tourists from all over the world visit Greece, drawn by the promise of days drenched in the sun, beautiful islands with white washed buildings, tantalizingly fantastic food, and a warm and welcoming people. You may ask why I would include a chapter devoted to the Greek spirit here and perhaps hastily conclude that it is because my own father was Greek, one born less than twenty minutes from Sparta or because I am enamored by this culture. Okay, that's undoubtedly true. However, for my purposes here, I seek to shed light on a code of conduct that has arisen from a people in existence for some five thousand years. In all they do, *Greeks celebrate life!* Such passion is baked into their spirits! What better way to showcase how we should appreciate our loved ones than by looking at a culture and people whose lifestyle is all about living life to its fullest? I'll share a few "fun facts" as well as a couple of family stories; then I'll outline some characteristics of Greeks which will prepare you to meet four persons who are particularly dear to me.

You may already know that Greece boasts of enjoying more than 250 days of sun and in its territory has some 6,000 islands, of which about 200 are inhabited. Statistically speaking, the island of Ikaria is known for having one of the world's top five longevity rates. I can say, "Olympic games" and "Greek mythology," and need not elaborate on their impact or import. Of course, you are aware that ancient Greece advanced cavemen past stick and stone and fire by introducing theater and philosophy to the world. Who wouldn't agree that democracy is her crowning glory? I recently learned that Greece has more than 4000 traditional dances around the country; that can't help but infuse joy in one's spirit! I am sure that one reason my mother fell in love with my father had to have been when she first saw him dance. In my mind's eye, I can imagine her transfixed, delighted, and moved to see such a free spirit hop, twirl, and lose self to soul.

How do these facts get fused into a nation's character? I really don't know; that part is all Greek to me, but I *can* tell you that, in general, Greeks are at once a joyful, independent, and freedom-seeking people. They are also generous, kind, watchful, and helpful. I've never met a more open people who are ready to speak their minds and give you their opinion, solicited or not. They can be pouty, but not for long, and they are not judgmental. I can still recall my Greek grandmother chiding me on the telephone for my not speaking Greek and expecting *her* to speak English; she quickly informed me in her screechy pitch that "*the Grik language the best language in the world! It has been around for a meeeeelllllllion years!*" Well, it turns out she was close: the Greek language is unique in that it has been in continuous use for more than 5000 years. This makes it the oldest written language still in existence and in use.

It is true that Greeks are profoundly proud of being Greeks, and yet, for those living in America, you'd be hard-pressed to find a group of people more hardworking and patriotic as they. You'll find the American flag waving and whipping atop the Greek one, high above their business establishment. They are a people who, even if they do their own thing on a daily basis, adhere to the r traditions with enthusiasm, and you can witness this most demonstrably and vibrantly in church and in celebration. That said, my own father is an example of an immigrant who came to America because of need, not from want. So, for him, regardless of the successes and accomplishments he made for himself in America, for him, Greece would always be home. In fact, in the last two decades of his life, he made his way back there as often as he could, like some homing pigeon drawn by its blood's memory and beckoning. Let me take *you* there now to meet my friends.

42. Petros

Meet Petros. I'll bet if I strung together all the hours he and I have spent together, they wouldn't add up to a single day, but for me, the lessons I've learned from this man will last me a lifetime. I've seen him on three different trips I've taken to Greece; each time I hired him as my guide for various hikes that he has plotted through the wiles and mountains in a section of southern Greece called Mani. Petros is not the stereotypical gregarious and bigger-than-life type of Greek your mind may conjure up when you think of this nationality. No, he is quiet, contemplative, and soulful, and he is as connected to the earth as a babe at its mother's breast, as the ancient stone in Delphi is considered the navel of the world. In him, there is no pretense, just power; nothing profligate, just pure. When you read about him, you will find a Homer who came home and to his senses when he realized that the life he was leading, one which is considered "normal" by the masses, was actually off-course. It occurred to him that keeping up the pace with ones who lived for leisure revealed a mindset that was both a shame and a waste. There *had* to be more to life than this! Like me, Petros doesn't want to miss out on a moment in life, so he probed his soul, discarded his superfluous stuff, and, undeterred, came back to his home village to start life anew. To hike with him in the unmolested and magnificent mountains of the Peloponnesus is to resurrect your spirits.

Do you have a friend or loved one that switched gears
and made a radical life change, one that celebrates
Nature and sloughs off narcissism? Maybe a midlife
crisis occurred prematurely, and he is all the wiser for it.
Do you know a native son who came back home and is
considered a local hero, but one who is as low-key and

unassuming as you' ll ever find? Have you thought of a way to thank him for being true to himself or her for following her dreams? How have they shown you what's noble and excellent that you may have dismissed or taken for granted?

Join me to meet Petros!

"[Driving], you [can] see Mani in three days; walking, in three months, and in order to see its soul you need three lives. One for the sea, one for its mountains and one for its people. I began to grasp one of the great and uncovenanted delights of Greece: a direct and immediate link, friendly and equal on either side between human beings, *something which melts barriers* of hierarchy and background and money, and, except for a few tribal and historic feuds, politics and nationality as well... Our glances say that *existence is an adventure* which we are in league to undergo, outwit, and *enjoy on equal terms* as accomplices, fellow-hedonists..."
— Patrick Leigh Fermor, emphasis mine

"In the woods, *we return to reason and faith.* [Here] a man casts off his years, as the snake his slough, and at whatsoever period of life, is always a child. *Within these plantations of God, a decorum and sanctity reign,* and the guest sees not how he should tire of them in a thousand years. I feel that nothing can befall me in life, — no disgrace, no calamity, — which Nature cannot repair. Standing on the bare ground, — my head bathed by the blithe air, and uplifted into

infinite space, — *all egotism vanishes.* The currents
of
the Universal Being circulate through me; *I am
part or particle of God.*"
— Ralph Waldo Emerson, taken from *Nature*
(1836) emphasis mine

July 7, 2019

Dear Petros,

The first time I came to K. in 2011, it took me no time to be enamored by this charming little town, and as my family and I explored, just beyond the complex of ancient K., we found a tiny hiking trail sign that pointed the way to the church of Saint Sophia. Little did I know how gratifying this adventure would be for my brother, sister, and me. After several hours of walking along this trail and taking in its Arcadian beauty, we then trekked through the boulders and rocks of the Viros Gorge, which eventually brought us back to civilization. As spent as I was, the appetite for this place was birthed in me to do and see even more here. Meandering back to the central part of town, I discovered your shop which promised the aid of a guide who could help one experience what I longed for: a lifetime of exploring this area. What is it about K. that proves so compelling? Is it the fact that K. is one of the oldest settlements in the Peloponnese, considered by many to have existed since prehistoric times, its name being mentioned in Homer's epic poem, *The Iliad*? Is it because it is close to my father's hometown of Gythion, a mere two-hour, achingly beautiful drive over the knobby knuckle of the middle Mani finger so as to get from its outer to the inner side? Little did I know that over the next eight years, returning to this spot three times would lead me to take three spectacular hikes with you as my guide. Considering the impact you have made on me in these hikes, how could I not take *you* on a short journey through my soul, if for no other reason than to reflect on the wisdom I gained from you and to celebrate the friendship we now have? I'll do so by recounting my hikes with you; my aim to share both what I learned from you and felt stems from thankfulness.

In 2015, the summer of my first hike with you, I signed up for the Exohori Hike, and though I was the only person going that day, you still kept the trip a go. Little did I know that this is how you operate: it's not the size of the group that matters; it's the satisfaction of the individual that counts. For our safety, you always lay the groundwork and dispense the rules of the road; to that end, I dread no mishap or misstep because what you carry in your backpack amounts to a mobile clinic. I was told beforehand to bring a liter of water, a snack, a change of shirt, and good hiking shoes. It doesn't take much to have a good time, and packing light with only the essentials is all we really need — well, that and the right attitude and a presence of mind. A lighter load can lead to a fuller heart when eyes are wide open, and souls alert. You told me to keep my hands free and to take regular, but conservative steps, that I should not try to bound ahead or to catch up because the quads are the largest muscle group. In fact, you said that if we don't tire out our thighs, we could walk forever, which is precisely how long I wished our hike would last. I'm not sure if you have ever read Ralph Waldo Emerson, but I think you are a transcendentalist to your core, and you help those who hike to slough off years of the city to "connect with the inner child...in a very spiritual way," as you taut on your website. Ever patient and even-keeled, you let me prattle on about this and that in my life before you then told me select bits and pieces of your own. I came to know that you are a man who experienced the loss of a father too early, who adores his mother — she who makes the world's best fried potatoes, and who remains close to his sister and her children. Initially not wanting to reveal your age because you maintain that "age is just a number," you proved to me that the life in your years is longer than the years in your life if you keep your frame and brain robust and unfettered from inconsequential matters.

You also shared the moment when your life pivoted, and you took the quantum leap of faith where purpose and direction were concerned. No longer did you merely want to exist, passing the time by accumulating moments of mere leisure. To sit and chit-chat with friends who smoke and drink their lives away in cafés or bars is no way to honor life! Surely, there is more than this! A radical change was called for! I can just imagine the moment when you told yourself, "There's *got* to be more in store for me; there's so much more than meets the eye, and I am going to seek it!" And find your path you did. I believe that the real love of your life is Nature; her beauty and eloquence quench you. I consider you a patriot of the purest sort. Attuned to the fact that Greece's posterity started before her actual history, you are protective of your ancient birthright, and it shows in how you preserve and promote your portion of the Peloponnesus. Dressed in deceptively simple hiking gear with the latest technology, I see a modern-day monk who dons himself in black, retains a dry sense of humor, possesses a free spirit, and grows in wisdom as he traverses his little corner of the world. You take delight in and respect Nature's treasures with every step you take.

Yes, you return to the city, but only for practical concerns, and the artist in you snaps up photos of passed-over moments there. Later on, I recall our resting by a small chapel. You rang its little bell as if you were subconsciously calling us to church because it was time to take our snack of a communion. We partook of bottled water and honeyed sesame bars. At that time, I took the opportunity to share the video of my recent baptism in Kavala, and you watched with avid interest, immediately giving your seal of approval by remarking, "Cool!" Yet it was your spontaneous smile and beaming, deep-set eyes that communicated a greater assuredness and joy than a thousand words ever could. You seemed to understand the import of my independently choosing the path to salvation rather than remaining content with an infant's passive bath. As we ambled on in the last leg of the hike, we headed toward another church, and you told me her age — centuries, of course — and although she'd long since seen use, I felt as if you and I were attending there. You suspended this moment and led me past to a dilapidated house, now a skeleton of its former self, just beyond which we would face the entirety of the bay of K. below.

We walked over its trusses like acrobats, and then you protectively held my hand so I could lean onto and look through the windowless frame to behold the splendor of the seascape just beyond. The sun was already beginning to melt into the sea, a roseate glow spreading over the water. The peninsula to the right juts out as if to hug the rays in a little longer. If it had been the pearly gates of Heaven I beheld, I could not have been more moved! This sacred memory I share only with you; you witnessed my tears of joy. With the hike finished, coming back to town felt like coming back to earth. We parted with respect and affection, and as I turned to leave, I was already planning my next arrival.

Fast-forward two years later to when I unexpectedly found myself in K. again. Naturally, I made a beeline for your store, and we picked up where we'd left off as if not even two hours had passed. This time, you told me you'd picked for me to hike Dubitsia, a wildlife refuge which towers above Vyros Gorge. Along with another hiker, I got in next to you in your van, and we three headed to our starting point. You prefer the quiet of the early in the morning to human voices, and so we drove in silence up those narrow, curvy roads, going up, up, and more up through golden shafts of early morning sunlight; it was as if angels were accompanying us. Your preparatory hiking rules were delivered, but this time, I inadvertently violated your warning not to jump and land on my feet. The seriousness of your response, a near scolding, let me know your alerts were intended to avert accidents — after all, the terrain could be ambiguous — and it showed you care. After an uphill walk with spectacular views of the gorge below, the Taygetos summit and other peaks punctuating the distant horizon and lush vegetation and wild landscape commanding our immediate vicinity, we arrived at a plateau. You pointed out where your village was, on the rim of even higher mountains in the near horizon, and I thought to myself, "Oh, to witness this heavenly view every day!" We then crisscrossed down through a mystical, dark forest where you showed us centuries-old, broad levels of terracing, now overgrown. Suddenly, we heard a rustle and stamp ahead of us; you stood as still as a deer and then smiled as soon as we three spotted a wild boar appear for just a split second before he stamped and turned to flee. Though I felt like an intruder, I was momentarily transfixed in an awed hush. It is so apparent that your mien of respect for Nature is a default setting; you possess a comity for all life around you, be it snake or stick. You respect the mountain like a native son. God may have been given man "dominion" over every living thing (Genesis 1:28 NKJV), but you remind us that to be a good steward means "not to hurt the grass of the earth, nor any green thing, nor any tree" (Revelation 9:4). Every now and again, you stop, look up, inhale deeply, and involuntarily make a "Hmm" sound, like some primitive and guttural "Amen." We continued on to end up in the dry riverbed of the gorge itself. As we return to Exochori, we step over ancient stones of a 2500-year-old trail that connected Sparta to K. Following you over this path, I feel ancient blood coursing through my veins; you are my commander, and we are off to defend our sons and soil. As we made our way back to town, another layer was peeled back, and the physician and philosopher in you explained the body-mind connection pertaining to the foods and experiences we ingest. Your diet is not a fad with tepid slogans like "go green" and eat "gluten-free"; you dive deep to the cellular level regarding what we take in and how deceptively simple choices impact the full spectrum of our spirit and life. Local gree -gold olive oil, mountain tea, and honey with wild thyme are yours for the taking. At the end of the hike, you took us up to a café in an eve more remote village, and the panoramic view there stole my heart and took my breath away: I felt like I was sitting in heaven with you! Parting once more at the foothill wasn't too terribly difficult; I knew I'd be back.

Sure enough, two years later, now just two months ago, after checking into my hotel, I walked right into your store, straight back to where you were at your desk as if no time had passed. You saw me, and we embraced. Then you let me know which was to be my next hike, adding with a smile, "You are going to *love* it!" Thus far, admittedly, the Ridomo Gorge hike has been the most challenging for me, perhaps because the pace was a tad faster since the couple with us was twenty years my junior. If this was apparent to you, you did not let on, but reflexively offered a helping hand, like some thick branch appearing from the foliage for me to take hold of whenever I needed support. You are an encourager who says, "*Bravo!*" when you've assessed our step or approach up a particular hillock to be wisely chosen. Each step we take in life matters, doesn't it? Once again, I got in to sit next to you in the vehicle, like it was my usual spot, and you quietly drove us to our starting point. You make wry comments about this and that, like how political elections are really a theatrical show, and this puts us as ease and makes us feel familiar with you. We waited for you to bike back to us at a little chapel after parking the Jeep at the termination spot where we began. I had just lit a candle, when, out of the corner of my eye, I saw you flash past on your bike. It was like I'd seen the Holy Ghost whizzing by! The rules of the road were again announced to us, and later, you quizzed us: the number one rule is to secure the area and for good reason. Then, with hard hats donned, we silently skimmed alongside the underbelly of the mountainside to avoid any potential mishaps or even an avalanche. Not once did I fear; I have utter trust in you. To quote your website, with every I hike I take, the bond between us gets "reinforced in a very spiritual way." To that end, I was so impressed by "the rich geologic features of the gorge, with its evident stratification of rocks, its burst of intense rock color palette in perfect match with its splendid greenery." How eloquent! How true! On this six-hour hike, I beheld the marriage between tree and stone, how they had fused together over the centuries, having had water rush through them, bringing sediment to cement the intertwining of two seemingly incompatible entities. Oh, what that man could learn from Nature and learn to exist in such perfect symbiosis! You and I had our picture taken there, and we mirror the harmonious fusion around us: side by side we stand. You placed one arm around me, your hand protectively resting on my shoulder, and your other hand was interlocked with mine, fingertips to knuckles, an unbreakable bond instinctively formed. I spied a cradle formed from gigantic tree roots nearby, so naturally, I lay me down as if to sleep, like I'd found an eagle's glen. After spotting a large chunk of driftwood, debris from some storm, you tied it to the bottom of your backpack, a memento for future use. You playfully played the air bongo on an old abandoned water pipe, then had us do target practice by tossing well-aimed pebbles at its opening. When we made our way through that deep, dark, and narrow passageway, at one point, spotting above us a several-ton boulder having gotten wedged between two sheer walls of mountains from some epic fall, I felt as if I were in a netherworld. Here droplets of water echoed loudly, primeval frogs chirped among pools of cool water, and shafts of sunlight penetrated hither and yon, a mystical mist faintly visible. The colors of the stones were spectacular, their varied hues on bold display because of being faintly wet. The sign we were returning to civilization the Koskarga bridge above us; it was our signal to climb to the termination point of this hike.

After drinking a Greek coffee to resuscitate zapped energies in a nearby square of a sleepy village, we drove back to town. On the way, upon observing how parched the land was, one of the others asked you what Greeks do if they spot a fire. You calmly but proudly informed us of an organized team of local volunteers who were trained for such emergencies, that you yourself had served with this brigade before. Then I asked you whom a person should call if an emergency arose, and without skipping a beat, you looked over and instructed me: "If you *ever* have an emergency, you call *me*!" I thought it applicable across the ocean, too! Touched, I smiled over at you in appreciation for such life insurance. All of us spent and content, the drive back to town held yet another surprise for us: you showed us some grand graffiti on a support wall done by a famous local artist and activist, and it, too, proved congruous with the surroundings. I was only sorry that I had to leave before I could see the exhibition of local photography which included some of your work. You have an eye for capturing the sublime in the simple.

Perhaps you are still wondering why I would recount our three hikes. After all, your job is to gratify your clients' hiking experience. Well then, for sure, mission accomplished! Even though we have spent no more than twenty-four hours and seven minutes together, your kindnesses, confidence, and concern have me considering you a friend for life. An acquaintance of mine wrote that only recently did she understand the importance of a few kind words. I certainly do, and these here are mine for you. May I say that I am already looking forward to our next hike, even if it's likely two years away? I hope I can make the pilgrimage to the roof of the Peloponnesus, the summit of Mount Taygetos, with you. Though not too long ago, I learned that this peak is mentioned *The Odyssey*, I've no doubt that should I get to do this, I will feel like I am with a modern-day Prophet Elias, the patron saint of high places. Like Elias, who climbed high to get away from it all, Greeks still crave light and seek the sun. You and I are such ones. Thank you for following your dreams, which brought you back home to the austere yet magnificent mountains between Messenia and

Mani. On these hikes, we also spot evidence of bygone hikers: here and there are short stacks of small stones, one residing atop the other on the base of some wide boulder. They indicate those who have passed before and have carefully placed their chosen stone balanced atop another, adding to the pillar of collective memory. Even Simon Peter said we are to be "a living stone, which... is choice and precious in the sight of God." (1 Peter 2:4). Please then consider this letter a token of my gratitude for the indelible mark you've made on my life.

Sincerely yours,
D. C.

43. Sophia

Meet Sophia. She is a fellow lover of travel and an educator; twice, Sophia was my tour director on student trips I lead to Greece and Italy. We are both intellectuals who enjoy exploring a range of topics, including ancient and modern history, linguistics, and pop culture. I think what makes our relationship unique is that we both exist somewhere on the continuum of Greek-Americans whose parents, my mom notwithstanding, can be classified as immigrants. And more profound than this, we are a little obsessed over what constitutes identity when life is in flux. It's as if the plane hasn't quite landed, and we don't know which airport we are to use in entering the city. Both of her parents are Greek to my paternal one. They chose to uproot their family and move *back* to Greece to raise their four kids. In contrast, my dad and his brothers emigrated *to* the States after the Greek Civil War, so when my dad married an American, he forever changed the trajectory of his children's Hellenistic concentration and values. It is his eldest daughter who takes much pride in and has a yearning for her heritage; in fact, she hankers to go to Greece as often as she can. There she gains sweet relief from the sense of wholeness within. The common denominator for both Sophia and me is that we have been on a similar quest to find home and to feel like we belong. For me, it seems as if we are siblings as much as we are friends, and I'm sure the feeling is mutual. Sophie is that zestful Greek with energy, intensity, and passion, so when she's ready to explore or go, you'd better be prepared to keep up. Her quick mind makes connections between ideas and places in no time flat; it's apparent that hers is a soul that is restless and seeking, and I believe we help each other find our missing puzzle pieces. I know she has found her peace *and* a home. We are both teachers, she of college students, but when I'm with her, I believe it is I who learn the most. We have a tacet affection for one another that is not dependent on time or place, so I'll miss her in the meanwhile until I book my next flight to Athens.

Who is someone you know that shares many a parallel or life experience despite your two being in different places? Since Sophia and I are a year apart, we grew up at the same time; we are of the same generation. Who is this person for you? Perhaps it took a life circumstance, event, or trip for your lives to intersect and cross. Whom are you grateful to have found, some new yet familiar friend, and one who is ready for whatever little or much time you can spend together? How might you thank this person for her insights and friendship? Have you met someone who has a similar ethnic background or shares a cultural connection with you? How can you develop your point of mutual fascination or personal parallel to take your point of contact from acquaintance to friend?

Read on to learn more about Sophia.

"Man is a being in search of meaning." — Plato

[20]Ποῦ σοφός?... [22]Ἐπειδὴ καὶ Ἰουδαῖοι σημεῖον αἰτοῦσιν, καὶ Ἕλληνες σοφίαν ζητοῦσιν... [25]Ὅτι τὸ μωρὸν τοῦ θεοῦ σοφώτερον τῶν ἀνθρώπων ἐστίν, καὶ τὸ ἀσθενὲς τοῦ θεοῦ ἰσχυρότερον τῶν ἀνθρώπων ἐστίν... [30]Ἐξ αὐτοῦ δὲ ὑμεῖς ἐστε ἐν χριστῷ Ἰησοῦ, ὃς ἐγενήθη ἡμῖν σοφία ἀπὸ θεοῦ... (ΠΡΟΣ ΚΟΡΙΝΘΙΟΥΣ Α)

"Where is the wise man? ... For indeed Jews ask for signs and Greeks search for wisdom; ... Because the foolishness of God is wiser than

men, and the weakness of God is stronger than
men... But by His doing you are in Christ Jesus,
who became to us wisdom from God...
— from 1 Corinthians 1:20, 22, 25, and 30

"There is an eternal landscape, *a geography of the
soul*; we search for its outline all our lives."
— Josephine Hart, emphasis mine

"Was that what I had searched for all my life?
My heritage? Who and What I am? Was that
what my wanderlust had been about from such
an early age? No guidebooks could hold that
key. *I felt changed in some inexplicable way.* I had
history. I had a people. *I had love that went beyond
my own lifetime and my own small life. A love that was
somehow ancient. That was connected to the beginning
of time."*
— From Thea Halo's *Not Even My Name,*
emphasis mine (2001)

July 14, 2019

Dear Sophia,

When I asked for your address, it is because I already knew
I would be writing you a letter, one that has been brewing in
me for some time coming. Don't worry; it's nothing as dramatic
as you might expect, but because you are my friend and one
with whom I share a covalent bond for all we have in common,
I wanted to gift you a little piece of my soul, a memento of
acknowledgment and of encouragement. You have earned
your Ph.D. and can boast of many other accomplishments and
accolades, but I wanted to dive deeper and brag on the "inner

man" in you I've come to know and treasure, like an ancient Greek coin of burnished gold that's come into my possession. From the moment I met you in the airport in Athens, along with a dozen eager students like ducklings behind me, I knew by your warm greeting that we were in for a treat! Little did I realize then just how much our friendship would blossom.

I'd run out of fingers were I to list all we have in common! We are the perfect puzzle-piece match where birth order is concerned; you are the youngest of three boys and a girl, I, the oldest of three girls and a boy. We both respect and adore our fathers. Our zeal for work and travel has become for us what a child is for others. We are philhellenists to our cores, and we will share with any and all who will listen to us the grandeur that is Greece. We are intellectuals who probe and discuss life's eternal questions, scratch our heads as we contemplate world politics and human nature, and gravitate time and again to affirm the impact that geography makes on the course of our lives. I am the southern Rebel to your Jersey Shore girl whose sections of Americana are stamped on our souls. We both share a passion and pride, vim and vigor, and an essential optimism and energy that many find either daunting or delightful. We are at least bilingual; however, my Russian pales to your f luency in Greek, Italian, and even some Turkish, and I eagerly lap up the many lessons you give in etymology and mythology. Where else would I have learned the unanticipated Germanic root of the word for "Greek" and the term "diaspora," which, in a single word, captures the effects of our fathers' odd odysseys? We speak of Greeks in Crimea or Cyprus as if they were long lost relatives yearning to return to the Greek navel at Delphi. I have hungrily read both of your dad's books. From them, I recognize a certain essential rawness and me tal vigor which finds its expression in you, and most recently, per your suggestion, I avidly ingested *Not Even My Name* and sensed the similar undercurrent in her search for identity.

When the central locus of the *famiglia* has been shifted, it is like we possess an internal compass that no longer points to the top pole; therefore, we check the coconut shell that contains the prize underneath but which has gotten moved out of order, so we become disoriented. Oh, to right ourselves! You and I are such ones, who, time and again, have put down roots for ourselves, but the phrase, "there's no place like home," remains hauntingly elusive. We carry our home in our hearts, so wherever we go — and go, we must — we look for other hungry hearts and find sanctuary in them, like an oasis in a desert or a makeshift tent in a camp of huddling refugees. You are no nomad, and I am no gypsy, but we have both felt like castaways, and this drive to set right the feeling of being exiled has somehow led me to you, and I am beyond grateful. I say "somehow" loosely, as if I believe it was by chance, fortune, or fate that we met, but I do not. I think that we had a divine appointment and that the God we both believe in, yes, each in our own fashion, set us on a course to meet, like two chess pieces headed for a lively exchange. Since then, you have not only read my *Connecting the Dots...*, but, eating lunch in a café in the village you now call home, you said you had questions for me; in fact, truth be told, I was quite humbled by the intentness of your interest. I thank you again for reading my clunky tome.

Looking back, I do not believe I quelled your bewilderment over my evocations of faith, a perplexing thought-reality for thinkers like us, or your puzzlement over my frequently mentioning the name "Jesus," as if He were my buddy. Of course, He is not, but He can be the Son *and* my Savior *and* Friend all in one. Like Peter, had I not had a personal encounter with Christ, which was as mysterious and mystical as it was momentous, I would not find myself saying, "I cannot stop speaking about what I have seen and heard" (Acts 3:20). I agree that it can seem not only unnecessary, but even disrespectful or vulgar to talk about the Son of God and say His name as if He were somehow common, but I had to debunk this myth in my own mind. No one knows me better and loves me more than my maker; that He came in the flesh to meet and redeem the likes of us surpasses history. It's destiny. If I seem boastful or oddly familiar, it is because He lives in me. The Church doesn't get a corner market on Him. Many end up promoting man's inhumanity to man, or, for those that do not, they fall short of the mark by making God out to be distant, uninvolved, or even non-divine. That said, my own local *ekklesia* where I live promotes both *koinonia* and His *agape*, which I hold as the banners for my life, but seeing is believing, now, isn't it? Action *must* speak louder than words. Therefore, with this letter you hold in your hand, I hope to offer another way of saying, *I love you*, Sophia, my great friend *and* my neighbor!

Daily I hit reset to try to "'love God with all my heart, soul, and mind'" (Matthew 22:36–37). I deliberate here because I feel I fell short in responding to your questions about my book, yet I acquiesce in recognition that, ultimately, it is His Spirit that massages and move our minds. He compels me to share. Since my impulse to write you is based upon an abiding affection I have for you *and* because I believe we are at a similar midlife juncture, a crossroads betwixt our careers eclipsing and our future slowly unfolding before our eyes, I wanted to hit pause and sing your praises. Why? Though we may *think* we know what our strengths are, we are not the alpha and omega, the author of our life, so it can be powerful to be reminded of the gifts and talents with which we are endowed *and* which we have put to positive use to impact others. This letter is my offertory for you. A heartfelt reminder and pat on the back can boost you to rev your drive for you to continue in your calling.

There *is* life after leading tours, and we stand boldly at the next threshold. I recall your telling me how important it was to get high marks on your evaluations; I have written two such for you, both filled with my own glowing remarks as well as testimonials from my students. Without a doubt, that fateful night we had to admit a very sick student into the emergency room to combat complications from her diabetes wreaking havoc on her young system sealed the deal and catapulted our relationship to another level. I have to back up and say that I was nervous about even knocking on your hotel door to inform you matters had worsened, as it was then approaching midnight, but without hesitation, you let me in, and the conference began. What I really liked was that I felt we were in this *together*; that you always asked me, "What do *you* think, Dimi?", such that I thought our brains and beings were one, and we, a united front, could solve any of the world's problems. Later on, in the waiting area of the hospital, you could have left all well enough alone and not involved yourself. You could have stood by and let me unknowingly sign this or that form in unwitting ignorance to perhaps expedite the care that my student was to receive. This was not the case because that is not who you are. In fact, a ferociously protective mother bear in you came out and gave the young technocrat receptionist behind the desk what-for, that I was not the one to sign anything! I felt like another baleful disaster had been averted. In my sleep-deprived and anxious state, I was informed that I had to remain; you and Bonnie were to go ahead and act in my stead. The agony, angst, and simmering fury I initially had somehow got transmuted into an acceptance of my plight; indeed, I got into a relaxed routine of sorts in my unanticipated hospital stay. Suspended in this state had the effect of increasing my anticipation of reuniting with the group and rejoining you. My eager heart swelled with euphoria when from the rooftop of our hotel outside Rome, I caught sight of you all in the distance coming up the drive. Like a reunion of lovers running in slow-motion toward one other on the beach, I felt elated the moment as I bound down the steps three at a time to greet my students. After a messy group hug with a blur of deliriously happy students all around me, I then embraced you, rocking back and forth, both of us laughing for joy. Our conversations, which had been rich and dynamic before, now got launched into the stratosphere of trying to figure out the next time we could meet, so clad was the bond we'd formed.

That you promoted my not only visiting, but perchance even someday residing in Kalamata said it all, and I was moved. Who else but you would send me ads from the local paper showing me apartments to buy there? You are an *all-in* kind of woman, and the type of support from you not only to explore more of my Greek heritage, but to claim and live it, is more than I've experienced, and for that I am beyond thankful. That we correspond with some regularity between our teaching and travels, be it through FB or your calling me when you visit your aunt in Florida, is a testament to our devotedness.

The next summer, I did come to explore Kalamata, and it was everything you reported it to be. Yet, it did not offer the work in the manner I anticipated for teaching, and this led to one of the many explanations you gave that helped me better understand the mind of a Greek. Having spent five months in Moscow at school and among friends enabled me to annotate to students how Russians view life; you are a similar personal curator for me. You have shed light on the psychological underpinnings of the Greek mindset by analyzing the cultural milieu of Greeks who live in Greece. I have listened to you, spellbound. Just to be enamored by Greece is not the same thing as to get under her skin, to see warts and all. I have yet to live here long enough to gain primary knowledge, but you have illuminated much for me with explanations kind. It wasn't until the last day of this trip that we got to spend what amounted to a full afternoon together, and without students trailing behind us or a set schedule to complete, you showed me a more avant-garde section of Athens. You expounded on a thousand and one things, including the reason for the many protests here; the failure of modern Greeks to practice economic accountability; and the fact that many rest on their ancient laurels. You have explained the geopolitical role of Greece in the global economy and the impact of western thinking — one which promotes self. Such a mindset has adversely, albeit indirectly, deleteriously impacted how Greeks raise their children. Let's not forget the many talks that spawned from our speculating over the implications for the latest refugee crisis there. In short, all manner of secular affairs affecting Greece you unravel; fortunately, my comments and conjectures have you ruminating as well. We are literally and figuratively all over the proverbial map, and I love our voyages! The meeting of our minds is a robust one, and I feel the charge of mental electricity spark with the free flow of information, yet it is our outbursts of laughter from unanticipated and spontaneous humor that seals the deal of our friendship. Oh, you and I are intellectuals who gravitate towards philosophy, economics, and psychology just as birds do to air.

Still, there's something in our natures, perhaps that deep love of freedom that breathes within the breast of every Greek, that makes our spirits soar. I recognize the mantle of rationalism we both don. In addition to evidencing a preternaturally active brain, intellectualism masks bruises borne in youth. Resultantly, I feel tenderness towards, comradeship with, and guardianship over you. When you dance, I discern a tempered restraint to your moves that speaks of a respect for the dance as well as measured modesty proven necessary from lessons learned in the past; we are of the same timber, you and I. Even if we are passionate and enthusiastic by nature, we are also politic and cautious in choosing whom we bring in close; therefore, for us to have found and set anchor with one another is all the more momentous. Speaking of dancing, you taught my students the phrase, "Italians sing, but Greeks dance!" and then you immediately brought the *show* to the *tell* for them! On both cruises, first the 1-day and then the 3-day cruise, my students saw a Zorba in *you*, a living, breathing *"Opa!"*, one who gave belly-dancing lessons 101 to delighted to girls and the like to awkward, bumbling boys, but I get ahead of myself. That was to come the next year, the year my trip to Russia was canceled, and I chose another Italy-Greece tour and expressly requested *you*. Looking back, I do not see this occurrence as mere chance.

The summer of 2018 was a special one for me: I was to have

shown my brother and two nephews Mother Russia; instead, we returned to the land of my father, and in their meeting you, you then became like family to us all. Once again, your desire to keep your chicks out of harm's way was demonstrated. In this case, it was my nephew who had such a severe case of poison ivy, that pus was oozing from open sores; his own father mocked him mildly for his furious scratching. You insisted on taking him to a Greek pharmacy and helped translate there such that a perfect remedy was quickly prepared and dispensed. Later, when our group — affectionately dubbing itself "Tennasota" — was plopped down in Samos during the wee hours of the morning with no plan in place, you swiftly orchestrated what little you had to work with behind the scenes. You conjured up an on-the-fly side-trip to a nearby famous cave that housed a church, and this was then followed by an excursion to the beach for a refreshing swim. You moved mountains without making a peep. Your desire for everyone's satisfaction — especially for that of the *other* group leader, whose affect made him seem like a crypt, so uncommunicative and bland was he — compelled you to arrange a détente to demonstrate your democratic concern for us all. You effectively separated the personal from the professional so he could see I held no privileged place with you. I only appreciated this tactical move later. On the "Greek Night" in Athens, you made sure those of us attending had plum seats to watch the spirited performance, and it made it all the easier for the kids themselves to go up and dance, and dance they did! Later on, when it seemed as if I had not seen a soul from our group all day, that eve ing at the cruise ship's Greek Night, whom should I spy first but you? My heart skipped a beat, and a smile spread across my face. Without either of us saying a word, it was as if our steps were ordained to run into one another; Greek music beckoned us there. Though conversations quickly commence, my immediate sense of euphoria confirms that our friendship is not based merely on the wealth of information we share — though that is rich in itself

— but on a pure love of life.

There is some primitive impulse we share, some zest for life, some curiosity, some keen pulse that keeps our souls restive and searching for meaning. Maybe we each try to overcome the kosmos' sacred-secular divide through our own efforts. Perhaps we're just curious Greeks. We recognize this pull and are drawn to one another. Of all the topics we track, be they related to mythology, history, world heritage sites, language, education, or travel, you and I, like ministers of peace in times of war, time and again, gravitate to the topic of diaspora. Why? We are the products of such ourselves, and the effects thereof have not only blistered the souls of our kinsmen, but, by extension, ours, too; therefore, we still ache for their pains and are compelled to honor them by sharing their stories; our wounds become healed. In your case, your academic contributions shine a light in this darkness in the form of working papers and presentation sat prestigious world councils, Oxford, and the like. I am magnetically and inexorably drawn to Greece. I share her with students as I continue to search for the missing puzzle pieces of my own heritage. With all I've got, I relish the pebbles I cross, every mountain I climb, every piece of spanakopita or pasteli bar I eat, every portion of the Mediterranean Sea I glide into, and every ancient temple I behold. And that's not including the gratification of being with my relatives! This search has become my living mantra, the crusade of my core. Who knows if I will experience residing here for a stretch of time to actually feel like I am home? You know first-hand what it means to be able to call "home" spots on two different continents, two countries. The "landscape of *your* soul" is multi- tiered, and that your work requires travel, at times, can make you feel all the more like a gypsy, a vagabond, or, as you put it, a "semi-nomad." Either way, with current events and family circumstances beyond our control, we both have also felt like migrants or orphans. Even if we had ruby-red slippers, we cannot click our heels and return to some Kansas or lost Atlantis, a time and place that were home for family we have never met. Is there value and worth in the seeking of it? From my core, I cry out, "Yes!" This search proves more primal than the restoration of bygone times or the reanimation of faded lives. The past can't be repeated, so a visitation boils down to our way of showing respect.

Thomas Wolfe wrote a novel entitled, *You Can't Go Home Again*, describing this phenomenon. Persephone never returned to her mother Demeter for the full calendar year, and Adam and Eve never made it back to Eden. For me, this quest, this longing is best rendered by T. Halo: it becomes the search for "who and what I am." Whether we sift through the tragic rubble and explore the genocide of the Pontic Greeks, Armenian, Ukrainians, or Native Americans, it's just one example after the next whereby people, hunted down like animals, are forced to find shelter and ultimately make their home elsewhere. Alliances and allegiances shift and blur. To disambiguate identities and untangle these agonizing and forced migrations, generation after generation, moving from one spot after the next, *ad nauseum*, is the business of historians. Every now and again, for lost puppies like us, we who somehow still seek asylum for ourselves, it is a topic that cannot be exhausted. Why? We long for the ultimate family reunion, and I have faith that this happens when we look not to man but maker, that is, when we take baby steps in trust and faith. Doing such delivers a poignant "peace ... which surpasses all comprehension" (Philippians 4:7). This is my olive branch, my hope for you, Sophia.

As I put the finishing touches on your letter, I'd like to tell you what I have resting beside my computer: my ticket stub to the Vatican Museum, which, as you know, depicts your favorite piece of art: Raphael's fresco, *The School of Athens*. I've read that it symbolizes the marriage of art, philosophy, and science. In a way, this captures the brilliance that's in *you*. The elderly teacher Plato points to the sky, reminding us that it is the spiritual realm that holds real meaning to the forms and shapes below, but his sage student Aristotle informs us of our need for the concrete evidence of the real world. This tension, this restlessness resides within you; you, too, are brimming with life that finds an outlet in bursts of enriching travel. I recognize and love this about you. You and I are like Lord Tenneson's Ulysses. You have made your home in a renovated domicile on ancient grounds just outside Greece's former capital, and I in the hills of east Tennessee. Regardless of the home and hearth we have sought and found, we *still* find ourselves pulled back out to the sound of the calling sea because you and I possess the "equal temper of heroic hearts, [which desire] ... to strive, to seek, to find, and not to yield." Home is where the heart is, and you, my compatriot, my friend for life, have a piece of mine.

With love,
D.C.

44. Voula

Meet Voula. She is my cousin, or, to be technically correct, my father's cousin's daughter, but in Greece, folks aren't so picky or particular about who is what to whom; you just know you are family. Since 2007, I've seen Voula probably close to ten times, and that means I've spent more time with her in my adulthood than with my four cousins who live Stateside combined, and that's no joke. Little by slowly, through my coming to Greece with regularity, she has become so dear that it pains me to be away from her during the bleak seasons of life, like now, for instance, as her mother just passed away. Her wise and kind mother was a survivor of that generation of Greeks who suffered doubly, both through WWII and the Greek Civil War. Voula is an only child, and her mother endowed her with the secrets of her soul, both the tragedies and cherished moments she treasured for a lifetime. Voula has a soft and steady soul, and when you're with her, her presence makes you feel like you're wearing velvet. For the past decade, she has been a guardian to her mother, husband, and her own spunky daughter. This is a labor of love that is both burdensome and rewarding, each in its own right. In the handling of my father's affairs way-back-when, a situation which brought about the transferal of a piece of family property to Voula, a relationship was set in motion between her and me, and it has blossomed into an abiding friendship, one founded on mutual trust. There exists an unwavering devotion and a sureness to her love I find quietly staggering; life is not always sunshine and baklava and vacation when you are a caretaker. It is a job that goes round the clock and puts self last at every turn. Therefore, when we are together, be it sitting on her balcony and gazing out at the bright blue sea, catching up on snatches of family news, or giggling together over a humorous moment, there is nothing stilted or stuffy about how we do life together.

I can hardly wait to see her again.

> *Who is a person in your life with whom you have a
> reciprocity or mutual purpose that has developed into
> a friendship? Have you met a relative — distant or
> otherwise — with whom you've become chums? What
> life stories have you swapped? Do you both have the
> same knee-jerk reaction to particular scenarios? Do you
> both laugh at the same things at the same time? What
> familial connection have you spotted that was hidden
> in the genes and got panned out and expressed in a
> way endearing to you? What solace do you provide one
> another just by being together, echoing nuances of love
> that need no words? Who is a caregiver in your family?
> Is it for the short-term or an extended period of time?
> Have you thanked or acknowledged what she does, day
> in and day out, which brings solace and sustenance to
> others? Could she or he use your help? Ask so she can
> receive.*

Read on to meet my cousin, Voula.

"This is Major Tom to Ground Control I'm
stepping through the door
And I'm floating in a most peculiar way And
the stars look very different today For here am
I sitting in a tin can
Far above the world Planet Earth is blue
And there's nothing I can do..."
From David Bowe's "Space Oddity" (1969)

"No act of kindness, no matter how small, is
ever wasted." — Aesop

"The two most important qualities in life
are *kindness and loyalty*, unlike love which is
instinctive and you can't help –kindness and
loyalty are matters of willful choice."
–Niki Goulandris, Greek philanthropist and
botanical painter (emphasis mine)

"Come to Me, all who are weary and heavy-
laden, and I will give you rest. Take My yoke
upon you and learn from Me, for I am gentle
and humble in heart, and YOU WILL FIND
REST FOR YOUR SOULS."
— Matthew 11:28–29

"'Έφαγα τον κόσμο να σε βρώ'."
~ "*I ate the whole world to find you.*"
— Greek phrase

July 21, 2019

Dear Voula,

What that I could fold and tuck myself up along with my letter inside this envelope to arrive at your doorstep so that I could be with and help you! The date above was my first day back in the States, and it is the beginning of a long stretch that will eventually lead me back to Greece, hopefully, the summer of '22. I find myself wanting to tell you that the dual citizenship I've attained is more than a document; in fact, it reflects a somewhat schizophrenic mindset. I've yet to take the plunge to plant myself there longer, so I see-saw and content myself with reasonably frequent visits. With every trip I make, I sense that you and I step a little closer together, and now, some twelve years since my first weeks-long visits there, having come to Greece seven more times since 2007, I feel like we are more than cousins: we are true-blue friends. I am aware of much that you balance and manage. Therefore, the fact that I am missing the means to help you from where I now am, please consider my letter a booster shot of Vitamin D! Here I will try to lift your spirits, or, if nothing else, to reassure you that someone else cares for you *very* much. I appreciate all that you do, day in and day out. I am not so naïve or overconfident to think that I have a real grasp of all the ins-and-outs of your life, including daily duties, hardships, and, of course, joys, but I *do* have an appreciation of all you are responsible for. Though you seek no applause, I want to tell you that from 5,500 miles away, I am cheering you on.

If I recall correctly, this is the time when you were hoping that insurance matters would get resolved such that you could obtain your doctor's clearance to be able to have the surgery to relieve the pain in your hip and back. I also know you will need much support while this procedure is taking place. Vastly inadequate though it is, here is mine in spirit for you today. I started this letter with a few seemingly mismatched quotes, so before I embark on my note of praise to you, let me first explain them. I know you are fond of David Bowie, as am I; in fact, you'd pick Bowie over the bouzouki any day, right? Although other songs of his are more upbeat, I am particularly fond of "Space Oddity." It captures the sense of powerlessness and disconnectedness we *all* can sometimes feel; plus, if I'm not mistaken, it came out the year you were born. Maybe it deals with modern man's lack of faith or his excessive reliance on technology such that he is left high and dry and alone, but that is not my focus.

I drive right on to the antidotes for Major Tom's despair, continuing next with the Greek wisdom of the mid-sixth century B.C., which I note describes your essence: *kindness*. And though you have commented on the shortcomings of the Church, I don't pretend to know the fundamental conceptions of your faith, so

I humbly offer you this verse from the Gospel of Matthew with reassurances. Why? Ultimately, we believe in the same man and Messiah; the sanctuary we occupy matters not. Leave it to a Greek woman to demonstrate kindness and loyalty, both of which are core attributes of yours. I know the final phrase may seem absurd or even comical. Still, I now see that my travels from the past thirty years to places all over the world have led me inevitably to Greece, the place of my heritage. Here I feel such joy and fulfillment, and, without fail, it also leads me straight to you, Voula. I would eagerly gobble up the world to find my way right back to you. Plus, we share the same namesake, so we are connected at the core of our identity, too, all the more so since my yiayia is the common thread between us.

We often joke about the fact that you wear many hats: you are a taxi driver for your husband and help him make his way about Athens for work, for your mom to go to doctor appointments, and for your daughter, everywhere else. From what I've witnessed, this is no small feat in Athens; plus, you have zig-zagged across town late at night to bring us back to Hotel C. too many times to count. You are now the manager of your apartment complex. Your "adventures" with neighbors show me that you are respected and trusted for your can-do ability and steady hand. You take care of things that go off course, be it someone's inability to pay rent on time, a hot water heater that has malfunctioned, or a tenant who comes a-knockin' at your door 'round midnight for something senseless. I recall the first time I saw your other apartment. It was as cozy as it could be, with comfy touches, warm colors, and twinkly lights adorning your balcony from which one could catch a glimpse of the Acropolis in the near distance; that night, the moon was bathing down her glow of approval. I also recollect a table with multi-colored tiles atop that you were working on, like some craftsman of ancient Greece making a mosaic; I really admire the artist within you. Today your daughter benefits from the treasures you allow her to have to foster her imagination.

Next, like Bonnie, there isn't much you can't fix or figure out, and I know you are always on-call to solve or remedy problems. Your relatively-recent role as mother has been a life-altering identity shift. I can see that it is fulfilling in a way that can't be put into words and yet has been intensified to a degree for your often having to do double-duty as a parent. And though you are uncomplaining and steadfast, I can't help but feel the weight of your world. Depression is a land that saps its inhabitants of their souls and strength, and where you have had to take up the slack for a man at times unavailable for his daughter has made you twice the mother. Your baby girl possesses such spunk and spirit, confidence and will; this indicates an active mind, a vivid imagination, and an impatience for life that pulses within her little frame. You passed on an energy to her that comes directly from your mother, her namesake.

That your daughter has utter trust in you and full belief in herself is because you have provided a marble bedrock of esteem and confidence. She will continue to blossom, and I will quietly tell you that I admire what you choose to ignore as well what you encourage in her. Please know that I mean no disrespect when I say that I believe that your decision- making as a mother has been influenced by difficulties experienced in your youth; as a result, you take pains to reverse the course so as to avoid unnecessary hurts. Your daughter will not have to prove herself to meet some unattainable mark of validation. There will be no push-and-pull, comparison-contrast, or hide-and-seek games your daughter has to play to earn your approval; your liberal love is free and ready for the taking! You reject the tendency of modern parents to depend on a digital screen's allurement for babysitting or convenience. This is a testament to your doing the right thing where the formation of your daughter's mind and emotional landscape are concerned. Playing with dolls and crayons and stickers and stones are the stuff our imaginations crave; electronic images are counterfeit substitutes. I am no parent, but as a teacher, I would say, "Brava," to you in your efforts to expand her scope while at the same time shielding her from a world that can show no mercy. To shift now from the aspect of mother back to adult daughter, I struggle to know where to begin to compliment you where your own mother is concerned, so much a dominant part of your life has she been.

I think the relationship betwee mother and daughter has got to be *the* most complex one we will ever have in life, and I would never be so presumptuous as to try to unravel yours. Though many of your features and gestures are replicates of your father, it is the strength and resilience from your mother I witness in you. Your large and luminous almond- shaped eyes are like those in the icons of the Virgin Mary, and your voice is like honey. I see a beautiful woman when I look at you; please know I ache for your pains, though you bear most in silence. I also love it when you get tickled; to share laughter with you is just the best! In our first visits there, it seemed as if you were some medium or diviner, translating and revealing to us anecdotes (or portions thereof) from your mother's childhood. It might have been humorous tales that involved outwitting her cousin, my father; struggles she bore over a lifetime dealing with her afflicted leg; or horrors witnessed during the war when she lost her own mother to murder. While she would listen to your recounting her stories, she would look over at me, nodding in silence, as if to confirm that what you described was not only true, but really just scratching the surface. Thanks in significant part to you, I have recorded many memories from our family's history; my dad left gaps and made errors in his jagged recollections. Although you sometimes have made the executive decision to leave much out or more left unsaid, I feel and respect your shielding silence of omissions; atrocities need not be given voice again.

On our very first visit to you and your husband's apartment, you lavished on us a spread of appetizers, and the four of us made the delightful discovery that we preferred a life of no pretense or privilege. We laughed easily among one another as your husband told jokes in broken English, explained the current political situation in Greece, and lamented over the more recent "degradation" of the Greek language from its purest form in a now weakened education system. If only my Greek were a fraction as good as yours is in English, I'd be ecstatic! I recall that after you had explained yet another fact about your mother to me, it was your response made about a person who had made some sort of negative remark about your mother, a fact in itself which stunned me: in defense of your her, you announced in a calm, cool, and collected voice, "If someone talks about my mother, *I cut their tongue*." I felt like I had a pirate in the family! I was thrilled and impressed to see such a protective streak. I would seek to investigate more of our background traits and characteristics later on. Fast forward to the last night of that year's visit. You, your husband, Bonnie, and I dined underneath the Acropolis at an enchanting restaurant. I felt as if we were eating like Greek gods in a renovated ancient temple, what with a gleaming tray teeming with fresh fruits brought to us after our meal. This was not our last supper; I knew we'd be back for many more visits in the years to come. I couldn't be more proud that we are family, grateful for how well we get along, and so content with our company and conversations; our roots run deep.

Back home in the States, I researched some of these backdrop connections we share and have come to learn that the same blood coursing through our veins — or at least those drops from your mother and my father — can trace its origin to relatives from the mountains of Mani. It turns out we are from a superstitious people, and that part of our ancient culture is associated with family vendettas; resultantly, we united and banded together when foreign invasions took place. Oh, to be locked in a tower with you during a time of trouble; I know no harm would befall us! I have also learned that we come from stock that has been termed "pure-blooded Greeks." As historian David Howarth states: "The only Greeks that have had an unbroken descent were the few small clans like the Maniots who were so fierce and lived so far up the mountain, that invaders left them alone." We can also boast of being from the particular part of the Peloponnesus where some of its women became an unmatched type of professional mourners, who, with their impromptu chanting and wailing, described the newly departed in eulogistic verse. If you go even further back, I read that this poetic impulse can be traced to choirs of Greek tragedies back in B.C. days.

I have never personally witnessed such an arcane display of grief, but I have lamented over the cleft in my Greek lineage. At times, it has left me feeling fractured over a loss of continuity in this vein of my heritage. No, I do not wail or moan or howl; my sorrow is borne in silence. I mean no disrespect to my own bright mother or what she passed on to me. My mind constructs a version of what it would yet like to experience and become within the woman you know as your cousin. With every voyage I take to Greece, that longing part of my soul takes a journey to a wondrous place where it pulses with energies restored as if resurrected from the dead. I can't explain why I feel as fully alive as I do in Greece. You don't hold it against me that my own history began across the ocean, nor do you judge me for my idealism or sentimentality. I am acutely aware I do not know first-hand the hardships Greeks bore then and endure now. The bottom line is we are cousins *and* family. Your generosity and acceptance of who and where I am in life is more than consoling. In fact, I have more of a relationship with you than I do all my other cousins. I respect and admire the fire within you to resist being bound to the past. You are a modern girl who looks to the present and future, all the while appreciating the past, and this leads me full circle back to your mother. Now you have become the parent to your parent. It's like a Greek dance we do from some collective memory, only now the handkerchief is in *your* hands. I hope you realize that I can commiserate and feel tremendously for you in this stage of your life. You know that I, too, have borne the bittersweet burden of looking after a parent who, bit by bit, has pieces of life snatched away, leaving him or her feeling robbed and us often frustrated. Our elderly parent gets stuck on a few tracks in their life's album, repeating and arguing with those closest with what will that still remains. Through it all, we also know that it is also an honor to do our parents right. I will now take your lead and, without delay, turn the page to a more pleasant place, namely those spots in Greece I have come to see, thanks to you.

In the summer of 2007 spent in Greece, I mixed business with pleasure; part of my plan was to deal with the sale of my dad's properties there. Even though my papou built the house on unofficial and unmarked land in the environs of O., over the decades, as you well know, it was *your* mother who became its practical proprietor. Up until then, the only glimpse I had had of my grandparents' house and property in O. was twelve years earlier. My brother and I climbed on the front gate and then precariously balanced ourselves, holding on to a tree branch for a few seconds if only but to pick a piece of its forbidde fruit — a kind of sweet apricot, if I recall. My dad may have burned bridges with his brother, but God had in store for *us* a future re nion and restoration.

No need to repeat how it came all to be in your possession, but your calm, patience, and understanding during that turbulent transaction let me know who my real family was. I am immensely relieved that things turned out the way they did. What that I could bend my uncle's initials welded in that dull red iron gate in front of the house into yours! Such a modest yet splendid place to restore your soul, one that has become another place implanted in your daughter's brain, as she, too, is making memories there, in fact, right under the daphne tree of *your* youth. That year, you also encouraged us to go to the just-completed and bold New Acropolis Muse m, and that was the first of many places you suggested we see. Along the way to this museum, we spied and became struck by the diminutive St. Sophia's Church of Acropolis, the very place in which I believe you said you got married.

The summer of 2011 was the first time I personally got to spend time at O., during which we also visited your parents where they were renting nearby. Oh, what a visit! We talked and laughed out on their balcony, so much so that the next-door neighbors shouted for us to be quiet; after all, it was Greek nap time! Through travels with the student tours I've led, I am pleased to have brought my mother and, most recently, Stephen and the boys for us to have small family reunions. You made these visits possible by coming to meet us over by Monastiraki so we could eat altogether, and I don't take for granted the effort it took for you to bring your mom out. Since then, you have let Bonnie and me stay at O. in June now two more times, and each stay there makes us more grateful than the last for the contentment we feel. While we were there this past June, we sense from you that the Spanish expression, "*mi casa es su casa,*" holds true. God willing, I hope we'll be able to come for another extended stay the summer of '22, the year when Bonnie hopefully will celebrate being five years free from cancer. Your love and acceptance of Bonnie mean everything to her, and I hope you know how much she adores you! She would and has helped me move small mountains to make sure O. looks its best for you after the precious time we spend there.

Returning back to the topic of new places, thanks to your suggestions, I have come to see special spots in Greece I might not have otherwise. This includes exploring the archeological ruins across at Evia and the Amphiareion of O. Amphiareion is a sanctuary that was dedicated in the 5th century B.C. to the hero Amphiaraos. Both times we visited it, Bonnie and I, its sole guests, felt like modern-day pilgrims seeking oracular nods or even a gift of healing. It may be no grand affair for you, but for me to inhale the scent of pines while I feel the heat of the sun kiss my face as I hear an orchestra of locusts chirping in the background, all the while knowing this was the same environ for those who attended the theater or sought sanctuary in its baths ages ago — brings history to life. I nearly tremble for feeling so alive! Bonnie and I have stood at the spring where its ancient stream of freshwater *still* trickles, and we imagine ourselves to be among the women washing their clothes or bathing there, gossiping and catching up on the latest bits of news. Back over in Athens, quite by chance, we discovered that it turns out you, too, prefer the Benaki Museum over the larger and more renowned ones, its vast array of Greek art displayed in a relatively small space. Plus, that fantastic view from atop its café above makes it doubly worth the visit. This past summer, I finally went to Olympia, not because of its obvious significance, but because you said you loved it. I see why! It's another place where one issuspended in the splendor of the past while retaining a sense of timelessness in its brilliant conception: the idea was to bring people together for peaceful purposes through grand games. I have yet to travel to the island of Delos, but that you recommended it was reason enough to visit the mythological birthplace of Apollo, the grounds of which I'm sure are still alive with its constellation of archeological wonders.

More important than any location we've been to, it is the place in your heart I hold dearest. You take care of us in a way that makes me feel totally at ease with you, and, for this, too, I am grateful. Truth be told, I think you are one of the least judgmental people I know, and the rare times you are critical, it is because you are looking out for the underdog. I can't even count the visits we have had together, including all the times we've eaten out on the way to and from Skala O. (and where I now know your favorite restaurants). Thanks to you, we feel as if we are kind of local there, what with frequenting the large grocery store (and pretty much all others) you've taken us to, daily enjoying a double Greek coffee and pastry where my grandmother used to patronize, and buying our produce at the end of town. We walk there daily, memorizing ever curve of the land as we round along the coast; even the lone horse there recognizes us as we go by.

Not only this, we have come to visit you in your neck of the woods in Athens in your hip neighborhood. Literally right around the corner from you, we've gotten to sit among a crowd of folks unwinding in the evening and enjoying any number of specialty appetizers, the plates often barely fitting on the table. To be with you sitting among a mishmash of relaxed Athenians feels like a mini-vacation within the day, though it couldn't be more normal an occasion for you. There you have asked me my opinion on this and that, and we make the discovery that not only do we have similar stances about values, child-rearing, and politics, but about various persons as well. I love that we laugh over many an irony and balk at those with guise. Our common enemy is pretense; snobbery leaves us cold. More than you know, I appreciate the two of us possessing a little savagery and primitive ways to keep things real in a world too smart for its own good.

Speaking of vacation, after all these trips and visits, we finally got to make our own holiday together, just the four of us! I felt like I'd really arrived, taking our first road trip adventure! Yay! To be next-door- neighbors staying in adjacent hotels in Gythion, like we'd been doing this our whole lives, and from our baloneys looking out upon the broad, bright harbor was *so* satisfying! And to witness your daughter's little gasp of pleasure when she pulled back the hotel curtains, unexpectedly awestruck by the gorgeous panorama, I will never forget! Her whole self was beaming! The next day, we drove up, up, up to the pinnacle of Panayia Yiatrissa; it happened to be my fourth time there, thanks to your telling me about its existence years ago. This instance proved *the* most special of all visits; it was a full-circle experience. Eight years ago, my forehead touched cool marble while I kneeled prostrate in prayer; I was alone in the tiny chapel, making an appeal to God for *you*; only the icons were my witnesses. This time, however, I felt a little shy, and I turned away to give you privacy as you lit your candle. Your daughter stood by your side, holding your hand as you made your own silent and holy supplications. I know that although *worship* with others is an engrained experience in Greece that includes many traditions and customs, I have also learned that evocations of *faith* for Greeks is an incredibly private matter. It is expressed while kneeling in a hushed icon corner of one's own home or praying in the inner-most recesses of one's soul. That said, I'm sure that God was glad we were all there together that sunny afternoon. No church is perfect, but I will quietly tell you here I am glad we are of one and the same Spirit. When we drove on to the fortress of Mystras, you asked me to walk to its summit with your daughter. Making our way to the top over ancient stones, walking hand-in-hand, was another milestone for me. Willful though shy, tentative, and not easily trusting, yet, little by slowly, she has become more at ease with me each visit. It has taken years of these short get-togethers for your daughter to warm up to and accept me; therefore, that afternoon when your daughter reached out and slipped her little hand in mine as we made our way triumphantly up the rugged path, I felt like I was on cloud nine before we ever reached the top. No words or translation was needed; we bonded, and that was that. Thank *you*, Voula, for this making special time together possible, and I hope for many more of such get-togethers in the future.

Can you tell I don't want to let you go as I linger here and write to you? I'll fade out now by having us imagine we're sitting on the beach at O. To have this place sown in the deepest recesses of your memory makes it all the more special. We know that this little piece of eternity lives on in your daughter, too. There are no waves here, just lovely, multi-colored pebbles beneath us, made soft with the waves' wear. Many may come here just for the weekend, but you'll stay there off and on for three months at a stretch. Even in the three weeks every few years I stay there, I get into a daily groove — running, cooking, eating a meal out on the balcony, cleaning, and just plain old living; I master every nook and cranny and corner I cross or clean. Every evening or before I have to depart, I walk over and say a vesper prayer of gratitude beneath the flags outside the little church of Agia Fotini. Each trip since then has inched our hearts closer, to the point where, other than land and sea, I now feel we have no distance between us.

Until our next visit, I hope you'll consider these thoughts shared I've here as a token of my affection, gratitude, and love for you, Voula.

A thousand hugs and kisses,
D.C.

45. Evangelia

Meet Evangelia. She is a Greek who has spent her whole life in America — in the deep south, no less, and she exudes a unique amalgam of Greek pride and American patriotism. She is a member of both her local Greek Orthodox parish and a national Pan-Hellenic Society, but she has no interest in going to Greece anymore. It has been close to forty years since her last visit when she was but a maiden. This woman lives, breathes, and ingests any- and everything Mediterranean, and yet she serves a portion of the population that parties and lives life like a wild teen on spring break. Evangelia's husband is also Greek, Greek to his core, and one who himself suffered hardship as a youth in Greece during the war, but you'd never know it today. He is a hunter, deputy, and a successful man of independent spirit; you can't be sure whether he'll be at the beach property with his wife or back home with his fellow hunter- gatherer menfolk. They are a husband and wife team who run a modest hotel in PCB, Florida, and in discovering it nearly eighteen years ago, it has become my home away from home in mid-July when I've a desire for R & R at the beach. My focus here, however, is on Evangelia: she took a shinin' to me right off the bat, and sometimes I feel as if I am the combination of a long-lost daughter, a friend, a fellow Greek compatriot, and her tenant all rolled into one. She is always working; there is not a lazy bone in her, and she runs circles around those she employs. She wears many hats and swaps them out swiftly and deftly, depending upon whether she needs to be concierge, reservationist, or cleaning lady; in short, she does it all. It is in the evening time when I have come back from dinner and the indigo evening is upon us, waves softly crashing in the near distance, and I spot the glow of her TV on behind the shutters that I stop by her office unannounced and plop down next to her to catch up on our day. Perhaps we will watch a little on the boob tube or eagerly view Greek videos on YouTube until we both get tuckered out enough to turn in. I adore Evangelia.

Do you share a handful of eclectic connections with a person that has created a special bond between you two? Who has become your friend through vacations spent year in and year out at the same place? Who is one who has served you for a decade or more such that you now have become friends? How has he or she been there for you in a way that has brought you ease and comfort?

Read on to read about the one-of-a-kind friend of mine that is Evangelia.

"Man is by nature a political animal."
— Aristotle

"The essence of America — that which really unites us — is not ethnicity, or nationality or religion — it is an idea — and what an idea it is: That you can come from humble circumstances and do great things."
— Condoleezza Rice

"We are what we repeatedly do. Excellence, then, is not an act but a habit."
— Aristotle

"Let food be thy medicine and medicine be thy food."
— Hippocrates

"Whatever you do, *work at it with all your heart,* as working for the Lord, since you know that you

will receive an inheritance from the Lord as a
reward. It is the Lord Christ you are serving."
— From Colossians 3:23–24 (NIV),
emphasis mine

July 28, 2019

Yassou, Evangelia!

I know this letter will come as a surprise to you, and, in a
way, I hope it is. There's not a lot that astonishes you in life. You
have witnessed much; plus, you keep up with what's going on
in the world, in America, and in Birmingham and Florida, as
if you were a roving reporter. My letter contains no current
events, but rather celebratory words of praise and gratitude for
you. When Hurricane Michael last struck and touched down
at PCB, we who love the Emerald Coast got reminded of the
fragility of life and just how flimsy are the structures we erect
when compared with the might of Mother Nature. So naturally,
prayerful thoughts of you and the Greco Inn swirled to such a
degree that even now, I am compelled to take a few moments
to write you. You and your husband have been in my life for
well over a decade; every year, you are one of the few who still
sends good, old-fashioned Christmas cards (and not just photos
of yourselves decked out). Here is an out-of-the-blue note of
thanks to you; I'll take my time and count the ways because I
don't think folks do this enough.

I'll start out by stating the obvious: I am grateful for the
haven you have provided me in the summertime; fifty paces
away from your property is what I come for year after year.
For me, the ocean is *the* best place to bask in the sun, splish-
splash about in powerful waves, and wash all the barnacles
from one's soul that have built up over the months. We feel
the Lord's strength, grace, and omnipotence as the tide rises
and washes back out. What could be better for restoration and

relaxation than hearing the crash of waves rolling in, observing the gulls suspended midair and cawing overhead, feeling the sun caress our skin, or the salt of the sea touching our tongues? You are proud to post pix on FB that reassure us that PCB is not only surviving this or that storm, but even if she has taken a hit, she's only momentarily down, not out; green flags are sure to be seen soon. There's a tranquility felt as you look down its long stretch of white coast; flanked alongside is the expanse of brilliant aquamarine water. And in the distance towards the west, just past the giant piers off to the right, we bear witness to the cadmium red, burnt orange, or chrome yellow of the setting sun. Such beauty! Every day, the miracles keep piling up. It's like we've got God's own tub mere steps beyond your pristine pool, and you are happy to share it all with us.

You may or may not know this, but I'll never forget the day I discovered the Greco Inn; it was a complete surprise to me, yet I felt like I'd come home. I had been looking for a different place to stay, not the other more crowded or popular highrises further down; plus, so many on the quiet end seemed rather sad and run down. Not yours. Admittedly, when I saw the bold red lettering above your office, how could I *not* wonder if the "Greco" of your inn traced its roots back to the ancient city of Sparta across the ocean? All I had to do was walk in your front door to know the answer was *yes*, it was. Above your nearly-hidden desk, I saw the familiar signs of a Greek in possession of this property. Protective icons adorn the wall nearby, the framed newspaper articles herald your establishment's history, and your parents' obituaries hang by the door as if frozen in time. In the near distance at the table where you eat is a bottle of ever-present olive oil. Your husband was on the recliner watching soccer, and he quickly popped up to greet me with a ready smile. You were working on your sizeable monthly schedule on poster board, deep in concentration, erasing a name here to pencil in a name there. When you stood up to greet me, my first impression was that a Greek statue had come to life:

your posture is perfect; your frame spare, and your carriage stately. You are a perfectionist in your own right, and Aristotle's comment on the habitude of excellence dwells in you, for sure! You'll laugh at this description because I know you'll focus on your hair unkempt, outfit plain, or face unpainted due to the demands of the summer's work. Still, anyone can tell that you are like a goddess who has temporarily suspended her state for the labors of hospitality due to us mere mortals. In short, to enter the expansive living room area, which also serves as your office and dining room, is like walking into a little piece of Greece. It is the pride in your heritage that I'll next reveal.

Like me, you were born and raised in the States, but having both parents being Greek meant that your outlook, temperament, and values reflect a Hellenism that runs through your veins as surely as does your blood. In the snatches of time we grab between going to the pier or beach, over the years, I have learned much from you. For example, the word "laconic" was not unknown to me, but you had me sit beside you as we peered together at the map of Greece, and you outlined that portion of the Peloponnesus where it lays. It turns out that you, too, trace your roots back to this area, and with my father being born in one of the port towns used by the ancient Spartans, I figure that this makes us neighbors. Though I may be driven to communicate at length, our ancestral desire for getting down to brass tacks fuels us *not* to beat around the bush when a matter is truly important. I would say your entire *modus operandi* reflects this efficiency and concision which has made it possible for you to care for two homes and serve hundreds who flock to the beach every year.

As a Greek-American living away, but not apart from my patrimonial estate, you have encouraged me to join the National Hellenic Society. I may have no dowry, but I do have a right to claim and keep alive millennia-lasting values. How are these values manifested in you? I see a commitment to the excellence of which Aristotle speaks, and it is reflected in your work ethic and health habits, which Hippocrates himself would applaud! You work circles around your cleaning staff, and though you may stop to chat, there is an internal buzzer that goes off deep in your brain and tells you not to tarry; there's cleaning to be done or guests to be attended to. Every corner of every cranny of your property is as clean as you can make it, and because you're never truly done, I expect you'll live a very long life for all that's left to finish. Your health habits leave the rest of us in the dust. While others thoughtlessly devour burgers or glazed donuts, you shudder and eat the fare from the Mediterranean diet that has kept us fit as a fiddle for millennia. It's like a scavenger hunt in the grocery store to have to wade through packages of pretty processed poisons to get to what's pure and right for us, but you are a soldier in this matter and are victorious every day. Knowing I am of the same mindset, how many times have I come up from the beach to discover a grocery bag of goodies hanging from my doorknob? I smile knowing you've brought me fresh radikia — red dandelion greens, perhaps a few pieces of spanakopita, or some other healthy and tasty Greek food that you didn't want to go to waste and know I'll appreciate. I think you are a little glad when I pick the fresh basil you've got planted around your pool. You are so attuned to the mechanism of your body that you often surpass modern physicians' treatments and find natural medicinal sources that flush toxins or maladies that might temporarily afflict you.

I do not want to leave the impression that it's all work and no play for you, but here again, it's the Greek that comes out to play, and such comes in the form of the entertainment you choose for yourself. Though you have no children, at times, I have felt like a daughter when you endow me with the treasures of your heart, including sharing better memories of the past or things of late that make you smile. You have also told me all about your brother, who, like me, loves Russian literature. And while I may not be fully fluent in Greek, I do know enough to be able to speak in code with you when there is cause to converse in hushed tones. Like a parent and my friend, you alone have taken me by the hand and slowly taught me Zorba's Sirtaki dance, and I tried with all I had to learn what your feet knew by heart. Not only this, but how many times have you and I sat together in your living room in the evenings, giggling while watching Greek comedians you have brought up on YouTube, one after another? Do you remember when we watched the old black-and-white version of *Antigone*? You and I cheered her on from the couch as we were transported to days in our own lives when we, too, challenged and proved to both man and father that we as women are worthy, that we do matter, and we fight for what is right. Some things don't change, but we don't blame Eve; we take up our crosses daily. Your love and attention are not limited to the ten days I stay at the Greco Inn in the summer. Oh, no! The way you demonstrate your love is by sharing morsels of what's vital in life, and you dispense it throughout the year. This reminds me of my father, who would do much the same if, for example, he saw a violinist or some program about cooking or traveling he knew I'd enjoy. He would be sure to alert me to turn on the TV, just as he would should warn me of impending inclement weather which forebode potential ill tidings for his daughter. Many a morning I have awoken to find that you have sent me any number of links via Instant Messenger; it's like receiving a small Christmas gift or a coin from the tooth fairy. They remind me of things dear to both of us: Greek song and dance, our faith, or our history and heritage.

Another aspect of you that is true-blue and bonafide is your patriotism for the U.S. of A. Your pride as an American is intensified because you also have a passion for politics. Therefore, I bring Aristotle into view again for reminding us that, despite the American warning *not* to discuss politics or religion, the Greek in you says not only, "Why not?" but "We must!", and you do. This is *your* land of sweet liberty, and you let freedom ring by reminding any who will listen that democracy works best when we put petty politics aside. Though you know where democracy was birthed, you pledge allegiance to *this* country because she stands the highest chance of seeing it come to full fruition; therefore, you keep up with current events because they reveal the health of our nation. You talk to the TV announcers as if they were your colleagues, heckle the reckless and feckless who get caught in some lunacy, and grieve for those who suffer evil or disrespect, be it an innocent bystander or the man who holds the highest office of the land. So many of our fellow citizens take their rights and liberties for granted, and even more, disregard the responsibility we all must shoulder to preserve and protect our sacred freedoms. You and your husband well know that Condoleezza Rice's words about the great potential and promise this country possesses prove correct because you have witnessed growth and greatness in your own lives, and you take nothing for granted. Your husband will never forget scavenging through trash bins for food when he was a starving lad back in war-torn Greece. Even today, some of the elderly there who have what amounts to pennies for pensions can be found silently sifting through garbage, ashamed but in quiet desperation. Oh, we live resurrected lives here. Maybe that's why when we watch your husband dance the lone eagle dance of Zeibekiko, we understand and respect his improvisations; they amount to powerful prayer. Even though the crowd may make it rain dollars on him, I have seen him in a trance, taking sacred steps and leaps that both celebrate and mourn the hard times he has faced. You and I know no such Greek tragedy, but I see you cherish your honorable Greek warrior who is also hunter, deputy, and dependable guardian.

I'll close by saying how much I admire that you waste not, want not; you make the most of every moment in life. As the Apostle Paul says in Colossians 3:23, you put your heart in all you do; you are mystified how the world could possibly otherwise. You love the stars and stripes, but I see you stand in attention to the Greek and American flags co-existing like banners waving inside you. I'm pretty sure I haven't told you this, but I have imagined standing beside you among a reserved crowd of Greeks outside a cathedral past midnight on some early Easter dawn down in Tarpon Springs, the light of the candles softly glowing on our faces as we sing "Christos Anesti." I whisper, "*What rapture!*"

All roads may lead to Rome, but you and I are heaven-bound, and so I wanted to say thank you for being my friend and neighbor. You deserve to know. I am looking forward to being there and seeing y'all this coming summer at your Greco Inn.

With love,
D.C.

August

The A, B, C's of Being a Teacher

Once a month, FTA students who dream of one day becoming a teacher meet with and ask us veteran teachers, we ol' battle-axes, for advice as to how *we* did and do "our craft," day in and day out. We look back at these young starlings, a little bleary-eyed and wizened, not knowing where to begin. We smile back affably and offer well-intended assurances. I will let you in on a little secret: when we see such students or interns with the same lofty or altruistic aims we once had, sometimes what we *really* would like to tell them is, "*Run! Turn away! Get out while you can! It's not what you think it is*!" I jest, but there is a kernel of truth in what I say because in a job like ours, you will get little thanks, less pay and not much support, and frequent resistance. Every year, the demands get greater, the social milieu more complex, and the latitude as to what and how we teach reduced. If by year seven, we don't get burned out, there is a good likelihood we will stand the test of time. Veteran teachers operate in a subsonic groove of providing; not much ruffles our feathers. Unlike online videos or courses that assist with remediation, we in the flesh not only explain, but we inspire. In fact, we crush it every day. We dispense knowledge, wisdom, guidance, and support like it was candy; they don't know it's gold. As a result, even if all cannot make the grade, we know that most are better off than they were, and that's a fact.

The overall success of our students cannot be quantified.

Their effort expended plus our input provided doesn't necessarily equate to the desired outcome of the grade earned or gains gotten. Ours is a soft career that confounds, but remember, we deal with teenagers, so whether they are scallywags or scholars, their need is greater than the total of what's dispensed in their textbooks. We deal with paradox and irony on a daily basis; therefore, Paul's words, "God has chosen the foolish things of the world to put to shame the wise, and God has chosen the weak things of the world to put to shame the things which are mighty" (1 Corinthians 1:27 NKJV), make sense to us. When we see a sea of eager, hopeful, curious, suspicious, blank, or downcast eyes facing us, we realize the magnitude of our burden. Therefore, when their lights turn on, we've deciphered their mood, or, many years later, when we receive a note of thanks, we *know* we've done right by them *and* made a difference. It produces a sense of satisfaction like no other. The teachers I've chosen to highlight this month are those whose harvest has been abundant, and I'm honored to have taught among them.

Do you personally know a teacher/educator, policeman, fireman, nurse, EMT, or veteran who bears the brunt of doing that which keeps our community safer, smarter, and in order? Have they ever shared with you a day in their life, and it left you stunned in not knowing how to respond? You can start with a simple "thank you."

Read on to meet Rachel.

46. Rachel

Meet Rachel. I have heard some teachers say that they refuse to care more than the student does. This statement rings hollow and smacks of something amiss; in fact, it is unbecoming for one in our profession to say such. I recall an older guidance counselor who once reminded me that we teachers are to hold ourselves to a higher standard, that we don't have the luxury of not caring; it is our calling and our duty. We must try to fill in the gaps when they can't seem to complete (or turn in) their assignments. Perhaps the students have a deficit, void, or sorrow within, the source or cause of which we need to ferret out; only then can we proceed to jumpstart or rev the potential that lies fallow or dormant within. Rachel is a colleague of mine whose ethical and moral standards are impeccable, and she takes her job seriously. There is something disarming about her which puts you at ease and can make you feel like you are in her good graces; as a result, it's all the easier to risk and try and do. This is an incredible gift for one who teaches. She needs not to perseverate, and where she can help it, she doesn't allow any student's past failures or present problems to intrude upon their future successes. She believes in them. There is something noble about Rachel, but at the same time, her unique and quirky sense of humor will endear her to you. Another mantra or maxim of us teachers is to "accentuate the positive and eliminate the negative," that is, to build one another up and not to tear each other down. Both as a teacher and our department chair, Rachel shows her faith by her works; her deeds *do* match her words. She turns her back to gossip, backbiting, and judgment, and her students are the beneficiaries of her kindnesses and goodness along with the subject she teaches.

Do you know one in the public eye who makes a concerted effort not to live by the ways of the world, but by those of a higher authority? Is he or she able to balance the needs of his or her own children while nurturing and leading those who are not? Have you met one who is at once sensitive yet strong, organized yet spontaneous, compassionate and principled, and forthright yet flexible when need be? Do you know a person who can serenade you with a song at the drop of a hat and make your day to boot? Does he or she use humor to leverage his or her power? What teacher do you know that is committed to excellence and maintains the highest of standards, yet is ever-ready for some frivolity? What convocation of complexities does this teacher possess and bring to the table that brings betterment to the world?

Read on to learn more about Rachel.

"I believe the children are our are future Teach
them well and let them lead the way Show
them all the beauty they possess inside."
— From "Greatest Love of All," by Whitney
Houston (1984)

August 4, 2019

Dear Rachel,

I can't think of anyone else in the world but you who would appreciate my juxtaposition of the erudite and common, the elevated and the simple, and the Puritan with the populist. You alone could jam to the fused verbiage here without getting whiplash! In homage to the beauty, originality, strength, and complexity that you possess, I decided to put pen to paper and write you a note of love using the vocabulary of Nathanial Hawthorne alongside select song titles of Whitney Houston. A moment of silence, please. Obviously for different yet, equally legitimate reasons, they each remain dear to us because they touch upon something pure and passionate within *us*. This is reason enough to serenade you using their words. I'll even toss in for free in some of the officious jargon with which we in education have become familiar.

I Get So Emotional when talking about the Greatest Love of All that we teachers attempt to endow within our neophytes. Our passion for and calling to instill a love of learning boils down to the fact that we try to uplift our students so that they know they can Count on Me in the classroom and beyond. Sometimes when perambulating through our red wing hallway, I have seen you at it in your classroom and noticed you've gotten so enthused. It's as if you were both showing and telling your class, "I Wanna Dance with Somebody"! "Whom?" you may ask. *Them*, our students, that's who! Why? What I have come to observe in and know of you is that in all you do for the students *and* for your co-workers, You Give Good Love. Yes, sometimes we have those days where we feel that, no matter what we do, It's Not Right But It's Okay, and we in the trenches get weary to the point where we may complain and tell ourselves, "I Have Nothing" or even speculate "Didn't We Almost Have It All?"; therefore, I've decided to take this One Moment in Time and relish just how much I Believe in You and Me. Even more, I want to explain How Will I Know that My Love Is Your Love. How is it that I have so much to say to you?

It's because I have been Saving All My Love for You! How better to reveal my unfeigned tokens of gratitude to you than through the diction of our own adored Nathaniel Hawthorne? I transition through the following pithy quote, which, "perforce, will far from throw a lurid gleam." Indeed, my own venerable one, know that I aim for you to ingest beneficence.

*"Hester felt or fancied that the scarlet letter had endowed
her with a new sense… If truth were everywhere to
be shown, a scarlet letter would blaze forth on many
a bosom besides Hester Prynne's. The symbol seared
Hester's bosom so deeply that perhaps there was more
truth than our modern incredulity may be inclined to
admit…"*
—from The Scarlet Letter *(1850), by Nathaniel
Hawthorne, emphasis mine*

I believe that the substance of these lines expresses what
it takes to be a successful and impactful teacher. Forsooth, it
is evident that you have become preternaturally imbued with
sagacity, fairness, and benignity. Unlike Hester, *your* "new
sense" comes from an ethereal source which makes you
replete with benevolence. Your physiognomy often reveals
your mirth, and I apperceive you to be precocious. When I
saunter into department meetings on designated mornings,
your congenial visage is often replete with a vivacity that
ultimately stems from your piety. This note may feel to you
like some apotheosis, but my gesticulations are not gratuitous.
When I look over the annals of our career as teachers, I am
neither palliating nor expiating the prattle of brazen hussies,
let alone the machinations of malignant or ignominious forces
that make us feel like we are walking the scaffold as if we
deserved the pillory. What we do is an enigma to denizens of
our community, let alone to the plebeians of society at large.
Through the vicissitudes of our careers, we have borne the
rankle and upbraiding of many a petulant parent to the point
that, perforce, we may desire to become recluses and avoid
the contagion of diabolic forces which tinge our society as if
from some sable malignancy.

Let me not linger on what is amiss. Although I may have
a propensity for loquacity, it takes no conjuring on this end
to say that, in my own past, I have betimes been an uncouth

heathen; resultantly, I have no right to play the acrid despot. Instead, I acquiesce that, as one of the brethren now, I must be unfeignedly scintillating, decorous, and devout; I see such sanctity in *your* mien, and I am buoyed up by your eminence as my department chair, comrade, sister, *and* friend. I seek no boon; I tarry but to enshrine my respect and affection for you. In short, we are not imps, and you are past being an airy sprite. In fact, I trow that I have also watched from the sidelines as if I were a grandam and have taken great pride in seeing the verdure and vivacity that motherhood has wrought to your personage! There is no ponderous process needed to deduce that your comportment is golden, not gilded, and your frame dauntless and dependable. We are two teachers who refuse to capitulate the stance that the sage on stage is inferior to the guide on the side. We can be *both* for *all*!

Betwixt us, we have seen some phantasmagoric changes in our field! We go way back and have experienced tumultuous times, including the advent of the likes of state testing, beginning with the grisly Gateway, and still, state testing knows no bounds. We have *always* attempted to leave no child behind such that he can read literature like a professor, yes, long before common core was imposed. When I look at the citadel of our career together, our vistas span enough time such that we have also borne witness to moving our adored faculty workroom to what used to be a computer lab, which, in turn, was a former classroom. We name our computer carts with terms that lack endearment, and we have witnessed many a dear colleague in our orb come and go for various and not always positive reasons. You and I have held real gradebooks which bore the ink of scarlet marks indicating success or failure *way* before we came to depend on the auspicious electronic portals of Aspen and the like.

We carefully traverse the labyrinth of the human psyche so as to disseminate our pearls of wisdom and knowledge which are propounded in time-honored speeches from our native language and classical literature, all for us but to bring forth, like some conjurer, the potential of each student. Many a wayward Antigone do we admire *and* subjugate for her greater good, erudition, and personal edification. With hopes as bright as our students, we look eagerly to the omens of the Magic Eight Ball, all but for the hope of a scintilla of respite to lift our spirits through the form of some wintry mix that keeps us homebound. Then we can catch our breaths and have a prayer of catching up on grading or dealing with the duties or exigencies in life. Yes, we have lost the sacred cow of tenure and gained new ones that label our students with acronyms indicating contagions in life that we are informed stymie, thwart, or smite their innate potential. As a professional, you bear no stigma; your reputation is pristine, and though I have endured the dark mark of infamy, it was solace through your proffered song, "Thy Will," that helped mollify my mood, and for that, I thank you still.

We live among heathens who might try to make us misanthropes baring the guise of malefactresses, but you and I remain devout. Our faith is immutable and indefatigable. We do not work in a utopia — no one does — but through it all, you stay a benefactress of positivity and hope. Even in your notes to our department that are laden with imperious or daunting tasks for us to complete, both collaboratively and individually, you take the time to celebrate our small successes and even mention us by name. In fact, you help replete us with merriment in your laughter and lyrics carefully chosen from the annals of your past.

So, please take note from your dually-certified colleague, from whose room in our hallowed hallway you may still catch the distant strains of *Fiddler on the Roof*: "Sunrise, sunset... Sunrise, sunset... Swiftly fly the years." No, "nevermore may return the traveler to the shore," yet still, my friend, let me encourage you to be "sustained and soothed by an unfaltering trust." Without a doubt, you will recognize these sagacious words from Longfellow and Bryant, but I come back to Hawthorne to capture *you*: you are our "sweet moral blossom." With this, I close my message dedicated to you by telling you that yesterday and today and forever...

I Will Always Love You,
D.C.

47. Veronica and Ashley

Meet Veronica and Ashley. They say Rome wasn't built in a day, and, well, neither is a child. These two are sisters in arms and ones of the same vocation; in fact, they are one hallway apart from one another, and they are friends as well as sisters and colleagues. I know them each in a different capacity, and the two together make a whole that adds exponentially to all whose lives they touch and teach. I am fortunate to count myself among their tried and true ones, and we have weathered much together. When cycles of administrators come and go, there is a tendency for some teachers to romanticize the past or vilify the present. These two look down the pike and at the bigger picture; they know when to hold out, but they never run. From years of experience, they understand that it takes new ones in power a couple of years to get settled and another two to have it running like a well-oiled machine. For me, the fact that these two women care so much about their fellow teachers that they would and have defended us, we who have become fatigued or forlorn or feel slandered or sullied, places them in a league of their own, like Nobel Peace Prize winners. They have put themselves on the line to blot out stains, clean up messes, and redress grievances when others withdrew or have or make no time. Of course, they are incredible teachers, each in her own right. I view them as a pair of queens in the classroom, and they position their students on their chessboards with winning strategy. They bring out the best in their students and make them feel like champions. Here I pause to curtsy to these ladies who go above and beyond to help our school run more smoothly, and, thanks to the fact that they support *both* the novice and the veteran, less of us are lost too early attrition or feel hamstrung in by policies that need to change. Veronica and Ashley are teachers and leaders *par excellence* if ever I saw any.

*Do you know siblings in the same profession or job site?
Are they complementary to one another? What type of
relationship do you have with each, and what does each
unwittingly bring out in you that is worthwhile, perhaps
even unexpected? In what way do you see them each as
catalysts for change and self- betterment in those around
you? Do these two complete each other's sentences and
bring merriment and delight to those who are with them?
If you find yourself stewing or fretting over something
in your world that has run amuck, are they less than
intimidated or daunted by the situation and find a way
to refresh your spirits by bringing your problem down to
size or to its resolution? How might you honor them?*

Read on to learn about Veronica and Ashley!

"We make a living by what we get, but we
make a life by what we give."
— Winston Churchill

"You never really understand a person until
you consider things from his point of view —
until you climb into his skin and walk around
in it."
— Harper Lee, *To Kill a Mockingbird* (1960)

"Let's groove tonight, Share the spice of life..."
— "Let's Groove Tonight" (1981), by Earth,
Wind, and Fire

"Be anxious for nothing, but in everything
by prayer and supplication with thanksgiving
let your requests be made known to God.
And the peace of God, which surpasses all

comprehension, will guard your hearts and
your minds in Christ Jesus."
— Philippians 4:6–7

"Words are perhaps they are the most powerful
weapons in the entire world... Teach your
students how to dream big dreams, broaden
their perspective and speak words of life to
your students."
Principal of Admiral High School to the Staff
(10-20-19)

August 11, 2019

Dear Veronica and Ashley,

Back in the fall of 2018 at the initial draft of this letter, the reason for writing you was unrelated to my decision to retire. I had no idea that this was going to be a possibility or an offer put forth; it also had nothing to do with health concerns or a significant shift in my life's direction. I just decided to launch a pet project of sorts, and the private impetus or reason behind this was to let a few people who are particularly precious know in detail how much they mean to me. You ladies are at the top of my roll for folks I intended to write to here at school; the time is always right for putting love on our list. Here it is, one year later, and my zeal and commitment to completing your letter have not diminished one iota. As a result of our teaching "in the trenches," as they say, we share a bond few do and fathom more than many might wish to comprehend. Therefore, I want to honor this portion of our lives and to commemorate a few particular memories I share with each of you. It is not only students who need words of life and votes of encouragement!

Ashley, being the elder of the two and the one whom I have known longer, I will start with you:

I inaugurated this letter with a relevant quote from Churchill, a man, no doubt, a hero of yours, he who knew the privilege and price for leadership that chooses *us*. To say you have a passion and care that cannot be quelled would be an understatement; in fact, I am sure you have more energy in your pinky than most folks do in their hearts, and you are a natural fit for what you have committed your life to. You are one of the few teachers I know who has retained her core enthusiasm, a sense of wonder and joy— not only for her subject matter and her students, but for life itself! For us in the consuming and honored field of education — a vocation we readily admit is both a labor of love *and* our charge — let me state that it is quite a feat to balance personal and professional duties. You are a zealot for both. When you are down, you are never out, and we all run to you when in need of a booster shot of hope. I celebrate this quality in you. You are more than a teacher; you are a leader and a conqueror of nations, and I have seen you in action. You bring history to life and have introduced thousands of students to many prominent historical figures as if you were on a first-name basis with them. You instill in your students a fervor for learning because it cannot be quenched in you, and I've no doubt that you've raised battalions and squadrons of curious students who have followed the Pied Piper in you. As a result, they inherit your broader and richer mindset that acknowledges we are a planet full of people, all with a host of differences, yet who each struggle and scratch and scrape to retain dignity in the face of adversity. We cheer at triumphs and mourn at losses because they are we and vice versa! What character! What a lasting legacy that is yours!

You also know that the best classroom is the one grounded on real life, so you show what you say: you have taken hundreds of students with you, boots on the ground, and brought history to life by having them walk in the footsteps of the greatest leaders as well as those of unknown soldiers. I'm sure your globetrotters in their own right have stormed the beaches of Normandy, crossed the Avenue des Champs-Elysées, and been silenced bearing plaintive witness to the ghosts that still haunt Dachau. Do you recall when we once literally ran into each other on a narrow street just past the hauntingly beautiful Notre-Dame? What are the chances? I say it was a divine appointment! And, of course, we can fondly look back on our trip to Mother Russia together! What a dynamic duo we made: I for majoring in its language and culture and you the superhero of history. To walk across Red Square with you; to peruse the Amory with its imperial jewels, crowns and furs, spectacular carriages, and even Faberge Eggs; and to step through the stately halls replete with masterpieces in the Hermitage and Winter Palace was like strolling the grounds with an American empress. Around every corner, this or that proved familiar to you, and you told many a back-story as if you lived and breathed among royalty. You ran toe-to-toe with our guides, and thanks to your own storehouse of knowledge, you made history real and relevant for us all. Do you remember making that PowerPoint presentation of our trip at your place shortly after that? Every slide told at least one story; you seamlessly connect the past to the present. There's nothing dusty or stuffy in your history lessons because you possess a playfulness and curiosity; plus, coinciding with your fascination with history is a readiness to exalt all moments of merit, both great and small.

You take nothing for granted, and with hawk eyes, you can see into the soul of a student, and instinctively, you know how to draw the best out of him and her without their ever being aware of it. Those who remain recalcitrant or unruly, you let them learn from the proverbial school of hard knocks; coddling can foster e titlement, and your disarming love and attention knock the chip off their shoulders. History teaches us that to the victor go the spoils, but the virtues of sacrifice, commitment, loyalty, and selflessness are the stuff of which true heroes are made, and there'll be no losers produced on your watch. Oh, we come from a vintage and generation that still remembers what it means to have pride in one's country, so to bow our heads and take a moment of silence as we place hands over heart still stirs us to the core. It seems to me that somewhere post-Watergate, we took a wrong turn at the crooked fork, and we have never quite righted ourselves. That's no matter; it's just another reason we do what we do: you become Rosie the Riveter because everything about you cries, "We Can Do It!" Your students can still be instilled with a sense of pride, purpose, valor, compassion, and righteousness, yes, even if progress that has led us all to lean a little too much on our own understanding (Proverbs 3:5). To be satisfied with self erodes our humanity and capacity for visionary thought and independent action. I am not knocking technology, and I know you are not one to shy away from the world of modernity, but you herald our need to be authentic; we only get one shot at this life. No one escapes your care, and the bold honesty and integrity you bring to the table and to your classroom let us all know you are on our side and will give us all you've got. And you don't just love people who are close to you or if it's convenient. I have seen you at Panera's helping a student study just a notch more to ensure her greater success on an A.P. exam; although the public might not ever know this, it doesn't go unnoticed. Your ready smile, lively eyes, affectionate nature, and quick wit are expressed through a thousand and one gestures as well as on your animated face. In fact, to read your expressions is to read a good book daily, and any who've partaken of you are left hungry for more.

I should also like to speak to your leadership qualities. For this, I can go back several administrations to say that I have watched you in admiration as you rally your department, back your teachers, and conduct negotiations with many an admin. team, all with such finesse and diplomacy. To me, it was abundantly clear whose brain and arm have helped bring both department and school a great leap forward. You also were instrumental in seeing to it that your more reticent sister was acknowledged for all she has done as educator and department chair, and so she earned her just deserts as teacher of the year. I appreciate your fierce loyalty, and no one doubts that when you're on their side, you're present and accounted for through any dark night. Regardless under whose helm we have served, we have weathered storms of both the powerless and the pernicious and have retained our dignity and purpose. Now we are right- side-up again and serve alongside those with vision, insight, and respect. We don't merely hark back on days gone by; with the sense of hope, resolution, and intentness the likes of which you abound in, there will always be brighter days ahead! The best leaders have the gifts of generosity and humor, and these you surely do. Few like you take the much-needed time to celebrate and refresh fatigued spirits with good old-fashioned fun. Often, you have knocked on my classroom door while I was lecturing (or imagining myself to be saying something important) because you couldn't wait to invite me to some concert or music event! Should I agree and say, "Yes," I would be in a conspiracy of vital frivolity with you! These bones still long to dance and shout and celebrate. They say youth is wasted on the young, but everything in you retains that vibrance and gaiety in life. Thanks to you, I've been a part of the pack that went to see Earth, Wind, and Fire as well as Kool and the Gang. You demonstrate all the best that a big sis can be. Time and again, I've seen you *be there* for your little sis, who is my colleague and friend here in the Land of English, so I now turn to face her.

Dear Veronica,

You are the perfect complement to your sister's gregarious nature, and, truth be told, we who go big and bold feel a little lost without the soft stability you provide; it steadies us through the bumps of life. Having been your next-door-carrel neighbor in our department for well over a decade, I now know that beneath the calm demeanor lies one who can weep and worry. Still, we don't see you tremble because you sense in your soul that "it is the stars, the stars above us, govern our conditions." Shakespeare may have penned this, but we know it is God who shields us. We who bustle about are jealous of your calm. When I read your favorite passage from Philippians, I am reminded of you because it so perfectly renders your capacity for putting faith into gear and action. We who love you know this through experiencing the protector guardian in you who have sheltered and shielded us from many a tempest in the night.

There remain few in the department whom I've known as long as you; we are of the old vanguard and can say we go "way back." As my fellow English teacher, may I say that I love the Anglophile in you? The literary geniuses of Shakespeare and Shelley notwithstanding and beyond our appreciation of diction perfectly plucked and placed is a respect in you for a nation known for its time-honored traditions, moral integrity, for restraint and discreetness, and for a liking for things to be kept proper and tidy. We admire them for keeping the stiff upper lip of stoicism in the face of adversity. (That said, you know I can read the reddening of your neck like it's some '70's mood ring exposing inner agitation.) Why is this? Because like Emma Williams, you concede that "if our hearts are not right, life will not be beautiful and bright."

Therefore, like holding onto a subsonic torpedo that no one would suspect you possess, what drives you is your pursuit of peace and tranquility. Because this quietude is in your core, we with frenetic energy are drawn to you as inevitably as a child who, kneeling by her bed every night, whispers prayers for the Lord her soul to keep. We feel safe and sound and tucked in with you. I need not count the ways and means that have been imposed upon us who happen to know precisely what we are doing in the classroom. Those who are dumbfounded as to why we can't seem to levitate the leviathan of the lethargic student are want to admit a malaise of mediocrity that blankets our culture and covers our kids. We still seek to instill a love of language and a passion for values that are imbedded within the lines of truth and fiction, and, by and large, proof or not, we know we do. It's a sacred charge we have and one that is still as intimate and real and as worthy as the students we face; they happen to lap up the spoonfuls we feed them, back and hungry for more the next day, yes, even with the usual grumblings aside. Why is this? We know just how to pour that spoonful sugar which makes our medicine go down. We are proud to be a little nerdy, a little bookwormish; therefore, it's no surprise that we likeminded ladies and colleagues once went to the mall *not* to go shopping, but to watch the movie version of *Hamlet,* played by Benedict Cumberbatch, no less! I'll bring us up to speed here by saying that, thankfully, we are past the two terms that brought about the Time of Troubles. It is the words from our current principal I've copied that stir my soul. I know you, too, subscribe to what he believes, and that is, beyond the content and form we expect from our students in their writing, we hope our words and ways foster dreams and give the breath of life to the students we teach. I know behind the veil of closed doors in the sacred chamber of your classroom, you do this, and for this, I praise you. Now, I don't want to give the impression that you are prim and proper or some Miss Priss. You have a dose of sassiness that comes out when rights are wronged, mendacity is detected, or yours have been hurt. I love that, to your core, you are a southern lady, and I have come to learn that "Bless her heart" would not be a blessing I would wish bestowed upon me. We wonder why the world can't run according to the ways and means and values that Atticus Finch instills in his daughter. And though we are middle-aged — hardly old — we still long for a simpler time when character counted for something. It brings a smile to my face to know that in your neck of the woods still exists a form of Mayberry R.F.D. Your parents, sister, and you live within a short radius of one another and would gladly vote for Sherriff Andy Griffith to be in charge of our community and beyond.

You come from a lineage of strong women, and though that

ship has sailed when I could call you my department chair, serving underneath as well as alongside you, this duality adds another dimension to our relationship. That title connotes an unenviable position, and I remember many a day when you would go home weary, also facing hard times there when you were the sole breadwinner. You never swerved or complained; instead, should someone ask, you might quietly request prayers, knowing that nothing is more potent or effectual. I confess I have offered mine for your mother. Because of our proximity in the workroom, I have seen you saddled during particularly difficult predicaments, be they dealing with colleagues who have faltered or fallen, to superiors who have acted inferiorly, or to the operation of our school during periods of duress and stress. Through it all, you have remained the epitome of grace.

If I were pressed to choose a favorite aspect about you, with pride *and* prejudice, I would say that it is the fact that you are my sister in Christ. I hope you know how precious is every prayer we've made together, heads bowed, bodies seated in some cold classroom, but hearts warmed by knowing we put our stock in the one who's *really* in charge. And, my, how He cares for and loves us, doesn't He? Even through times of uncertainty, when we were wandering through the desert, I always looked to you. You are also one who seeks to keep her candle of faith lit. You possess what Arthur Parker describes as "a living flame which pierces the clouds and banishes night"; resultantly, you, *too*, walk in Byronic beauty. May I also now thank you again here for the classic devotional by Oswald Chambers, which you gave me mere days after the day of my salvation? Such a treasure-trove of His wisdom and penetrating insights!

Well, ladies, sisters, and colleagues, I'll put my quill down now; in fact, recollecting the two of you has now made me ready to give you both a bear hug! Somewhere in time, ages hence, when we look back on this joint venture of a career we share in common, I hope you recollect in fondness the better days we've had here in our school named after Rear Admiral

David Glasgow Farragut. I've since learned that the Battle of Mobile Bay of 1864 is the one which he issued forth his now famously paraphrased command, "Damn the torpedoes, full speed ahead!" which enabled his fleet to move beyond the range of some gunners. Let us, too, go all out for love in life! You are two who already do.

Much love and praise to you both,
D.C.

48. Tammy

Meet Tammy. There's not a doubt in my mind that in her twenty- plus years as a teacher, she, like me, has heard the top two quotes of all teenagers, "It's not fair!" and "But you don't understand!", too many times to count. And yet, Tammy remains nonplussed *and* not dismissive, also a feat when patience wears thin. At a casual glance, she might seem aloof, but don't let that fool you. Tammy is one who would astound you with her patience, her uncanny ability to read students, and the peace and calm she brings to the table and the classroom, year in and year out. She is one of the few that sets the bar high in terms of standards, but her expectations are more realistic than most, so she doesn't get cranky or all in a tizzy when students falter or fail. "Practice makes perfect," we tell them time and again. She scoops them up, dusts off their knees, and sets them back at the task at hand. I hear so many jaded teachers gripe about students being knots on logs or apathetic, when, in fact, kids are just being kids, often trying to scrape by or escape drudgery. I'll reveal a mystery that keeps Tammy and me young at heart: we never forget that we *choose* to be here — after all, this is our career; however, they *have* to be there. Not a month goes by, but that I don't casually, but sympathetically mention in class that sometimes they may feel incarcerated; they smirk and giggle because it's the truth. I can share this with Tammy, and she gets it. For other teachers who complain and snip that their students are grabbing or grubbing for points and don't want to work, Tammy and I sigh and shake our heads at these misguided ones; we assume nothing and start from square zero or scratch if need be every day. You won't find it in any pedogeological course or evaluation form, but it's *also* our job to lift our students up. We tell ourselves in private that it's no wonder kids cringe; your average C students often don't know how to study. They'll forget what's unimportant to them (e.g., documentation of any kind) and take the most expedient route every time. Tammy and I also roll our eyes and count to ten *ten* times in dealing with the sometimes exasperating, but lovable creature that is the teenager, they whose brains won't fully be completed with the finishing touches until they are in their mid-twenties. Therefore, how can we *not* give them our best and root them on during this four-year block of education? In the scheme of things, it's a short gestational period. Tammy and I also know not to go it alone; we swap stories, collaborate, and plan together because we know it's essential to support one another, and that starts with planned time just being together.

Do you have a friend or coworker who has a real pulse for the people she serves? Is she able to select the most salient points and present them in a fashion that is both compelling and significant? Is she empathetic, and does she make it a daily habit to put herself in another's place, all the while never skipping a beat or shirking her responsibilities and giving it all she's got? Whom do you know that is a team player and, without being prompted and of her own accord, helps others complete the requisite tasks at hand, going above and beyond without skipping a beat?

Read on to meet the ever-considerate Tammy.

"No, I have the misfortune of being an English instructor.
I attempt to instill bunch of bobby-soxers and drug-store Romeos with reverence for Hawthorne, Whitman and Poe..."
— Blanch Dubois from Tennessee Williams' *A Streetcar Named Desire* (1947)

"I felt that I wanted the world to be in uniform
and at a sort of moral attention forever; I
wanted no more riotous excursions with
privileged glimpses into the human heart."
— Nick Carraway from F. Scott Fitzgerald's
The Great Gatsby (1925)

"For just as the body without the spirit is dead,
so also faith without works is dead." "Mercy
triumphs over judgment."
—James 2:26 and 2:13

August 18, 2019

Salutations, Tammy!

Here it is mere weeks before the birth of our Savior, and
we are at school scurrying about and busying ourselves as we
complete tasks thrust upon us from above. You may wonder why
I am writing you out of the blue. For starters, you should know
that I am listening to your annual Christmas CD, thoughtfully
made and quietly slipped onto our desks, a goodie for the soul
that you mixed and made beforehand for your colleagues, we
who are also weary this time of year of short days and long to-
do lists. You have inspired me to give back to you; only I will
use words, not songs, and I've enough stored up to present you
a letter of love that you, too, would not have anticipated. We
are not of a profession that compliments itself or that has value
matched by monetary means. In fact, we are grateful for what
we provide for one another, usually in the form of sugar. Still,
every now and again, a single letter or two will come back to
us from a grateful student who has come to realize that what
we give is more than what they thought they got, and we are
touched. Now it's this teacher's turn to rivet her attention to you,
and, as Mr. Keats instructs his boys in *Dead Poets Society*, "carpe

diem"; I want to count the ways that I think *you* are great. We are not promised tomorrow in life or in labor, so I'll take my lead from you and pass it — a love unexpected — forward.

You are of a generation closer to the age of mine than any other English dept. member, and I'm probably the only one who knows that you are housed in the Green Wing because you came on board at a time when we were bursting at the seams and had to make use of another wing to provide the necessary classrooms. That you have made your home over there makes you no less dear to me; I'm glad you have a family of colleagues who are your next-door-neighbors as well as us who are your family that share your love of language and literature. Cliché though it may be, behind closed doors, it really is all about the kids. You and I know timeless truths about education and teenagers which transcend the dictums or platitudes put forth by well-intentioned, yet far-removed entities or personages that attempt to tweak this or to introduce that so that we might achieve some measured growth or gain. We have seen trends and countless curricula — all with their own cutesy acronyms and logarithms of value — come and go and then come again anew full circle, like some bad déjà vu. Oh, you and I had rigor in our curriculum long before any state task force concocted common core standards; we were hardly idle or biding our time, waiting on *their* exams to cover that which we had long since tested. As has been the case for me, I know you, too, have had to cut corners because standards have changed, and we must do more in less time; accommodations of all sorts must be met. Things have run amuck and afoul.

I don't mean to suggest that we haven't witnessed positive changes in education regarding what goes on in our hallowed halls since when we first started. I am not implying that by recording scores in physical gradebooks, by getting mail in boxes rather than being inundated by emails, or having evaluations done every now and again, rather than multiple times per year, that I consider the status quo then adequate. Oh, no, we are of those who witnessed on TV the 1999 mass shooting at Columbine, which left our country in the wake of a trail of tears that *still* hasn't ceased. Such a turning point that was! Havok was wreaked! Problems *still* persist, and deferred dreams *do* explode. The world is upside-down and topsy-turvy; in fact, it seems as if the pendulum has swung off the clock. How so? Adults are the ones who often act like brats, and our youth possess power and privileges that should be privy to parents only. Thus, through our teaching and giving of selves, we try with all our might to keep our young Hamlets from experiencing great falls. You and I are the real catchers in the rye because we seek to snatch those who start to go over the cliff by keeping their heads afloat and spirits bright. We do the best we can with what we've got to better the many who often have little. I would be remiss if I didn't give a nod of acknowledgment to the fact that you and I have been through similar trials by fire, ones we never saw coming, and we are survivors. That's why for me, your keen sense of humor, your go-to mode of verbal irony, your greater perspective and resultant calm, your persistent optimism, and groundedness in faith make you like our own Flo on the Progressive insurance commercials. With you in particular, I feel the guarantee that His will *will* be done: you are already there, taking comfort and courage in the peace and power God alone provides through our ultimate insurer, His Son.

I also wish to speak to the fact that you are an extremely private person, and I want you to know how much I respect the quiet Christian soldier you are, you whose actions speak louder than words. I *so* admire the humility, steadfastness, and good cheer *you* walk with through life's green pastures *and* shadowed valleys (from Psalm 23). Your being chronically ironic cloaks you in humor and has filled me with glee too many times to count. Some let their frustrations out by using foul language, gossiping, or deprecating others. Others broadcast their woes or share their personal affairs as if the world needs to gawk at the airing of dirty laundry or to know their business. Not you.

In all you do, I see you follow God's top ten, so whe man or child violates our rights, rules, or expectations, you know who's got your back, and so you stand your ground and weather life's trials. You and I know what it's like to have the earth rumble beneath or feet and feel our livelihood suspended in mid-air until the terminus reaches its conclusion. To be pushed off-kilter and to have the wind knocked out of us at the very place where we aspire to show a little kindness, give a little tenderness, and teach students a few facts about their native language or stories from literary their heritage boggles the mind and hurts the heart. So, we press into our faith with all we've got, come what may. Not for all the tea in China would we ransom our souls to be anything but good to those little bundles of joy we serve. We here in the thick of things have seen the changing of the guard and have wondered while we wandered in the desert, at times feeling abandoned by man, but never forsaken by the Son of Man. For this and to you, I extend my hand in sisterly support.

Speaking of His commandments, I observe your taking the honoring of your parents with all due diligence, and I want you to know I admire the relationship you have with each. Your kindnesses to me personally cover the gamut from my receiving them at home and at work, so I thank you. You have transported me hither and thither to the airport and back, more than anyone else, and regardless whether the transit was in the wee hours of the morning or close to midnight, you were always dependable and in spry spirits. I'm not even sure anymore how you and I came up with our terms of endearment for one another, where we slur our first and surnames together into an original alloy, but I like to think that it is because the whole of us has become so dear to each of us. I know you are for me. During our requisite collaboration meetings, an artificial constraint imposed upon us with the express purpose of keeping us in check and in tune, because of your humor and efficient compliance, you actually make it the real deal that is intended. I always learn from you, and, truth be told, I welcome these meetings if for no other reason than to be able to touch base and bump noggins. That you take on chairing our meetings, share your intellectual property (e.g., tests and quizzes and the like) via Google Drive, and ready us for the tasks we are obliged to execute is made amenable because of your good cheer, willingness to assist, and respect. You may be the leader, but we are all equals. Though you don't know a word of Russian or any term from the Soviet Union, you are certainly one I consider my comrade; furthermore, you possess that volunteer spirit for which our state is nicknamed. "*Go team!*" I can hear you say with that quiet irony that endears us all to you. Your generosity literally extends out to the football field, where week after week, in the chill of fall air when teen spirit is its most potent, I have eagerly ferreted you out, knowing I'd get a hug served along with a bag of popcorn you've provided me. Such is the perk I sought.

You and I may be "old school," but at the same time, we are also forever young because we aren't sapped by the demands of motherhood. According to the Rules for Teachers in 1872, each teacher will "bring a bucket of water and a scuttle of coal for the day's sessions." Thankfully, we are no longer such scullery maids. Although we balk at an exacting code which would have us dismissed if we married or engaged in "improper conduct," there is something to be said for us few who, by and large, have chosen to divest our life's energies onto *others'* children. We do not lead monastic lives, but one may find purity and sacredness in a life devoted to the progress and promotion of babes neither innocent nor astute, and daily we turn the other cheek. That said, we are no martyrs. We thrive on being a mother hen to our clutch of chicklets, and, by and large, we are proud of the strides (i.e., baby steps) they advance in the march against darkness. I see you as a kind of lady liberty, holding her lamp of knowledge for all who pass through your classroom. I like it that when we swap sets of final essays to grade; you are quick to concur that we should "err on the side of mercy" when deliberating on a final score. A little kindness goes a long way; therefore, your students will unknowingly be leaps and bounds past the rest, all while having ingested the likes of American authors you and I both adore.

I'll end with where I started because I haven't yet touched upon my selected quotes for you. Although we can surely commiserate with Blanche DuBois' assessment of just how *not* fascinated our students can be with this or that author we love, truth be told, there is a kind of lyrical innocence in them that moves us as if they were living books. And like it or not, yes, we often get those painful "privileged glimpses" into our students' lives. Yet, if need be, you don't shy from taking them to task; oh, they must at least *try* to toe the line. For me, what sets you head and shoulders apart from others and keeps you joyful, pure, and young at heart is that your living works of mercy work wonders in *everyone's* life you touch, and that has included mine, too, so I wanted to let you know how grateful I am for your being a part of my life.

Much love and affection,
D. C.

49. Beth

Meet Beth. She is one of our school's art teachers, and I have admired her from afar for many years. Her reputation precedes her: she is a perfectionist who not only has a passion for her subject, but she cares for her students very deeply. There is nothing that takes the place of that. She, too, doesn't waver and would astonish you with the conditions in which she has had to work. Through no fault of her own, she makes do with less, and her meager classroom, limited storage space, and the underwhelming amount of supplies which she's provisioned seem more like leftovers. Such might leave the heartiest feeling dispirited. Not Beth. She finds a way to make the best of a bleak situation, and she tirelessly communicates her needs. She's finally being heard. To understand her plight better, you've got to realize that for those of us who teach an "elective" like art, it can feel like the subject is nonessential or of little consequence, as if the topic you teach is a stepchild compared to more sturdy ones like science or math. Beth and I are of one mind because we know that *what sets man above beast is his ability to create*, so why not spruce up the facilities of a place that invigorates students' often parched souls and nourishes those who live for art because art brings life to them? Although she has a calm demeanor, she has a laser-focused mindset, and every day employs her privilege by taking students on a journey to a new frontier: the plains of their imaginations. For those students who feel on the fringe or the edge of failing a class, Beth deems that they may be on the cusp of greatness elsewhere. Sometimes you have to show rather than tell, and what more sanctified and revelatory way than through art? Remember that we all drew and painted long before we formed a single letter or number. Beth gives credence to how much she believes in her students by showcasing their art wherever she can, including her ceiling panels, now festooned by her own Van Goghs. Beth is also an intuitive person, and, like some bloodhound, she sniffs out nonverbal clues in her students' body language and facial expression to read what may be garbled in their speech. Whenever we perchance meet, she and I always have conversations of a philosophical nature, and I suspect that she tells herself, "We cannot grow faint or weary. We are accountable." Therefore, I will cheer her on and lift her up to be a light as she colors our world.

Do you have a friend whose job some might take for granted? Do you see the value of what she does? Here I have chosen one who teaches art, but in terms of other careers taken for granted, it could also be anyone in the service or manufacturing sector. What people do you know who promote the arts in their community, be it a preservationist, a historical society member, or a quilt maker, that is, any who celebrate and promote the visual arts in real and practical ways? Do you know a teacher or a coach or an educator, who, unlike the bulk who subscribe to "tough love" which sometimes can give one a license to be cruel, would rather die than humiliate or belittle another, knowing that sarcasm can be as fatal to the soul as a bullet to the heart? They see beauty whenever a child has peace of mind and are sure to make them feel loved.

Please read on to learn more about my friend and colleague, Beth.

"The word which came to Jeremiah from the Lord saying, "Arise and go down to the potter's house, and there I will announce My words to you." Then I went down to the potter's house, and there he was, making something on the

wheel... Then the word of the Lord came to me
saying, "Can I not, O house of Israel, deal with
you as this potter does?" declares the Lord.
"Behold, like the clay in the potter's hand, so
are you in My hand..."
— Taken from Jeremiah 18:1–6, emphasis mine

"*We artists are indestructible*; even in a prison, or in
a concentration camp, I would be almighty in
my own world of art, even if I had to paint my
pictures with my wet tongue on the dusty floor
of my cell."
— Pablo Picasso, emphasis mine

"Only God creates. The rest of us just copy."
"I saw the angel in the marble and carved until
I set him free."
— Michelangelo

August 25, 2019

Dear Beth,

If I may, I'd like to pick right back up where we left off at
the end of the faculty meeting this past November — you know,
the one in which our esteemed principal sounded more like a
pastor than an administrator and reminded us that our life has
a purpose. He told us that we are neither victims of our past
nor of circumstance and that we matter more than grains of
sand in the ocean. Like you, I was struck by the fact that he
was complimenting us beyond the perfunctory niceties we hear
regarding our value as a teacher. Secondly, the manner and
mood with which he honored us revealed he truly respects us
as individuals *and* the calling placed upon us. He acknowledged

that our job taxes us, but he went deeper and paid due deference to the One who made us. Therefore, what might have been penciled in as a "pep talk" on a bullet point for an average leader was obviously not stock and store for our principal. For these golden moments, he spoke intently and quietly to us, and slowly, we wary ones discerned his sincerity; his words were not stale and did not trivialize. In fact, I dare say, they took our breath away. We were unexpectedly uplifted by his telling us that we are not here by accident, that we each matter, and that what we do with and for our students is of utmost importance; it is a sacred charge from a holy vocation. There has *never* been an administrator who delivered such an existential sermon of sorts to us. We were all moved; no one uttered a word. For whatever reason — perhaps it was divine intervention, I could barely contain myself to wait for the meeting to end so as to make a beeline for you. I wanted to stress the veracity of all he said, particularly as it applied to *you*. Maybe I discerned your dismay or doubt, but my intent was pure; conviction prompted me. I realize you were not a little overwhelmed at my spotlight on you, but as I didn't get to express all that was on my heart, if I may, I'd like to continue here in this more intentional way. "Why?" you might ask. Oh, how could I *not*?

In our short tête-à-tête after the meeting, you asked me if I had ever taken an Enneagram Test, or did I know my "number." In ignorance, I thought this was some version of numerology to which you were referring, so out of curiosity, I went online and took a test. It turns out that I am a "1" and "7" to your "4" and "6," which confirms attributes we already know about ourselves. Among other adjectives, I found "disciplined," "perfectionistic," "adventurous," and "high energy" versus your being "individualistic," "creative," "prepared," and "devoted." I confess that well over a decade earlier, I had our department members take the Meyers Briggs Personality Test so we could identify and better deal with underlying manners and motives which often had us locking horns. My score indicated I am an INTJ; its more common label has been classified as the "Mastermind." You probably know that the origin of this test is based on Jung's typology. Earlier as a youth, I scoured the newspaper to read my horoscope to see what was in store for this Gemini. If we go further back to the fifth century B.C., the Greek physician Hippocrates was also mulling over human nature. He theorized about the early body-mind connection and stated that certain moods, emotions, and behaviors were caused by an excess or a lack of body fluids, which he called "humors." The ideal personality was one that balanced the complementary characteristics; usually, one of the four temperamental categories dominates, thereby creating an imbalance of the paired (i.e., opposite) qualities. In fact, I've even heard that the characters on *Winnie the Pooh* are more or less representatives of the types we know as "sanguine," "choleric," "melancholic," and "phlegmatic," each named for one of the bodily humors. No wonder the choleric or sanguine in me seeks the melancholic or phlegmatic in others. Don't you find this to be true for yourself? And then there's the whole left brain–right brain explanation as to why we think and act the way we do, and I confess, I am fascinated by such analyses and hypotheses. There are scads of other tests and indicators, but my point in touching upon these here is to state what strikes me as obvious: that *man seeks wisdom* and a suprarational knowledge because the child within him never gets his fill of "Why?"

I will go out on a limb, dive deep, and point to the source I believe in and love with every atom of *this* Adam: our divine maker. God not only loves us and creates all; He desires for us to seek Him. Since man is made in His image, then every exceptional characteristic and excellent quality he possesses are attributes that originate from his Maker. Therefore, our fascination with shades and nuances of our disposition is a confirmation that we do not come from naught! We are modeled after perfection, and so we stew and fret and wonder why things aren't quite so down here. The most exquisitely creative force that exists outside of time and matter, yes, He who is eternal and every perfect Omni out there, has made us *expressly* and *seemingly* lacking so that we might turn to and seek Him for fulfillment and acknowledge Him as absolute! That's what love *does* and who God *is*! Oh, our attention easily gets diverted by the shiny and beautiful things down here. That we contemplate our nature and our navel is only natural. Ultimately, our theorizing and systematizing is another form of child's play, fascinating and fun though our puzzles and blocks may be. Only when man reaches to Maker does he find the warmth and light he s been craving all along, and His blanket of love inspires us in endless ways to reach and out and do the same for others.

When it's all said and done, that is why we teachers can say with mysterious and sure authority that it's not *what* we teach but *how* we teach that matters. We literally live to love, and it comes out through the unique ways we have been fashioned and positioned as well as through the topics, talents, and temperaments instilled in our minds and embedded in our hearts. We are never more like our Maker than when we create, so I tip my hat to you, Beth, because art is not merely your area of certification; it is your raison dêtre. I love how Picasso attests that you can't *not* paint or create. My mother was an interior decorator, as the career was called in her day. Being brought up by her was like living in an issue of *Architectural Digest;* I became fluent in the language that deals with design, light, and Fengshui. Like her, I know shades of color like some girls can rattle off hues of nail polish. In elementary school, I volunteered to draw portraits of any willing classmate who might prefer not to play kickball that day. When I got to college, I took a basic drawing class that introduced me to terms like "plasticity," "chiaroscuro," and "negative space," the latter of which blew my mind in terms of the perspective it provided. It taught me that space is never empty, and what we can't discern by sight is as vital as all that's visible. I also gulped down a course on the history of modern architecture — another elective — like a man lost to drink. And in graduate school, I waited two full years for a particular course taught on Byzantine Art and Iconography. It was my younger sister who was our family's artist; in fact, she majored in it, and though it was her territory and role in the typecast of my family, I, too, am drawn to beauty. As Emily Dickinson says, "Beauty... and...Truth — Themself are one."

In terms of personality type, you and I may be at opposite ends of the spectrum, but in the realm of fine arts, I want to celebrate the divine bond we share, you, of course, as its artist and I as her admirer. I have come to your ragged kingdom of a classroom in school, a maze of mismatched rooms that have no semblance of logical connection, and have observed your supplies literally bursting from their storage spots for there not being adequate room. You more than make do; it's a miracle that every day you spin gold from straw. Your students mill about before they settle in for the lesson that will have them launch into their own opus. Having experienced the liberation of being in an art class, I, too, have felt the lifting of my spirits and the surge of creative juices flowing. I know that the haven you provide, the instruction you give, and the confidence you instill are like precious few rooms in school, and what they draw and do for you will be with them forever. Decades later, I still remember the resurrection of my mood and manner as I headed to my

A.P. art class after having left physics. Tears of frustration and a sense of ineptitude were replaced by a glow of satisfaction from the batik or pastel drawing I'd completed. I have seen that same look of accomplishment and pride in your students, too, one that can only come from a job well done when effort, talent, discipline, training, imagination, and vision all serendipitously converge.

As a teacher who is still a student of life, I want you to know that I learn from you. Several times, I've gone outside to where you were conducting class in a distant field, the smell of smoke in the air, as you have the students fire their various pieces. Like some welder or master craftsmen, you are all beans and business while you oversee your students in the production phase that leads to being able to display their final wares. Who knew they'd learn chemistry, *too*? From you, I also discovered that in raku firing, all of nature's elements are used: earth, fire, air, and water. How incredible! The forced rusting whereby the iron gets oxidized creates a different effect each time, and so, we all wait in wonder in eager anticipation to see how the crackled glaze or striking metallic effect is going to manifest itself in the object made. The technical result may be copper oxide, but I call it amazing. This spontaneity and unpredictability of outcome remind me of what we teachers attempt to achieve in our students. We do not know the outcome of how all the elements of influence will manifest themselves as we apply heat and pressure to our students; we hope none break, and so we handle them with kid gloves. Those who are not directly involved in an actual school cannot appreciate that students are flesh and blood and brain and soul. They are not tidy products whose gains or growth can be quantified or measured by mere data, let alone manipulated by methodologies. Many in the outfield of the field of education need to come to visit us more often. And like your raku pottery, the term I learned literally translates to "happiness in the accident," our students' outcomes and achievements are not solely dependent on nature and nurture, but gift and gumption.

As one whose passion is clay and like the potter who throws earthen clay on her wheel, you help shape the lumps of students who come to you; it's both visceral and spiritual, tactile and cerebral, and all so wonderfully messy. In a certain respect, are we not like Pygmalion, he who attempted to give life to his own stone creation — our Galateas — and in so doing, correct in marble the flaws and mars we note in flesh and blood? The parallel ends with outcomes differing between our truth and this Greek myth. The primordial slime from whence we came and the dust to which we return are all so because we have a master potter who saw fit to create and craft His clay into being, into the very vessels we are. No two pots are alike, and He makes no mistakes. I believe He broke the mold with you, Beth, you who are "fearfully and wonderfully made... [and] my soul knows it very well" (Psalm 139:14).

There are many other interests we share in common, but I'll start out by affirming that you and I value traveling, and we seek to see the world because we have a sense of wonder, curiosity, and love of life that cannot be quenched or contained. You have permitted me to visit your classes to recruit for my tours abroad — now too many times to count. I see this as a testament to your understanding the value of what lies beyond the here and now. You do not mind the time I take to paint a mental picture for the students of what they might see and experience on such a trip. Truth be told, while in Greece, I have often wished for you to be my curator in the Museum of Cycladic Art because I know you could explain the significance or symbolism of many a vase, figurine, or pottery piece. I intuit that you, too, have a great appreciation for the more primitive impulses, abstract expressions, and primal tones and veils in art as well as life. That said, there is an exquisite sensitivity in you, a perfectionism that is transported when art becomes life at its finest. I have seen Michelangelo's *David* as well as his *Pieta* and stood transfixed, struck dumb for being so moved, tears running down my cheeks as I see Mary mourn while the blush of life leaves her son, our Savior. The ideality of David's physique, especially the grace and strength witnessed in his hands, is matched only by his bold look of confidence and defiance. What that we could be so encouraged to face our giants! You and I are not ones to shy away from foes or threats, and years ago, with no foreknowledge or pre-planning, we both signed up to be on our school's safety team. I looked forward to sitting next to you as strategies and plans were put in place to make our school and its environs safer and sounder. Turns out, unspeakable tragedies did strike; our own were not left unmolested, and so we continue to maintain our vigil with a watchful eye, putting better nets in place.

Another trait you possess and we both share is that the teacher in you still has the student in her who loves to learn; such is not age-dependent. Therefore, I applaud you for taking the needed time to re-energize and get re-inspired by attending classes at A. School of Arts and Crafts. And though our phones can often be too smart for our own good, I say to you with all earnestness that in the months when our brains met in the electronic halls of Words with Friends and Chess with Friends, I relished our interplay of focus, calculation, and strategy, like it was a mental dance we did. So many times on Facebook, I have seen you pictured on your bike going who-knows-where, undoubtedly on a trek that will involve many mountains or miles. To me, it is as if you have your own flying machine as conceived by Leonardo DaVinci! I have seen your happy countenance and noticed the daubs of green in your eyes, your irises the color of moss, and such might compel one to focus on an earthiness that's an intrinsic part of you. However, I spy with my little eye an intent look of zeal, concentration, and exhilaration in you, which I believe springs from a love of flight, speed, momentum, and thrust that is hardly virtual; your spirit revels in freedom. So whether you are on your bike, in the classroom, in a studio, or in the privacy of your home, what you add to life and to us all who know you is rich and real, and I for one want to thank you and praise you for being exactly the way you are and who you are.

With love, a big hug, and much respect,
D.C.

September 2019

Nearest & Farthest, Consummatum est

The moment before He drew His last breath on the cross, Jesus declared, "It is finished." As I now round the corner to take my last lap and herald my three remaining persons, I feel a sense of giddy anticipation at completing my project. Consummation is commencing. God *knows* I mean no disrespect! This has been both exhausting and fulfilling; taxing and liberating. The motivation for this labor, this exploit of love, has been to honor those who are particularly precious to me, and I intend to end strong. Bob Goff sagely states that "*the love you leave behind you will be your legacy*," so the way I see it, communicating my gratitude and lavishing love is the *least* I could do. In fact, I can't get over how much is stored inside me that wants to come out as I meditate over the ones I love. The notion of "nearest and farthest" about the men that follow has to do with the fact that, on the one hand, I feel a particular affinity with them. We share a unique connection that is dear to me. I am beholden to these men because they have poured into or shared a portion of my life, and I am the better for it. Where "farthest" comes into play is because there exists a cleft that divides us in some marked way, yet the schism creates no rift. A year ago, when I started writing these letters, the differentiation of the two persons in September's category referred to geographical distance and a spiritual split. Now, I will expand upon this division and explore those whose life choice, experience, or state is so distant and remote from mine that they astound me. Regardless of what is similar between us, as a result of the time I have spent with these men, the net effect is that *I am not the same woman* because of them. What that you might make the most of vital contact with dynamic people, become inspired to give back to folks in need in a way that's natural for you, and hope never to cease improving and learning. The following men's lives echo and prove true the words I teach of Henry David Thoreau: "If one advances confidently in the direction of his dreams and endeavors to live the life which he has imagined, he will meet with a success unexpected in common hours." That sounds like victory to me! Thanks to these lives here — and one man in particular — I am triumphant.

Come and take my hand. We' ll visit my final three men.
May their merits move you, too.

50. James

Meet James. He is a former colleague of mine from the good ol' days of the first half of my career. Unlike others who teach American lit., James and I shared a not-so-secret affection for the Puritans, and we were not a little glad to extol their pious values and virtues, all the more so because we see that much in the world has gone wrong. I don't consider us old-fashioned or fuddy-duddy; righteousness and goodness never really go out of style or favor. Our students happen to live in a day when anything goes; freedom has no restraint, no governor, so he and I quietly toed the line, even if it meant they saw the error of their ways through how we graded their papers. With red pen held in hand, poised and ready to strike, and our heads bent down in concentration, we plowed through piles of papers. Meanwhile, for far too long or often, our loved ones were denied the pleasure of our company. If you don't teach — or if you do, but not English — you will not understand this type of sacrifice and commitment. Grading essays is more than just calling *"Foul!"* when we spot infractions made in grammar and the like or find errors when focus shifts or organization is lacking. Writing is *incredibly* personal as it comes from the wellspring of spirit as well as intellect. Therefore, how we evaluate has more of a profound impact than, say, the assignment submitted for a physics class or an economics project. When essays have been graded and as we pass them back, James well knows the expectant look on students' faces; they are scared in the way a child is who is thinks he's getting coal on Christmas morning. The stroke of our pen can stab their souls, and none likes to face such discordant or cacophonous music. All that said, faith cannot thrive in a vacuum, and James was being convicted by His Spirit to align form and function. His frame of mind changed from imperceptibly to undeniably as the sanctified life he was trying to lead at home could not be put on the shelf or on hold just because he came to work. Knowing that James could not tell the students how to conduct themselves or plea with them that their comportment mattered more than they could imagine, I believe he felt increasingly troubled by this ambiguity. In fact, he couldn't stand it. It was as if, in his silence, he was giving tacit approval to those who wore unseemly outfits, to those who took pride in their surliness, and to those who unapologetically said,

"No," to His Lord and Savior in everything they said and did. Their sins of commission continued through his one of omission, and James no longer would turn a blind eye or appear neutral. He had qualms. Such blatant disregard was an affront to him, and how he dealt with this was more important than conforming to the duties of his job, so he drew a line in the sand and gave up the ghost there. He stayed true to himself *and* his Lord. Like John Proctor, he is left with his name intact and reputation unsullied, and for this, I will always admire him.

Do you have a friend who quit his or her job over principles? Do you know a person whose values matter so much that they would do anything to see that they are upheld? Have you ever had your senses assaulted and sensibilities shocked by an incident? Did you stay? leave? speak up or out? Do you realize just how much people watch and observe how you react to this and that, especially when things aren't the way they should be? What sacrifices have you made to be true to your principles?

Read on to meet the remarkable James.

"*Do not love the world nor the things in the world.* If anyone loves the world, the love of the Father is not in him. For all that is in the world, the lust of the flesh and the lust of the eyes and the boastful pride of life, is not from the Father, but is from the world. The world is passing away, and also its lusts; *but the one who does the will of God lives forever.*"
— 1 John 2:15–17, emphasis mine

"If your hand causes you to stumble, cut it off..."
— Mark 9:43

"All mankind is of one author, and is one volume; when one man dies, one chapter is not torn out of the book, but translated into a better language; and every chapter must be so translated.... As therefore the bell that rings to a sermon, calls not upon the preacher only, but upon the congregation to come: *so this bell calls us all.... No man is an island*, entire of itself... any man's death diminishes me, because I am involved in mankind; and therefore, never send to know for whom the bell tolls; it tolls for thee."
— From Meditation 17, by John Donne (1624), emphasis mine

September 1, 2019

Hello, James!

I can't tell you how overjoyed I was to see you at my book signing last fall! Though I saw your two youngest and now nearly-grown children at the local farmer's market selling fresh produce — an occurrence that brought unexpected delight for my detecting in them the stamp of you I have yet to spend any time with you since you took the road less traveled, that is, the high road, His path of peace. I imagine you sitting in a simple-spooled cedar chair, one long leg crossed over the other, like some lanky Abe Lincoln mulling over a document as you ponder my words. My purpose here is to honor the man God made in you, and I choose to do so this way because you are not a man to seek vainglory, let alone a stray compliment. You know the stains man bears; therefore, you would shrink away or swiftly change the subject should I praise you directly, as opposed to, as Dickinson would say, telling the truth "slant." Do please let me linger for a moment and cherish the son He saw fit to create in you, my former colleague and forever friend with whom I share the same faith.

I start out my reminiscences by fondly recalling some humor we teachers mete out and share when students aren't around. We, too, need a dollop of frivolity to balance the seriousness and purposefulness we bear to ensure that they buckled down and press into their studies. Sitting in silence in our little cubicle, deep in grading mode, red pen held poised and ready to make the mark that reveals transgressions made in mechanics or some missed point in meaning, we hover, alert and prepared to judge. Students view our final assessment of letter or numeral recorded as the signal of our having the power of life and death over their essays, and, by extension, over their all-too-often fragile self-esteems. You and I have spent countless hours in such a posture, and you well know the hundreds of hours into which this part of the job seeps and can dominate our private lives. We who take our jobs seriously, we who crave the light and thus point the way to enlightenment, subconsciously seek balance for ourselves and, yes, a little levity. If memory serves me correctly, once when we were in the thick of grading, you crumpled up a piece of paper intended for the trash, and, instead, chose to lob it over the carrel, so that with any luck, it might tag me on the head and break my concentration. The launch was a success, so the battle was on, and what fierce fun we had. All work and no play makes Jack a dull boy, so we made way for a coveted chuckle or giggle. That seems like ancient history to me now. And rather than refer to one another by our given names, in our department, we would sometimes call one other by nicknames that Lord only knows how they sprung up. To my already polysyllabic surname, another syllable was added, and it made me sound like a type of dinosaur rather than a fellow sapien. For your sobriquet, I uttered a rhyme of endearment in my thickest fake French accent and would call out, "*Croissant!*", and who but you would come a-running? It fits you precisely because you are so *not* pretentious!

You and I took pride in being *the* two A.P English teachers of our large department, I the junior to your senior, and we held standards in high altitudes, evidently too high for others' liking. In the name of equity and efficacy, we were indirectly requested to reconfigure the bell curve in order that the wave crested earlier and waxed wider so that the first two letters of the alphabet were in greater supply and met market demands. We went with the flow, but, in reality, we did not change our standards: our students still toed the line, grew sturdy, and were all the better for it. I'll bet you still can rattle off from memory a slew of the code of Harbrace numbers used to indicate the particulars of grammar that need tending and mending. The elements of fiction and literary or poetic devices are the nomenclatures of studying our literary language, and, should we choose to analyze or pour over some classic we've read, I'm sure you are still fluent. So many aspects of teaching are held up to close scrutiny, and we are called to task, but in this fertile field, we know that the whole is greater than the sum of the parts, and the lives we touch and the minds and hearts we move are our trophies in unseen, but honored halls of fame.

If I were asked to pick a literary character to symbolize you, it would be Levin in Tolstoy's *Anna Karenina*, the co-protagonist and landowner who deliberately chose the more austere life of labor in agriculture to that of sophistication and culture. Like Levin, you eschew modern man's means of measuring success by worldly standards, which promotes a lifestyle that seduces with its ease and convenience but also fosters lethargy and wantonness. Your pursuing a purity whereby convictions are mirrored in manner grew in you by degrees; your core of righteousness that started as a spark combusted into flame. You *had* to make your escape before you got scorched by corruption around you. The choice to put your profession on a funeral pyre and leave the world behind I see was a wise sacrifice. How could you live with yourself and claim you were who you said you were if you didn't try to put a halt to far greater transgressions than what we spy on essays? To turn a blind eye is tantamount to an unspoken acceptance of what is foul far beyond the state of Denmark. Sins of omission are no less lethal than those of commission. Therefore, while we may take some satisfaction in reducing the latter, if we say or do nothing while we witness folly and foolishness, we give tacit approval to what He condemns. In this case, silence is sinful, not golden. As the Apostle Paul so often says, "*May it never be!*" How could you *not* exit stage right and announce your curtain call?

We share more than just academics at school and our profession. Over a dozen years of working together naturally led to dealing with situations that had nothing to do with school or students. In a sense, we also did life together. I bore witness to pains in your personal life, including your losing your mother, taking phone calls to quietly chastise your children when your wife was at her wit's end, and also your leaving for the hospital when your wife became deathly ill. I felt close to you as you were bearing these burdens. I've also been to your home, broken homemade bread with you, and seen the "building," what amounted to your barn for grading and other ascetic or scholarly endeavors. Therefore, the year you left, I felt like I'd lost a limb; I knew an era had ended, but I had only the best of well-wishes for you. When we parted, you truly started, and how fitting that it should be within a community that bears the same name as that of our earliest settlers?

That you moved to a town named after the first permanent English establishment in the New World at first seems fitting, but unlike those whose motivation then and there was to expand English trade and gain a broader market, your impetus was a nobler one. To better capacitate your family and enable yourself to be angelically refined, what better way than to join a group of like-minded ones who sought in all their ways and means to do His will, 24–7? You chose to pass by the world, which is already passing away at an alarming rate. There's no need to cut off extremities when you've made your home and hearth among fellow modern-day disciples of His. In fact, you share more in common with our earliest pilgrims from Plymouth, whose lifestyle was marked by cooperation and hard work, than you do with those from Virginia. No longer do we have to conte d with fighting Indians, suffer disease, or battle the elements of the wilderness; today, it is Satan's battle for the mind and his seduction of the flesh that we have to worry about, so why not decrease the odds?

My only remote experience with observing a similar lifestyle has been when visiting relatives up in northern Indiana; there is a town known by its Indian name, Nappanee, which is called Amish Acres. Although there are shops and markets and an auction at which these Amish sell their wares, I prefer to drive up and down the straight-as-an-arrow long drives on which their acres'-rich property holds their plain, hale, and starched-clean homesteads. The yards are adorned by bright and cheery flowers, windows by home-sewn lace curtains, and farms with

Clydesdale horses driven by capable young men. Children are out in the yard or barn working their measure's worth right alongside their parents; a grandsire may be seen mowing the lawn while his aged wife helps her daughter-in- law inside with the canning. In short, all work is holy, and every member has intrinsic value and worth and purpose. Each person respects the other and loves his Lord. Such a tightly-knit community united in pursuit of the fruits of His spirit I admire. Perhaps I'm a little jealous.

In short, I want you to know that I have always respected your self- discipline, your work ethic, and your daily walk in Him as you try to carry the torch and live by His standards the best you can. There's no love lost for the world because He's got you in the palm of His hand. Early on after you'd moved there, you visited and brought your family to one of our department's Christmas gatherings. By that time, you and your family were already donning the distinctive dark dress, demarcating you as separate from the others in His earthly kingdom. To some, you probably looked like an updated version of Grant Wood's painting, *American Gothic*. Not for me. What I saw was a family unified, quietly content, and flourishing in its modesty and its calling from God, still very much in the world, but not of it. Year after year, your wife has been faithful to send an unadorned card soon after Christmas, packed with the past year's facts of your life to help those of us who still know and care for you to keep up. I eagerly await my note, too. I know that you read either Scripture or theological studies that augment your understanding of His word, but I can't imagine that you would ever forget the likes of our dear Reverend Mr. Dimmesdale. You, too, have that "lofty and impending brow" that bears witness to "native gifts and scholar-like attainments." I appreciate that grading was hardly gratifying; the soul needs fresh air! I'm also sure you can recall John Donne, the famous sixteenth-century poet as well as the foremost preacher in the England of his day. I couldn't help myself in choosing the famous passage I did from

Donne. I know you still appreciate the extended metaphor that captures the fact the we who believe in Him are chapters in His book waiting for a better translation. Donne was actually in physical decline when he heard the tolling of a passing bell, and he dared to ask if it applied to him. What that we were all that courageous and bold in seeking what we still can do for Him. You do daily. Therefore, that renowned metaphysical conceit, which is used by many a high school commencement speaker, you live out in the mystical body of Christ, a veritable beacon nestled in our land of liberty.

You and I are still connected and covered; this time, by the blood of the Lamb. I hope in the not-too-distant future, I may come and visit you and your family where you now reside. To do so would be no less than the taking of communion for me. Until then, may your crops be copious, your spirit robust, and your love for Him *and* your loved ones overflowing like milk and honey. Grace and peace to you!

Your former colleague and sister in Christ,
D.C.

51. Boris

Meet Boris. He is a man of my father's generation, but unlike my father who died eleven years ago, this octogenarian is still alive and doing well. I have not actually seen him in nearly two decades. Yet, like pen pals from distant countries, we two have an unspoken pact between us, and we continue our relationship through written correspondence. This man is somewhat eccentric, and I suspect he lives as a recluse or hermit, but despite our not visiting one another, what he means to me is more than many might know. One bond Boris and I share stems from the universal language we speak: music. I am the major to his minor; we both play the violin. He taught me to whistle like a bird. Though I met him many years before, when I went to college, he became my violin teacher. I soon came to sense in him something akin to my father. I could tell by the questions he asked that he cared about me more than just how I was coming along with a piece I was learning, and I loved that he joked around or teased in his wry manner. He seemed to understand my untamed gypsy spirit and encouraged me whenever he saw my "Greekness" come out. As a man born and raised in Ukraine, he'd been around the world a time or two and recognized "otherness" when he saw it, but his own soul was tinged with a cynicism that, at the time, was a mystery to me. What had happened to him such that he could turn from gaiety to gloom in a flash? Maybe it was that sad Slavic soul of his, which buoyant Americans cannot fathom. Our second connection proved to be a double-whammy. Here I was majoring in and enamored by all things Russian, yet except for what I'd read in books, I was ignorant of the antipathy Ukrainians felt towards Russians as a result of centuries of atrocities committed against them by Russians, the worst of which had occurred under Stalin. Do not worry;

Boris let me in on a thing or two. Like my father, here was a man who had witnessed unspeakable horrors during the war and was emotionally scarred by a toxicity borne in youth. Therefore, when he played his violin, you could tell it was like medicine to his soul; it reached his hurts unhealed. When his bow crossed the string more slowly or his vibrato widened, I felt privy to his private agonies and ecstasies. Compared to what Boris and my father experienced, I feel like any problems I have are minuscule — mere child's play — so I give myself a good talking to and tell myself that I am not entitled to a life without deprivation or affliction, and I hush.

Do you have a friend of your parents' age who has given you new insights and a better appreciation of the outlook and values of a generation different than yours? What have you come to understand better about your mom or dad through your relationship with this person? Even if you don't play anymore, do you share the bond of music with someone that keeps you connected? Think about a person who has been like a mother or father to you. What did or do they provide you that was missing or unavailable to you in your own childhood? How can you thank them?

Read on to learn more about Boris.

"Ukraine, an important space on the Eurasian chessboard, is a geopolitical pivot because its very existence as an independent country helps to transform Russia. *Without Ukraine, Russia ceases to be a Eurasian empire.*"
— Zbigniew Brzezinski, emphasis mine

"When you play a violin piece, you are a
storyteller, and you're telling a story."
—Joshua Bell

September 8, 2019

Dear Boris,

No doubt, you'll see the date above and think I've moved
to another continent in a different time zone or that I've lost
my marbles, but never you mind; I haven't! Just look at it
as a delay from the intended date I'd hoped to write to you.
Anyway, here it is the season of Christmas, our appointed time
of annual correspondence, so I duly take note that this is my
sign to put pen to paper, to wear my heart on my sleeve, and
to deposit this letter in your hands via the U.S. Postal Service.
Do you realize that ever since I graduated from college back
in 1986, with no forethought or plan to do so, you and I have
kept in touch? That's more than three decades! Although I
am hardly Catherine the Great and you are not Voltaire, that
we communicate but haven't seen one another in well over
two decades brings to mind these two historical figures who
corresponded for fifteen years. They never once met, and I,
for one, find that remarkable. The single time I did visit your
home, now a lifetime ago, I recall now your beating me at
billiards, and you played music on the now outmoded reel-
to-reel player. In commemoration of our friendship, this time,
I'm sending you a bonafide letter to convey sentiments not
found in any Christmas card.

You are not one who seeks fanfare or attention. In a recent
email, you wryly quipped that your "twinkling eyes have
dimmed considerably, and [your] wit has soured." You also
announced to me that this year, you would be an octogenarian,
so I also wanted to send you a birthday gift by jotting down
a note of congratulations and thanks by telling you what you

mean to me. I won't miss the chance, and I hope not to miss my mark. There are many life accomplishments you've had cause to celebrate and to take pride in; however, this note is not one intended to sing just your worldly praises. Plus, I would be remiss if I pretended to be acquainted with a fraction of your personal life, let alone professional achievements. You are a particularly private man; therefore, I set my chin on its rest and place the angle of my bow just so as I relate the story my spirit tells, *expressivo*, *largo*, and *con spirit*, using words instead of notes.

There's no way you could know how captivated I was the first time I saw you. Who was this slight, spry man sauntering across the stage who had blond hair, ruddy cheeks, and a face accentuated by a Cheshire cat grin? I was informed that you were to be our city orchestra's guest first- chair violinist one weekend. You seemed both mysterious and merry, not like the majority of middle-aged men who were deadly serious or pompous. I was then in my early teens. Mesmerized and watching with avid interest, I carefully observed how you played. I noticed that your bow glided across the strings with pressure evenly sustained, your wrist was relaxed and loose, and you lay your head on the violin in a manner that seemed to indicate your soul had found a home. You employed vibrato of both arm and wrist, slow or fast, depending on what and when you deemed it was called for. The melody came to life because your violin was an extension of you, and you made it look so natural, so easy. Maybe it was because I noticed a certain parallel between you and my own violin teacher at the time who was Dutch. Perhaps it was some old-world European aura that I was fascinated by, but the point is that I was drawn to you then. My own father also had that uniqueness that separated him from the local yokels among whom we lived and with whom he tried in vain to fit in.

Fast-forward to the fall of my freshman year at my audition for the university's orchestra: I was a nervous wreck, but I somehow managed to scratch out a song for you and the head of the music department. I looked forward to weekly private lessons with you. I was transformed from a rigid board comprised of a bundle of nerves and energy, to a softer, more supple self which you somehow brought out of me through simple scales, a doleful song, or a spirited movement. I watched us both in that mirror, mirror on the wall. I made an effort to release my bow arm and wrist to achieve a more relaxed posture; I hoped for any sign of approval from your eyes. Flow can't come when we're stiff. You were always loose as a goose, and as you'd lean back seated in your chair, violin tucked under your neck, eyes fixed on some unseen point outside your window, you'd model and play with ease whatever I was fumbling at on my fiddle. You challenged me to do better.

It's no secret that I was never going to be a virtuoso, but I felt that you understood a part of me better than what I appreciated I possessed. You frequently joked with me or made references to things that would please this Greek, be it about baklava or asking about how my father was. I can still see you making your way to or from the music building in your ruby-colored Cadillac, yes, a small guy in a big car, but for me, such a mighty man. When my parents' rift became the great divide and our family felt its fallout, you didn't know it, but my honeyed hour with you was where angst ceased, and music soothed the savage beast in me. Once when you performed Vaughn Williams' *The Lark Ascending* as the soloist with the university's orchestra, you transported us all to supernal vistas, far above the riffraff and into a stratosphere where sacred beauty exists, unmarred by us mere mortals. You, too, are that charming and elusive. Like Vaughan William's lark ascending, it seems to me that you also fly alone, ever independent, forever soaring, even if the days have passed since you serenaded anyone. Although a solitary man, you are not a snob; when you return to earth, you are ready to take delight in something that has struck you as funny, wicked, or absurd.

That this Greek majored in Russian doubled our connection; you are a Ukrainian man who is all too familiar with Russia, which has been no mother to you. Your own cold war with the Soviet Union was based on the loss of your family's flesh and blood. The regime of Stalin that starved out something like eight million people — your own grandfather among them — left a bad taste of Mother Russia. You told me that because of this, people welcomed the Germans until they found out that there was little to choose between the two. You said you were lucky to escape. Fifty years later, you recognize the rapacious nature in Putin and wryly remark that everyone still wants the breadbasket of Europe. Like my father, you know the horrors of war, and they stay locked in the vault of your heart, gone but hardly forgotten. He also took such a ship to better shores. I want to thank you for sharing with me what my own father could not, and so I've recounted it here; it's the same song as for him, just a different verse. Nothing is lost on or escapes me as I honor and recall one of the experiences you wrote for me:

> I still remember the "lights out" and the
> bombs coming down on the refinery close to
> our house, or the sirens, and the trek to the
> basement of a bank or similar structure. The
> towns in rubble vividly remain in memory.
> The bloody toes of a barefoot child walking
> on a tank's chewed-up asphalt have not been
> forgotten. And best of all, the mysterious night
> arrival of soldiers in trucks with white stars will
> never be forgotten. The travels from D.P. camp
> to D.P. and the 6-week ocean voyage now
> seems like a distant memory. By all accounts,
> we were luckier than most. I am sure that your
> father had similar stories to tell. As I watch the

> news of today, the posturing, the threats, and
> the building up of nuclear arsenals, it is clear
> that the memories of all seem to be fading
> away.

As these memories fade, I am glad to know you still pray. I do, too. The world needs our prayers. I recently shared with you that I taught my Russian class to sing, "Dark Nights," a Soviet song that speaks of the longing a soldier has for his wife and child, and his recollection of them serves to sustain him. I want my students to know that even heroes hurt. To tell you the truth, I have felt like an ignoramus around the likes of you and my father. I never wish to witness such loss, despair, or brutality, but the fact remains that I haven't seen manunkind at its worst like you two did. You are five years younger than my father, but you are both of that displaced generation whose life was torn up by its roots and transplanted over here in America. Thankfully, your daughter still has you; sadly, this daughter no longer has hers. The impression I have of feeling fractured or not quite complete was a trait I acquired, like some accidental inheritance. That empty-stocking sensation inside had me subconsciously seeking the means to satisfy my longing for a living heritage. What "took" for me was Russian culture, and it carried me off by storm; I was hooked. It was as orthodox for me as faith is to others. Of all people, somehow, *you got that*, and, subsequently, you continued to take an interest in me; maybe you were also fascinated as to how the major I'd chosen would pan out for me later in life. Therefore, when I went to graduate school, I found that my time, energy, passion, and attention, which up to then had been divested in music, got supplanted. My new focus replaced instrument with tongue and music with language. You didn't mind because you understood me, and we continued our relationship as modern-day penpals who reconnected every Christmas. You kept up with me as a teacher, and one who traveled with students as well.

Fascinated, you would ask me where I was off to next, be it any of my eleven trips to the Soviet Union and Russia — both as a student then and with students now — or to other places in the world. I have even been to Kiev during the first few weeks after she gained her independence in '92. Such jubilation and singing in the streets! Brzezinski had it right when he spoke of Ukraine's unique geopolitical importance. You also cheered me on when I returned to the land of my ancestry, one which boasts of giving the world Aristotle's logic, Archimedes' screw, and Athena's wisdom. I should also like to share with you that over the years, you are one who has been a recurring person in my dreams; for me, this is neither sick nor strange. It just shows that you are in my heart's core. It's not frequent, only familiar. And though I am no famous or celebrated author, you were quick to congratulate me on my recent literary endeavor. As of this past May, I want you to know that I retired, but I now continue on teaching in a half-time capacity. These are the last days of thirty years of teaching Russian; only English is left.

Although cynicism can sometimes run deep, hope and love still pulse through your veins. I have been the recipient of quite a few of your Christmas presents, mailed faithfully every year from across town, yet seemingly as distant as if they came from the North Pole. Nestled next to my Russian stacking dolls are your Ukrainian Christmas cards, which have depicted on them dear-to-me icons of the holy moment of Jesus' birth, with Mother Mary lying supine in a cave holding her baby, our King. Were you in my li ing room, you would notice that balanced atop your homemade wooden candlesticks, I have placed brightly-painted, wooden Ukrainian Easter eggs. How apropos! That you did such woodworking was shocking to me because you put your violinist's fingertips in harm's way for other creative endeavors. Year after year, I have shared with many a Russian class the ivory leaf you gave me which contains music for the Mass of Confesor Bishop for Psalm 132. In this psalm, David assures us that the Lord will bless; He has prepared a lamp forHis anointed. Oh, Boris, you are undoubtedly one of His! So, I say to you, "Христос Рождається"! Christ is born! May you have a merry Christmas and a bright New Year!

My very best wishes to you,
D.C.

52. Emmanuel

"For Christ also died for sins once for all so that
He might bring us to God, having been put to
death in the flesh, *but made alive in the spirit...*"
— From 1 Peter 3:18, emphasis mine

"I am ... the *living* One; and I was dead, and
behold, <u>I am alive forevermore...</u>"
— From Rev. 1:17–18, emphasis mine

Meet Emmanuel. For many, this man needs to introduction; his reputation precedes him, and he outdid himself for you and me. The calendar we all go by is based on his birth year. That aside, he was present and accounted for long before any of us or anything was in existence. He goes by "I am" still. In keeping with this chapter's title, I'll first state the obvious: Jesus was just as much of a person as you or me, but then that's it; similarities cease. He is also God, but I'm going to leave it at that for now. In the divine sense, he *is* far, but do let me tell you just how near he is. Perhaps you are like me, in that, as a youth, you were not introduced *to* this man; you just heard *about* him. I used to associate him with his followers, and I found them less than inspiring, to say the least. I became dismissive of and disinterested in this man; frankly, he wasn't on my radar. Out of close-mindedness and intellectual arrogance, I put no stock or credence in what the *Bible* said of him, so it was pretty much a closed case against him. However, behind the scenes, little by slowly, his spirit *was* working on me; the search for *more* and *why* was still on; I just didn't let on. Admittedly, I had enough faith to believe in *God*, it's just that it took time for me to get warmed up to Emmanuel as being more than mere man.

Fast-forward to the month shy of my turning fifty. After

meeting a pastor who piqued my interest in Jesus, I pressed on with the curiosity of a child. *And then it happened!* I had an encounter with Jesus, and it was vivid and real and intimate! Who was this man with outstretched arms and a smile on his face looking right at me? How could I *not* say, "Yes," to his honest invitation of love? Without hesitation, I gave myself to him. It's not something you *do*; it's a choice you make, and the rest will follow. When you let yourself receive a love that's made for you, surrender is what you *want* to do; this is what happens when you fall in love. *I did.* This is no mood or phase; it's a birth, and I *have* been born again. If you see me blush or my eyes shine bright, it's because I still feel a glow within. Truth exists, and it will *always* matter; therefore, I won't fill you with facts you can read, I'll tell you the truth instead. The rest is my short history: I turned aside former ways and allegiances and accepted him for who he said he is: "the way, and the truth, and the life" (John 14:6). I pledge allegiance to *him*. These are facts that attest or prove that I am a Christian, that I follow a man *not* bound by time and space; flesh aside, he cannot be anything *but* alive. Yes, of course, he was murdered, but he returned to the father in the supernatural and permanent state he existed in before what we witnessed here. Need I remind you there's no end to eternity?

We simply don't have the language or possess the faculty to capture or comprehend this. Jesus doesn't expect us to get it, and he doesn't leave us, his followers, empty-handed. When we accede, we attain his spirit, and this bond is a done deal, secured forever. There are no take-backs. Have you ever noticed that when Christians talk about the r leader, it's as if he is alive and not some smart dead guy with wise rules for righteous living? Jesus gives us eternal life *and* a better way to live! It's not a "one and done" situation; He'll be back. Speaking for myself, Jesus is more a part of my life today than when I got saved. In fact, his love fills me to the point that my love spills out to you; you're holding evidence of it in your hands. Just recently, Pastor Mark and I had a conversation I found so helpful. He said that perception is *not* reality. My relationship with Jesus is very much real and personal, *not* because I imagine it or because I think it is so; a proof stands before you: my joyful surrender *has* led to a new life *in* and *with* him. As the old Merle Haggard song says, "*He walks with me, and he talks with me. And He tells me I am His own…*" *This* is the personal relationship and intimacy I have with Christ. No, there's nothing you have to or could ever do; it's already been done. Is *your* mind open to possibility? Read on so I can share with you my final letter. You'll see for yourself just how wonderful and real and living is the man I address.

If you are a Christian, I would like to invite you to join me in prayer <u>while</u> you are reading my letter. I've no doubt it' ll flow. If you are not a Christian, that doesn't matter to me. Please do read on! I ask you to consider this letter and book as a hint of His love meant for <u>you</u>. Ultimately, I hope what you read here will serve to inspire you to seek Him and experience an unmatched joy and promise, such that you would want to share this passion with others. What could matter more?

"Everything inside me cries for order... Someone tell me I am only dreaming Somehow help me see with Heaven's eyes... Before my head agrees, my heart is on its knees. Holy is He. Blessed am I. Be born in me. Be

Order my steps in Your Word, dear Lord Lead me, guide me, every day Send Your anointing, Father, I pray...

Humbly I ask Thee, teach me Your will While You are working, help me be still Though Satan is busy, God is real...

Bridle my tongue, let my words edify.

born in me... I'll
hold you
in the beginning,
You will hold me in
the end.
Every moment in
the middle, Make
my heart your
Bethlehem.

Be born in me..."
— Taken from "Be
Born in Me (Mary),"
by Francesca
Battistelli (2011)

Let the words of my mouth
be acceptable in Thy sight.
Take charge of my
thoughts, both day and
night.
Please order my steps in
Your Word...
— Taken from "Order My
Steps," by Glenn Burleigh
(1991)

"Now all this took place to fulfill what was
spoken by the Lord through the prophet:
"BEHOLD, THE VIRGIN SHALL BE WITH
CHILD SHALL BEAR A SON, THEY
SHALL CALL HIS NAME IMMANUEL,"
which translated means, "GOD WITH US."
(Matthew 1:22–23, emphasis mine)

Septembe 15, 2019

Good morning, Jesus!

Right off the bat, I can hardly wait to say *I love you*! I thank God
I've got eyes that see, ears that hear, and a heart not hardened
so that, even though you liked to call yourself the Son of Man
— after all, you were entirely so when you walked among us,
I clearly see the Son, the one- and-only who is one with God,
therefore, God with us and *you* with *me*! You've been here since
before the start; you testify that you are "the bright morning star"

(Rev. 22:16). Honestly, there are no words to adequately convey what happens when someone comes to know you, but for me, it's like you are in every cell of my system and then some, and, in part, I seek to partake of you by sharing you with others, like some happy show-and-tell, except this is no game. Can you see that I have been trying to encourage others through these letters? You have watched me teach my students that there are at least five words for "love" in Greek, and right now, if I could, I would come up with a few more to capture the reverence, gratitude, amazement, stirring, inspiration, motivation, peace, and tenderness that I feel for you. It's a love that doesn't stay put in its seat; it squirms and wiggles and makes me itchin' and rarin' to go for you. When I said, "Yes," to you, now some seven years ago, when I finally answered the knock at the door and let you into my heart, my world was rocked, and my life hasn't been the same since. I can't see it myself, but some folks tell me I've changed, and I think they mean for the better. No, I am no longer a babe lost in the woods or an infant drinking your milk. I hope not to be repetitive; after all, you already know all about the dots I've connected. No one wants to be irrelevant, and we can't run on fumes, so I still mine for your precious gold, crusade as your pilgrim, and do not settle for the good. You are on my mind all the time, and I can't get my fill of you; it's like I'm in love, yet this is a love that doesn't want to be kept in a box. It's dynamite! The letters in this book are actually your love flowing out of me. As my two middle typing fingers both fumble and fly across this keyboard, I've got to admit that it is so weird to be aware that you already know what's on my mind, already know what I'm going to say. However, you stay still and seated right here beside me, whether or not I'm aware, yes, just as you do for *every* believer. That's no empty rocking chair next to me in this warm womb of my office — oh, no, that is your throne, and I am at your feet! You're never not on call and are always ready for the asking and taking, and that's for forever and wherever! You already know that I am smiling inside and out from both sheer delight and the enormous gratitude I have for you! Though every leaf here has been an outpouring of love for people in my life, as I write, I am quite aware that I've saved the best letter for last: *yours*, King Jesus!

At the moment, you can see that I'm re-reading the ἀποκάλυψις, a sneak preview of your rapturous return; John's book of Revelation includes a welcomed spoiler that lets us know how the story is going to end, or rather, to be continued. I'm glad to report here that there are no longer any conflicting notions within me about the Trinity. I don't wonder whether I ought to face and speak to God the Father; whether I should snuggle up and whisper just to You, my Savior; or whether I should let the most astonishing gift I'll *ever* get, Your Holy Spirit, do my talking for me when I do *or* don't know what to say! Thankfully, you told us that although you "exist in the form of God, [you] *do not regard equality with God a thing to be grasped*" (Philippians 2:6, emphasis mine). I no longer stamp my feet in impatience when I hear that "what I do, you do not realize now, but you will understand hereafter" (John 13:7). That's a promise and blessed assurance, and you keep your promises.

You know I respect and revere you with every fiber of my being, but I just plain old love talking to you. I don't think that you mind. I may sometimes sound like a gush bucket with my words, but the fact that you call me, a believer in you, your *beloved*, that you called your ordinary disciples "friends" has me feeling giddy and a little like John did when he beheld you on Patmos: he fell like a dead man! Most of the time, I end up sounding more like a kid in a candy store, but it's a woman who is pleased to be on call for you. I am not trying to sound calm, cool, and collected; anyway, you get me when I'm muddled or mute because you've got me. Obviously, you don't really want us thunderstruck; that's why you keep telling us not to be afraid. Being flesh and blood, we sometimes burn out, turn astray, or get stuck, but, Lord, let me never fall away. Please help me get back up and stand firm even if I'm down and out; your hand is ever-ready and outstretched for the taking! You have had me to stew and suffer, look and learn, so I'll see and say just who you are to me, and now this living stone is securely set in your building. I am *joyfully* yours, cross my heart, but will *never* die. No, I have never hung on a cross, but I'll take up whatever is mine for you. I want to count the ways I love you so that others can be in on what's no secret to me, which is that you are my Number One; no others follow. Some say that "it's the thought that counts," but I couldn't disagree more, so I'm going to make my prayer here visible with ink, and I hope it's as sweet as incense for you.

Mentioning incense makes me think of the Greek Church, where I was first presented to you as an infant and where I make an annual trek every Easter. I am drawn to her Byzantine tones, candles, icons, and mysterious veils as we all worship your majesty and the Miracle, but, oh, you well know from where I get my daily bread. In fact, the bride you've positioned for me to attend is just around the bend, and she is bold, accepting, vibrant, and messy, but there is more of your love there than in any other church I've attended. I sense your presence there, and I am mightily moved; you meet me there weekly, and I hear you clearly through my pastor who has your pulse of love. I also have brothers and sisters I love now and with whom I'm doing life. In fact, I need them. That's *your* doing, and so, I thank you for placing me on this path and letting me be a part of our church's life. I'm hooked, but of my own free will, and I feel your Holy Spirit bolster, soothe, and warm me from within as I abide and obey.

Like the seventeenth-century Puritan poet Edward Taylor, I ask that you "clothe therewith mine understanding, will, affections, judgment, conscience, memory, my words, and actions, that their shine may fill my ways with glory and thee glorify." I, too, crave for you to squeeze all you can out of me, yes, every last drop; I just hope I can get out of the way. May

I also thank you not only for what you've already done in my life, but what you're going to do? You haunt me with your ways. You are just as enigmatic and confounding and attractive as you ever were! Part of me still contemplates on how it can be that I will never die. And yet, I am not vexed; without a tremor, I am not afraid because I know death will only bring me closer to you; flesh will fall away. I'm in a worshipping way now and yet want to be as real as can be; I am humbled by your glory and power, yet feel invigorated by how you love me. I matter to you, and I am more than enough because your "grace is sufficient" (2 Cor. 12:9). I proudly wear the beautiful garland you've given me, and I have fountains of the oil of gladness (Isaiah 61:3). Lord, I exalt you!

You may ask me why I started out this letter with a couple of songs, neither of which is on my playlist of favorite Christian tunes, hymns, and Orthodox vespers. I tell you, Jesus, even as I was writing the last few notes to others, your letter was already rolling out like some scroll in my brain, and it just happened to be the time of year when we were approaching the day of your birth, so I was relishing listening to Christmas music. You already know my favorite ones which I'm moved most by, those older ones with achingly beautiful lyrics: Hark, I *do* hear! Silent Night... Oh, Holy Night! These ones included here, however, were tunes *new* to me this year, and because I feel made so fresh and so clean, like some vestal virgin, I chose those that match what's in my heart.

I'll now tell you the second odd circumstance I noticed. I have neither given birth nor have been a mother — a fact you do not hold against me, but when I first heard, "Be born in me," I froze in my tracks! I felt the truth in the lyrics as if I were in that manger two thousand years ago holding you close to me. Even though I wanted to protect you back then, I know it is you who saved me now. I am confiding my innermost thoughts to you as I confess that, though this vessel came equipped to birth a baby, I do not recall those stirrings or yearnings to bring forth a child. Rather, you tailored this woman more like Anne Bradstreet, who longed to deliver her "rambling brat (in print)." That said, I *do* feel a type of nurturing maternity for those whom I teach; some call me a "life coach," but if that's so, it's by your rule book I play. In a way, writing feels like some sort of immaculate conception taking place because words come from things said that do not spring from me. Emily Dickinson asked her readers to "judge tenderly of me!" However, I don't worry about that with you because I'm covered by your precious blood. Nothing is more powerful or primal. You have seen me experience afflictions — no, thankfully, not any real ailment, pain, or infirmity — just ridicule and rejection. You certainly are no stranger to scorn; people still forsake you. When I finally did reach out and seek you, you didn't turn away or shun me. Quite the opposite. I well understand what that hemorrhaging woman must have felt when you told her, "Daughter, your faith has made you well" (Mark 5:34). I, *too*, have that peace, and it *is* well. And may I say that there's *nothing* I'm more proud of than being Your daughter. My own father, who is with you now, would understand and approve. Such is my ecstasy in you!

The second song I chose is no carol, but you know I love listening to spirituals because their pitch hits my pain like a balm to my soul. Every word of "Order My Steps," I sing to you. I pray I bring you glory as I walk in faith in what you've laid out for me; therefore, I wish for my words to bring others cheer, not pain. To show obedience to you is hardly a hardship; you show no chauvinism and love me no less than you do your sons. There's freedom and power and liberty in submission to you; to do so delights me. There's no "if"–"then" conditional clause or bargaining on my end; I just want to be ready for all you've instilled and inspired me to be and do. You have made me a passionate, positive, and enthusiastic person by nature; I bob and bow with joy, but I also feel agony for a world of woe, for ones who live in constant sorrow. This seeming discrepancy whereby I can concurrently feel happiness and elation but still be drawn to the melancholic makes sense to you. That's how you fashioned this little Greek girl to be. Though I've never fought a day in my life, there's a Russian soldat *and* a Spartan warrior within me, so daily I lay down my life for you. I just pray for courage to match my discipline and for sweetness, softness, and gentleness to complement my strength. This song has me chomping at the bit to tell you how much I relish your Word!

I am no different than billions like me. Heavens! You've thought of *everything*, and I never tire of marveling at how piercing your ideas are at every read or turn of page. You've ordered in me a desire to see your magnificent creation, and I'm so very grateful for all the places you've allowed me to visit; you know all my favorite sunny spots! There's no need to quote Scripture to you about this or any matter. Jesus, I think my favorite trait of your teaching is how you use counter-intuitive wisdom and irony to blow away leaders who tout stale platitudes; you bring Truth to the table every time! Because of you, I seek wisdom over knowledge, the likes of which I had not before: a kind that is spiritual over worldly, and that's something for this Greek! Recently, when I read, "The fear of the Lord is the beginning of wisdom, And the knowledge of the Holy One is understanding" (Proverbs 9:10), another poem rushed out of me that I hope captures and explains what wisdom from you means. I share it here for others:

> To fear the Lord doesn't mean you're scared.
> Revere Him more; you know you're spared! Put
> faith into action and knowledge into gear.
> Others will see it 'cause it's to His holy ways you
> adhere. Keep your eyes on the prize;
> You'll move, mature, and become more wise.

Jesus, as a leader, you never ask us to do what you wouldn't and didn't do yourself; no one but you can and did save us from ourselves, from that dreadful, eternal separation. I'm so, *so* sorry for the pain, suffering, and humiliation we brought on you as a man! The shortlist that you've etched in my heart is that goodness is an inside job; mere show and appearance are facsimiles of what you want. Our motives matter! You seek our obedience and ask us to respect our fellow man — especially the least of these, and I tell you, I smart from being far from where I want to be in how I address and treat those whom you elevate in the Beatitudes! You ask us to turn the other cheek and not to seek vengeance, to love those who scorn us, to show mercy rather than judgment, to put self last because it's all about *you*, and to let our actions speak louder than our words so that others might look past the dim and the din and see you.

Oh, I want to do right by you! Even if you don't keep score anymore, I am still culpable and accountable. Faith cannot be forced, or it would not be legit., and as a late-blooming believer, I am a living testament to that. Jesus, thank you for never giving up on me! Can I tell you that, thanks to you, I am not afraid; because of you, I am not in peril! Seven years out, I don't simmer or stew or fret over questions anymore, but you know I still seek discernment and *your* wisdom. Your spirit holds my hand and guides me in these moments. You have transformed what may seem mundane and routine in my daily life such that I recognize the countless opportunities I have to little-by-slowly be a part of illuminating who you are to others, especially ones who don't know you. I want others to see there is nothing drab, droll, or dingy in a life with you, you who are the "radiance of His glory" (Hebrews 1:2). To walk in faith towards the frontier you've given your sons and daughters is to be a part of something eternal and majestic, dazzling and amazing, rich, and rewarding. I do not want to be redundant or irrelevant, but it begs for me to restate that during harrowing moments when the Enemy lies to me, takes the wind out of my sails, or steals my joy, that you are that guiding light and beacon I reach for and cling to. Sometimes, lying Lucifer makes logical appeals that make sense to thought and f lesh, and, before I know it, he has clawed his way to my weak spots and momentarily stuns. I may weeble and wobble, but with you, I don't fall down. Jesus, help me come to you before insecurities and isolation distort what I know to be good, right, true, and fine. Although I may not have experienced the misery many other people have, I learn from the glint or gleam in their eyes how to be steeled through a strength that only you can provide. *That* is a triumph! Praise God! I praise *you*!

I want to thank you right here and now for hearing my humble prayers I've made for these fifty-two selected persons. You understand that this is actually a drop in the bucket. You know their needs, as well as my desire to refresh them with a draft of your love through encouraging words *you've* provisioned. Not all of them know that you went from a cradle to the cross for us. I hope you realize that in my not wanting to be so obvious in my appropriation of you that you know I have addressed some incognito to ever-so-slightly turn heads so that they might experience a little of your light and love. *Thy* will be done! I also hope you can see how I relish turning on the spigot around those who do know and love you, too! I am grateful for your putting breath in these lungs and fashioning me just the way you wanted; you make no mistakes or misfits, and I marvel at how you allow me to live in abundance every day. Oh, my cup runneth over for all the good you've put in my life! Thank you for the opportunity to teach so many youths, to show and tell through traveling just how great thou art, to use this mouth and mind to go tell it on the mountain that *you are our Lord.* Can I tell you how excited I am for the opportunity to return to Jerusalem, this time with my pastor and ride-or-die friend, Mark, as well as a dozen or so other members from my church, not to mention my BFF, Bonnie? You set all this up beforehand such that the very man who introduced me to you in the compelling way you created him to be *and* through the work of the Holy Spirit that drew me to accept you as my Lord and Savior, would be one you'd have me show new places? You are so generous! Partly because of your faithful servant, Mark, and entirely because of your atonement, I will someday see you in Heaven! Therefore, how incredibly awesome is it that you've positioned me to show him some heavenly spots down here, including Paul's stomping grounds in Greece and now, God willing, your Holy Land?!? Would it be commonplace or disrespectful for me to say that I know it will be such fun?

Did you notice last summer that I was stopped in my tracks as I caught sight of the Garden of Gethsemane? Why, I saw you kneeling beneath that thick olive tree right over there. How many times have I imagined your anguish and loneliness the night you said, "Yes," to your Father, acquiescing to take that horrible hit for us? So many times, during your mission to make it possible for us to reunite with your Father, you intentionally suspended your infinite might. Anyone else would have used that trump card of divinity if they had it. Not you! You are *such* a family man! To sway alongside masses also eager to see your place of nativity in Bethlehem put me and us all in a trance; we were spellbound to see your first point of contact! Then to drive through the desert with a guide pointing just over yonder at the mountain where you were transfigured was mind-blowing. To climb up, up, up the Mount of Temptation, then gaze down far below, where Satan sought for you to plummet to your death made me shudder and gasp. I loved breaking pita with my fellow travelers at that restaurant by the Sea of Galilee which boasts of fish served as in the days of Peter. You know I love Middle-Eastern food, and I relished everything I ate, knowing that you'd partaken of the same. The desert heat that hit my face you, too, felt, but that haunting call to Muslim prayer playing over the city's megaphone you did *not*, and yet when I caught its cry, it moved me to want to drop to my knees right then and there to revere *you*. Yes, I realize that they've dammed up the waters to make the Jordan river wax broader and deeper for your contemporary co-heirs who want to be baptized there just like you were. Sitting and watching believers line up, I squint and glance up in the near distance. In my mind's eye, I can just see the Spirit in the form of a dove lighting on you. I can hear the unmistakable bass voice of your Father announcing, "This is My beloved Son, in whom I am well-pleased" (Matthew 3:17). We all are, too, and I am still. You surely don't need me to tell you about other places where you were, but I know you understand that where I am in life right now, that my visitation there and the prospect of soon returning with my church family are keen on my mind. The fact is, you dwell in me where I am, and your Holy Spirit is with me wherever I go; such is this permanent and unalterable state that assures me of a love like no other.

Jesus, I don't know how much more clear you could be about who you are; I'm just grateful that every "I Am" statement you made hits me square between the eyes; it's like someone shot me with an arrow in the heart. You know I seek to please you and bring You glory, so I pray I say, "Yes," to the many opportunities you've already prepared for me to walk in. I am His "workmanship," indeed, Jesus' own "poema" (Eph. 2:10)! And though it is my hope that the letter you now hold your hands will be read by others, this is no message in a bottle; it's my love letter to *you*. No, I do not sway and rock and weep when I pray, as I witnessed others doing at the Wailing Wall, but you know I love being with and talking to you anywhere and everywhere; you're always and already there! Jesus, I thank you for saving us and for loving me! *I love you!*

Yours always,
D.C.

Epilogue

A Final Note To The Reader

"Anxiety in a person's heart weighs him down,
but an encouraging word brings him joy."
— Proverbs 12:25 (NET)

"Be kind to one another, tender-hearted,
forgiving each other, just as God in Christ also
has forgiven you."
— Ephesians 4:32

"Finally, brethren, farewell. Become complete.
Be of good comfort, be of one mind, live in
peace; and the God of love and peace will be
with you."
— 2 Corinthians 13:11 (NKJV)

Dear Gentle Reader,

Though I haven't met you, you are no stranger to my world, so I thank you for reading this book; in fact, I now turn to address *you*. In completing this odyssey, you have become acquainted with my dear ones; therefore, you, too, have become tangentially connected to this undertaking. You have become privy to my feelings and perceptions of these people; an interchange has taken place. What was formerly private, unseen, and known but to me has now been made public and evident to *you*. More than anything, I pray that you have been inspired to do something similar for *your* precious ones, too! Are you curious as to what my recipients' responses were upon getting their letters? Of course, I'll never know *precisely* what they felt the minute they opened their letter and sat down to read it. Still, I suppose it would be something akin to having someone toss you a brand-new football, but upon catching it, you discovered that it was as heavy as lead, and it caught you off-guard for its weight. Perhaps they fell to their knees, fainted, or fumbled. That's what I *imagined* happened. For all I know, initially they might have thought I was terminally ill or something. Though I sought and expected nothing in return, I *did* receive the full gamut of responses. I got everything from no response at all to texts thanking me. I got emails from those saying they didn't know what to say, but that they appreciated it. A few confided that they had been moved to tears; others told me that they were grateful and that the letter had come at "the perfect time." One person, a child, wrote me back a message in kind. I've been told by some that their letters will be kept in a secret place where they can easily access it should they need a boost in morale or a pleasant reminder of how good it made them feel. This makes me glad! Truth be told, the honor is all mine. Accentuating the positive in others does not make you one with your head stuck in the clouds; it helps you become kinder.

Do you mind if I tell you what the *original* title of this book was? I thought about calling it *Best Left Said* because it piggy-backed off the adage, "better left <u>unsaid</u>." The latter is a caveat for us *not* to reveal things that might injure a person or harm a relationship if peccadillos were revealed, criticisms were uttered, or, in be ng "frank," we cross the line and become crass or cruel. I concluded that its counterpart or inverse would hold true, so I proceeded to state its opposite in full measure. I would focus on building *up* the other person by focusing on the best characteristics and revealing how fabulous he or she is. You need no rose- colored glasses to say the good that's in your heart about the ones who mean so much, just a little time to expound the ways. In fact, though it may be hard to start, you may find it hard to stop, as was the case for me. That this endeavor would seem awkward or weird shows just how <u>unused</u> we are to giving or receiving words of affirmation on a steady basis. Trust me: people don't care if you do or do not have a way with words; they're touched by your thought and effort. I discarded this title when I realized it sounded like a warning, and I wanted no associations with admonitions. In fact, it was the Holy Spirit who tapped me on the shoulder and had me focus on His bigger, brighter picture. These are not just people upon whom I am to bestow my personal praise. These selected chosen ones have been expressly created by *Him*, and He loves them beyond measure; they need to be told *this*, too! In short, God inserted Himself in my letters because anywhere love is, He is involved. How could He *not*? He *is* love!

You may contend that whether it be one or one hundred letters written, the fact is that I picked people I love, therefore, it would be easy and delightful to shower these ones with honeyed words. That's no challenge, you might argue. You may say that it's easy to love the loveable. Why, you might even quote Scripture to me and remind me that "if you love those who love you, what credit is *that* to you? For even sinners love those who love them. If you do good to those who do good to you, what credit is *that* to you? For even sinners do the same" (Luke 6:32–33). I don't disagree. You might up the ante and remind me to do something else Jesus commands us to do, one which is only the hardest thing ever: "love your enemies, do good to those who hate you, bless those who curse you, pray for those who mistreat you" (Luke 6:27–28). Who *says* to do that? Jesus does, and I have been put on notice. Yes, you are correct here as well, but *it doesn't and oughtn't to take away from the merit of loving those right in your path and right under your nose.* Sadly, the ones we love the most are often the very ones we take for granted, pass by, or even dismiss; although technically, we are around them the most, they may be receiving our love and attention the *least*!

Oh, heaven forbid, we feed them our leftovers! I have been rightfully called on the carpet for doing just this. Therefore, I chose to heed Him and obey, so I disciplined myself in *this* way to *really* stop and smell the roses in my life and treat them as if they were exotic orchids. They are! We are each so unique and precious in His sight! That was the charge of *this* task. Some might contest that these letters don't actually *do* anything, but I would counter that this is the devil's argument; after all, he is in the business of squelching or squashing love when and where he can. Do not be sullied or stilled by his trying to put jaded thoughts into your mind! I tell my students all the time that when they are being cynical, it doesn't make them look wise, smart, or more mature, just old and spent. Mercy should *always* be our mission, yet when you look around, don't you find it sorely lacking? Loving on your precious ones sometimes can be a challenge because they are the ones most deeply embedded in the folds of our memory. They became a part of us way-back-when, when our brains were in their freshest, most sponge-like state, so we've ingested their disappointments, mistakes, and pains as a part of us like some sort of ingested silt and debris. We weep when they fall; we roar when they become beasts. Our expectations for those closest to us are also higher than they are for others. Never forget that this fact also holds true about you for them.

Consequently, another lesson I learned in this process is just how much I need to be in the habit of forgiving; this is love, too — love at its best. Anyway, down here on planet earth, there will be seasons of love where you will feel flummoxed when life seems to be in limbo or when your loved ones seem to be heading in the wrong direction. *Let it go* and love them where they are, modeling how you'd hope they'd be in their own way and in the future to come. Perhaps *you've* been the one in such flux, stuck in a holding pattern or bent on nursing some grudge. It's hard but *so* worth it to *try* and be the first to extend an olive branch. There is such sweet fruit to bear. You'll change your brain and heart as well as their life. Now *that's* crushing it!

Should any person re-read his or her letter here, I want to reassure him or her that by including it in this compilation, nothing we have and share together is diminished. What I experienced while I was writing the letter or what you felt as you were reading it is *still* sacred and private. I hope the recipients can appreciate that my end goal enhanced the means and process: my <u>co</u>-purpose was to find a way to inspire *others* to love on *their* loved ones, too! There ought to be no particular reason like a birthday or holiday to write; ideally, your love letter should come out of the blue to touch them unexpectedly and strikingly. There are a coupleof other by-products that came from writing these letters: the first for me was overwhelming *gratitude*. Focusing on and sharing my fondest recollections and opinions with these persons has improved my relations with them. Now they have no doubt that I care *deeply* for them! Okay, it may not be a dramatic game-changer, but at least each person possesses a piece of the rock of my appreciation, a tangible reminder of just how I how much I value and love them. There are *so* many things that your loved ones may not actually know you feel. Writing forces you to slow down to express that which typically would not be spoken because of the lightning speed it takes for our ideas to travel from brain to mouth to word. We possess the original computer. Then, practicality has us reflexively go for stating just the facts, Jack; therefore, much gets missed. I wanted to be ponderous, intentional, and generous and delve into the many things that move me about them, and, for me, this best takes place when I purposefully slow *way* down and revel in the memory and essence ofthem.

This exercise has helped me put myself in the frame of mind to be more mindful about looking for the good in *all* people. A critical spirit is not one that readily gives positive reinforcement, and an indifferent soul overlooks a lot in life. Living without love makes for a cold house to come home to. While I was writing this, I was praying that I would foster the habit of love through this labor of love. God manifests Himself in infinite ways, but the most potent and palpable way is through people comforting others. I promise you that you'll be right on time when He's involved you in this mission *possible*. God uses people to bring about the best in each other *and* gives glimpses of Himself in the process. All roads lead to Him if one drives with eyes wide open. I challenge you to do the same. Let me also invite you to *talk to Jesus*. Though you can't see Him, He is on standby and on-call for you round-the-clock; you need not dial 911; He's everywhere always. I hope you experience the same love I have and share it with others. Nothing and no one else but Jesus could have stirred me to undertake this lavishing of love. And no matter what you're going through or have already experienced, He can have us seeking to give *and* receive the fruit of the Spirit: "love, joy, peace, patience, kindness, goodness, faithfulness, and gentleness (from Gal. 5:22–23). I hope that like me, you, too, will be inspired to partake of the love I have felt and you will express *your* love with *others* more!

God's love will awaken something in you, and before you know it, it will have you reaching for His Son. Don't let Hallmark do your talking for you; you are better than that! So are they! In fact, you have a date with destiny to share the love you have with others. I close by asking you a question: what if *you* wrote fifty-two letters? To whom would they be addressed? What if you wrote five? *What if you wrote just one?* Your chosen one would feel the rush of love and encouragement that ultimately comes not from you, but from *Him*. Isn't it time to begin *your* love letter? Yes, now *is* the time, *your* time! Show and tell your love!

Afterword

"When I am afraid,
I will put my trust in You. In God, whose word
I praise, In God I have put my trust;
I shall not be afraid.
What can mere man do to me?"
— Psalm 56:3–4

"I am with you always, to the very end of the
age."
— Matthew 28:20 (NIV)

"For God has not given us a spirit of fear, but
of power and of love and of a sound mind."
— 2 Timothy 1:7 (NKJV)

As it would turn out, during the final stages of preparing my book for publication, the pandemic of the coronavirus disease (COVID-19) is now upon us. We find ourselves in unchartered waters and living through unprecedented times. At times, I feel like I'm in a free-fall, as if we are facing some impending and invisible tsunami; I sometimes crave escape. I am *also* experiencing a settling and persistent calm that I can only attribute to Jesus, the living God and bedrock of my faith, yes, He in whom *I* trust. Only He is *semper fidelis*. No, it doesn't mean I don't check the news, and I certainly do hope people will heed the advice of experts and that our leaders will make prudent decisions. It doesn't follow that I haven't procured for myself physical provisions, but *I do not fear*. For me, this is just another piece of evidence that my Lord lives *in* me and *with* me, and so I state it here for you and for the record. I find it fortuitous and not an accident that Pastor Mark just started his series on Proverbs and wisdom; we'll be seeking

his doses of this and Him. I'll let you in on a secret. This book of love letters, which was prompted by an urgency only God could bring about, has made itself apparent as to how and why the sense of imperative and propulsion came about in the first place. Time *is* of the essence! He *will* have His will made known through me in this fashion. If you have finished this book and are reading this page, you are a survivor! I selected the Scripture above because these are ones that particularly speak to me during our harrowing age; I would suggest you find your own. I do not intend to isolate; at least for now, we can communicate through the world wide web, and, for that, I am grateful. You will also find me in steady prayer. In mere moments, I will send out this offertory, this opus of love, from the living stone I am. . .

Postscript: Just now, a little over a full year has passed since the Covid pandemic struck, and we are rounding the corner, coming up for air with our hopes renewed, and taking tentative but eager steps back to a sense of new normalcy. A month ago, I got an unexpected email from the husband of Emily in this book, asking me only for my phone number. Not a promising sign. When he called, I could tell by the split-second delay what was coming next. He was sorry to have to tell me, but *Emily had passed away* two days ago. Then he explained that Emily's cancer had returned two *years* ago, but that this time, she chose *not* to share her news even though she had since undergone numerous cycles of chemotherapy, all to no avail. Reeling at the information and the fact that she had been struggling for two years, I did the math and asked him if Emily had gotten my letter that I mailed her. I could feel him smile as he replied warmly, "Oh, *yes!* She *loved* it! Thank you! Then, like a child, I asked him, "So then, she *knew* how much I loved her?" to which he quickly and softly confirmed, "Oh, yes, she *did!*" I think he and I were both crying by the end of that hard phone call, but I choose to share this moment with you now to attest to you that sharing *your* love, especially memorialized in a letter, will be so worthwhile. You'll both be glad you did.

9 781954 932555